SHARE THE MAGIC OF
A REGENCY CHRISTMAS

You are cordially invited to delight in the enchanting romance, partake of the splendid feasts, and experience the sheer joy of a traditional Christmas in Regency England. In these six wonderful stories by six bestselling authors, romance sparks and flares as suddenly as a fire in a holiday hearth; and its consequences will just as surely warm your heart!

Join the characters as they romp on sleigh rides, exchange gifts, sing carols, waltz at candlelit balls, and kiss at midnight under the mistletoe. You will almost be able to taste the eggnog and hear the crackling of the yule log. Certainly, you will fall in love with the dashing heroes, perhaps even sooner than the heroines do!

So curl up with A CHRISTMAS DELIGHT and let Jo Beverley, Sara Blayne, Anthea Malcolm, Elizabeth Morgan, Dawn Aldridge Poore, and Lois Stewart transport you to a Christmas of yesteryear . . .

A Christmas Delight

ANTHEA MALCOLM   LOIS STEWART
JO BEVERLEY   ELIZABETH MORGAN
DAWN ALDRIDGE POORE   SARA BLAYNE

ZEBRA BOOKS
KENSINGTON PUBLISHING CORP.

ZEBRA BOOKS

are published by

Kensington Publishing Corp.
475 Park Avenue South
New York, NY 10016

Third printing: September, 1992

Printed in the United States of America

CONTENTS

Twelfth Night
by Jo Beverley

"Ah, there you are at last."

Lady Alice Conyngham looked up from her papers and grinned at her brother. "Yes, Roland, here I am in my study. The last place you would look, of course."

"Well," he said as he came to perch on the edge of her desk. "It's going to be the last place I look today. Why would I keep looking when I've found you?"

Alice chuckled and rolled her eyes at him.

No one would ever doubt that they were brother and sister. It would not be hard to suppose them twins, though Lord Masham was four years his sister's senior. Both had fine-boned features, wide, humorous mouths, and sparkling hazel eyes. The difference lay in their hair. Lord Masham had dark blond unruly waves; Alice was blessed with a thick, heavy mass of chestnut which fell die straight past her hips.

When newly emerged from the schoolroom she had suffered hours of curling and crimping to achieve a fashionable look, but these days she was wiser and let it be. When she was informal, as now, she simply tied it back with a ribbon.

She looked at her brother severely. "Now that you've found me, Roland, state your business and go away. We've thirty-three guests arriving on Christmas Eve and I have work to do."

"Thirty-six," he said.

"Thirty-three," she repeated firmly. "I should know, since I have the task of allocating bedrooms to them all."

"Thirty-six," he said again. "Forgot to tell you. Invited three fellows before I left Town."

"Roland!"

"Come on," he said beguilingly. "We can't actually have run out of space. Bumped into Lord Ivanridge and Thornton Ewing at White's. Clear they'd nothing particular laid on for Christmas, so I invited them here. After all," he added coaxingly, "they're both war heroes, Al. Bad show if they were left to spend their first Christmas after victory by a lonely fireside."

"I believe I have seen both names mentioned in reports of battle," admitted Alice. "But they're total strangers, Roland, and they must have family."

"Not total strangers," he pointed out. "I was at school with 'em. They were both on the Town before they joined up—you must have met them somewhere. In fact, I rather thought Ivanridge came to a Twelve Days once."

"I don't remember him . . ."

"And I'm not sure they do have family," Roland continued. "Close family, that is. Ivanridge's parents died when he was young. He inherited his uncle's title a few years back and the old man was a bachelor. Anyway, the people invited here aren't exactly orphans, Al. They come because Conyngham Christmases are famous."

Alice sighed but gave in, as she usually did with her brother. And it was true that the twelve-day Christmas festival held each year at Conyngham Castle was a renowned festivity. Invitations to it were prized. The fact that it had not taken place last year because of the death of Alice's mother, the Countess of Raneleigh, made this year's celebration even more anticipated.

It also meant that Alice had the running of it for the first time. The earl and Roland loved the event and could be depended on to organize activities once the guests arrived, but they had no patience with the tedious preliminary work of allocating bedrooms and stabling, ordering supplies, and making sure those guests arriving by stage or mail would be collected. Even with an excellent and experienced staff, Alice had her hands full.

"Very well," she said and frowned at her lists. "But I truly am not sure where to put them. All the good bedrooms are taken."

"Double 'em up," said Roland blithely. "The younger men won't mind. I'll take someone in my room. Bed's big enough for five."

"Invite any more impromptu guests," warned Alice, "and you'll be testing out that theory." She scribbled changes to her room list. "You said three?"

"Ah yes," said Roland, suddenly developing an interest in the winter scene beyond the window. "Well, he was with us, Al. Could hardly leave him out, could I?" At her questioning look he said, "Standon."

Alice stared at him. "Roland. Tell me you're teasing. Please."

He did color up a little. "Devil a bit. Come on, Al. It's six years. Surely you two can meet on good terms."

"Of course we can," she snapped. "We've been meeting on good terms ever since. It must have been the most civilized jilting ever!" Alice pressed her hands together and forced the shrill tone out of her voice. "That does not mean I want Lord Standon here for Christmas."

"Not like you to hold a grudge," Roland reproved. "Fellow's all alone. Parents dead, sister in Canada with her husband . . ."

"But *Christmas,* Roland," Alice pointed out, experiencing familiar exasperation with her brother's insouciant disregard for details. "It was during Christmas at Conyngham six years ago that I jilted the man!"

"Oh," he said with mild surprise. "That must be why he hesitated about accepting. But I made a big thing about how welcome he'd be, Al. Can't fob him off now."

Alice shook her head. "I suppose not," she said bleakly. "But if he does something cakish like offer for me again I shall make you deal with it, Roland."

11

"You could do worse," he pointed out. "Than take up with him again, I mean."

"Doubtless," she replied tartly. "However, my sentiments have not altered."

"Nor have his, I suppose. Why else hasn't he married? He's turned thirty and has a duty to his name. Don't like to make a point of it, Al, but you're twenty-three yourself. If you're not careful, you'll end up an old maid."

Alice looked him in the eye. "Roland, one thing I promise you. I will not end up an old maid. Now go away and check guns or billiard balls or something."

Recognizing her irritation, he went. Alice rested her head on one hand. Damnable, damnable situation.

She'd made her curtsy at seventeen, highborn, well dowered, and passably good-looking despite the impossibility of holding her hair in any fashionable style. She had been a mild success in the Season of 1809 and, in her mother's opinion at least, it would have been vulgar to be anything more. Let the impoverished and the parvenus seek to be a Toast; a Conyngham had no need of such extremes to marry well: that is, within the inner circle of the *haut monde*.

It had been made quite clear to Alice which were the gentlemen most suitable for her consideration—suitable in terms of politics, wealth, and bloodlines. Most of them were familiar, having been houseguests at Conyngham.

During that Season Alice had enjoyed herself with all of them and waited for love to strike. When that mythic emotion had failed to appear she had happily settled for fondness and accepted Charlie Dearham, Lord Standon, whom she had known from the cradle. He had been, still was, an easygoing man with a gentle wit and a kind heart. She had always enjoyed his company though she had not, in fact, been in a great hurry to wed. The ceremony had been set for May, 1810.

Of course Charlie had been invited to Conyngham for Christmas that year. And that was where it had all fallen apart. All because of a rogue called Tyr Norman. Captain

Tyr Norman, newly commissioned to the 10th Light Dragoons, a Hussar regiment, magnificent in his blue dress uniform with silver braid, the dashing fur-trimmed pelisse swinging from one shoulder.

During the Twelve Days at Conyngham the guests were required to wear medieval garb, but Lord Raneleigh made an exception for serving officers. Perhaps that was what had made Tyr Norman so dazzling to her eyes, the fact that he was in a real uniform and soon to be posted to the Peninsula, whereas most of the other men had been playacting.

He'd been growing the necessary Hussar moustache, she remembered, and had laughed disarmingly about the fact that he couldn't yet twirl the ends like an old hand . . .

It had taken just twelve days of Tyr Norman to turn Alice's life upside down.

Charlie had never understood why she suddenly broke their engagement. She knew he and others had waited for her to show the new attachment which must surely be the cause. She had not been able to explain to him except to say that she found she did not love him as she should.

The truth was that Alice had found that love was not a myth but a painful, maddening reality. But how could she tell anyone that she had given her heart to a rogue and then her virginity, too, and that the rogue had taken both and decamped, leaving her without honor or heart to offer to another?

In the end, unable to bear the burden of guilt, she had confessed all to her mother. Lady Raneleigh had been deeply shocked but surprisingly gentle. She had explained the possible consequences, but when Alice's courses had shown that she was not, at least, pregnant, her mother had recommended that she get on with her life. She had strongly urged a reconciliation with Charlie, using a whole battery of logical arguments.

It had been no good. Tyr Norman had proved a rogue of the first order, but there had been something between them, something extraordinary. Alice had found she could

13

not bear to wed without it. Her mother, she knew, thought that her experience had been distressing and had turned her against marital intimacy. Honesty told Alice that it was quite otherwise. She could not now bear the impersonal couplings her mother earnestly promised her.

Alice was shocked to feel the dampness of tears on her fingers and angrily brushed them away. It was over. It was ancient history. Tyr Norman was probably dead.

She had guiltily searched out the few mentions of his name in military dispatches — he had distinguished himself at Talavera, she remembered — but all mention had ceased two years before. She must have missed his name in the casualty lists. She had had after all, moments of sanity when she refused to look. She hoped he was dead. He deserved to die in a muddy field somewhere . . .

More tears were squeezing past her lids. Oh damn!

Alice grappled for composure.

Tyr Norman, dead or not, would never show his face at Conyngham again. Charlie Dearham, she reminded herself, was a civilized man and wouldn't create any embarrassment. It would all be all right.

And now, she thought, pulling another sheet of paper closer, she had twelve days of celebration to organize.

Christmas Eve was the usual merry chaos, but Alice was relieved to have it come. The hard work of organization was over and now it should be fun. Even the minor calamities, like the stranding of the Duke and Duchess of Portsmouth ten miles away due to a broken axle, could easily be taken care off.

Conyngham Castle — a twelfth-century castle to which pieces of each succeeding style of architecture seemed to have stuck — was lit from cellar to attic. Inside it was festooned with greenery and ribbons and made cozy by roaring fires. Cheerful servants dashed around, for they loved the celebration as much as anyone, and plenty of extra hands were always hired so the workload was as light as possible.

Besides, the vails were always extraordinary.

Guests arrived all day, breath steaming, laughing and chattering. There was a buffet of hot and cold food set up in the Yellow Saloon, and familiar guests knew to make themselves at home. Alice, her father, and her brother were on hand to look after the less experienced and make them welcome.

Alice had just befriended shy Lady Podbourne, whose new husband had abandoned her when he became caught up in a discussion about fowling pieces, when the doors swung open again to admit a gust of crisp air and new batch of guests.

She introduced Lydia Podbourne to the Beasleys then went to welcome Mr. and Mrs. Digby-Rowles. Behind them she saw Charlie.

The Digby-Rowleses were regular guests and merely waved a greeting before putting themselves into the hands of the bevy of waiting servants. Alice turned to the man she had jilted.

She knew there was nothing he would hate more than any mention of it. "Hello, Charlie," she said and accepted a cool kiss on the cheek. "Lovely to see you here again. I'm afraid you'll have to share a room, though. I've put you in with Lord Ivanridge. I hope that's all right."

"Of course," said Charlie with no hint of awkwardness. He was pleasant by nature and pleasant by looks. He had soft brown hair and a smooth face, fine, kind eyes, and a shapely mouth made for smiling. "We traveled down together. Found we'd both been here once before as well, so we're old hands. No need to fuss over us." He indicated the man behind him and Alice turned with a smile.

Which froze.

"What the devil are you doing here?" she said.

It was, thank God, said softly.

The dark-haired man's courteous smile cooled. "Delighted to meet you too, Lady Alice."

Charlie said, "Is something the matter, Alice?" but his

voice seemed faint and far away.

He looked the same and yet different — leaner, with shorter hair, and no trace of the moustache of which he had been so proud.

It was impossible to do as she wished and have him thrown from the house. She'd kept her secret for six years. She could surely keep it for twelve days more. "No," she said with a shaky laugh. "I'm sorry. Things are at sixes and sevens and I'm losing my wits. It's just that I thought this gentleman was dead." Remaining coherent by force of will, Alice swallowed, extended a hand, and said, "It is Mr. Norman, isn't it?"

He acknowledged her hand with the briefest of touches, his mouth smiling, his eyes cool and watchful. "Lord Ivanridge now, Lady Alice. That is doubtless why you were taken by surprise."

"Indeed," she said. "Congratulations, my lord. As you will have heard, I have had to put you to share a room with Standon. I hope you do not mind." At last she could turn away to summon a maid. "Hattie will show you up. I'm sure you will remember that we leave our guests to suit themselves until dinner." She turned an impersonal smile on the group. "I will see you later, gentlemen."

It was only as she walked away that she registered that there was another man in the group, doubtless Major Ewing, and she had ignored him. She could do nothing about it now. She had to escape.

With a smile fixed painfully on her face, Alice walked composedly across the hall, mounted the stairs, and progressed along corridors to her bedchamber. Once there she turned the key in the lock with unsteady fingers and collapsed on her bed.

Tyr Norman was here, sans moustache, sans uniform, but still able to drive wits to wildness in a second. How could he have done this to her?

Would he have the decency to make an excuse and leave?

Why should he? she thought with a bitter laugh. He, at least, must have expected this confrontation.

What could his purpose be?

Had he come to gloat over his long-ago conquest?

Had he come to try to repeat it? She'd see him dead first.

Devastating thought. Had that riotous tumble in his bed been so long ago that it seemed of small importance to him? Perhaps so. After all, he'd surely spent the past six years engaged in warfare, killing and wenching his way across Europe. Why should he remember one silly seventeen year old?

Alice bit on her knuckle. Perhaps he didn't even remember. She found that insupportable. She'd lived with the memory, bittersweet though it was, every day and night since.

How hard he had looked. Where was the young man with the laughing dark eyes? Latin eyes, her mother had said dismissively. Where was the smile which had melted her bones? Swallowed up by war?

She rolled over and buried her head in her hands as the memories flooded back as if it had all been yesterday. The way those dark eyes had become even darker, and yet brighter, when she had shyly slipped off the top of her gown to expose her breasts.

Where had she gotten the boldness to do such a thing? she wondered. From twelve days of festivities and an excess of mulled cider. It was as if she'd been another person that night.

She remembered the soft music of his voice as he had told her how beautiful she was and calmed her anxieties; the sight of his magnificent torso, bronzed by the firelight except where it was darkened by his hair; the feel of that body beneath her hands. That had been the hardest to forget, the feel of leashed power beneath her hesitant fingers.

When he'd gone, abandoned her, and she'd realized that she could never marry, that had been the hardest part — to know that she would not experience that again, the feel of a man's body beneath her hands . . .

There was a scratch at the door.

Alice leapt up and quickly washed her face, trying to

wash away her wicked thoughts along with the tear stains. Had she learned nothing in six years? She went to the door to open it. A maid was there.

"Sorry to disturb you, milady, but Mr. Kindsy says there's a problem with the Countess of Jerrold's room. She says the chimney smokes." This was reported with a resigned tone. Every year, Alice's godmother, the Dowager Countess of Jerrold, found something about which to complain. Once soothed, she settled to be an acceptable guest.

Alice put her moment of wildness behind her and went off to deal with her godmother.

This event would not be the disaster she feared unless she allowed her wanton heart to make it so. In the hectic, crowded days to come it should be easy enough to avoid Tyr Norman, Lord Ivanridge.

It might be possible to avoid Ivanridge, but it seemed impossible to keep him out of her thoughts. As she dressed for dinner that evening, Alice found herself wondering what he would think of her gown and was instantly annoyed that she would care.

Six years ago, however, she had been just out of the schoolroom and her clothes had been chosen by her mother. They had all been of the highest quality and the finest cut but demure. For day there had been the universal light muslins, for evening plain pastel silks.

These days, having resigned herself to spinsterdom, Alice dressed to please herself. She had discovered a taste for strong colors and unique designs and wore them for her own pleasure. Her mother had not approved.

Christmas Eve at Conyngham was the last night of modern dress, and Alice's gown for this evening had been chosen weeks ago — a bright royal blue of simple cut, trimmed with silver braiding on the bodice and braided leaves around the hem and down the long sleeves. The plain style might not be the current vogue, but she thought it suited her, for she was tall for a woman and had a shapely figure.

Her maid swept her hair up into a coil on her head and surrounded it with a silver bandeau. Silver and sapphire jewelry completed the outfit.

When she checked the final effect in the mirror, however, Alice was shocked to realize how much her outfit resembled a Hussar uniform. It was the blue with the silver braid which created the effect and was a poignant reminder of Tyr Norman all those years ago. Surely she had never intended this when she'd designed it. Had she?

Would anyone else notice?

She forced herself to be sensible. Even if anyone did, there was only one person who would think it of any significance and he could go to hell.

Alice draped eight feet of silver shawl over her arms and swept out to her first evening as hostess of the Conyngham Twelve Day Festival.

Conyngham Castle was a genuine medieval home. Though it had been extensively added to during the last six hundred years, it retained the original castle at one end — or at least, the bottom two floors.

The lower floor was still used for storage as it had been when first constructed in the twelfth century, though now the cool wine cellars were floored and plastered. The medieval top floor had been greatly altered to make the family chapel. The middle floor was the old Great Hall. This had been preserved in its original form except for the addition of glazing in the windows and more efficient fireplaces, and it would be the center of the medieval Twelve Day Festival.

Tonight, however, was the last night of modern living, and family and guests were gathered in the Blue Saloon which was one of the finest examples of the work of the Adams brothers. Alice reminded herself that she'd designed her gown with this room in mind, not with any thought of a dashing Hussar.

Alice's father came over to her — a tall, hearty man with

19

the same heavy brown hair as his daughter, but muted now by gray. "Everything's as it should be," he said with a wide smile. "Your mother would be proud of you, Alice."

"Thank you, Father, but it is mostly the staff, you know. I think they could run this on their own. They doubtless only consider my instructions unnecessary interference."

"Don't downplay your hard work, my dear. Capital job. Fine company." He beamed around. "All the old favorites and enough new blood to keep us on our toes, eh? Glad to see Standon here." With a slight frown he added, "Bad business, that." Alice wondered if after all these years her father was going to choose this moment to upbraid her for her conduct, though he did not know the whole of it.

She should have known better. He and Roland were very alike. "Seems to have kept him away for some reason," the earl said vaguely. "Shame. Always liked Standon."

He wandered off to have a word with Lord Standon. His place was soon taken by Roland. "What the devil have you got against Ivanridge?" he asked. "Fine fellow."

"What do you mean?" responded Alice coolly.

"You've put Ewing in my room—I'd rather have had Tyr, by the way—and he says you tried to throw him out. Tyr, I mean."

"Nonsense," said Alice with deliberate lack of interest, though she'd just had a paralyzing thought. "I was a little surprised, that's all. I wasn't aware that he'd inherited a title and so I didn't expect him."

"No reason to swear at him. Quite shocked poor old Ewing."

Alice could cheerfully have wrung poor old Ewing's neck, and tension had seized the back of her neck. "He must have misunderstood," she said shortly. "Go and mix, Roland. There must be some quiet souls who need bringing out. And," she added, "don't think of changing your place this year. I've put you by Miss Travis, who's very shy. Look after her."

"Shy girls are a terrible bore," he complained with a twinkle.

"She's tolerable enough when she relaxes. Relax her."

He gave a snort of lewd laughter, and Alice felt her color rise. She remembered a man holding her close and saying, "Relax, *puella miranda*. Relax," as his hand and voice had brought relaxation of the sweetest kind. As if drawn and caught, she found her gaze fixed on Tyr Norman across the room. He returned her gaze pensively.

Alice dragged her eyes away. The thought that was torturing her was that she had carelessly put her seducer and her jilted betrothed to share a room and a bed. She wouldn't put it past Ivanridge to use the occasion to make trouble.

She became aware that she was standing among the company like a wax dummy. She couldn't do anything about the situation at the moment, but tomorrow she'd either find a way to throw Ivanridge out or find him another room, even if it had to be the coal cellar.

Dinner was announced at that moment, and everyone progressed, chattering, into the magnificent dining room with its walls and ceiling painted by Laguerre. A string trio played softly in an anteroom, invisible but audible through the open door.

Despite this grandeur, the tone of the Twelve Days was informal, and so there was no head or foot to the long table and the family was scattered among the guests.

As she took her place, Alice checked and was relieved to see Roland assisting Miss Travis to her seat. Their mother had indulged his yearly game of rearranging places so he was seated by some racy young matron. Alice would have no part of it.

She was seated between the Reverend Herbert, the Conyngham chaplain, and Sir George Young, the local squire. They were the two most boring guests and so she had taken them for herself. As she took her place her attention was all on last-minute checks that everything was in order and everyone was comfortable.

It was only as she settled with relief into her place and pulled off her long white gloves that she realized she was seated opposite Tyr Norman. She'd given no thought when she arranged the table to putting Lord Ivanridge opposite her own seat. Now she cursed the mischance.

He raised a brow, as if implying she had arranged this seating deliberately. She gave him a frigid glare and turned to engage the chaplain in a lengthy discussion of the actual date of Christ's birth.

". . . So you see," he was saying some time later, "that it was unlikely to be the year zero, Lady Alice, even if there had been a year zero . . ."

Alice saw nothing, for she had only been pretending to listen as she kept a watching brief on Ivanridge. It had occurred to her that he was a very dangerous man, and she had carelessly placed him between two susceptible young women.

On his right was her friend, Rebecca, Lady Frederick Stane. Rebecca was a widow and should know what she was about, but Rebecca had been granted only two months of marriage before her husband had sailed off to the Peninsula and death. That had been two years ago, but she had taken the loss hard and was only just resuming a social life. Also, Alice knew Rebecca was lonely and possibly susceptible to a handsome rogue.

On Ivanridge's left was Miss Bella Carstairs, a local beauty who considered herself up to every trick. Alice was not convinced, and she mistrusted the glittering excitement in the girl's eyes. Had she once looked at Tyr Norman like that? She prayed not.

Surely not, or no one would have been mystified when she threw over Charlie.

Bella was ignoring both the food and the gentleman on her other side. She was not only hanging on Ivanridge's every word but leaning all over him as well. Her bodice was shockingly low. If the table were less wide, Alice would have kicked the chit on the shin.

As best she could tell, Ivanridge was not encouraging either lady but then, Alice remembered, he hadn't appeared to encourage her either. Though he had changed, he was

22

still the sort of man who could draw women to him without any effort at all. Perhaps more so. The sheer anticipation of life which had shone so brightly six years before was muted, but in its place was an aura of achievement, experience, and power.

Alice caught herself up. It was merely a rather showy kind of virility.

"Lady Alice? Lady Alice?"

Alice snapped back her attention to Reverend Herbert. "I'm so sorry, Reverend. I thought there was trouble with the wine." She dredged her mind for the last thing she had heard. "You were referring to the reign of Herod . . ."

"Ah, yes," said the gentleman with a twinkle in his eye.

Alice grinned back at him. That had doubtless been ages ago. "I'm sorry," she said. "I feel I have to keep my eye on so many things."

She resolved to ignore Ivanridge and all his doings. After all, there was nothing she could do about him short of telling her father the truth and having him thrown out on his ear. In that case, however, Roland might feel obliged to call Ivanridge out. She shivered at the thought of that unequal contest.

By the time the meal drew to a close, the situation had given Alice a headache. The music, the chattering voices, the smell of food and candles were all making it worse. If she had not been hostess, she would have slipped away.

At last the meal was over and her father took over the managing of the affair. "My friends," said the earl, "we are set to enjoy twelve right merry days here at Conyngham, but let us not forget the cause of the celebrations. We are here to celebrate the birth of our Saviour."

The candles in the huge chandeliers were extinguished and people put out the table candles nearest to them. Ivanridge reached forward to pinch the one between Alice and him. The room was left dim except for the lamp stands in the corners of the room and the burnishing light of the leaping fire. All was quiet.

Led by the earl and the musicians the company sang the

old carols, the holy ones—"O, Come all ye Faithful" "While Shepherds Watched" and "Unto Us is Born a Son." Then began the solos. Lord Raneleigh started with his own setting of Robert Herrick's "What Sweeter Music Can We Sing than a Carol?" Roland obliged with "The Burning Babe," a somewhat startling Puritan hymn which appealed to his sense of humor. He particularly relished the line, "So will I melt into a bath to wash them in my blood!"

There was a pause and then the Duchess of Portsmouth sang, soon followed by others. Now there was no set program and the singers were unaccompanied. All went well, however, for everyone knew the musical standard was high at Conyngham and those who chose to perform were gifted amateurs.

Then Ivanridge rose to his feet. Alice caught her breath. She had never heard him sing—had no idea whether he could. What was he up to? Mixed in with suspicion was an absurd protectiveness. Was he about to make a fool of himself?

His voice was not remarkable, but it was a pleasant baritone. The song was one she had not heard before but clearly very old. "There is no rose of such virtue as is the rose that bore Jesu. Alleluia. For in this rose contained was, Heaven and Earth in little space. Res Miranda . . ."

Miranda! Alice felt her face flame at his use of that name, the one he had murmured in the dimness of his bedroom. *Puella miranda, deliciae miranda . . .* Wonderful girl, wonderful darling. She looked down at her hands and fought to keep her face blank and at least deprive him of the satisfaction of knowing his weapon had found its mark.

For it must have been planned, this song. He had been given plenty of time to prepare for this evening while she was still trying to cope with the shock.

There were three more songs and then Alice saw her father's sign and rose. It must be close to midnight and for the last ten years she had been the last performer, singing the haunting old carol, "I Sing of a Maiden."

Her contralto voice was naturally excellent and had

been trained by masters. It filled the beautiful room:

> I sing of a maiden that is makeless.
> The king of all Kings to her son she chese.
> He came all so stille to his mother's bower,
> As dew in Aprille that falleth on the flower.
>
> He came all so stille where his mother lay,
> As dew in Aprille that falleth on the may,
> He came all so stille where his mother was,
> As dew in Aprille that falleth on the grass . . .

Despite her intentions she found herself looking at the man opposite, permitted the foolishness by the fact that he was now looking down. His face was mysterious in the half-light—dark hair, dark eyes, dark shadows like blades across cheek and jaw. She remembered singing this carol six years ago. He had looked up at her then, over half a room, bright-eyed and moved. That was when her heart had first trembled for him.

As the resonance of her last notes faded there was a hushed pause suddenly filled with the sound of distant bells. The servants threw wide the windows and the pealing bells of the village church rippled in on the frosty air.

The candles were lit again, the lamps turned up. "Merry Christmas!" called Lord Raneleigh. "Merry Christmas all!"

It was picked up by the whole company and everyone embraced their neighbors. Bella Carstairs will like that, thought Alice sourly, grateful she had not by mischance put Ivanridge beside herself.

Then the earl led them all in "Christians Awake" as they made procession into the old part of the house and up the worn stone stairs to the chapel. It was soon packed with the guests and most of the servants, but all found a place to kneel as Reverend Herbert led them in the Christmas service.

Alice loved Christmas. She felt the familiar peace and joy settle in her heart and swell out to encompass her family, the guests, and even Lord Ivanridge. It had all been so long ago. If she had been a naive seventeen, he had only been twenty-one. Mistakes had been made but should be put behind them, and that choice of song had doubtless just been an unhappy accident.

When the service was over the company surged down to the Chinese Room for a nightcap among the scarlet and black lacquer and bamboo-style furnishings. Alice whirled around in high spirits, making sure everyone had their choice of caudle or posset or hot spiced wine.

She was standing and surveying the company with satisfaction when Roland came over, the center of a merry group of bachelors. "Aha!" he declared. "Look where she is, my good men!"

Alice looked at him, then up and sighed. She'd taken a spot under one of the many bunches of mistletoe. "Fair catch," she admitted.

Roland moved forward, but someone else was before him. "We can hardly start Lady Alice's Christmas with a kiss from a mere brother," said Ivanridge. "Allow me."

Alice took one step back but realized in time it would be unpardonable to retreat. But how dare he do this to her? She sent that message full force with her eyes.

As his head came down to hers he murmured, "I've charged an enemy battery, Miranda. Your flaming eyes won't stop me."

It was an appropriate Christmas kiss, just his lips soft and warm against hers, his hands resting light on her shoulders. Alice stood rigid, turned to stone by his brutal use of that name. The song had not, after all, been an accident.

He let her go. "Merry Christmas," he said coolly as he reached up to pluck a berry from the bunch. His eyes were shielded, but she sensed he was not as cool as he wished to be. Could Tyr Norman at long last be experiencing guilt? She prayed for it.

"Now can a mere brother get a peck in?" asked Roland and swung her close for a merry buss.

Major Ewing took his turn next, stiffly but thoroughly,

then it was Charlie. His lips were butterfly soft against hers, but his eyes were kind. "Merry Christmas, Alice."

"Merry Christmas, Charlie." If she had any sense she'd marry him, smirched honor or not. She shrugged off the thought. She accepted three more kisses then looked humorously up at the bush. "We certainly made inroads into that one, didn't we? I think you should all go off and assault some other lady." She looked around and then at Ivanridge. "I see Bella Carstairs posted hopefully beneath a kissing bunch, my lord."

"So she is," he said with a smile. "And Christmas kisses don't mean a *lasting* commitment, do they?"

With that he walked away and Alice, by dint of great will power, did not glare after him. As she wandered around checking on her guests, however, the thought rang through her head like the Christmas bells. How dare he taunt her with his own callousness? How dare he?

She'd been wrong. Christmas peace or no, she couldn't have Ivanridge here for twelve long days. She would have to get rid of him, and now was a good time to tell him to go. As the guests began to disperse she longed for her bed too but lingered, hoping for an opportunity to speak to him in private.

It looked for a while as if the younger men were going to make a night of it, but then Roland reminded them they'd be expected to be out early the next morning in medieval garb to find and cut a yule log.

As they began to disperse, Roland said, "You don't have to stay up, Alice. I'll make sure all's right here."

She gave in. It had been sheer desperation which had made her think of confronting Ivanridge at this hour, and it was clearly impractical. As she headed for her room she tried to think of a reasonable way to throw him out without raising anyone's suspicions. The more she thought about it, the less likely it became.

Then, as she walked along the upper gallery, she saw him going down the opposite stairs, which certainly did not lead to his, or any other, bedroom.

27

She slipped down a different set of stairs and followed.

For a moment she wondered if he was up to no good, thievery even—nothing was too low for this man—but then he turned to a candle in a wall sconce and lit a thin cigarillo. Trailing wisps of aromatic smoke he turned into the conservatory.

Alice followed as if drawn by magnets but hesitated at the doorway. Now that she had come this far, she wasn't at all sure what she was going to say or that this encounter was wise.

She took a step of retreat. He sensed her and turned with alert speed, then relaxed but only slightly. "It's unwise to creep up on a man not long away from war. What do you want?"

The terse rudeness of it brought heat to her cheeks. "I might be here to tell you we do not permit the cigarillo habit in the house."

"Are you?"

Alice felt a fool. "No."

"Didn't think so. Your brother smokes 'em." He blew out a stream of silver-gray. "So?"

He had the manners of an undergroom. Alice grasped her courage. "I want you to leave."

"The conservatory?" he asked mildly.

"Conyngham."

"No."

She hadn't expected such a blunt refusal. "Why not? The situation is damnable. You cannot have thought before you came here."

There was only the moon through the steamy glass to light them, and he seemed shadowed in spirit as well as flesh.

"I thought a great deal before I came here."

"Then why did you come at all? A moment's thought must have shown you how . . . how *improper* it is!"

She saw his teeth glint white in a cruel smile. "It won't be improper unless you start tearing your clothes off again, Miranda."

Alice took three steps forward and hit him with all the rage and pain of six years. He allowed it. She knew that as if everything had slowed down. She watched the angry mark flare on his cheek. She noticed that except for the jerk of his head under the force of her blow he did not move. After a breathless moment he raised the cigarillo to his lips and drew on it. He said nothing.

Alice had no idea what to do or say. Anything would be feeble. "So you refuse to go," she said at last.

He blew out smoke. "I have ghosts to exorcise," he said. "Judging from your performance to date, it should be easy."

"You cannot judge me," she cried. "You took my innocence. You *abandoned* me!"

"Did I? Even so, I would have thought you'd had your pound of flesh."

Alice stepped back, away from his coldness. "I? I have had nothing."

His lips curled up in a smile that didn't reach his eyes. "You've had a good swing at me at least. You can't deny that." He crushed out the cigarillo in a potted fern. "Good night, Lady Alice." With that, he walked by her and was gone.

Alice awoke the next day with a feeling of dread, and this was Christmas Day, which she'd always loved. Had she slept at all? It didn't feel like it, and she remembered countless restless hours tussling with rage, loss, fear, and a twisted, bitter kind of excitement.

Things were better once her maid, Hobly, brought her coffee—the day was now underway and she could pretend, at least, to be in control. It was better still when Rebecca popped her head around the door. "May I come and drink coffee with you, Alice? We'll never have time for a coze otherwise."

Rebecca was a slender blonde whose sweet disposition was written all over her face. It wasn't right, thought Alice with a spurt of anger, that Rebecca had been robbed of her loving husband by a war which had left Tyr Norman untouched.

"Oh yes, do! You can go, Hobly. I'll ring when I'm ready to dress." Alice leapt out of bed and led Rebecca into her small sitting room.

"This is so comfortable," said Rebecca as they sat in the chairs in front of a new fire. "Perhaps I should demand something like this now I am back at home."

"Why not? I decided, since I will not marry, I might as well have my comforts."

"Will not marry? Alice, of course you will!"

Alice tempered her words. "Let us say, it's beginning to seem unlikely, and I'm well content. There's space enough for me here even when Roland marries."

"What about Standon?" Rebecca asked tentatively. "He's such a lovely man, and I'm sure he still cares. I never did understand—"

"Oh please!" Alice interrupted as cheerfully as she could. "It's such old history. I'm still fond of Charlie, but I assure you I will not change my mind about marrying him. Surely you," she added gently, "who knew real love, can appreciate that fondness is not enough."

Rebecca looked into the fire, her delicate face unwontedly sober. "I don't know, Alice. Frederick seems so long ago. I'm lonely, and love . . . love exposes us to such terrible pain."

Alice closed her eyes, but she could not shut out the knowledge that she too had loved and been deeply hurt.

"Oh Alice, I'm so sorry!" Alice opened her eyes to see Rebecca's concerned face. "I swore I wouldn't be a shroud at the feast, and here I am giving you a case of the dismals."

Alice gathered her friend in for a hug. "Don't act for me. Don't ever act for me." They smiled at each other somewhat tearfully, then Alice leapt to her feet. "But we must be up and about if we're to inspect the men at their work."

"Cutting the yule log? But Alice, it's supposed to be

the fair maidens who go out to tease. I'm no maiden."

"I prefer to interpret it as the available young ladies. After all," she added with a wicked look, "who's to say all the unmarried wenches hereabouts have kept their maidenheads?"

Rebecca gave a startled giggle and hurried off to dress.

Alice rang her bell for Hobly, reflecting that she was going to have to bridle her tongue or she would end up spilling the truth. Having Tyr Norman here had not only brought old feelings to the surface but was prompting her to speak of matters best left unaddressed.

With Hobly's help she was soon dressed in medieval style, ready for the first of the twelve days.

It was the custom at Conyngham for all to wear twelfth-century dress during the festival though some guests were loose in their interpretation. Houpelands and even farthingales had been seen, but generally the loose, comfortable lines of the early middle ages were the norm. The family, of course, had extensive, authentic wardrobes, and there were ample spare costumes for the unprepared guest or one who ran out of appropriate garments.

Alice was soon dressed in a long linen shift, a gunna of finer linen in a rich buttery cream embroidered in brown and red, and a knee-length tunic of warm red wool. The tunic was trimmed at neck, sleeves, and hem with braid. Alice knotted a silken rope around her hips and Hobly braided her hair into two long plaits interwoven with ribbons. This was one time when her hair came into its own. Alice pulled on stockings and then the long loose braies necessary for riding astride. Low red leather boots completed her outfit.

She glanced in the mirror and was satisfied. She loved these clothes. She sometimes thought she would have been happier in medieval times, but then she remembered the cold, harsh castles, the chancy supply of food, and the almost incessant warfare, and was pleased to live in a civilized age.

She picked up her brown cloak lined with vair and went

off to collect Rebecca and gather up the other young available ladies.

Rebecca was ready in shades of blue. Miss Carstairs was found to be in a form-fitting outfit more of the fourteenth century than the twelfth, and Alice doubted that even then they had cut the neckline quite so low. The girl was going to freeze for though she had a warm woolen cloak she was leaving it open to display her attributes.

Susan Travis was anxious in a nondescript garment of brown wool tied around the middle. It was, thought Alice, quite authentic if she wished to play the part of a downtrodden serf. She resolved to take the shy girl on a foray through the Conyngham wardrobes later. For now, she merely supplied a warm cloak, which Susan lacked.

Before leaving the house, however, Alice had a word with a maid to check the state of the clothes of Miss Travis's parents and to offer additions if required. Then she guided her company to the stables.

It was a beautiful morning, clear and crisp with the frosted grass crunching under their feet. It was a miracle, thought Alice, but it seemed that Christmas Day was always beautiful.

Bella Carstairs shivered. "It's so cold. Where are we going?"

"To find the eligible men," said Alice and pinned the girl's cloak close around her. "They are off finding and cutting the yule log. We will go and tease them."

Bella cheered up. "Will Lord Ivanridge be there?"

"I suppose so," said Alice.

When they arrived at the stables she said, "In the twelfth century ladies rode astride, but you may choose sidesaddle if you wish." Bella and Susan earnestly assured her they did, and Susan asked for a quiet mount.

Rebecca said to them, "I relish this one chance to ride astride. You should try it, and your modesty is safe." She raised her skirt to show the linen leggings she already wore.

Susan gasped. "Heavens! What are they?"

Alice replied. "Leggings, braies, hose. Call them what

you wish." She produced another two pairs from under her cloak and waved them temptingly. "Are you sure you don't want to try?"

Bella and Susan were very clear that they did not.

Soon they were mounted. Alice had come to love her annual experience of riding astride, though she always paid for it with complaints from muscles unaccustomed to the work. Now she wanted to race off at full tilt, but she could see Susan was a nervous rider and Bella was in no mood to hare around, being more concerned with draping her yellow silk skirts and white cloak to greatest effect. Silk, thought Alice, shaking her head. The girl wouldn't wear silk in the morning ordinarily, so why now?

"Where will we find the men?" Bella asked.

"In the Home Wood somewhere," said Alice. "It's not far. A few trees have come down there in the last year which will be suitable for burning."

She eventually got her party up to a canter and began to enjoy herself.

They entered the wood and stopped to listen. There were voices over to the right but no sound of work. With a sign to her companions to be as quiet as possible, Alice led the way. Bella opened her cloak again. Susan giggled.

"Good morning, gentlemen," Alice said. "Having difficulty?"

Six men looked up at the four ladies. As well as Roland, Standon, Ewing, and Ivanridge, there were Lord Garstang and Mr. Noonan. The latter was a little old for this, but he was unmarried and so entitled to take part. It was a shame, however, that he'd chosen to wear the fitting hose and short jacket of the fourteenth century, for he was short and plump. He'd have been much better off in the braies and knee-length tunic worn by the other men, and more comfortable as well.

"Not at all," said Roland, pretending offense, though the scene was played out much the same way every year. "We are just resting the saw."

The two-handed saw was propped against the huge tree

trunk into which they were cutting. They appeared to have gotten halfway through before stopping to refresh themselves from tankards of ale.

"Don't let it rest too long," said Rebecca with a grin. "We need the yule log today, you know."

Roland scowled at her. "Saucy wench. All right, men, whose turn is it?"

"Mine and Standon's," said Ivanridge, shrugging out of his cloak and going to take one end of the saw.

Alice remembered him taking part in this tradition six years ago, but he'd been in uniform. He'd taken off his jacket and worked in shirt sleeves. He'd been dashing no matter what he wore and still was. His medieval clothes were simple homespun browns, but with his forged hardness and his dark hair slightly long, he suited them perfectly. He could have stepped out of a previous century.

He and Standon began to operate the saw, pushing and pulling smoothly. She dimly heard Rebecca leading the other two maidens in humorous taunts about the men's performance. Even Susan was beginning to get into the spirit of things. Alice was dumb.

She told herself she couldn't actually see the muscles under that loose clothing, so why could she sense the power of them, imagine them beneath her fingers?

She broke the spell he was casting on her. "Really, Lord Ivanridge," she called out. "Is that the best you can do? You're hardly making any impression at all!"

He turned with a challenging smile. "Come and assist us then."

Alice felt as if she'd stepped into a trap. This wasn't part of the script at all, but everyone was greeting this with huge merriment.

"You too, Lady Frederick," called Standon. "Come and lend your strength at this end!"

Rebecca complied instantly, so Alice had little choice. She slid off her horse and walked stiffly towards her tormentor. "What do you think you're doing?" she asked, but quietly.

"Cutting a yule log," he said.

He was startlingly unsafe in his loose, homespun garments. As if he sensed her disquiet, he stripped off his tunic to reveal a thin linen shirt. It was slit down the front and showed dark hair curling over hard muscles. Alice's mouth dried.

"Hot work," he said as he tossed his tunic aside.

Alice found herself within his arms, back pressed to his hard body. She swallowed and grasped the handle of the saw.

"Put your hands on top of mine," he said softly against her ear. "We wouldn't want you to get a blister."

"What of your hands?" she asked.

He spread them momentarily and she saw the hard skin and callouses. "Sabers and other instruments of death," he remarked.

He gripped the wooden handle, and Alice put her hands on top of his, seeing how delicate her white hands looked over his. She wasn't going to do much good in this position, but then that wasn't the point. This situation had been devised to torture her. Or seduce her.

She looked up and saw Rebecca and Charlie on the other end of the saw, laughing. The look Rebecca flashed up at her partner was surprisingly flirtatious.

Right, thought Alice. Tyr Norman isn't going to have it all his own way. She relaxed against his body and let her hands flex against his. "What now?" she asked, deliberately using a husky tone.

"Push and then pull, Lady Alice." He leaned against her so that the saw slid toward Standon. Then the saw was pushed back, forcing her against his body. Push and then pull. Push and then pull. Alice allowed her body to fall hard against his at the end of every pull . . .

He suddenly let go of the saw and stepped back, releasing her. "Whew," he said, wiping his arm against his damp brow. "I think an armful of such beauty saps my strength instead of adding to it."

He said it jokingly, but he was serious. Alice felt a triumphant smile tug at her lips but controlled it. Ivanridge caught it, however. Alice saw the flash of anger in his eyes, followed by a reluctant gleam of admiration.

Ewing and Garstang demanded to try the same system and Bella and Susan were persuaded to assist. Alice strolled back towards the horses.

"You always were full of surprises," Ivanridge said behind her.

She turned and met his eyes. "Best you remember that, Lord Ivanridge."

"Oh, I remember it well, Miranda."

"Stop calling me that!"

"Why? You are certainly a creature of amazing surprises."

Alice closed her eyes briefly. "Why won't you just go away?"

"I told you why."

She glared at him. "I can make your life extremely difficult, Lord Ivanridge."

He laughed shortly. "That's an old weapon and worn very blunt." He turned away dismissively. "They're almost through. Amazing what the presence of a few suitably appreciative damsels will do to a man's strength."

Alice watched him stroll away knowing she was perilously close to tears. She fought them away and pinned on a smile. But what did he mean about an old weapon? She'd never made his life difficult . . .

A triumphant shout told that the task was accomplished. The men mounted their own horses and everyone rode back to the house together. Egged on by Roland, Alice at last indulged in a flat-out gallop, but she noticed that Ivanridge lagged behind with Susan Travis. Now, what was he about?

In the stables she lingered until he arrived and sought another moment alone with him. "You will please leave the young and innocent alone, Lord Ivanridge," she told him.

He led his and Susan's mounts over to a groom. "Am I not allowed simple converse with the female sex?"

"Not with the likes of Susan, no. If you are feeling amorous I can recommend a couple of the matrons who are not averse to variety."

His look was slightly disgusted. "You've added pandering to your hostess duties, have you?"

Alice winced, knowing she deserved that. "You make me behave like this," she said despairingly. "Please, won't you leave?"

"No. And Lady Alice," he said with precision, "I have never *made* you do anything in your life."

He walked away, and Rebecca took his place. "What's the matter? Lord Ivanridge looked . . ."

"Looked what?"

Rebecca thought about it. "Like a soldier, I suppose. One about to kill."

Alice shuddered slightly. That was what she sensed in him. A leashed killing anger. Why?

As Christmas Day progressed, Alice found she had little time to herself, and the little she did steal was spent trying to think of a way to force Ivanridge out or at least change his room. She could come up with neither. There were available rooms, but they were all inferior or very out of the way and she could think of no excuse for the change.

Instead, over tea, she sought out Charlie and probed for details as to his interaction with Ivanridge.

Charlie considered her. "What's up? Anyone would think you suspected the man of being a murderer. Or a madman."

"Of course not," Alice said gaily. "I just feel a little guilty for asking you to share with a stranger."

"It's no problem, except that he's a restless sleeper."

"Then he is making it difficult," she said, thinking she saw an excuse presenting itself.

"Not particularly. Once asleep, I sleep soundly." He apparently felt obliged to reassure her. "We discussed it this morning and he's agreed to wait until I'm asleep before going to sleep himself."

"What was the problem?" Alice asked, knowing she

would be wiser to hold onto ignorance.

"War dreams, I suppose," said Standon. "Don't say anything, Alice. I'm sure he wouldn't want it spoken of."

So Tyr Norman had nightmares about the war, did he? Served him right. But Alice was bitterly aware of a desire to hold him in her arms and bring him to a sound sleep.

That night was the Christmas feast, held in the Great Hall. The lofty stone chamber was hung with banners and ancient weapons, and the tables were set down the two long walls. At one end of the large room sat a high table on a dais and at the other stood an enormous fireplace.

The first order of business was for the unmarried men to drag the yule log to the fireplace while being urged on and tormented by the maidens. Alice deliberately let Rebecca lead the ladies and kept well in the background herself. She was giving Ivanridge no further opportunity to harass her.

Once the kindling was lit beneath the log, there was a great cheer and everyone took their places. Alice, Roland, and Lord Raneleigh sat at the high table, but the two central seats there were left vacant for the king and queen of the feast. Alice saw Ivanridge take a place down one side. She had arranged for him to be out of her direct line of sight and between Mrs. Digby-Rowles and Lady Jerrold. Extremely safe.

As soon as everyone was seated, the earl rose, magnificent in a full-length tunic of plum velvet trimmed with fur. "Our first duty this night," he explained, "is to choose our rulers. Here in these chairs we will enthrone a king and queen for our festivities, and within this hall their word shall be law for twelve full days. Behold, here come buxom wenches and bonny lads bearing gifts—gifts for everyone! But one gentleman and one lady will find a bean along with their trinket. They will be our monarchs of mischief!"

To the accompaniment of foot-stamping music, laughing maids and footmen in period costumes entered and passed around the tables, handing out beautifully wrapped boxes, and kisses for those who asked. Most did.

Though the family did not receive these gifts, Alice had had her eye for some time on a particularly fine specimen among the staff, and as he crossed the hall in front of the high table, she called out, "Ho, sirrah! I may not receive a gift, but should I be deprived of a Christmas kiss?"

The handsome fellow grinned cockily. Alice had no doubt he was a devil among the maids. "T'wouldn't be fair, would it?" he replied. Instead of leaning across the table, he came round and swept her up for a hearty kiss. The hall erupted in cheers, though some of the ladies looked a little shocked.

Alice laughed. "And a merry Christmas to you too, Peter." As she resumed her seat, however, she told herself she should have learned she was no hand at managing men.

Then she realized that the king and queen had been discovered, and Rebecca and Tyr Norman were approaching the table.

Her father leapt to his feet as trumpeters blew a fanfare. "Behold our monarchs! Welcome, Your Majesties!"

Roland was already on his feet, waiting to drape the rich crimson cloak edged with ermine around Rebecca's shoulders. Alice forced herself to her feet to perform the same task for her nemesis. She couldn't believe it. Why was this happening to her?

He was tall and had to bend slightly to allow her to put the cloak on his broad shoulders. As he sat she saw how poorly the mustard color of his outfit went with the cloak, and she took spiteful satisfaction from that. As she'd said earlier, he seemed to be driving her to a mean pettiness of thought and deed.

He examined the enameled card case which had been his gift. "Your family gives handsome gifts, Lady Alice," he said pleasantly. "What a shame you receive none yourselves."

"We exchange gifts privately," she said, thinking that at least in this seating arrangement she didn't have to look at him.

"And perhaps gifts find their way to you later? Let me

see. Last time I was here I believe I received a jade pin."

He'd given it to her at some point during the night. She'd thrown it in the lake.

Alice ignored his taunting, determined to be a perfect lady. "Do you have any commands, sire?"

The silence from her right stretched so that in the end she had to look at him. "Come to my room later," he said.

Alice met his cold eyes. "Your commands only hold in the hall, sire . . ."

He smiled. "Intriguing."

". . . and you share a room."

"Beginning to regret that, are you? I'm sure you'll find a way around the problem."

Alice turned to the front and fixed a polite smile on her face. "If you think," she said between her teeth, "I have the slightest intention or desire to visit your room, Lord Ivanridge, you are sorely mistaken."

"Have other game in your sights this year, do you?"

Alice found she had the sharp eating knife tight in her hand and that she was full of desire; the desire to plunge it into him. "Talk to your queen," she said tightly. "Invent some mischief. I am sure you are very good at that."

He proved to be. As the platters of food—fowl, suckling pig, boar's head, peacock, and all the sundry accompaniments came around, he and Rebecca conferred and commanded.

Various guests were ordered to join the musicians and play or sing. Others were ordered to perform a trick or offer a puzzle. Alice noted, however, that no one was asked to do something they could not, and the shy were left in peace. Rebecca's doing, she was sure.

Then Ivanridge turned to her. "Lady Alice, we would have you do Salome's dance for us."

Alice had no cause for complaint. This, like the somersaults Roland had just performed, was part of the tradition. She had been doing her version of the dance since she was fifteen, but for the first time she felt uncomfortable about it.

40

She went out of the hall briefly and put on her veils—one around her head to cover the lower part of her face and one over her hair. She settled her jeweled girdle lower on her hips. At her signal, the professional musicians began an Eastern melody, and she swayed into the hall.

When she'd first had this idea at fifteen, her version of the dance had been more like a solo country dance, but since then she had researched it and even taken advice of the Persian Ambassador's wife. She knew the moves, though a mild version of the real thing, were suggestive, but that had never bothered her before.

As she swayed her hips and played with her veil she tried to remember dancing like this six years ago. But on Christmas night six years ago Tyr Norman had just been a handsome young Hussar and Charlie had been more on her mind than he. Alice couldn't remember feeling embarrassed to be doing the dance before Charlie.

She tried her hardest not to look at Ivanridge, but it was impossible if for no other reason than that she was supposed to be persuading him to give her the head of St. John. Once she looked, she was captured by those dark eyes. Forbidden passions began to fuel her dance. She danced closer to him, moving her shoulders and swaying her hips, wanting to break through his hard coldness and see desire in his eyes.

So she could laugh in his face.

Though she watched like a hawk, no flicker of emotion showed to reward her. Was he made of stone?

The music stopped and she sank into a curtsy as thunderous applause broke out.

"We will grant you anything in our power," said Ivanridge huskily.

Alice rose. "I would have a rogue's head, sire." With her eyes she told him whose she wished it could be.

A brow twitched, but he said, "Point out the rogue, you luscious wench, and I will call the headsman."

Alice looked around, drawing out the suspense. She'd fully intended to get petty revenge by picking Ivanridge.

41

Now she thought of choosing Charlie, but people would read all kinds of things into that. In the end she pointed to Major Ewing.

Four footmen leapt on the startled major, and a fearsome giant — a local laborer who enjoyed his part in the festivities — stalked in bearing a huge, authentic-looking ax. It was, in fact, authentic, and Alice was always a little nervous the man would handle it carelessly and lop off something or other. Ewing was dragged forward and guests new to Conyngham began to look ill at ease. The rest chanted, "The head! The head!"

At the last moment Rebecca leapt to her feet. "Stop! I am queen as much as this man is king and I will not let an honest man die at a strumpet's whim!"

Alice covered her face in exaggerated shame.

"Release him!" commanded Rebecca. "Good man," she said to Ewing, "resume your seat and enjoy the feast without fear. And you," she said to Alice sternly, "go strip off your veils and act the proper maid."

Shrieking with mock tears, Alice fled the hall. She heard Ivanridge say, "Isn't that just like a woman to spoil a little harmless fun?"

She took a moment to compose herself and to let the hall settle. The scene had gone better than ever. Of course, both Rebecca and Ivanridge had seen it before; sometimes a newcomer was chosen monarch and had to be prompted by her father and brother. Both Rebecca and Ivanridge had showed real dramatic talent.

But then, she knew him to be a facile deceiver.

She slipped back into the hall and to her place.

"Your dancing's improved," he said casually.

"Your acting's as good as ever," she said in the same manner.

"I believe the queen commanded you to act the *proper maid,* Lady Alice."

It sounded like a calculated insult.

There was the dancing to get through. Roland and she demonstrated some simple steps, which were not so very different from the familiar country dances, then they were joined by three couples well used to the business for a more complicated demonstration.

Soon all were on the floor stamping and clapping to the merry, earthy dances.

Alice was glad to lose herself in the dancing. It was true that she had to partner Ivanridge now and then—everyone partnered everyone else at some point—but these were not dances to encourage intimacy but to express the joy of living and moving.

There was an endless supply of wine, punch, and more benign thirst quenchers. There was a buffet of food, and nonstop dancing.

Some of the older people began to drift off to bed, but most of the company stayed on. Chess and backgammon games started up, and some people took breaks for conversation. The kissing bows were stripped of their berries; tomorrow men wanting to steal a kiss would have to seek out the more cunningly hidden ones, which were also the ones well situated for more lingering embraces.

Alice would be sure to avoid them.

Tiredness was beginning to fog Alice's mind when she realized she was *waltzing* with Lord Standon. "This dance is very anachronistic, Charlie."

"But a lot less exhausting. If the king and queen don't object, what are we poor lesser folk to do?"

Alice saw Rebecca waltzing with Roland, while Ivanridge partnered Bella. There were a dozen or so other couples drifting in lazy circles, and Alice supposed the hard-worked musicians were also relieved to be playing more familiar fare. Charlie's voice startled her out of a pleasant vacuum.

"I'm going to embarrass us both, Alice," he said, "but I need to know. Will you reconsider the decision you made six years ago?"

Alice sighed. She'd feared it would come to this. "Charlie, I refuse to believe you've been nursing a broken heart. You've kept a very handsome mistress these last few years."

"True," he said without embarrassment. "Are you holding that against me?"

"Of course not." In desperation, Alice returned to the argument she'd used six years ago. "I just don't love you, Charlie."

"I don't think I love you either," he said, which startled her considerably. "Not as the poets describe it, anyway. But I like you. I admire you. You were a charming girl, and you've grown into a beautiful woman. I need to marry, Alice, and I'd rather marry you than anyone else I know."

Alice looked up at him. "I'm not sure whether to be amused or insulted."

His smile was friendly but held some steel. "As you pointed out; it would be absurd for me to be protesting an undying passion. When you ended our engagement, I naturally assumed there was someone else. That appears not to be so. Since neither of us seems likely to be hit by Cupid's arrow, it would be sensible for us to marry. You can't really want to grow old as a spinster, and I still think we'd suit very well. Perhaps love would grow."

Put that way it did seem suitable. Alice was aware that in some secret part of her heart she'd been waiting all these years for Tyr Norman to return with an explanation and protestations of love, but now he was back and clearly no answer to her problems. "I don't know, Charlie," she said at last. "May I think about it?"

"Of course. But not for another six years."

As the dance ended Alice was again aware of that steel beneath his courteous surface, and she liked him better for it.

When the music struck up again, she was swung into the dance by Ivanridge.

She resisted. "Let me go!"

His arms were like iron. "We are in the hall, and I am king. Dance with me."

Alice glared up at him and decided the time had come for attack. She would not be his toy in this cat and mouse game. She relaxed and allowed him to twirl her in the dance. "What exactly are you up to?" she asked.

"Dancing?"

"I mean," she said, "why did you come here, why have you stayed, and why do you keep forcing yourself on me?"

His eyes smiled down at her, full of hard-edged admiration. "The bold approach. But then that was always your strategy, wasn't it?"

Alice couldn't bear his look and turned her head away. "As a strategy," she remarked, "it leaves something to be desired. It hasn't gained me an answer."

"Left you dissatisfied, you mean? We can't have that, can we?" There was a weight of meaning to the words which she could not fathom. "Let me see," he continued pleasantly, "I came here because I was invited. I stayed because I found unfinished business. I keep forcing myself upon you because you seem to dislike it. If you can convince me you like it, Miranda, I'll avoid you like the plague."

Alice looked at him in shock. "It's as if you hate me," she whispered. "What have I ever done to you?"

"Very pretty," he approved. "It's all the theatricals, I suppose. Cuidad Rodrigo," he said as he twirled them around. "Badajoz. Albuera."

Alice's head was spinning and with more than the twirling. "Are you saying I drove you to war? You already had your marching orders when we met."

"Was that part of my appeal?"

She hit back. "I suppose we're all fools for a uniform."

"You must be grieving the war is over."

Alice fought him and stopped the crazy spinning. "You still haven't answered my question, Lord Ivanridge. If you found you didn't like war, you can hardly lay that at my door."

"There's war and war, Lady Alice," he said, and at that moment the music meshed with their action and stopped. "If you don't know that, your uncle certainly does."

He was gone and Lord Garstang was asking for a dance. Alice made an excuse and escaped into an empty corridor. What had all that been about? The uncle he referred to

45

must be her mother's brother, Gen. George Travis-Blount. As one of the senior men at the Horse Guards, he certainly knew all about war. Was Ivanridge suggesting that she ask him about it? Was he using the horrors of war as his excuse for the cruel way he was tormenting her?

There was no need for Alice to seek out her uncle. She had heard enough frank talk to have lost any romantic illusion about warfare. It was a bloody business usually prosecuted desperately in large amounts of mud. The most surprising thing was that the survivors often seemed to enjoy the memory.

Ivanridge, she suddenly remembered, had nightmares. She shuddered and hugged herself, though the corridor was not particularly cold.

But he could not possibly be accusing her of sending him to war. That decision had been made before they ever met. And whatever horrors he had seen and experienced did not excuse what he had done before he saw fighting at all.

Perhaps, she thought for the first time, he was mad. She had heard of men whose minds broke under the stress of war.

Major Ewing came strolling down the corridor, humming a song, clearly a little on the go. "Ah, the lovely Salome! Damn fine dance, that."

"Thank you, Major." Alice linked arms with him. "I suppose you and Ivanridge know one another well."

He looked at her glassily and shook his head. "Different regiments. Anyway, Tyr Norman was a hero. I kept my head down."

Alice felt there was a mystery here that she had to solve. She steered the major to a widow seat and he seemed happy enough to collapse there.

Alice sat beside him. "What do you mean, a hero?"

Ewing made a generous gesture. "Derring-do. Single-handed exploits . . . Sort of fellow who seeks out the most hellish spots." He shook his head. "Madmen, usually. Don't last long. But then they seem to have a death wish."

Death wish? Alice began to examine the notion that Tyr

Norman had been so guilt ridden over his treatment of her that he'd tried to get himself killed. No matter how she looked at it, it didn't fit. If he'd felt guilty, he could have tried to make amends. He certainly would have no reason for assaulting her now as if she were the enemy.

Ewing was humming again and she guessed that he was soon going to drift off to sleep. "Major Ewing," Alice said to catch his attention. "How do you think Ivanridge survived?"

"Luck," he said simply. "There's a devil of a lot of luck in war. And he came to his senses. Last few years, I never heard of him acting crazy." He gazed, without focus, at the tapestry on the opposite wall. "Could have just been a way to make it up the ranks, if he was desperate enough. Hear there wasn't much money there . . . Made it to colonel with his craziness, so . . . crazy or not?"

His lids began to droop, and Alice left him there. So much for her melodramatic imaginings. He hadn't been awash with guilt. He'd just been ambitious.

So, what had he meant when he'd mentioned her uncle? Did he know that Uncle George would be coming after New Year's Day to enjoy the last few of the Twelve Days?

Alice looked into the hall. Couples were still dancing. She saw Roland flirting with Bella and Charlie dancing with Rebecca but no sign of Ivanridge.

She couldn't make herself enter the half-lit chamber, where he might be waiting in the shadows to pounce on her. She went quickly to her bedroom, a fugitive in her own home.

By employing tactics worthy of her uncle the general, Alice found it possible to avoid Lord Ivanridge.

It was no longer necessary for her to sit by his side at the high table, for after Christmas night the king and queen were expected to command whom they willed to sit there, and it was custom that the honor be spread around.

Alice complained to Rebecca of the waltzing so that she

not be in danger of that intimacy again, and she ensured her safety by escaping from the hall revelries as often as she could. When Roland questioned her, she told him tartly that it was his fault for inviting Lord Standon. Then she felt terribly guilty about maligning Charlie's behavior.

Through days of skating and treasure hunts, charades and riding, she maneuvered with the sole purpose of avoiding Ivanridge even though she had no clear evidence she was being stalked. She resented it deeply. The man was completely spoiling her Christmas. Even her father noticed how strangely she was behaving.

"Anything up, Alice?" he asked her on New Year's Eve. "You don't seem to be in the thick of things like you used to be. Not feeling quite the thing?"

"I feel perfectly well, Father," she said, knowing that any other answer would have the doctor at the door. "I just feel I have to keep an eye on things."

"Nonsense!" declared Lord Raneleigh. "Everything's going marvelously. No more of it, now. Roland's organizing Snapdragon for midnight. I expect to see you in there grabbing a few, my girl. All right?"

Alice sighed. "Yes, Father."

That night as everyone waited for the approach of midnight and the beginning of the Year of Our Lord, 1816, Roland entered the hall bearing a great shallow earthen dish. Rebecca followed with a lighted taper. There was clapping and cheering, but all Alice's attention was on Ivanridge to be sure he stayed on the other side of the room from herself. He seemed fixed in the company of Lord Garstang and Miss Travis, however, and so she relaxed a little and allowed herself to join in the fun.

Her brother ordered the lights extinguished. Soon the room was plunged into darkness, except for the glow from the fire at the far end and that from Rebecca's taper. There was expectant silence as she touched the flame to the bowl. When the eerie blue flames danced up, Roland carried the dish of flaming brandy-soaked raisins to the high table and Alice started the traditional chant,

Here he comes with flaming bowl.
Don't be mean to take his toll,
Snip! Snap! Dragon!

Rebecca blew out her light and the lurid flames of burning alcohol were the only illumination as everyone gathered round to see who would be the first brave soul to risk their fingers.

Looking suitably devilish in the strange light, Roland flexed his hand. Quick as a flash he grabbed a raisin and popped it still flaming into his mouth and bit down. There was a cheer.

Take care you don't take too much,
Be not greedy in your clutch,
Snip! Snap! Dragon!

Major Ewing went next, then the Duke of Portsmouth who fumbled and burnt his fingers. There was a groan of derisive sympathy.

With his blue and lapping tongue
Many of you will be stung.
Snip! Snap! Dragon!

Alice was about to demand a turn when she thought to check on Ivanridge again. He wasn't where he'd been before. She searched the crowd, but it was amazing how different people looked in the strange blue light. She felt a prickling between her shoulder blades but stopped herself from looking behind. She'd had enough of letting him spoil everything. If she wanted a raisin, she'd take one!

She stepped boldly forward and plucked a raisin from the flames. There was a cry. Before she could pop the raisin in her mouth it was slapped away. She was grabbed from behind, spun, and crushed to a hard chest.

"Damn you!" she cried in disbelieving fury that he would attack her so in public. She kicked at him, then understood.

The smell of burning silk and velvet told the story. He relaxed his arms cautiously, and they both looked down to where her loose silk sleeve had burned away, singing his velvet where he'd smothered the flames.

Alice swayed with the shock of what might have been. She looked up at him numbly.

"Are you all right?" he asked as if he cared.

She nodded.

"Are you burnt?"

She felt a mild pain and looked down. "Just a little. It's nothing."

He relaxed. "Getting off lightly again," he said, the familiar edge returning to his voice. "You never learn, do you?"

By then her family and others were gathered around. "Good Lord, Alice," said Roland, "I didn't think I had to remind you to beware of trailing sleeves!"

"I didn't think—"

"I don't know what's the matter with you, Alice," said her father testily, which showed he was upset. "You're not yourself. Our thanks to you, Ivanridge. Damn quick thinking."

"I just happened to be closest."

"Nonsense. Fine bit of work. Learned it fighting Boney, I suppose." Lord Raneleigh looked at the younger man closely. "Fancy you were here a few years back in Hussar uniform, yes?"

Alice wondered if the sudden tension came from Ivanridge or herself. It was only then she realized that though she'd turned to face her father she had done so within the circle of Ivanridge's arms. She made a move to escape, but his hold was like steel and no inconspicuous movement was going to free her.

"Yes, Lord Raneleigh," said Ivanridge levelly. "That was before I inherited the title."

"Ah, that explains why I didn't recognize the name. Been bothering me. Don't usually forget people. Norman!" he announced with satisfaction. "That's it. Tyr Norman. Fine name for a fighting man. Thought so at the time. The Norse god of battle and the warlike race that conquered this island. Heard you lived up to your name, too. Good show. Good show."

50

Roland had turned back to supervise the game again and cheers and squeals indicated success or singeing, but Alice's father had put his considerable bulk between her and the table so she could not see what was going on. It also meant that the small amount of light was blocked. In that private darkness, Tyr Norman's arms settled more thoroughly about her. Again she thought about struggling, but instead she gave in to temptation and relaxed back against his hard body.

"Thank you, Raneleigh," Ivanridge said smoothly, as if nothing was untoward. "But it was more the case of seeming to find myself in situations which called for heroics. I did not set out to gain a reputation."

"Just lucky, hey?"

Though she knew she shouldn't, Alice raised her hands and laid them on his over her midriff. Sweet heaven, but this felt so right. There was no reaction.

"You could put it that way, I suppose," said Ivanridge dryly. "Certainly my destiny was shaped by some force, malign or otherwise."

She wanted to turn in the circle of his arms and taste his lips again . . .

"Otherwise, my boy!" declared her father. "Look where you are today. A fine reputation, a title, and a pretty woman in your arms." He peered at Alice. "Still look a bit shaken, my girl. But you can't cling to your rescuer all night." Alice hastily moved her hands. "Let him at the raisins before these greedy people have them all!"

Ivanridge took his arms from around her, but before she could gather her wits, he grasped her uninjured wrist and pulled her forward to the bowl.

"I deprived you of your raisin," he said. "I'll get you another one."

Knocked off balance by the sweetness of those intimate moments, Alice didn't know what to say, and she still couldn't read him. Had he really been concerned for her safety? Had there been sincerity in that cherishing hold? "There's no need," she said.

51

"I don't want to be in your debt. Ready?"

Without waiting for her consent, he reached out and snatched a flaming raisin. He brought it rapidly to her mouth. Alice hesitated for a fraction of a second, thinking it would serve him right to burn his fingers but then repented of such petty spite and opened her mouth. She closed it quickly on the delicious burned-brandy sweetness.

He sucked his fingers, but she had no way of telling whether he was soothing a burn or enjoying the remains of the brandy. He looked at her and in the uncertain light appeared much more the warm-hearted young man with whom she had fallen in love. She recognized the danger of it. No, she told herself desperately. She wouldn't play the fool again.

"Now you should get one for me," he said.

"After I was almost burnt to a crisp?"

"You were only slightly singed." He smiled slightly and without bitterness. "I'd be interested to know whether such a brush with danger puts you off or whets your appetite for more."

He *was* trying to seduce her again. Alice lost control of her breathing. "I'd be mad to want to catch fire a second time . . ."

He released her wrist and slid his hand around her until it rested in the small of her back as if they were alone in the world, as they might as well be in this dim light and playful mayhem. "Rather depends on the fire, doesn't it, Miranda?"

His hand felt like a burning brand there, and flames were spreading from it along her nerves. *No, she wouldn't let him do this to her!* She moved away from the heat, but that only took her a step closer to his body. She looked up at him. "What do you want?" she whispered desperately.

"Sweet, spicy fire in my mouth," he said softly. "I thought you were a courageous lady."

Alice was at the end of her strength. "If I pick you a raisin, Tyr, will you please leave me in peace?"

Something flashed in his eyes — anger? pain? — then dark

52

lashes shielded it. After a moment he looked at her again and all she saw was kindness. "Yes, Alice. The war's over, isn't it? We all deserve some peace."

Alice nodded. He released her and she stepped close to the almost empty bowl. This time she made sure that her sleeves were well out of the way, then she picked a raisin and popped it in his ready mouth.

"Mmm," he said as he swallowed. "Delicious." He caught her hand and slowly licked the trace of sweetness there. "You have to admit, Miranda," he said almost wistfully, "we are very good together." His smile was gentle as he kissed her knuckles. *"Pax tecum, deliciae."*

With that he left her and Alice knew the persecution — if it had ever existed at all — was over. Everything was over, except the Twelve Days. There were six more to go.

Alice moved through the days as if her head, her heart, and her body were separate. Lack of comment told her that her body was doing all the appropriate things. Her head struggled with the fact that she still loved a rogue and would go to his bed again if he snapped his fingers. Her heart ached because she wouldn't allow herself to do it.

She survived by counting away the days until he'd be gone. But she couldn't stop watching him like someone who stores scraps against a coming famine.

She could see no dark side to him now. He was still harder and tougher than he had been six years ago, but he was more relaxed. He was very popular and was kind and warm to everyone.

Except herself. He ignored Alice as if she didn't exist.

On the fifth of January Rebecca came to Alice's room to share morning coffee again. With Rebecca being Queen of the Revels, they had not found much occasion for chat.

"So here we are at the twelfth day," said Rebecca. "I must say that you work your guests hard, Alice."

"The penalty of being a monarch," said Alice, staring into the fire.

"Are you sure you are quite well, Alice?" Rebecca asked

with concern. "You seem in very low spirits."

Alice looked at her friend, knowing Rebecca would see more than most. "I am perhaps a little tired, Becca. But please don't fuss."

"It's only that we care, dearest. I wondered whether you had burned yourself more seriously than we thought on New Year's Eve."

"No, honestly. It was nothing." Alice pulled back her sleeve. "See. There's not even a mark."

"Lord Ivanridge acted so quickly, didn't he? At first I thought him a little cold, but having to be with him to think up new mayhem, I have developed a warm regard for the man."

Alice looked at her friend in horror, aware of a stabbing pain suspiciously near her heart.

"Why do you look like that?" asked Rebecca, then she laughed. "Oh, not in that way, Alice, though why you should look as if I'd suggested self-immolation, I don't know. We have just become friends. I like him, and I think he's a man I could trust if I needed to."

"I suppose so," said Alice, feeling she had to say something.

Rebecca considered her. "It is my opinion that the gallant hero is not indifferent to you, Alice. I've seen him look at you once or twice in a very meaningful way. And it's amazing how often he turns the conversation to the topic of one Lady Alice Conyngham."

Alice felt her face flame. "You must be imagining it."

Rebecca grinned triumphantly. "You're *not* indifferent! I knew it. Why on earth are the two of you avoiding each other? It would be an excellent match on both sides."

"Heavens! Do you have us married already, and we've scarcely shared a sentence?"

" 'Methinks the lady doth protest too much'."

Alice scowled at her friend and sought a retaliatory weapon. "And what of you and Charlie, then? You're living in one another's pockets."

Now it was Rebecca's turn to blush. "I . . . I do find I

like Charlie very much." She looked anxiously at Alice. "I have no desire to hurt you, though."

Alice gaped. She had taken in the fact that Rebecca and Lord Standon were often in company without truly absorbing it. "I have no interest in Charlie," she assured her friend. "But you said you liked Ivanridge, too. Are you becoming a flirt, Becca?"

Rebecca smiled thoughtfully. "I like Ivanridge, but if I were to never see him again after tomorrow, I wouldn't give a fig. If I never saw Charlie again, I . . . I would miss him."

Alice absorbed her friend's words and stared into the flames again. She realized her feelings were the exact reverse of Rebecca's. The thought that Tyr Norman would leave Conyngham tomorrow, possibly never to be seen again, was unendurable.

"Oh, Alice," Rebecca said, interrupting these anguished thoughts, "you *do* care. You must know that I would never steal Charlie from you."

Alice felt as if she had been dreaming and had suddenly woken up. What had she been thinking of? She couldn't let Tyr Norman leave her life a second time or not without a battle. And she desperately needed to know what was behind the dark bitterness he had brought to Conyngham. She sensed that there she would find the key to her heart's desire.

She looked directly at her friend. "I don't want Charlie. I want Ivanridge."

"*What?*"

Alice leant over to take her friend's hand. "Becca, you are not to tell a soul. Promise?"

A wide-eyed Rebecca nodded.

"I jilted Charlie six years ago because I'd fallen in love with Tyr Norman."

Rebecca gasped. "But why did you never tell anyone?"

Alice lied without a twinge of conscience. "My mother wouldn't permit such a mésalliance." In spirit it was true. The Countess of Raneleigh would have had to be tortured in her own dungeons before she would have agreed to her only daughter marrying a mere captain.

Rebecca knew this and nodded. "But everything's changed now, dearest. Why are you avoiding him?"

"Because everything's changed," said Alice cryptically, rising to her feet. She felt as if she were singing with new purpose and power. "But I can't give up without a fight. I intend to use every weapon in my arsenal. Don't ask questions, Becca, but will you be ready to help if I need it?"

"Need you ask?" Rebecca chuckled. "But this has the feel of one of those scrapes you were forever leading me into in our schoolroom days."

Alice shared a grin. "It does, doesn't it? But I promise, this one is going to be a lot more exciting. And a lot more rewarding."

The first thing Alice did was cut Charlie free. She drew him aside after breakfast. "Charlie, I am very flattered that you are still willing to consider me as a wife, but I think we both deserve better than mild affection." She did not miss the flash of relief in his eyes.

"I think you're right," he said, adding perceptively, "Is there finally someone else, Alice?"

Alice smiled. "Perhaps. You can be sure, if you hear of my nuptials, the relationship will not be based on mild affection." She reached up and kissed his cheek. On impulse she said, *"Pax tecum,* Charlie."

"Peace be with you too, Alice," he said and went off to speak to Rebecca.

Having tidied her house, Alice considered the next part of her strategy. She couldn't be sure that simply throwing herself in Tyr Norman's arms was going to do any good, despite the declaration of armistice, and she still had to solve the mystery of his behavior.

That was necessary in order that she know how to approach him. It was also necessary for her own peace of mind. Love, she discovered, had little use for pride, and she would forgive and forget his treatment of her if she had to.

She would prefer, however, to at least understand it.

The obvious point of attack was Gen. George Travis-Blount who had arrived two days before. She ran him to ground smoking a pipe in her father's study. He was a sinewy, hawkfeatured man who bore a great resemblance to Alice's mother.

"Ah, Alice," he said without particular warmth. He'd never been a demonstrative man, and his manner to her had become stiffer as she had left girlhood behind.

"Good morning, Uncle," said Alice, taking a purposeful seat opposite him and arranging her flowing blue skirts. "I wanted to talk to you about warfare."

He scowled at her. "What the devil for? Not a suitable subject for a lady."

"Since men fight to keep us safe, Uncle, I would have thought it appropriate that we take an interest."

"Nonsense. Men manage war best without women dabbling their fingers in it."

That seemed to be said with some meaning, but Alice couldn't fathom it, so she stuck to her guns. "But when men return from war, it is often women who have to cope with the consequences." At his blank look, she added, "Wounds."

"Oh. I suppose so." He scowled at her. "Not thinking of marrying a wounded soldier, are you? Damned stupid thing to do."

Alice realized she didn't like Uncle George very much. "I would have thought it noble," she said.

The only reply he made was a snort of disgust.

Refusing to permit a distraction, Alice continued her advance. "Is it true, Uncle, that some soldiers are wounded in mind as well as in body?"

He puffed on his pipe. "Only weaklings."

"But some of the things that happen in war must leave horrible memories. Perhaps," she added, "give people nightmares."

He took his pipe out of his mouth and glared at her. "And what do you know, missy, of men's nightmares?"

At that moment a number of terrible revelations came to Alice in a flash. She was silent as she struggled to sort through them.

"Eh, missy!" her uncle barked. "Been up to your old tricks? Eh?"

Alice was too shocked to be embarrassed. "Mother told you."

"She did indeed. I'm pleased to see you have some decency and haven't taken your shame to an honest man's bed."

Alice felt as if her mind was like a blade—clean, sharp and deadly. She easily ignored his words and aimed for the heart. "Why did she tell you?"

"Eh? What?"

"You and my mother were not so close. She would not have told you without a reason."

His eyes slid away, and he made a business of fiddling with his pipe. "She was considerably distressed," he muttered.

Alice arranged her information like the battalions of an army: her mother's nature and her uncle's; Tyr Norman as she had known him six years ago and as she knew him now; his words as they danced on Christmas night. Major Ewing's description of his military career.

She waited, absorbing it all, until her uncle uneasily turned to look at her.

"You tried to kill him," she said.

His face twitched angrily, and he muttered words too foul for her to truly understand. "I'd have called him out but that your mother feared the talk. Don't know how he survived."

Alice wanted to scream foul words back at him, to claw at his sharp-boned face, but she was icy as she asked, "Why did you stop?"

"Wellington!" her uncle spat. "Damned jackanapes took a fancy to the rogue. It was made clear that I was to cease my meddling, so don't screech at me, girl. I did my best. You and your mother near broke me, and none of it would have come about if you'd just kept your knees together."

He was upset because he'd failed, not because of what he'd done. Alice could see no purpose in talking to him further. She stood stiffly. "He's here," she said.

Her uncle was goggle-eyed. "What! Tyr Norman?"

Alice nodded. "He's Lord Ivanridge now. You played billiards with him last night." Some of her anguish escaped. "Didn't you even know what he *looked* like, this man you were trying to kill?"

"Why the devil should I?"

Alice held his eyes. "If," she said with cool precision, "Tyr Norman has a heart big enough to forgive this family for what they have done to him, I am going to marry him. If you ever harm a hair of his head again, Uncle, I'll kill you myself."

With that, she left her uncle gaping.

Alice's urge was to run to Tyr and pour out the whole story, to persuade him that she'd known nothing of the foul plot, but she sensed that would be disaster.

For one thing, the Twelfth-Day tournament was underway, and the King of the Revels would be busy all day with the arrangements and taking part. For another, it would be better to consider her approach carefully, for there were traps to avoid.

It would be easy, for example, to slip into upbraiding him for leaving her without a word. It would be equally easy to scold him for his cruelty during this visit, even though she now understood. These things were irrelevant when set beside the horror which had been visited on him.

She remembered his words, now so meaningful. "It was more the case of seeming to find myself in situations which called for heroics." "My destiny was shaped by some force, malign or otherwise." She wondered when it had dawned on him that the fact he constantly found himself in the most hellish situations of the war was not simple bad luck.

No, she simply wasn't ready to talk to him yet. Tonight. She would speak to him tonight. On Twelfth Night. It seemed appropriate.

Before she went down to the tournament, she changed into her most becoming gown, a flowing gold wool worked with brown embroidery. She set a filmy veil of silk gauze edged with gold over her long plaits, fixing it with a gold circlet. She added a gold collar around her neck and heavy gold bracelets of medieval design. These bracelets had more commonly been worn by warriors, but that seemed appropriate. Alice was dressing for the fight of her life. The fight for love.

The tournament was held in the large meadow below the east walls, and a stand had been erected for the ladies and the elderly gentlefolk. Around the other three sides, ropes held back the local people who were all cheering for their favorite knights.

Even though the lances and swords were blunt, Alice had her heart in her mouth as she watched her beloved fight. She almost burst with pride at the sheer skill of the man. Roland was fit and trained for this medieval warfare. Major Ewing was a hardened, competent soldier. But Tyr had a spark of genius in the way he handled weapons and mount so that he carried all the prizes.

No wonder Uncle George had found him so hard to kill.

Rebecca slipped into the seat beside her. "Could I guess, perhaps, why you are dressed so beautifully?"

Alice took in Rebecca's very fetching blue and cream costume. "Doubtless the same reason you look your best."

Rebecca blushed and laughed. "But I fear Lord Standon is not cut out for bloody warfare." They both winced as he was neatly unhorsed by Roland.

Next, Roland fought Tyr. Tyr won.

"Alice," Rebecca said softly, "you're looking at the man as if he were a flaming raisin you want to snap up."

Alice burst out laughing. "A flaming raisin! Becca, what a thing to call such a magnificent specimen."

Rebecca smiled and shook her head. Alice looked back to find that Tyr's attention had been caught by her laughter, and he was looking at her. She wished he were the sort of man who could be read.

He had been once, before her uncle and her mother had put him through hell.

She swallowed tears. The desire to run down and enfold him in her love was almost overpowering, but she controlled it. She must wait. She could never let him go, though. She'd tear her clothes off again, if that was what it took.

The light was going by the time the last tournament prizes were awarded. Now the huge bonfire was lit — the final celebration of light in this midwinter festival which was as much pagan as Christian.

Whole carcasses of ox, sheep, venison, and pig had been roasting all day. Now the mulled cider and the wassail bowl came out and a feast began for all — servants, tenants, tradesmen, neighbors. Anyone who cared to attend. There were all ages, from babes to centenarians, and all having a good time.

Alice kept a longing eye on Tyr, her need to be with him warring with her self-control. It wasn't practical to think of speaking here of meaningful things. He was always the center of a merry crowd, and she had her duties to perform, ensuring that all the guests were content.

A band of fiddle, pipe, and drum tuned up, and country dancing started. Alice danced with whomever asked as a clear full moon rose up to light the crisp winter landscape.

Alice noted that Bella Carstairs had finally gotten some sense and dressed herself in a becoming but warm, red woolen gown. She had apparently abandoned hope of Lord Ivanridge and was flirting purposefully with Lord Garstang.

Susan Travis was pretty in a cream and brown outfit from the Conyngham wardrobes and had come out of her shell considerably. Alice saw her dancing with Tyr and looking radiant, but it didn't bother her. She knew it was just the glow of being relaxed and admired and a sign of Tyr's kindness.

Rebecca and Charlie were together more often than not.

It was not in their characters to be demonstrative, but Alice, who knew them well, could sense the warmth that was comfortably growing between them, and was delighted.

It was clear that Tyr was deliberately avoiding her.

After a while this became intolerable and, fortified by a considerable amount of cider, Alice seized her beloved and dragged him into the circle for the next dance. It was just a country dance, but at least they were together and able to touch now and then.

After a momentary resistance, he didn't fight her, but it was as if he were walled off from her by glass. There was a polite smile on his lips, but she couldn't read his eyes. It was frustrating and frightening how little she could read him. It was alarming and exciting how even the fleeting unavoidable touches of his hand against her waist or fingers was turning her dizzy.

She was going to have to break through this barrier soon, to discuss delicate matters with this intimate stranger, and the thought terrified her.

He seemed to sense her unease and cautiously lowered his guard. "What's the matter?"

"I need to speak to you before you go."

The barrier slammed up again. "I don't think that's a good idea, Lady Alice."

The dance ended, and he was gone. Alice wondered if she would have to take him prisoner and lock him in the dungeons to speak to him. If that was what it took, she would, though she didn't know how she was going to explain it to her accomplices. And she certainly would need accomplices to overcome Tyr Norman.

Close to midnight the fire began to die. With the end of the fire, the Twelfth Night would be over. When the Twelfth Night was over, the Twelve Day Festival would be over. Everyone would leave, including Tyr.

Lord Raneleigh and the farmers went off singing to do homage to the trees and assure good fruiting in the coming year. As the midnight bells rang from the village church,

62

gun shots and horns were heard from the orchard as the men saluted the oldest apple tree. The Reverend Herbert studiously ignored this pagan rite.

Slowly, sated people began to drift home, either to village or castle, still singing as they went.

It was time. Alice looked around for Tyr.

He had disappeared.

In a blind panic, she ran to the stables, imagining that he'd already whipped a team up to speed to carry him away from Conyngham. But when she arrived, she found everything peaceful. She leant against a stall to catch her breath, wondering if she had finally run mad.

A sleepy groom came to see what the matter was, and she had no sensible answer for him. She merely shook her head and headed up to the house.

On Twelfth Night everyone was a little reluctant to admit it was the end and go to bed. People were scattered all over the castle—a few in the billiard room, others in the library, some playing instruments in the music room, others playing cards in the Chinese Room. There was even a supper laid out in the Great Hall for the few with an inch or two of space in their bellies.

Alice could not find Tyr.

Casting desperately along a first-floor corridor, Alice came across a couple twined together in a window embrasure. Without hesitation, she interrupted them.

"Rebecca, have you seen Tyr?"

Rebecca was rosy with embarrassment, and Charlie looked cross. "Damn it, Alice—"

But Rebecca stopped him with a gentle touch. "He said he was retiring," she said.

"Oh, Lord," muttered Alice.

Rebecca looked understanding. "Charlie could go and tell him you want to speak with him."

After that earlier rebuff, Alice knew that would do no good. "No," she said. "It's all right. Sorry to have interrupted."

Charlie watched her hurry away. "I'm beginning to worry

about Alice."

Rebecca gently regained his attention. "There's no need, love. She'll be fine. Now, before we were interrupted . . ."

Alice progressed briskly towards the chamber she had allotted to Lords Standon and Ivanridge, not allowing herself time to lose her nerve. This all felt eerily like that night six years ago, except then she had been much more tremulous. Tonight she felt like tempered steel.

At the polished mahogany door she raised her hand to knock but decided that would be a poor tactic. She turned the knob and walked in.

He was lounging on the bed with only the fire for illumination, cradling a glass of brandy. He looked up sharply, then sighed. "Go away, Alice."

Alice shut the door and leaned against it. "I need to talk to you."

"This isn't the time or the place."

"Last time you left at the crack of dawn."

He looked down and swirled the spirit. "With the passing of Twelfth Night, the magic fades . . ." He looked up at her somberly. "What do you want? An apology for living?"

Alice gripped her hands together. "I have come to offer an apology, Tyr. An apology for all that has been done to you by my family."

There was no reaction. His gaze rested on her steadily. "Accepted," he said at last. "Now go."

Alice bit her lip. "Tyr, I knew nothing about it!"

He closed his eyes and leant his head back against the headboard. "Alice, I came here full of bitterness with thoughts of revenge. I've managed to rid myself of it. It's over. Just leave me in peace."

Alice walked forward until she was standing by the bed. His eyes remained closed. "If you don't listen to me," she said, "if you don't talk to me, Tyr Norman, I'll start tearing my clothes off again."

Those dark eyes snapped open. "You never did fight fair, did you?"

"I don't want to fight at all, Tyr. I love you."

Their eyes held as if locked. "You said that six years ago, too."

He was frighteningly hard, impervious. Alice could feel minute tremors shake her body and wondered how long she'd be able to stand, what would happen when she collapsed onto the bed. "I meant it six years ago," she whispered, "and it never changed, though I hated you at the same time."

"That doesn't make much sense."

"Six years ago you said you loved me. Did the love die when you started to hate?"

He broke the gaze and looked down. "One tends to displace the other."

"Which is in you now?" she asked softly.

He took a swig of brandy. "I am gratefully numb with alcohol."

Alice grabbed the glass and sent it crashing to flare in the fireplace. *"Talk to me!"*

His eyes flashed and he grabbed her, pulling her down to his lap. "What of, Miranda? Love? War? What the hell do you *want* from me?"

Alice knew she should be scared, but she felt as if she was finally back where she belonged. "I'm asking you to marry me," she said.

His grip relaxed in astonishment.

Alice grasped the initiative and placed her hands on his shoulders. "I fell in love with you six years ago, Tyr, and it seems to be a permanent affliction. I can't bear to let you go without using every weapon I have."

"Do you know you have a very warlike turn of phrase?"

The muscles beneath her hands made no movement, gave her no indication of his feelings. She tightened her hold. "Do you know you are the most shielded, guarded person I have ever met? *Show* me something of yourself, Tyr, before I lose my nerve!"

His mouth came down on hers, hot and spicy with brandy. He wasn't gentle, as he had been six years ago. Instead he crushed her to him and seared her with a passion capable of destroying both of them.

When the kiss ended, Alice looked up at him, shaken almost to fainting. "Thank you," she whispered.

With a crack of laughter, he pushed her aside and leapt off the bed to stand by the window. He rested his head on his hands there. After what felt like an endless silence, he said, "Tell me exactly what went on six years ago, as you know it."

With wisps of hope and considerable fear that heaven might yet escape her, Alice obeyed. When she'd finished she added, "I have to admit that I started this by telling my mother what happened." There was no response from that broad back, and so she carried on, determined to get it over with. "I must also confess that I didn't quite tell her the whole story."

He turned then, a touch of humor in his shadowed face. "I suppose you omitted little details such as declaring your undying love and tearing your clothes off."

Alice nodded ruefully. "But I never imagined she would seek revenge. I feared Roland or my father might call you out, but Mother . . ."

He leaned back against the window frame arms crossed. "First rule of life. Never underestimate a woman."

His protective shell was cracked, but Alice was far from sure of success. She still couldn't tell what was in his head. "Don't you believe me?" she asked.

"I just wonder why you had this insane urge to confess to your mother at all."

Surprise brought her up to her knees. "You abandoned me! I needed to talk to someone. I was terrified I was going to have a baby!"

He stared at her blankly. "You thought — For God's sake, Alice, you couldn't be that naive." He walked over until he stood by the bed. His gaze was both searching and disbelieving. "Miranda," he said gently, "I never even took my breeches off."

Alice gaped. "You never . . . ?" She searched her memory, seeking detail amid dizzy ecstasy. "It was all rather hazy . . ." She felt hot color flood her cheeks and hid them in her hands. "Oh heavens, I fear I was just that naive." Then she looked up again, wide-eyed. "You mean there's *more?*"

He started to laugh. He leaned against one of the solid bed posts and laughed; there was more than a little wildness in it. At last he regained control of himself but kept his head against the post. He shook it now and then.

Alice swallowed. "Is there any point in saying I'm sorry?"

He looked at her, his eyes still damp with mirth. "It's always worth saying you're sorry. I should have realized, I suppose. You were such a darling innocent. But how could you think I'd leave you without a word if I'd taken your maidenhead?"

Alice was swamped with guilt for that lack of faith. She hesitated then put the question. "Why didn't you . . . ?"

He sat on the bed, leaning against the post, arms around one raised knee. Ghosts of humor still relaxed his features. "I had my orders, Alice. I sailed for Lisbon on the tenth. You enchanted me from Christmas Eve on, but I had to keep my wits for both our sakes. Not only were you a Conyngham while I was nothing, but you were engaged to marry a fine, wealthy, titled man. The only thing I could do for you was to spare you my inappropriate devotion." He smiled wryly. "I'd have done it too, if you'd behaved like a proper maid."

"I fell in love," she said softly, sending words across a gap she didn't quite dare to bridge. "I couldn't bear the thought of you leaving me. How could you bear the thought of leaving?"

"What choice did I have?" he asked simply.

"I would have broke off with Charlie in a moment. I did break it off with him. You should have known that."

"I never did have much faith in miracles. The closest I ever came to one was when the girl I adored came into my room and shyly begged for my love. I knew I mustn't take everything she offered, but I couldn't resist something to carry away to war. I was honored to be the first to show you

67

the magic of love, Miranda."

Alice rose to her knees and worked her way down the bed until her legs brushed his. At last she dared to tease. "And succeeded so well that I never even noticed you kept your breeches on. Truly noble restraint, my lord."

"I'm glad you finally appreciate that." He plucked off her gold circlet, slid back her veil, and began to unravel first one plait then the other.

Alice's heart was thundering. "What are you doing?"

"In filthy mud, when deafened by cannons, choked by smoke, and surrounded by the dead and dying, I held a picture in my mind. Miranda with her hair long and loose around her . . ." He threaded his fingers through the heavy mass of it, letting it drift down around her so the ends trailed softly on the counterpane.

His hands slid beneath to circle her neck, cradling her skull. "Do I get to set the date, then, since you proposed? Not that it was much of a proposal . . ."

Joy bursting within, Alice pulled out of his lax hold and fell to her knees beside the bed. "Oh noble hero, mighty warrior! Honor this humble maid by giving her your name and heart in return for her everlasting devotion and love. Shield me in your strength and let me wrap you in the warmth of my tender love . . ." She had begun in parody but ended in honesty. "Please, Tyr, let me chase all the shadows from your eyes."

In a heartbeat he was on the floor beside her, and she was in his arms, wrapped again in the power of his kiss. After a satisfying interval Alice fought free to gasp, "Does that mean yes?"

"Did I ever have a choice?" His eyes were warm with laughter as his lips hungrily sought hers again.

The door burst open. Lord Raneleigh, Roland, Charlie, and Rebecca all pushed into the room.

"Damme!" spluttered Alice's father.

"Rebecca!" accused Alice. She began to scramble to her feet.

Tyr snared her and kept her in his lap. "Very comfortable

carpet you have, Lord Raneleigh. Won't you join us?"

"Damme!" said Lord Raneleigh again. Roland and Charlie began to laugh.

"Sorry," said Rebecca unrepentantly to Alice. "I thought I'd make sure you didn't muff it this time."

"Muff what?" bellowed Lord Raneleigh. "Damn it, girl, get out of his lap!"

"I can't, Father," said Alice. "He's very strong. And anyway, since we're to be married, I suppose I should obey him."

Her father glared at her. "Well, of course you're going to be married when I find you rolling on the bedroom floor with him. What I want to know is why you couldn't go about it in a more normal manner. First you throw over Charlie, now this!"

Tyr suddenly stood, carrying Alice with him, then setting her on her feet. "You're completely correct, Lord Raneleigh," he said. "The only thing for it is to get her married before she changes her mind again. I think two weeks from now would do nicely."

"Two weeks," said Alice's father blankly. "You can't be married in a fortnight!"

"We don't want a big wedding, Father," said Alice, "and it's long past time I was wed." She smiled up at Tyr. "In fact, I think twelve nights would be quite long enough to wait."

His arms tightened. "Twelve nights it is. Did I ever tell you twelve is my lucky number?"

"Mine too," said Alice against his lips. "In fact Twelfth Night will always have a very special place in my heart."

"Damme," said the earl. "They're at it again!"

The Lords of Misrule
by Sara Blayne

"Maggie Willoughby, you cannot mean that!" exclaimed Charlotte Fenwick, eyeing her cousin in disbelief, who was sprawled on her stomach across the fourposter bed.

"Charlesworth and Oliver Crandall are two of the most sought after bachelors in England," continued Charlotte. "Any hostess would simply die to have them counted among her guests. And they are coming here to Willoughby Hall for Christmas. Why, it is a feather in your mama's cap, and yet *you* claim you could do just as well without their presence! Anyone would think you were a candidate for Bedlam for saying any such thing."

"Nevertheless, it is true," Maggie insisted, her brown eyes stubborn. "Christmas is meant to be a family affair, and now that the earl and his brother have condescended to accept Father's invitation, what has Mama done but get it in her head that she must invite the Winterbottoms, the Brewsters, the Thomas Smythes, the Guthries, *and,* heaven forbid, Her Grace, the Dowager Duchess of Almouth."

"Maggie, how *could* you!" Charlotte could not quite suppress a startled giggle, half-amused and half-scandalized. "You know very well Almouth is pronounced with an 'oo,' not an 'ow.' "

"Yes, but you have seen her. And worse, been forced to *listen* to her prose on forever about the merits of her daughter. Oh, yes, did I tell you? Lady Gwendolyn is to favor us with her presence as well. No doubt in spite of the fact that she is sister to a duke, she will be all too happy to cast her lures at a mere earl, especially since he is reputed to have an income which surpasses that of His Grace."

"Now you really are doing it much too brown," Charlotte insisted, flopping down on the bed beside the other girl. "It is not at all like you to be concerned over such things as incomes and titles. Why, if I did not know better, I should think you were jealous of Lady Gwendolyn."

"Jealous? Of Lady Gwendolyn? Charlotte, you must be mad. What in the world should I possibly find to envy in her?"

"Well," Charlotte considered, propping her chin in the palm of one hand, "she is thought to be quite beautiful, an Incomparable, in fact, with a fair wit and unexceptional manners. A diamond of the first water, if you will."

Maggie wrinkled her short nose in disgust. "Oh, she is beautiful all right, like a sculpture in ice or a porcelain figurine. I think her face would crack if ever she indulged in a real laugh instead of that tinkling sound she makes whenever she is beguiling some poor devil. As for her wit, you know as well as I that it is barbed, and while her manners may not be brass, they are most certainly polished steel. She has demonstrated the cutting edge of her tongue on more than one occasion of which I can think."

Charlotte's gaze abruptly wavered and fell from her cousin's. From the dark flash of Maggie's eyes, she had known instantly that uppermost in her mind was one particular occasion when it had been so. A blush stung her cheek at the painful memory. "Yes, well," she murmured quietly, "that was a very long time ago." She lifted her head, though she did not yet look at Maggie. "We were only children. You must learn to disregard it, Maggie. As have I."

Maggie bit her tongue to keep from blurting out a denial. They might have been children, but the memory was as fresh as if it had happened only yesterday. Nevertheless, it would do neither of them any good to dredge it all up again. The last thing she wanted was to hurt her cousin. Dearest Charlotte, who had never hurt anyone.

"Oh, you needn't worry," Maggie said, giving her curls a toss. "I have forgot all that long ago. In fact, I have come to view Lady Gwendolyn's presence at Willoughby in the light of a cloud with a silver lining. It is my one consolation that with her in our midst, the earl and his brother are hardly likely to notice me. I shall be free to go my own way, while *they,* no doubt, will be thoroughly occupied with Lady Gwendolyn."

Charlotte, taking in her cousin's lustrous brown curls and matching eyes, could not but have her doubts about that. Maggie, if she only knew it, was far more attractive than the duke's sister with her pale good looks. Besides having a fetching figure, smooth, unmottled skin the color of ivory, and cheeks with a rosy glow that came not from the rouge pot but from her affinity for the outdoors, Maggie was blessed with a natural warmth and vitality, which made her the life of any gathering. People were naturally drawn to her, something which Maggie herself seemed never to notice, no doubt because she'd never been farther from Willoughby Hall than ten miles. In Maggie's mind she'd never gotten the chance to put her popularity to the touch beyond the confines of home. Had she not been forced to forego her come-out last spring because of her mama's lying-in, she doubtless would have discovered herself at least the equal of Lady Gwendolyn, who, after all, was in her third Season and still unattached. Indeed, it was entirely conceivable that Maggie might find the earl and his brother not as indifferent as she hoped.

Turning over, Maggie bounced off the bed to embrace with wide open arms the sunshine streaming in through the bay window. Having vented her disapproval of her parents' invited houseguests, it seemed she had returned to her normally good humor. "Charlotte, did you ever see a more beautiful day?" she said expansively, flashing a look over her shoulder at her cousin. "It seems a positive shame to waste it, does it not?"

Charlotte, who had seen that look before and knew what it portended, sat up in alarm. "Oh, no," she warned, slowly shaking her head. "You know your mama said you were not to leave this room. Had you not put up such a fuss about singing tonight for the guests, you would not have been denied permission to attend Chloe's impromptu skating party. And, truly, I cannot think why you should have done, when you have a perfectly lovely soprano and play the pianoforte so well. One can hardly blame your mama for wanting to show you off, especially since she already blames herself for causing you to miss your come-out in London."

"Oh, but that's just it, don't you see? A come-out is one thing, but Christmas is quite another." Dropping down on her knees before the other girl, Maggie clasped Charlotte's hands earnestly in her own. "Dearest Cousin, next spring I shan't cavil at being paraded before all the dowagers, matrons, and eligible males. It is one's duty to marry, after all—as little as one might like it—especially when one has three younger sisters. But this was to be my last Christmas when I was gloriously free, and I do not intend to allow it to be ruined." Giving Charlotte's hands a squeeze, she sprang to her feet. "*I* am going skating," she announced with an ominous sparkle of defiance. "Are you coming with me?"

Charlotte, who did not understand at all her cousin's rejection of two eligible gentlemen, could only shake her head in wonder. Obviously Maggie did not have the least inkling what it was to have one's heart suddenly quicken at the mere appearance of a certain someone in a room or to know the delicious quiver of one's nerves at the accidental touch of a strong masculine hand. Maggie, it was quite certain, had never been in love.

"Maggie, pray do not look at me that way. You know I cannot," Charlotte said. "You forget. You may be free, but I am not. I am betrothed now. I dare not do anything that might reflect badly on my future husband. Besides, Felix is waiting. I promised him a drive."

"Are you quite sure? Everyone will be there," Maggie persisted, unable to keep the disappointment from her voice. For as long as she could remember, she and her cousin Charlotte had been closer than even sisters ever hoped to be. Now that was all changing, and she felt powerless to stop it. But then, that was the way it was when people set themselves up to be married. Only in this case, she had hoped against hope it would be different. Still, it was not Charlotte's fault, she reminded herself upon seeing the very real distress in her cousin's face. Charlotte, she realized with an odd little pang, did not love her any less simply because she loved Felix more.

"Oh, very well." With an effort she summoned her old, impish grin, which brought enchanting dimples out in either cheek. Playfully, she shoved her cousin toward the door. "Go for your drive. Though I daresay we should have had more fun stealing an afternoon at the pond. Oh, pray don't bother your head about me," she added, sensing her cousin's hesitation. "You may tell Mama that I have learned my lesson and shall be exceedingly pleased to perform after supper. Now, go."

Charlotte, smiling her relief, gave her cousin a quick hug and fled, free to enjoy her afternoon with Felix now that Maggie had apparently come to her senses.

No sooner had the door closed behind her, however, than Maggie was tugging on her cashmere pelisse trimmed with fur and covering her brown curls with a sealskin hat. Then, slinging her skates over her shoulder, she peeked out the door.

It was scarcely an hour since nuncheon, and the old

manor house was buzzing with last-minute preparations for the anticipated arrival of the guests. She could hear her father's good-natured raillery issuing from the Great Hall below, where, under her mother's watchful eye, he was in the process of hanging the kissing bough. Suddenly she grinned as her little sister Winifred's delighted squeal rang out.

" 'Lizabeth, look! Papa's kissing Mama!"

"The children, Mr. Willoughby, and the servants!" came her mother's scandalized reproach, which fooled no one, least of all her errant spouse.

"Now, now, Effie. You can't fault a man for stealing a kiss from the prettiest girl in the house. Especially when she stands so fetchingly beneath the mistletoe."

"Prettiest girl indeed. Such flummery. I am a woman of eight and thirty and the mother of a grown daughter," she did not hesitate to inform him, though Maggie was quick to discern the gruffness in her tone that clearly bespoke her pleasure at such a compliment.

Unexpectedly Maggie felt a lump rise in her throat. It was all a game. Everyone knew it. It had been the same every Christmas for as long as she could remember. How absurd that this time the antics of her parents should make her feel perilously close to falling into a fit of the megrims. Indeed, were she honest with herself, it was likely a twinge of conscience she was feeling for having precipitated the argument with her mama. Sneaking out of the house was not about to make matters any better. Still, she was eighteen. Old enough to decide things for herself. The fact was, she had not meant to be impertinent. Indeed, it seemed patently unfair to be punished simply for voicing her opinions on the subject of unwanted houseguests at Christmas.

Angry with herself without really knowing why, she firmly pushed such thoughts aside. It was the season for merriment, and she would be dashed if she spent it sulking indoors.

"Now be so good as to take yourself off," her mama was saying, shooing her husband from the room, no doubt, with the hem of her apron. "I've no time for such foolery."

Mr. Willoughby's laughter rumbled through the house, and Maggie, who had stolen out to the head of the stairs, backed hastily into a shallow alcove. Too late, it seemed, as her father, emerging from the hall, suddenly halted and glanced up.

She could have sworn the keen blue eyes looked straight into her own. Indeed, she could not mistake the significant arch of a single assessing eyebrow. The next instant to her surprise, she heard him noisily clear his throat and then, without a word, turn and stride off in the direction of the foyer, apparently for his morning ride.

No sooner had Maggie breathed a long sigh of relief than her lips quirked whimsically in a lopsided grin. With his twinkling blue eyes and his rather substantial figure garbed in a bottle green riding coat and buff unmentionables, her papa might have been Father Christmas himself. Truly, he had ever seemed to embody the spirit of the season with his hearty appreciation of all that was best about it—the drawing together of family, the observing of time-honored traditions, the warmth, the love, and, of course, the rollicking good fun. Surely he, of all people, must have realized how she felt.

This time next year, Maggie would already have made her come-out, and Christmas would never again be the same. She would either be betrothed or, worse, an acknowledged failure. In either case, her carefree days of girlhood would be gone forever. Not that she viewed her passage into womanhood with trepidation, she firmly told herself. But it had been so much *fun* growing up at Willoughby Hall! She was simply in no hurry to have it all behind her. She had made her feelings on the matter quite plain to Papa. She'd assured him that she was in no way devastated at having her come-out postponed by the birth of her new baby brother but had seen it as a sort of reprieve. Which was why she simply could not understand how he could have ruined everything by inviting Charlesworth and Oliver Crandall to Willoughby for Christmas!

Unfortunately, some quirk of fate had caused her father to suddenly desire a matched set of grays for the old landau. And of course, nothing short of Tattersall's in London would do for the acquisition of such a pair. But why did Charlesworth and his brother have to be there on that particular day? And if they had to be there, why did they have to strike up an immediate acquaintanceship with her father? And apparently they had hit it off very well indeed for her father to have invited them to join the family for the holidays. As to why two such noted gentlemen about town should have accepted was simply beyond her comprehension.

The fact remained, however, that they had, and standing around moping about it would change nothing. It would only mean she had wasted a perfectly glorious afternoon that she might have better spent skating. Firmly relegating the troublesome matter of the earl and his brother's impending arrival to the back of her mind, she turned and made her way quickly down the gallery to the back stairs and from there, out of the house.

December that year had been unseasonably cold with early threats of snow, but today the sun was out, and though there was a definite nip in the air, it was only enough to bring out the roses in Maggie's cheeks and a sparkle to her eye. There was a bounce in her step as well, as she made her way along the track, which led through a spinney of oak and down a low, rolling hill. By the time she had reached the bourne where it widened into a pond on the outskirts of the village, she had forgotten all about Charlesworth, Oliver Crandall, and Lady Gwendolyn.

She was not surprised to see the pond crowded with skaters. It was not often that the ice was thick enough before the first of January to allow for this favorite winter pastime, and she had known everyone would be of a mind to make the most of it. No sooner had she got her skates strapped on and launched herself with long, sure strides out on to the ice, than she was surrounded by a bevy of friends, all laughing and badgering her for news of her illustrious houseguests.

"No, they have *not* arrived yet," she announced to the obvious disappointment of all the female contingent. "And so I cannot say whether they are handsome or not."

"Oh, but my sister Marilla assures me they are quite dashing. Especially Mr. Crandall, who waltzes divinely."

"Oh, no, you are very much mistaken, Chloe. *My* sister, Rosalind, had the pleasure of dancing with Charlesworth four years ago when she had her come-out. It is her opinion that no gentleman displays to greater advantage on the dance floor than his lordship."

"Well, I, for one, could not care less which is the more dashing—Charlesworth or Crandall," Maggie declared with a grimace and, freeing herself of their clinging hands, propelled herself backward. *"Or* the handsomer or the anything else. Indeed, if you must know, I find the entire subject not a little bit tiresome."

Having made her escape, Maggie cut a neat turn and found herself staring into the eyes of a gentleman mounted on a prime bit of blood at the edge of the pond. She was given the impression of crisp blond hair topped by a curly brimmed beaver and having a definite tendency toward the rebellious, a strong, rugged face, which was nevertheless boyishly handsome, and indecently broad shoulders which showed to advantage beneath a many-caped greatcoat. Her first thought, that she had never seen a handsomer creature or one more obviously sure of himself, was quickly supplanted by the realization that he must have overheard everything she had said. Unaccountably, she blushed. Upon which, to her mounting confusion, he did the unpardonable — smiling in obvious amusement, he bowed his head and tipped the brim of his hat to her.

Maggie only just managed to stifle a gasp. How dared the coxcomb make fun of her! Obviously, he was arrogant and conceited. And, worse, he apparently thought her something less than a lady. A gentleman, after all, did not make overtures to a female to whom he had never been properly introduced, not, that is, unless he believed such overtures would be welcomed. Instantly, her head came up, her eyes flashing dangerously. Well, she would show him that his most definitely were not.

Head held regally high, she glided past him without deigning even a single glance his way. Unfortunately, she failed to take note of two boys on a sled careering on a collision course straight for her. She was just congratulating herself on having put the odious stranger in his place, when a grip of steel closed ruthlessly about her arm and, yanking her unceremoniously backward, spun her around.

An exclamation of purely feminine outrage burst from her lips as she found herself clasped ignominiously against a hard masculine chest.

"How *dare* you!" she gasped, struggling to free herself as she fought to get her head up to see just who *had* dared to assault her person.

She had time only to recognize the handsome features of the stranger who had insulted her when the sled whizzed by, missing her by inches, and her skate slipped, catching the gentleman behind one booted foot and sweeping his leg out from under him.

Together they tumbled to the ice.

For what seemed a long moment but was actually no more than a heartbeat or two, Maggie lay stunned atop the gentleman, her brown eyes wide and staring on his, scant inches from her own. All at once a frown puckered her brow.

"Gentian," she pronounced musingly. "No, most definitely lapis lazuli." Then, at the quizzical upsweep of a pair of blond eyebrows: "Your eyes," she explained kindly. "They are a most astonishing shade of blue, but then you must already know that. No doubt any number of people have told you they are the color of lapis lazuli."

"Oh, indeed," he agreed with only the slightest quiver of amusement. "Any number. But none with as convincing candor. Tell me, do you always begin conversations with complete strangers by making such pointed observations? If so, you will not mind if I return the compliment by observing that *your* eyes are the color of fine brandy as seen in the reflected glow of firelight, a comparison which you have doubtless come to view as trite, having heard it many times before."

"Then you would be quite mistaken." She grinned, the dimples peeping forth like twin imps in her cheeks. "The truth is, my eyes are plain brown."

"Brown, perhaps, but never plain, my girl," objected the gentleman. "I am not in the custom of dealing in Spanish coin."

"Are you not? Odd, I should have thought the females of your acquaintance must be well-supplied with just such a treasure trove. But then, I have very little on which to base any such assumption—only, in fact, that you are holding me unconscionably tight and in a position which shall soon prove compromising should you not immediately release me."

"I was wondering when you would notice that," he replied reflectively, making no discernible move to unbind his arms from around her waist. "And just when I was growing accustomed to making light repartee while lying prone on my back on a sheet of ice. I had begun to believe it was a local custom perfectly acceptable in the circumstances."

She could not stop the startled bubble of laughter that

83

rose to her lips.

"How perfectly absurd," she gurgled, firmly disengaging herself as she rolled to one side and sat up. "You must know very well that it is not. Any more than it is the custom for gentlemen to cast unseemly glances at females with whom they are unacquainted," she added, recalling the incident which had been the inadvertent cause of their present state of affairs. "It is all your fault I was nearly run over."

"Oh, but I beg to differ," rejoined the gentleman, propping himself on one elbow the better to observe her as she attempted to straighten the sealskin hat atop her delightfully disheveled curls. "*I* was only paying homage to the local scenery. I suggest that if you wish to avoid such future mishaps, you should refrain from skating with your lovely nose in the air. You know what they say about 'an haughty spirit.' "

Startled, Maggie's eyes flew to the stranger's, which were studiously lacking in mirth. For an instant their glances locked in sudden, mutual understanding. Then, together, as if on cue: "It 'goeth before a fall'!" they blurted, falling into helpless peals of laughter.

"Oh, you really are quite abominable," Maggie gasped when she had caught her breath again. "How dare you quote the *Bible* at me."

"It was an unforgivable lapse. One for which I most humbly beg your pardon."

Maggie, who was quite sure she had never seen anyone less humble, nearly choked.

"Even so," drawled the gentleman, smiling in complete understanding. "And, now, since it would seem we are about to have our privacy invaded, I think perhaps you should allow me to help you to your feet."

Startled, Maggie glanced over her shoulder. It was true. The young ladies of her acquaintance were hurrying toward them, their expressive faces a mixture of curiosity and concern. Inexplicably she sustained a sharp stab of disappointment that her unlooked-for adventure was so soon to come to an end.

"Maggie Willoughby!" exclaimed Chloe, the first to arrive, though it was to be seen she was not far in advance of her governess, who was serving in the capacity of gooseberry to her young charge as well as to the six or seven other young ladies crowding in close on her heels. "I saw everything. I was simply paralyzed with horror when I beheld you on the point of being struck down by a runaway sledge. And most certainly you would have been had it not been for this gentleman's daring rescue. I pray you are not hurt."

"On the contrary, I am perfectly sound of limb," asserted Maggie, keenly aware of the ogling eyes and the titters as the gentleman in question, having climbed to his feet only seconds before, reached down to lift the rescued damsel to hers.

"Then, sir," the governess interjected, sending a quelling look at the overloquacious Chloe, "we must all be very grateful to you."

"Not at all," the gentleman replied smoothly. "I am only too glad I was in a position to be of some assistance to Miss Willoughby."

"Indeed you are too kind, sir," murmured that young lady, the very picture of demure femininity with her eyes lowered to the ground—the better to hide the glimmer of pain in their depths. To no avail. The sharp-eyed governess apparently missed nothing.

"Maggie, dear," she said in immediate concern. "Are you certain you are quite well? You appear to be favoring your right ankle. Perhaps we should send someone to Willoughby for a carriage to take you home."

Maggie, who was indeed suffering acute discomfort from what gave every evidence of being a twisted ankle, was nevertheless certain that the *last* thing she wanted was for someone to send to Willoughby. "Oh, no, Miss Hinkle. It is very kind in you to be concerned.

However, I am sure it is nothing."

"Nonsense, child. You are gone quite pale. Obviously, you are in no condition to walk home. Only allow me to send one of the village lads—"

"On, no, really," Maggie blurted, then blushed at her unseemly interruption. "I-I beg your pardon. But truly it is not necessary."

There was a momentary uneasy silence, during which Maggie sought frantically for a convincing argument to deliver her from her dilemma. Oh, what a bumblebroth she had made for herself! It had seemed such a simple matter at the time to steal out of the house and then back in again without being seen. The possibility that she might sustain anything so absurd as a wrenched ankle had simply never occurred to her. It was not punishment which she feared but having to face the disappointment in her Mama's eyes.

Still, she supposed it was what she deserved for behaving so childishly. As she drew breath to inform the governess that she would be only too glad for someone to go to Willoughby, the stranger interjected.

"Miss Hinkle is right, you know," she heard him say. "You really are in no condition to walk. And since I feel partially responsible for your indisposition, it is only right that I should offer you my services." Without waiting for the amazed Maggie to reply, the gentleman turned smoothly to address the governess. "There is no need to send for a carriage, Miss Hinkle, as I shall be only too glad to take Miss Willoughby home."

"Oh, I don't know, sir," exclaimed the sorely beset Miss Hinkle, her thin face creased in a worried frown. "I am responsible for the young lady. She is, after all, here at Miss Chloe's invitation. I fear Mr. and Mrs. Willoughby could not approve."

"Oh, you needn't worry on their account," replied the gentleman. Bending down to catch Maggie beneath her shoulders and her knees, he swept her up into his arms before Miss Hinkle could do aught but gasp. "The fact is, I am their houseguest. Indeed, Miss Willoughby and I are old acquaintances."

"What a hum," whispered Maggie as he blithely carried her off the ice and toward his waiting chestnut. "I hope you realize we cannot possibly get away with this. Whatever possessed you to tell such a taradiddle? I've little doubt that when the truth becomes known, I shall find my reputation in shreds."

"Now, there's a fine thank-you," responded the gentleman, apparently unmoved at the prospect of her imminent ruination. "You will pardon me if I gained the impression that you were somewhat less than eager to have word sent to your parents. It did occur to me, in fact, that you found yourself in something of a coil. If I was mistaken, however, it is not too late. Perhaps you would prefer I left you here in Miss Hinkle's capable hands."

"No, though I am quite sure I should," Maggie admitted grudgingly. "If you must know, they would not be in the least pleased to discover I was here."

"I rather fancied that was the case." Setting her down on a low hillock of grass, he knelt to remove her skates. "And where, I cannot but wonder, are you supposed to be, Miss Willoughby? Confined in a dungeon on a diet of bread and water?"

"I wish you will not be absurd," Maggie said, wincing a little as he gently explored her ankle for any broken bones.

Inexplicably her breath caught as he glanced quickly up.

"I'm sorry, did I hurt you?"

"A-a little," she answered. "Nothing to signify." Hastily she averted her head, mortified at feeling a blush stain her cheeks. How absurd that she should suddenly be so keenly aware of the subtle scents of clean linen and shaving soap at exceedingly close range. Or that the mere

87

touch of strong, sensitive fingers could make her feel peculiarly queasy inside. Faith, what a ninnyhammer he must think her. And, indeed, she could not have explained even to herself why, as he stood and held out his hands to help her to her feet, she should feel her heart begin to behave in a most alarming manner.

"I don't think anything is broken," he said, helping to steady her as she balanced herself on her uninjured foot. "A slight strain, no doubt. I suggest, however, that you refrain from putting any weight on it for a day or two."

"A day or two!" she blurted before she could stop herself. "But that is out of the question. How can I possibly explain a strained ankle when I have been supposed to remain in my room all afternoon? Oh, it is simply too horrid to contemplate. Besides being forced to miss the bringing in of the yule log tonight, I shall, no doubt, find myself consigned to do embroidery and tatting enough to supply a couturière for a lifetime."

"A hideous prospect," agreed the gentleman, a suspicious twitch at the corners of his lips.

"Well, it is," Maggie insisted, nettled at his attitude of male superiority. "Being a man, you cannot know what it is to be forced to sit for hours doing something so detestable as handwork. Especially when one would much rather be outside doing practically anything else. I have never understood why it is thought admirable in a female to be accomplished in something which is so positively boring."

"Perhaps it is meant, Miss Willoughby," said the gentleman, clamping strong hands about her tiny waist, "to keep her out of trouble." Lifting her, he set her across the front of the saddle.

Maggie uttered an indignant gasp. Her glance flew to the handsome face. The stinging retort that had risen to her lips, however, suddenly died there as she found herself staring into blue laughing eyes.

"Fudge," she exclaimed, a rueful gleam lighting her

own lovely orbs. "I know a complete hand when I see one. You are roasting me, are you not?"

"While I am in complete sympathy with your dislike of tatting, it has occurred to me that you might be something of a trial to your parents." Vaulting lightly to the saddle behind her, he took up the reins and set the chestnut in motion. "What you need, Miss Willoughby, is a husband to curb your propensity for falling into scrapes."

Maggie, who had not been prepared to suffer a sudden, unsettling shock at having her waist encircled by a pair of strong muscular arms, was momentarily silenced. Indeed, it did not even occur to her to question how he knew in which direction lay their destination. She was far too occupied with the novelty of finding herself cradled snugly in the hollow of a firm, masculine arm where it connected most satisfyingly to the shoulder. Consequently, it was not until some time later that she was recovered enough to summon a reply.

"Do you not think you are guilty of having come to some rather hasty conclusions?" she ventured at last, as much to take her mind off the unfamiliar sensations coursing through her as to break what was fast becoming an unnerving silence. "Just because you happen to have caught me out in what I admit to have been a foolish error in judgment does not mean I am in the habit of landing myself in a briar patch. The truth is, you know nothing about me."

For the briefest instant he appeared to reflect. Then, "On the contrary, I know a great deal about you," he had the insufferable gall to answer her. "I know that you are impetuous, headstrong, and stubborn, qualities which are bound to lead you into trouble. Fortunately, however, you are possessed of a lively sense of the ridiculous, which enables you to laugh at your own foibles as well as at those of your fellow man."

"But how very charitable of you to grant me at least one virtue to offset all my obvious faults," said Maggie, stung in spite of herself. Nor was she in the least gratified that he had managed to come so close to the truth.

"Did I say they were faults?" he queried in apparent surprise. "The truth is I haven't the least use for a female who does not have a mind of her own."

"Then no doubt I must be gratified that I do not fall into such a category. How devastated I should be to think I failed to meet with your approval."

"I suspect you would not be in the least perturbed," he countered easily, his voice resonant with humor. "A circumstance which can only add to your credit. At the risk of sounding the veriest coxcomb, I confess I have had a surfeit of simpering misses and their matchmaking mamas to last for a lifetime."

"It does make you sound rather puffed up on your own consequence," she replied. "What else have you observed about me?"

"Little devil!" he said feelingly. "Besides being brutally honest?" He paused. A sudden hard gleam in his eye inexplicably made her stomach clench. "That though you must always attract immediate attention wherever you go," he supplied, as though measuring his words, "you haven't the least notion of how very beautiful you are."

If it was his intent to get in the last word, he had succeeded magnificently. Maggie's eyes widened on his in startled disbelief. Then, in confusion at the blue intensity of his gaze, they precipitately lowered.

What was happening to her? she wondered, utterly distractedly. Had anyone told her that a mere look could send her temperature rising or cause her heart to beat with alarming rapidity, she would never have believed it. But how absurd. Surely it was not the look but the unsettling observation he had made which was the cause of her discomfort. It had been a remark intended, no doubt, to put her in her place, she told herself. He had not meant it. Indeed, he could not. The truth was that, in allowing herself to reply with such freedom to a complete stranger, she had behaved in a manner wholly unsuited to a lady. She had, in fact, sunk herself beneath reproach. It naturally followed that her elevation both in temperature and pulse was due not to a reaction to blue eyes like steel points of flame but to simple mortification at where her unruly tongue had led her.

She was jarred out of her reverie at that instant by the sudden realization that they had come to a halt. It was, in fact, more of a jolt than a jar.

"Faith, are you mad to bring me to the front door?" she exclaimed upon finding herself at the very threshold of Willoughby Hall. "Pray put me down before we are seen."

"I suggest it is far too late for subterfuge," drawled the gentleman, insufferably cool. "Or had you imagined Miss Hinkle, not to mention her numerous charges, would miraculously have the entire matter struck from memory? The truth is there was never any hope of keeping our little adventure from your parents."

"Of course there was not," she retorted, blushing furiously at his sarcasm. "It was possible, however, that they might have remained in ignorance until *after* the holidays. If you must know, Chloe and her entire family are departing for Twitchen in the morning to spend Christmas with her paternal grandparents. Not that it matters now," she groaned as a landau bearing the crest of the Duke of Almouth swept into the drive and came to a halt a short distance behind them. "The fact of my ruination is about to be broadcast to the world."

Had she expected to impress him with the hopelessness of her plight, she was soon to be disappointed. There was, in fact, an unholy gleam of amusement in his eyes as he stepped easily down from the saddle. Nor was that all or the worst of it. After closing strong hands about her waist to lift her down to the ground, he had the further audacity to swoop her off her feet into his arms at the very moment that the Duchess of Almouth and her daughter were helped to disembark from their carriage.

Maggie's gasp of protest was silenced by the stranger's warning arch of an eyebrow.

"You have only to trust me, Miss Willoughby," he said quietly, "and play your part."

There was little else she could do in the circumstances. No sooner had the Duchess of Almouth lifted an ivory-handled quizzing glass to her eye the better to observe them than they were confronted by Mr. and Mrs. Willoughby, who, in the company of a handful of servants, had emerged from the house presumably to greet the arrival of their guests.

"Why, I believe it is Miss Willoughby, Mama," crooned Lady Gwendolyn's silken voice. "And, am I not mistaken, the gentleman is . . ."

"Charlesworth, my boy," boomed Maggie's father, striding forward with a beaming smile. "Good to see you, lad. I believe you are acquainted with the duchess and Lady Gwendolyn, her daughter?"

"Oh, indeed, sir," the blond beauty answered for him, her green eyes coolly amused beneath luxurious dark eyelashes. "We are old friends, are we not, Lord Charlesworth?"

Unaccountably Maggie, who was still reeling from the shock of discovering her rescuer was Charlesworth, clenched her teeth. Lady Gwendolyn's look would seem to bespeak of a more than intimate acquaintanceship.

"But of course you are old friends," rasped Her Grace, the dowager duchess. "Charlesworth went to school with your brother, after all. Spent one of his holidays at Brierly as a boy."

"I remember it well, Duchess," drawled his lordship, as if it were perfectly natural to exchange pleasantries while supporting a female in his arms. "How is Reggie? Still away on the Continent with his new bride?"

"Indeed, yes, the young scalawag. Couldn't bring himself to come home even for Christmas. Can't imagine what he's about. You may be sure his father did not fritter his time away gallivanting about in a lot of foreign places."

"I am quite sure he did not," agreed Mr. Willoughby, who was well aware the former Duke of Almouth had preferred frittering away both his time and his fortune at the gaming tables in London. "And, now, Charlesworth, since you have already met my daughter, you must allow me to present to you my wife."

For a moment Maggie thought she must be dreaming as, next, she beheld her mama coming toward them simply radiating pleasure.

"Welcome, Lord Charlesworth, to Willoughby. I do hope you found something in the local sights to entertain you. I am sure I could not have been more pleased when Mr. Willoughby informed me you had enlisted our daughter to serve as your guide."

"Nor could I have been better entertained, Mrs. Willoughby," his lordship assured her. "Though I fear Miss Willoughby has sustained a slight injury to her ankle. I feel sure it is nothing serious. It did seem advisable, however, to keep her off it for a time."

"Maggie, my poor dear," exclaimed her mama, all solicitude. "I did wonder if there was not something wrong when I saw his lordship did not put you down at once. Perhaps you would be so kind, Lord Charlesworth, to carry her inside. Indeed, everyone. Why do we not all go into the house?"

"Really, Mama," said Maggie no little time later, "this is not at all necessary." In dismay, she stared at the rickety wheelchair Mrs. Willoughby had caused to be dragged down out of the attic. It was inconceivable that she was actually expected to appear in such a thing. "It is only a *slight* strain," she ventured, struggling not to wince as she attempted to put her weight on the injured ankle.

"I am sure I can walk the short distance downstairs to the dining room."

Her mama, looking elegant in a pale green jaconet evening dress, her brown hair combed back and caught up in curls at the top of her head, finished fastening her pearl necklace around Maggie's slender neck.

"Nonsense, child," she said, cocking her head to one side as she studied the effect of apricot-colored lutestring against Maggie's ivory skin. Suddenly she blinked as a mist threatened to cloud her vision. Never had her sweet, impossible Maggie looked so grown-up before or so lovely. *I must be getting old,* she thought, half smiling to herself. All at once there were so many things she would like to tell her daughter. Wisely, she held her tongue. When the time was right, Maggie would know without being told, and then, no doubt, she would understand that not everyday could be Christmas, that, indeed, there was a great deal more to life than skating parties and figgy pudding.

"I'm sorry, dear," she said, that thought having recalled to mind the hundred and one responsibilities that awaited her below as hostess to more than forty guests. "Your papa agrees with me that we must not chance any further injury."

Maggie groaned.

"But I shall be made a laughingstock, wheeling around like old Aunt Agatha with the gout. It simply does not bear thinking on, Mother."

Mrs. Willoughby's delicately arched eyebrows shot up. "Oh, so it is 'Mother' now, is it? Well, Miss Margaret Willoughby, it will do you no good to set your back to the wall. Either you will resign yourself to sitting in this chair and letting Carleton convey you downstairs, or you will remain in your room and miss everything. I shall leave you to decide which it is to be."

"But, Mama . . ."

"No, Maggie," said her normally tolerant parent, her

94

patience apparently having uncharacteristically worn thin for the second time that day, "I am in no mood for an argument. Indeed, I haven't the time. You must simply ring for Carleton if you make up your mind to join us."

Maggie, left standing on one foot in the middle of the floor, stared at the closed door with the feeling that the whole world had gone suddenly topsy-turvy. Could it have been only that morning that she had awakened, tingling with anticipation of the events that lay before her: assisting her mama in preparing the plum pudding; spreading the boughs of evergreens interspersed with rosemary and holly through the house; Chloe's skating party, followed at long last by the bringing in and lighting of the yule log? Somehow it had all gone awry. Indeed, she could see now that it had been doomed to failure from the moment the Earl of Charlesworth had agreed to honor her papa's invitation with his presence.

"It is all *his* fault," she announced aloud to the room, unreasonably affixing the blame to the earl for having accepted the invitation rather than to her father for having extended it. "And now that I am once more confined to my prison on his account, he, no doubt, is enjoying himself immensely in the company of Lady Gwendolyn." Apparently having forgotten that only that morning she had been hoping for exactly that very thing, she now found herself growing increasingly more incensed at the thought.

It was all patently unfair, she fumed. The brown eyes staring back at her from the looking glass flashed sparks of resentment. Well, if it took appearing in a stupid wheelchair to show him she did not care a whit that he was making eyes at the "Ice Queen," she would do it.

Hopping on one foot to the other side of the room, she gave the bellpull an emphatic tug—too emphatic it seemed, as the tapestried cord plummeted to the floor, one end left dangling from her closed fist.

"Ohh—*fid*dle-faddle!" she blurted for want of a better

word. *"Now* what am I to do?"

Having already determined that the one thing she would not do was remain exiled in her room, it was not long before she was assaying to make her way along the gallery in her less-than-elegant conveyance.

She got no farther than the head of the stairs. Feeling absurdly helpless, she searched in vain for Carleton, the footman, who was not at his usual post near the door. He had no doubt been recruited to help with the serving, she realized with a sinking heart.

"Oh! I simply cannot conceive how it is that in a house full of servants, there is none to be found when one needs one."

Hardly aware that she had spoken out loud, she was considerably startled when a deep voice from behind her replied: "Know exactly what you mean. Damned unreliable, the help one gets these days. Perhaps I can be of some service?"

Maggie, starting violently, accidently caused the chair to lurch forward. She was only just saved from hurtling down the stairs by a quick hand grasping one of the handles on the chair back.

"Hold on, little miss madcap. You cannot possibly be in such a hurry as to wish so precipitous a flight as that would be. Only wait, and I shall be only too happy to make sure you reach your destination in safety."

"Oh, indeed!" Maggie uttered witheringly, having been given in the dim light of the hall lantern to glimpse boyishly handsome features topped by rebellious blond hair fashionably brushed in the windswept. "I seem to recall a similar promise only this afternoon, and just look what has come of it. I find I am now confined to a wheelchair. Just what do you have to say to that?"

A gleam of amusement leapt in the eyes the color of lapis lazuli.

"I say it is a damned shame. Why? What would you have me to say?"

"Well, you might say that you are the tiniest bit sorry," she answered, gazing beyond the tall figure garbed handsomely in a dark brown coat and white unmentionables above gleaming brown Hessians. "But since you obviously are not in the least concerned, indeed, since you fail to show that you feel in the smallest responsible, I should prefer that you say absolutely nothing."

"I see," said the cause of all her troubles, appearing to ponder the matter. "And naturally, as a gentleman, I should respect your wishes. It does seem, however, that such a restriction would put something of a damper on polite conversation, would it not?"

Maggie gasped, torn between indignation and an unwitting appreciation of the humor of his observation. Nor did it add to her equilibrium to detect a slight quiver at the corners of his handsome lips.

"Oh, what an abominable creature you are," she choked, unable to keep the tremor of laughter from her voice. "I suppose you think I owe you my gratitude for having rescued me not once, but three times today."

"No, did I?" he queried, apparently much struck at the notion. *"Three* times, did you say?"

"I do wish you will cease to play the gaby with me," retorted Maggie irritably, wondering at just what game he was playing. "You know very well you did. First at the skating pond, when I was nearly struck down by the sledge, then when you brought me home, and again just now, when you saved me from hurtling down the stairs."

"Oh, well, then, I suppose you do owe me some sort of thanks, though I was laboring under the impression that you held me in some way at fault for your apparent misfortunes. Tell me, just as a matter of curiosity, do you normally find yourself in need of deliverance any number of times in a single day?"

In spite of herself Maggie blushed. How very absurd he made it all sound.

"Not until you came into my life," she retorted darkly.

"Since that time I seem uncommonly prone to mischance!" Immediately she bit her tongue in consternation at where it had led her. He had, after all, gone out of his way to render her aid. "I beg your pardon. I should not have said that. The truth is I have only myself to blame for everything that has happened. Furthermore, I am well-aware that I am in your debt for your repeated kindnesses. Though," she added, reminded of at least one grievance that owed its source to him, "I confess I cannot but hold *some*thing against you."

"But of course you do," agreed the gentleman, encouragingly. "Don't be afraid to open the budget. I was beginning to suspect you had turned into a reformed character, and how very dull that would be."

Maggie choked. "Oh, you really are quite impossible," she gasped, struggling not to laugh. "I warn you. I have no intention of allowing myself to be distracted, not after what you have done. To have my parents discover me upon their doorstep, clasped in the arms of one whom I supposed to be a stranger, was bad enough, but to have the duchess and her daughter witness what I naturally assumed was to be my imminent ruination was quite beyond bearing."

"The duchess, you say, *and* her daughter." He clucked his tongue in sympathy. "A hideous prospect, I must admit. I daresay you may have been wishing me at Jericho."

"As a matter of fact, I was. You must have known how mortifying was my position. Why did you not inform me that all was well, that my father had, as I presume he must have done, sent you to find me? Faith, why did you not tell me that you were Charlesworth?"

He smiled apologetically.

"But how could I, my dear Miss Willoughby, for so I must presume you to be, when I am *not* Charlesworth?"

"Not Charlesworth?" she repeated in no little astonishment. "But of course you are. Indeed, who else could you be?"

Maggie, who knew as soon as the words were out, clapped her hands to flaming cheeks. "Oh, dear, what an utter gudgeon you must think me. And you would be quite right: It is Mr. Crandall, is it not? Mr. Oliver Crandall?"

"Right you are, Miss Willoughby. You are mistaken, however, do you believe I could ever think you the least gudgeonish." Taking her hand in his, he bent his head to salute her knuckles. "On the contrary." His eyes lifted to look straight into hers. "I am exceedingly charmed to make your acquaintance."

"Are you?" queried Maggie, supremely conscious of the fact that this was the first time a gentleman had ever kissed her hand. It was, she decided, a not altogether unpleasant experience. Indeed, she supposed she liked it very well. "It is very kind in you to say so, especially since I am afraid I treated you quite shabbily."

"Not at all, though I daresay brother Milt's ears are burning." He grinned appreciatively, a wholly engaging smile that made him appear not only much younger than his reputed eight-and-twenty years but an absolute devil as well. "The truth is, Miss Willoughby, that I have seldom been better entertained."

Maggie, however, was only half listening.

"It is the absurdest thing," she said, unable to take her eyes off his face. "I knew, of course, that you and Charlesworth were twins. I simply never dreamed you would be so very alike. Indeed, I should marvel if your own mother could tell you apart."

"Very often she cannot," he admitted, "a circumstance, which, I confess, we have used to our advantage on more than one occasion. There are certain compensations for being one of identical twins—take now, for instance."

"Now?" she echoed, her smile uncertain.

"Indubitably. You see, I should not have had the pleasure of viewing as lovely a pair of eyes as it has been my privilege to see were it otherwise."

99

"I beg your pardon?" Maggie queried guilelessly, well-aware that he was teasing her but liking him nonetheless for it. "I'm afraid I fail to see what the one has to do with the other."

"But it is quite simple," he answered with studied gravity. "It is only natural for twins to inspire a certain amount of curiosity in people who normally would be too polite to show it. Take the case in point: you, my dear, have been staring at me quite unaffectedly for the past five minutes, a circumstance for which I can only be grateful, since it allows me the opportunity to stare back at you."

"Now you are bamming me." Maggie laughed, not the least embarrassed. "Indeed, I very strongly suspect that where females are concerned, you, Mr. Crandall, are not to be trusted."

"And you would be quite right in your assessment," agreed a voice, wholly unamused, from the foot of the staircase. "It would seem, Ollie, that Miss Willoughby has you pegged."

Irritated to find that the mere sight of a masculine figure with indecently broad shoulders encased in a tightfitting coat of blue superfine had the power to make her heart begin to pound, Maggie frowned.

"No more so than in my assessment of you, Lord Charlesworth," she retorted, irrationally taking her anger at herself out on the earl.

"I should beware, Milt, old boy," grinned Oliver Crandall. "I have been given to witness just how lowering that opinion is of you."

"Then," observed the earl, mounting the stairs to them, "I must take it to mean that Miss Willoughby has yet to forgive me for this afternoon. I should, no doubt, have told you who I was from the very beginning."

"Yes, you should," agreed the young lady, refusing to look higher than where white unmentionables hugging muscular thighs went into the tops of brown Hessians polished to an unnatural shine. Not for the world would she have him see how easily he upset her equilibrium.

"I see. And would it make any difference were I to tell you that I have come expressly with the wish of making it up to you?" Maggie started as his tone noticeably altered. "They are about to bring in the yule log, Maggie, and I have not forgotten how much you looked forward to it. Will you at least allow me to take you downstairs?" Her eyes lifted at last to his and held.

So intent were they on each other, that neither noted Oliver Crandall bend a suddenly penetrating glance on the two of them.

"Well, I—" Maggie began, confusion flooding her cheeks most becomingly with color.

"Why, she no doubt agrees that is a capital notion," Mr. Crandall unexpectedly finished for her. The next thing she knew she had been swooped up into a pair of masculine arms and was being carried down the stairway. "Bring the chair, will you, old boy?" called Mr. Crandall cheerfully over his shoulder. "Miss Willoughby and I shall be waiting for you in the Hall."

Maggie, after glimpsing the earl's face, white-lipped with anger, hardly knew what she felt. One thing was for certain. She was careful not to look back again. She was filled with an even greater confusion, however, a few moments later, when she was borne, protesting with laughter, into the presence of her parents' houseguests. For a moment she had a sinking feeling of déjà-vu as she looked up to find the dowager duchess's magnified eye regarding her through an ivory-handled quizzing glass. Maggie swallowed.

"Mama," she pronounced, singling out the one in the room most likely to be sympathetic, "Mr. Crandall, as you see, has been kind enough to bring me down. And here is his lordship with my chair, so you need not worry that I am likely to do any further injury to my ankle. I do hope I am not too late."

"On the contrary, Miss Willoughby," purred Lady Gwendolyn. Waving her tortoiseshell fan gently to and fro, she watched as the two handsomest men in the room went to great pains to see the little Willoughby comfortably seated. "I should say you have your timing down to perfection."

Fortunately, the clamor of voices and the sounds of hilarity issued just then from the foyer.

The door burst open to admit Mr. Willoughby at the forefront of a jovial band, ranging in age from Uncle William, Grandfather Willoughby's younger brother, all the way down to little Jeremy Brewster, who was not above five. Into the room they marched, bearing with them a barrellike log, having a girth greater than the armspan of a sizeable man.

"Mrs. Willoughby, honored guests," announced the lord of the manor, his face rosy-cheeked from the cold. "Let the bowl of cider be brought in honor of a truly magnificent log. Hazel it is, circled by nine bands, one each for the unmarried maidens who wait to see who shall be the first to the altar. And for the consolation of the gentlemen, my vow of a new bowl of cider for each snapping of the withe."

A shout of approval shook the ceiling beams at that pronouncement. Mr. Willoughby bowed, then, lifting his arm, signaled the promenade to begin.

"Thrice around the room, merry band," he commanded, filling his glass from the bowl of cider mixed with brandy, which the footman had brought. "Thrice around and then into the hearth."

When the march about the room had been accomplished with a great deal of hilarity and the yule log had found its place on the flagstones of the fireplace, Mr. Willoughby poured over it the libation to the spirits of those who had passed away. At last, little Winifred, the youngest of Maggie's sisters, was brought forward. With a brand from the previous year's log clutched tightly in her freshly washed hands, she knelt to light the yule log.

Maggie, her eyes rapt on the flames leaping up to ignite the withes that bound the sticks of hazel to the log, found herself wondering who would be the lucky girl to claim the band that broke first. Not that she placed the least credence in what was only an absurd superstition. The order in which the bands succumbed to the flames could not possibly predict the sequence in which the single females would be married. It was simply that it was traditional. And waiting for the bands to break, with a loud crack that could be heard all over the house, added a spice of excitement to the evening.

"Oh, Maggie, isn't it marvelous?" exclaimed Charlotte, coming to grasp her cousin's hands. "I have drawn the thinnest of the bands. There, that one near the end. It is almost certain to go first. Caroline Guthrie, who has only just had the banns announced, was simply devastated at drawing the fourth one from the left."

"Oh, dear, and who can blame her?" Maggie said, entering into the spirit of the thing. "It is clearly the widest, save for that one, nearest the middle."

"You will be happy to know, dearest Maggie, that we have saved that one especially for you," Lady Gwendolyn informed her as she inserted herself neatly between Charlesworth and Oliver Crandall. "Miss Willoughby," she confided to the two gentlemen, "has made it plain that she is not the least interested in matrimony. She once informed me herself that she would far rather remain here at Willoughby."

"Once—a long time ago," Maggie answered, wishing she might scratch the older girl's eyes out. How like Lady Gwendolyn to dredge up something she had said as a mere child in the heat of anger! "And, indeed, I should never deny that I love my home."

"But of course you would not, my dear. No one would expect you to. After all, the country suits you so well. I, on the other hand, fear London has absolutely spoiled me for more rustic pursuits. One grows so used to having the opera, the theatre, and Bond Street, of course, close at hand, not to mention the society of one's own friends. Do you not find it equally so, Lord Charlesworth?" she inquired of Charlesworth.

Maggie's hands clenched with resentment. Lady Gwendolyn had managed with her usual adroitness to turn the knife. This time she had made her out to be a positive looby in the eyes of everyone present. That she might be concerned about one particular pair of eyes did not occur to her. She merely reacted out of hurt.

"Indeed, Lord Charlesworth, tell us," she said. "No doubt you find us as quaint at Willoughby as does Lady Gwendolyn. We are so terribly provincial, are we not?"

"If by that you mean you demonstrate at Willoughby a charming appreciation of the simpler things, such as ice skating and a traditional observance of Christmas, then, yes, Miss Willoughby," he answered, the blue eyes unwavering on her face, "I should say you and your family have managed, happily, to remain untouched by the cynicism of many of your contemporaries."

Maggie blinked, while Lady Gwendolyn blanched, the green eyes hardening to frosty points.

"Here, here," applauded Oliver Crandall, grinning, "Couldn't have expressed it better myself, Milt. And now that that is all settled, I propose, Miss Willoughby, that you allow me to take you into supper."

Maggie, still a trifle dazed at his lordship's tribute, was not given time to answer, as Oliver Crandall swept her in grand style off to the dining room.

Dinner was a merry affair. Oliver Crandall, seated to her right, kept up a steady banter with Maggie and with Charlotte, who sat on his other side. Indeed, he kept her so well entertained that Maggie was only occasionally conscious of Lady Gwendolyn and the earl sitting across the table from her. The one time Maggie let herself look at his lordship, he appeared wholly engrossed in conversation with the blond beauty. She did not look again. Consequently, she was not to know how often the nobleman's glance strayed her way, to linger speculatively there.

Lady Gwendolyn, however, noticed it. Indeed, by the time Mrs. Willoughby rose to signal it was time to leave the gentlemen to their brandy and cigars, the young beauty's smile appeared peculiarly frozen on her lips.

"Faith," whispered Maggie to Charlotte as they watched the Ice Queen sweep from the room. "What could have happened to send her into the glooms, I wonder."

"If you were not such an innocent, Maggie Willoughby, you would realize that *you* are the cause of Lady Gwendolyn's ill temper. You can hardly expect to monopolize the attentions of the two most eligible bachelors in the company without incurring the wrath of the reigning beauty, after all. If I were you, I should watch my back from now on. She is not likely to take this lying down."

"I wish you will not be absurd. Mr. Crandall was only being kind, and as for Charlesworth, he paid no attention to me at all."

Charlotte, who thought she detected just the slightest pique in Maggie's final words, hid a smile. "Then you must be blind," she said, positioning Maggie in front of the fire. "His lordship appeared noticeably distracted to me."

"Indeed, he did to me, too," Maggie countered snappishly. "With Lady Gwendolyn. Now, no more of such talk. I haven't the least interest in Charlesworth—or Lady Gwendolyn either, for that matter. Tell me about Felix and your ride this afternoon."

"Yes, do tell us, Charlotte," murmured an insinuating voice at Charlotte's elbow. "I understand felicitations are in order. I confess I was surprised. A man like Felix Dorsey, after all. But then he naturally is well enough off not to require a bride with a marriage portion."

105

"My dearest Gwendolyn," said Maggie with exaggerated sweetness, "I think you will never cease to amaze me."

"Quite possibly not," agreed the duke's sister, waving her fan tranquilly in front of her face. "I should think it remarkable if I did not loom beyond your powers of comprehension."

"Maggie . . ." Charlotte muttered, giving her cousin a warning nudge.

"No, no, Charlotte. You must not interfere. I believe Maggie had a point to make."

"Only that once before you tried to get at me through my cousin. I think I should warn you not to try it again."

"Or you will do what?" Lady Gwendolyn laughed. "Poor Maggie, apparently you have allowed your momentary popularity to turn your head. It pleased Charlesworth to be kind to you. And why would he not when you appear so charmingly helpless? Really, Maggie, only you would think to use a wheelchair to win the attention no one would dream of paying you otherwise. And I must admit, if you are going to feign a wrenched ankle, a wheelchair is an inspiration. A limp is so very unattractive, is it not? And quite utterly lacking in grace."

Smiling, she started to turn away, only to pause and glance back again.

"Oh, yes. Do not fool yourself into believing you have made a conquest in Mr. Crandall. To him you are nothing but a new toy of which he shall soon tire. As for Charlesworth, my dear. I warn you. *He* is mine. I suggest you keep your distance."

Just then, simultaneous with the earl entering the room a little in advance of his brother, a thunderous crack rent the peace and quiet.

"Faith, would you look at that!" exclaimed Charlotte, pointing with no little excitement to the fireplace. "It was yours, Maggie. The very first to break. Who would ever have believed it?"

"Not I," said Maggie with a straight face, though her eyes on Lady Gwendolyn's were brimful of laughter. "But then, stranger things have happened, I must suppose."

Lady Gwendolyn drew in an audible breath. Then, sending daggers in Maggie's direction, she turned with her head in the air and went to intercept his lordship.

"Miss Willoughby," smiled Oliver Crandall, who had wasted little time in working his way across the room to Maggie. "And Miss Fenwick. How fortunate I am to find two lovely ladies unattended."

"Only one, I fear, Mr. Crandall," demurred Charlotte, giving Maggie a knowing wink. "I'm afraid I must ask you to excuse me. I see Felix has been cornered by Mrs. Winterbottom."

"A ghastly fate," agreed the gentleman, observing Mr. Dorsey in the company of a matronly lady of mammoth proportions, made more daunting still by orange curls and a beaked-brimmed bonnet fully twenty inches or more in height.

Maggie giggled.

"Quite so," murmured Crandall. Unaccountably, his gaze, swinging back to her, made her catch her breath. The next moment, however, he was smiling again, the engaging grin that had ever the effect of disarming her. "I am almost disappointed," he said, "to find I am apparently not required to rescue *you* from some unforeseen peril. I can hardly be content, after all, to rest on my laurels when my brother is one up on me, can I?"

"Oh, but how can you say so?" Maggie replied, her eyes dancing with pleasure at his teasing. "You, sir, have already saved me from what might well have been a very dull evening. And, besides," she added, her glance straying unconsciously to Lady Gwendolyn, who appeared in rapt conversation with his lordship, "in spite of the fact that the children have been sent to their beds, the night is still young. Who knows what trouble I may yet get myself into?"

"Ah, the Ice Queen, is it?" remarked the gentleman, then laughed at Maggie's startled glance. "No, infant, it is not so obvious as that. It is just that I know her so well. Well enough, in fact, that I should never let her throw dust in my eyes, and neither, might I add, should you."

Maggie wrinkled her nose at him. "How very easy that is for you to say. You, however, have not had to put up with her for as long as you can remember. When we were children, the duchess used to have us—Charlotte and me, that is—to Brierly to serve in the way of entertainment for her darling daughter. Perhaps you will understand better when I tell you there are seven years separating Lady Gwendolyn and the duke, her elder brother."

"She is, I believe, rather used to having her own way," Crandall observed sympathetically.

"She used to order us about as though we were servants. I did not mind so much for myself. I was well able to give as good as I got. But, Charlotte—" She stopped herself, realizing how close she had come to divulging a good deal more than she had intended. "Forgive me. How very silly of me. You cannot possibly be interested in anything so mundane as my childish feuds with Lady Gwendolyn."

"You might be surprised how interested I am in anything which concerns you, Miss Willoughby."

He said it with such spellbinding seriousness that Maggie was quite taken aback. It suddenly struck her that Mr. Crandall was not at all as her initial impressions had led her to believe. Indeed, she suspected there was a deal more to him than the charming rogue he pretended to be.

Almost as if he realized he had slipped out of character, he immediately laughed and chucked her playfully under the chin.

"You must not frown, infant," he teased. "Besides making wrinkles, it is wholly out of keeping with the spirit of the evening."

Maggie, who was reeling under the impression that his touch had sent a small shock wave coursing through her, could only be glad that her mama chose just then to command their attention.

"Ladies and gentlemen, it is Christmas Eve. How fitting it must be, then, that two of the young ladies have agreed to entertain us with music. Lady Gwendolyn, dear. Perhaps you would be so kind as to start us off with a few selections on the harp?"

"But of course, Mrs. Willoughby." The young beauty smiled up at Charlesworth, quite obviously pleased with herself, Maggie thought wryly. "I should be only too glad."

Maggie normally enjoyed the sweet tones of the harp, and she would have been the first to admit that Lady Gwendolyn played with more than a mere competence. She could not deny either that the blond beauty poised gracefully, her long slender fingers running effortlessly over the strings, and presented a perfectly stunning picture. When Lady Gwendolyn finished playing and rose to make her bows, Maggie applauded as heartily as anyone present.

Her applause notably faltered, however, as Lady Gwendolyn, lifting her head, shot a look of cold triumph deliberately at Maggie.

Suddenly it came to her that it was all true. Compared to Lady Gwendolyn, she was a plain little dab of a creature who because of her temporary disability had attracted a deal of unwarranted attention. And who had asked them to shower her with their pity? Not she, she told herself. She had never wanted them there from the first. All at once her mouth thinned to a firm line. Very well then, she thought, a rebellious glitter springing to her eyes. If it was an insignificant little songbird they expected, she certainly had no intention of disappointing them.

Lady Gwendolyn had been chosen out of deference to her rank to perform first. Maggie, as the eldest daughter of the house, was invited next. She coolly refused Mr. Crandall's offer to convey her to the pianoforte, preferring instead to wheel herself there. A slight flush touched her cheeks at his suddenly searching look. Then giving a defiant toss of her curls, she left him staring after her.

Having instantly discarded her planned program of Mozart, Maggie was careful not to look at her mama as she launched herself into a lighthearted rendition of "Here We Come a Wassailing," followed without pause by any number of folksy Christmas songs, the earthier the better. Perhaps it was some slight sense of having sunk herself beneath reproach which prompted her to finish up with "God Rest Ye Merry, Gentlemen." Or perhaps it was only an instinctive realization that it was the only ending possible in the wake of what had come before. Having been carried, at any rate, on a wave of rebellion, she now came to the uncomfortable realization that she was about to be greeted with a stunned silence of disapproval.

She could not have been more surprised, then, when, launching into the part about everyone singing praises, her clear, lilting soprano was joined as if on cue by a deep baritone. Startled, her eyes flew to the back of the room to Mr. Oliver Crandall, whose manly voice seemed perfectly to complement her own. But that was as nothing when compared to the chorus of voices that chimed in on the final refrain. Indeed, she doubted that the Great Hall had ever before reverberated with such resounding "tidings of comfort and joy!"

She hardly knew whether to laugh or to cry with relief as she bowed her head to acknowledge the enthusiastic applause.

As she looked up, however, her glance happened to fall on a pair of indecently broad shoulders encased in a

110

tightfitting coat of blue superfine as they left the room in the company of a gloating Lady Gwendolyn. Inexplicably, her mood suffered a sudden blight.

So much so that she could hardly wait for the noise to die down that she might retreat to a quiet corner. Suddenly she felt inordinately drained and most unaccountably irritable. The last thing she was in the mood for was an impromptu game of "My Lady Coventry," which someone was trying to get up or any other card game, for that matter. She rather thought she would find Carleton and ask him to carry her upstairs.

She had almost made good her escape when she was stopped by a tall figure looming over her.

"Not thinking to run away, Miss Willoughby?" queried Oliver Crandall, his blue eyes quizzing her. "Not after your triumphant performance. You must tell me sometime what possessed you to take such a risk. Or did you know all along you could choose no better repertoire with which to follow Lady Gwendolyn's classical renditions?"

"No," Maggie answered shortly, vaguely confused and wanting only to be left alone. Immediately, she relented. "Yes—perhaps," she added, regretting her rudeness. "I don't know. It-it was all a foolish impulse, nothing more. Suddenly Mozart simply did not suit my mood." A wry grin tugged reluctantly at her lips. "No doubt I have you to thank for delivering me from my own folly."

"Don't be maudlin, I beg you," he said with an abruptness wholly out of keeping with what she had come to know in him. "The truth is you were a *succès fou* and would still have been had I interfered or not."

Hurt by his harshness, Maggie felt her cheeks grow flushed.

"Nevertheless, I do thank you," she retorted, turning her face away. "And now, if you will excuse me, I was just going in search of Carleton to take me upstairs."

"Maggie, wait!"

Maggie, who had leaned down to push the wheels forward, suddenly froze. It was all very absurd, but she could not stop her heart from its ridiculous pounding. Indeed, she was beginning to wonder if she had been stricken by some strange malady the symptoms of which were brought on only by blond-haired men with eyes the color of lapis lazuli. Chiding herself for an utter idiot, she forced herself to look at him.

"Maggie, I—"

At her look, he broke off whatever he had been about to say, his eyes probing hers with a curious intensity. He appeared to shake himself just when she thought she could not bear it anymore.

"There's no need to summon Carleton," he said at last, gruffly. "If you are set on leaving us, I shall take you."

Maggie shook her head.

"No, really. I shouldn't want to put you to the trouble."

He ignored her protest. Leaning down, he lifted her bodily into his arms. And all at once her temper snapped.

"Put—me—down!" she gasped, shoving with all her strength against his chest. "Have you the least notion how many times I have been snatched up into a man's pair of arms today?"

A gleam of humor flashed across the lean countenance.

"Two, is it? Or three, perhaps," he replied, appearing to reflect even as he tightened his hold on her. "Of course it could be more. I can't be held responsible for what you did when you were not in my company."

"This makes *four,*" she said in triumph. "And not once was I consulted beforehand. Contrary to what you apparently think, I am not some plaything which you and your brother are free to manhandle in any manner you deem fit. I am a person with a mind and a will of her own."

"As you have repeatedly demonstrated any number of times since I met you," he conceded with obvious feeling. "You, my girl, are not only impetuous and incorrigible,

112

you are utterly lacking in commonsense. And if you do not cease to struggle at once, you are going to make a spectacle of yourself."

It was true. In spite of the fact that the company had thinned to a mere dozen or more, the rest having departed either to the parlor where the bowl of cider resided or to the rooms set up with card tables, they were undeniably beginning to attract attention to themselves.

Immediately Maggie went still in his arms.

"I am *not* incorrigible, I'll have you know," she whispered fiercely. "And I promise I am possessed of a deal of commonsense. Which tells me there cannot possibly be a good reason to remain standing where we are."

Incredibly, he grinned.

"Oh, but I am afraid there is, Miss Willoughby. One superlatively good reason."

Mistrusting the sudden gleam in his eye, Maggie knitted her brow in a frown. Short of the unlikely possibility that he had thrown his back out when he picked her up, she could think of nothing that would prevent him from carrying her on upstairs.

"Oh, very well, Mr. Crandall," she said in exasperation after a moment. "Please be so good as to tell me."

"It is hanging over your head, Miss Willoughby."

Maggie's heart skipped a beat. She did not have to look up to know to what he was referring. Above them, suspended from the chandelier, the kissing bough hung in all its glory.

"Oh, no," she said slowly, shaking her head.

"Indeed, yes, Miss Willoughby," he answered her. "It is, after all, a very old custom, one which you surely, of all people, would not refuse to honor. Unless, of course, it is only that you are afraid?"

The devil! thought Maggie, her mouth suddenly dry. He was baiting her. What was worse, he knew she would die first before she appeared craven. A dangerous spark leapt in her eyes. Very well, if it was a kiss he wanted, he would have one.

"On the contrary, Mr. Crandall," she said, doing her best to feign a cool indifference, when in reality her stomach was doing flip-flops. "I am not in the least afraid. Indeed, why should I be? It is only a kiss, is it not?"

Determined to suit action to words, Maggie tilted her head back and, closing her eyes, promptly pursed her lips in readiness.

Thus she did not see the swift leap of amusement in the handsome face or know when the amusement faded to be replaced by a slow, searching intensity. Deliberately the blond head bent toward hers.

Maggie had seen her mama and papa embrace any number of times—a sweet buss on the cheek or a light brushing of the lips followed very often by her mama's cheeks flooding becomingly with color should she happen to discover they had been observed. But nothing she had ever witnessed had prepared her for the sudden shock of emotions that shot through her at this, her very first kiss from a gentleman.

It was not a very lengthy kiss and certainly could not be characterized as one of great passion. Indeed, compared to those about which she had read in the more lurid romances, it must have been categorized as disappointingly gentle, almost tender, in fact. Why, then, she wondered, did she feel as if she had just suffered the onset of a heady fever accompanied most alarmingly by symptoms of delirium and every indication that she might be on the point of succumbing to a swoon? It made absolutely no sense. But then, it seemed that nothing had since it had been her misfortune to have the twin Lords of Misrule drop into her life. Her eyes looking dazed and more than a little bewildered, she blinked up at the handsome face looming over hers.

His lips curved in a smile that unreasonably made her heart flutter.

"I'm afraid, infant," he said apologetically, "that I shall have to ask you to retrieve the token. My arms are full at the moment."

"I-I beg your pardon?"

"The berry," he chided her. "Surely you have not forgotten?"

Maggie blushed. She *had* forgotten. It was, of course, traditional to pluck a berry from the mistletoe in token of the kiss they had exchanged.

"No, of course I haven't forgotten," she lied. "I-I just wasn't sure I could reach it."

As it turned out, however, the gentleman's height of six feet three inches was more than enough to have allowed her to pluck any number of berries with ease had she been so inclined. Indeed, doubtless it was the altitude at which she found herself that made her absurdly dizzy, she wryly concluded as she pulled one of the white berries from the bough.

"There," she said, closing her fist around it. "Now, if you don't mind, I really should like to go upstairs."

"Are you sure I cannot change your mind?"

Maggie shook her head, quite certain she had experienced enough unsettling events for one evening. "No, please. I am rather tired."

Maggie, who was acutely conscious of the silence that had fallen over them as he carried her up the stairs, could only be glad when at last they arrived at her room. Discovering she had left the door open, he took her straight inside and without a word, set her on the edge of her bed.

"Are you sure you will be all right by yourself?" he murmured, studying her averted profile. "Is there someone I could send up—a maid, perhaps?"

Maggie smiled nervously and shook her head.

"No, I shall be fine," she answered, wishing he would cease to look at her with those disturbing eyes. "Thank you."

For a moment it seemed he would say something more, then apparently he thought better of it.

"Good night then, Miss Willoughby. I shall have Carleton bring your chair up."

"Thank you, Mr. Crandall, and good night."

Maggie waited until the door shut behind him. Then with an explosive breath, she flung herself backward on the bed.

Maggie sat curled up in the window seat in the dark, her chin propped on knees bent to her chest. Haunted by the image of identical handsome faces with equally disturbing blue eyes, she had given up trying to sleep some time before. Indeed, the hall clock was just striking two when she was startled by a soft scratching at her door.

"Maggie?" Charlotte whispered thrillingly, sticking her head in. "Maggie, are you awake?"

"Charlotte? Good heavens, what is it?" Maggie exclaimed, alarmed at the telltale quiver of excitement in her cousin's voice. "Wait. I'll light the lamp."

"Never mind the lamp." Closing the door softly behind her, Charlotte groped her way across the room to the window seat. "Br-r-r." She shivered and pulled her dressing gown tightly around her as she squeezed in beside Maggie. "Quick, let me under the quilt. It will be just like old times when I used to steal into bed with you after one of my silly old dreams. Only this time I wasn't dreaming, Maggie."

"Gudgeon, whatever are you rattling on about? What weren't you dreaming about?" demanded Maggie.

"About Charlesworth and Lady Gwendolyn, but never mind that right now. First, I want to hear all about you and Oliver Crandall."

Immediately, Maggie drew up. The last thing she wanted to discuss was Oliver Crandall, or Charlesworth, for that matter. She had been doing nothing but think of

116

them for the past two hours, wondering if she were going out of her mind. Indeed, she was on the verge of a splitting headache without having come to any conclusions except that she was very nearly certain she wished them both to the devil for having cut up her previously ordered existence.

"If you are here to tell me that Charlesworth has offered for Lady Gwendolyn, I promise I couldn't care less," she declared with the greatest outward manifestation of indifference, though, inside, she was experiencing a suddenly queasy sensation. "As for Oliver Crandall, I'm sure I haven't the least notion what you are talking about."

"Fudge," Charlotte retorted. "Everyone saw that Oliver Crandall was paying marked attention to you tonight. Indeed, he could not have been more obvious if he had announced it to the world. Faith, Maggie, he kissed you!"

"We were under the mistletoe. What did you expect him to do? I'm sure it meant as little to him as it did to me."

"Maggie, this is Charlotte to whom you're talking. The girl who grew up in the same house with you. We swore an oath once never to have any secrets between us." Charlotte's hand felt ice-cold as it closed about Maggie's wrist. "When Papa shot himself because he couldn't pay his gambling debts, and Mama and I came to live with you, you said we would always be like sisters. No matter how many times Lady Gwendolyn and the others reminded me of-of what happened, you always stood my friend. And that is why I have to know, Maggie. You do like Mr. Crandall just a little, don't you?"

Startled, Maggie peered at the indistinct silhouette of the other girl against the window. As if by tacit agreement, the subject of Charlotte's father was one that neither of them ever mentioned.

"Well, yes. I suppose I do. A little," Maggie confessed gruffly. "Though what it has to do with anything—"

"It has a great deal to do with your future happiness," Charlotte interrupted. "Now tell me the truth. Do you not like Mr. Crandall more than just a little?"

Maggie drew in a deep breath and harshly let it out again.

"Yes. No," she said, flinging up her hands. "Oh, Charlotte, how can I possibly tell you that when I don't know myself what I feel? I liked Mr. Crandall even when I thought he was Charlesworth. And then when I discovered he wasn't, I was relieved. Oh, he is a dangerous flirt, I told myself. Someone to have fun with but never to take seriously. Then after supper, when the gentlemen joined us in the Hall, he seemed suddenly different."

"Different?" Charlotte prodded. "What do you mean?"

"I don't know," Maggie replied testily. How could she tell her cousin that after supper was when her strange malady had manifested itself, occurring before only when Charlesworth was around? Indeed, how could she tell her that it was not Crandall who had changed but apparently herself? "Suddenly he just wasn't the same anymore. The way he looked at me, the things he said. He was just . . . different. I don't know what else I can say."

"I think, whether you will admit it or not, that you like Mr. Crandall more than a little. Indeed, I think you like him a lot. The trouble is, I think you like Charlesworth more than a little, too. Be honest, Maggie," Charlotte said gently. "Isn't that what is bothering you?"

"I wish you will not be absurd," Maggie retorted, still stinging at the memory of Charlesworth stealing out of the Great Hall with a triumphant Lady Gwendolyn on his arm. "Indeed, I don't know where you could have gotten such a ridiculous notion. I'm sure I haven't the least interest in the earl."

"You will pardon me if it seemed to me you were suffering some slight pique at his marked attention to Lady Gwendolyn at supper. I collect that I was mistaken. In which case you will not mind that Lady Gwendolyn is plotting a trap for his lordship. In fact, she is in his room this very minute, waiting for him to turn in. No doubt she will claim that he lured her there, and if no one believes her, it will hardly matter. However it is interpreted, he will have no choice but to offer for her."

Maggie recoiled as if she had just been struck.

"Charlotte, you cannot be serious. Not even the Ice Queen could be so calculating."

"Oh, but I am perfectly serious. I saw her slip into the earl's room myself, just as I was coming here to see you."

"Then we must stop her somehow. Indeed, we must find Charlesworth and warn him before it is too late!"

She was already off the window seat and hopping across the room to find flint and steel to light a candle. As the wick caught and flared, casting weird shadows against the walls, she saw Charlotte looking at her strangely.

"It *is* Charlesworth, isn't it, Maggie," she said. "You fell for him the first time you saw him, did you not?"

Caught off guard by her cousin's pointed question, Maggie faltered in her hurried attempt to dress. Could it be true? Had she fallen in love with the arrogant nobleman the first time she had set eyes on him at the skating pond? Indeed, was that why she could not bear the thought of his falling into Lady Gwendolyn's trap?

The memory of his arms around her, the strong body next to hers, was so vivid as to bring a blush to her cheeks. But then, no less vivid was the recollection of Oliver Crandall's lips touching hers and the bewildering flood of sensations they had caused to sweep over and through her. An image of blue, laughing eyes rose up to haunt her, but whether they were Charlesworth's or Oliver Crandall's, she was not certain anymore. As though they were one man, in her mind, she could not separate one from the other.

The devil! she thought, wishing she had never set eyes on either one of them. She was doing it because she owed

119

it to Charlesworth to warn him, she told herself firmly. And that was all there was to it.

"Never mind that now," she said briskly, returning to the task immediately at hand. "It does not matter what I feel. The important thing at the moment is to stop Charlesworth from going into that room. Do you know where he is, Charlotte?"

"He was partnered with your papa in a game of whist when I left Felix. But we dare not approach him there. As little as I care for Lady Gwendolyn, I should not wish to see her ruined. Besides, such a scandal could only reflect badly on your parents."

"Faith, I hadn't thought of that. You are right. They mustn't know, especially Mama. She would feel bound to tell the duchess, which would only make things exceedingly uncomfortable. Still, we cannot simply do nothing!" exclaimed Maggie, who was well-aware they could not be found lurking outside his lordship's door at such an hour.

"Well, there is Felix," Charlotte suggested doubtfully. "Though I cannot think it would be at all proper for me to go to his bedroom, even if we are betrothed. His mama is a great stickler for the proprieties."

"No, Felix is out of the question," Maggie declared decisively. "You go to your room, Charlotte, and stay there. I am afraid I shall just have to confront Lady Gwendolyn myself."

"Maggie, no! You will both be ruined."

But Maggie, having given up in disgust the hopeless task of fitting a shoe over her swollen foot, was already limping barefoot out the door.

For once she was almost glad to see the odious wheelchair outside her room where Carleton must have left it. Her ankle was paining her like a thousand toothaches. Fortunately, the suite assigned the earl was on the same floor as hers, and she wheeled herself resolutely down the corridor.

She was soundly questioning her own rationality as she

120

drew near the earl's closed door some moments later. She had encountered no one on the way, but luck had a way of turning on one, she noted wryly. Very likely she would find herself in deep waters before all was over and done with. And it would be all the fault of the odious earl for having upset her peace and tranquility. His and Oliver Crandall's, she amended, willing to give equal blame to that gentleman, who had only complicated matters more. If feeling utterly confused and finding oneself constantly on the verge of disaster was what love was all about, it was greatly overrated. And yet she could not deny that she had never felt so tinglingly alive as she had those fleeting moments with Charlesworth at the ice pond and after. Or as she had, for that matter, when she found herself beneath the kissing bough with Oliver Crandall. Faith, she *could* not have lost her heart to both of them — could she?

That meddlesome organ leapt at the sound of voices on the stairs at the far end of the corridor. Taking a deep breath, she reached for the door handle and turned it.

The room was dark after the lighted corridor outside, and in spite of the glowing embers of a fire in the Adams fireplace, Maggie was momentarily blinded.

"Lady Gwendolyn. I know you are in here," she called out in a low voice. "You might as well show yourself. I shan't leave until you do."

There was a rustle of silk and a light step, then a tall, slender figure in a shimmering white negligee detached herself from the shadows next to the draperies.

"Maggie Willoughby. Fancy meeting you here." Dangling a ring of keys in front of her, which she must have stolen from the housekeeper, she smiled frostily. "Had I known you were coming, I should have locked the door behind me. As it is, you can just turn your chair around and get out. I did warn you to keep your distance. I mean to have Charlesworth, and there is nothing you can do to stop me."

121

"Perhaps not. You have never demonstrated the least concern for the feelings of others, after all, but this is coming it much too strong. Faith, Gwendolyn, do you care nothing for yourself, you might at least consider what such a scandal would do to my parents, not to mention your own mother—and, I might add, your brother, the duke."

"My brother, the duke?" Lady Gwendolyn's laughter sounded brittle in the quiet of the room. "Good God, you *are* an innocent. My brother cares nothing for me. He never has. And as for my mother, she has made it clear on more than one occasion that I am a very great disappointment to her. Nothing would please her more than to awaken tomorrow morning with the discovery that I have managed at last to ensnare a husband. I doubt that she could care less how I managed it."

Unexpectedly Maggie felt a surge of pity for the other girl. How strange that she had never realized in all the times that she had been to Brierly how lonely Lady Gwendolyn's existence must have been. No doubt it was because Maggie had never wanted for the one thing Lady Gwendolyn had always been denied—a family like the Willoughbys, noisome and squabbling at times but never lacking in warmth or love! Indeed, it seemed that a great deal was made clear by those few bitter remarks.

"Is that what this is all about?" she asked, feeling her way. "Pleasing your mama?"

"Pleasing Mama? Heavens, where could you have got such a nonsensical notion. I would do anything to be free of her pursestrings, and Reggie's. As it happens, Charlesworth would seem admirably suited to provide just such a means of escape. He is reputed, after all, to be as rich as Croesus."

Maggie shivered. "Is that all there is to it? Faith, have you no true feelings for the man?"

"I pray you will not be absurd. Feelings have nothing to do with it. Marriage, after all, is a business arrangement. Although," she added with something resembling puzzlement, "I have discovered since coming here that his lordship is rather more entertaining than I had previously thought possible. In spite of the fact that I should be marrying beneath myself, I begin to think we might deal very well together."

Somehow that revelation did little to hearten Maggie. Indeed, it seemed she might very well be meddling where she had absolutely no business to be. Obviously the earl was not entirely indifferent to Lady Gwendolyn. On the contrary, if he had managed to break even the smallest chink in that ice-clad heart, then he must have gone to great lengths to woo her. In which case, she, Maggie, was an utter idiot ever to believe he might care in the least for a nobody like herself. All at once she wanted to be anywhere but in that room with Lady Gwendolyn.

"I-I beg your pardon. I did not realize—" she began, only to be interrupted by the echo of footsteps in the corridor. Her heart in her throat, she wheeled her chair around. Her eyes froze on the door handle as it began to turn.

A shaft of light lanced through the open doorway, nearly blinding her. As she flung up her arm to shade her eyes, two startled exclamations rang out: "Maggie! What the devil!" and "Oliver Crandall! What are *you* doing here?"

"Yes, Mr. Crandall, what *are* you doing here?" Maggie demanded as soon as her eyes had adjusted sufficiently for her to make out that the coat molded to indecently broad shoulders was indeed unmistakably brown.

"No doubt you will find this exceedingly odd," drawled the gentleman, imperturbably propping one of those powerful shoulders against the doorframe, "but that was the very question I was about to put to you ladies. You see, whereas I was assigned this room and as such would seem to have every good reason to be here, I can conceive of not a single one why the same would apply to either of you."

"Your room?" uttered Lady Gwendolyn in astonished accents. "But that is impossible. I was told this was where your brother was lodged."

"Oh, well, if it's *him* you want, I suppose that puts a different complexion on things. As it happens, my brother has a distaste for being awakened before noon, especially by sunlight streaming through an east window. Which is why I agreed to take this room. You will find him across the hall, two doors down."

"Thank you, Mr. Crandall," said Lady Gwendolyn, stepping in front of him. "And now if you will excuse me, no doubt you and Miss Willoughby have a great deal to discuss."

"Gwendolyn, wait—!" Maggie exclaimed. Too late. Mr. Crandall had already stepped aside, allowing the Ice Queen to sweep past him out of the room. The next instant, to her horror, the door slammed shut, followed by the ominous click of the key turning in the lock.

Abandoning the cumbersome wheelchair, Maggie hopped frantically on one foot to the oak barrier.

"Gwendolyn," she called in a harsh whisper. "Gwendolyn, open this door!"

"I am sorry, Maggie, dear," came from the other side of the barrier. "I did warn you, however, that nothing would stop me from getting what I wanted. Now I must bid you good night. No doubt it will occur to me to send someone to let you out, but if not, please do enjoy yourself."

"Now see what you have done!" Maggie uttered furiously as she turned to face the gentleman, who observed her with utter sang-froid. "She means to compromise herself with his lordship. Surely you must have guessed what she was up to. Why in heaven's name did you let her go?"

The masculine shoulders lifted in a shrug. "There seemed little point in stopping her," he had the gall to answer her, "especially since to achieve just such an alliance was one of the reasons we accepted your father's invitation."

"The reason you accepted . . ." Maggie faltered to a stop, her mind reeling with the inevitable implications of that startling announcement.

"Does it trouble you so much, Miss Willoughby?" Crandall asked carelessly. "I promise you my brother has long entertained an affection for the lady. In fact, he has assured me on more than one occasion that no other female will do to be his wife."

"Then no doubt we must be very happy for him," Maggie retorted in bitter accents. "It would seem he will have his wish."

What a fool she had been not to have seen it all before. Lady Gwendolyn had been right. Whatever small kindnesses he had shown her had been motivated by pity, nothing more. And as for Oliver Crandall, no doubt she had been right about him as well.

Then all at once did the greater significance of her situation strike her. "Good God!" she cried, turning once more to tug frantically at the door handle. "They must not find me here!"

"Maggie!" She froze as a strong slender hand planted itself against the door next to her face. "It's no use, infant. You will only call attention to yourself."

Maggie swallowed, made suddenly and acutely aware of the warmth of his body so close to hers. Then, more maddening still, her heart began to pound as if on cue and her temperature to rise most alarmingly.

"Then what do you suggest we do, Mr. Crandall?" she said in a strangled voice. "Perhaps a game of pinochle to pass the time until we are discovered?" She struggled against an insane urge to giggle. "And then what? Try and explain to my parents and a houseful of guests that it was all perfectly innocent?"

"I hardly think that would suit, Miss Willoughby," he replied with the barest hint of amusement in his deep voice. "As a matter of fact, I am quite sure it would not. Naturally, I shall ask your father for your hand in marriage. Surely you did not imagine I should do otherwise?"

Maggie clenched her eyes shut in mortification. "No, how could I?" she replied miserably. "When you have been so good as to rescue me from one stupid blunder after another? Really, it is simply too absurd."

She winced at the touch of his hand on her arm, firmly but gently turning her to face him.

"Would it surprise you to discover," he said, a finger beneath her chin forcing her to look up at him, "that I find nothing absurd in the notion of having you as my wife?"

She was startled into a nervous burst of laughter. "On the contrary, I should be surprised if you did. It is hardly a laughing matter, after all, to be trapped into marriage. Oh, it is all *his* fault. *Why,* if your brother was so set to wed Lady Gwendolyn, did he not simply ask her? Surely there was never any doubt that she would accept the honor of becoming his countess?"

An odd sort of smile twisted at the handsome lips. "You are right of course. She would never have turned down a coronet. Unfortunately, my brother is not an earl. *I* am, and I have not the least desire to marry Lady Gwendolyn."

Maggie, who had the sensation of having just been struck by a lightning bolt, felt her knees go suddenly weak beneath her.

"Maggie. You must believe I never meant to break it to you so suddenly." Strong hands reached for her to keep her from falling. "I was a bloody fool ever to agree to change places with Oliver."

This time she was too quick for him, however. Prompted by some instinct for self-preservation, she slipped from his grasp and, with something between a hop and a skip, managed to get the sofa between them.

"Then why did you?" she blurted, poised for further

flight should it prove necessary. "If it was to have fun at my expense, then you succeeded admirably. No doubt you will both have a fine laugh at my expense. Faith, what a fool you must take me for!"

"You, my dear, are foolish beyond permission if that is what you believe," declared Charlesworth, moving purposefully toward her. "It was nothing like that, I assure you."

"Was it not?" Maggie backed warily, never taking her eyes off him. "Come no closer, Lord Charlesworth. I warn you."

"You know it was not," he answered, taking another step. "Lady Gwendolyn made it obvious she would never let Ollie close enough to breach that well-guarded heart of hers, not so long as she thought she had a chance at a title as well as a fortune."

"So you came up with the brilliant idea of trading identities," Maggie concluded bitterly as she rounded the corner of the sofa. "And why not, when it gave you the perfect opportunity to amuse yourself at my expense."

"You are wrong in both instances, Miss Willoughby. It was Ollie's idea to exchange coats after you left us to our cigars and brandy, and it was never my intent to hurt you. I am well aware I should never have given my word not to tell you, but as it turns out, the plan worked beyond our wildest expectations. Lady Gwendolyn may never be a countess, but she will have a husband who loves her and a fortune not even she would sneeze at."

"No doubt you are both to be congratulated. Unfortunately it would seem that *you* got more than you bargained for. Or would you have me to believe you planned for the eventuality of a wife you could not possibly want?"

Her heart leapt wildly at the sudden glint in his eye.

"On the contrary, Miss Willoughby," he drawled dangerously, facing her with only the width of the sofa between them. "Lady Gwendolyn was only *one* of the reasons we came to Willoughby. You, my dear, were the other."

"I?" Maggie gasped. "Now you are doing it much too brown. You never set eyes on me before coming here."

"Oh, but I *had* seen you before, once, on a particularly memorable day at Brierly. I was on holiday from school with Reggie when I happened on you and your cousin involved in a heated exchange with Lady Gwendolyn. Perhaps you don't remember. You could not have been more than eight or nine at the time. That little girl, however, made a permanent impression on me. Having judged her to have grown at last into womanhood, I confess I was curious to see if she was still the same little spitfire who so courageously stood up against the duke's sister in defense of her cousin."

"That was you?" Maggie stared at him with slowly dawning recognition. He could not have been above eighteen at the time, a tall, slender youth who even then had had a commanding air about him. Lady Gwendolyn had not deigned to introduce him, not to Charlotte, whose father had died in disgrace and left his family penniless. It had been the first time either she or Charlotte had heard the truth of her father's untimely demise, and even now she could not bear the anguish that she had seen in her cousin's eyes.

Abruptly she turned away. "And now you have had your curiosity more than satisfied, have you not?" she said around the sudden lump in her throat. "I am that same impetuous little nobody who cannot seem to keep from becoming embroiled in one coil after another. Well, you need not worry that you will be made to pay the price of my folly. It would be asking far too much of you."

"Perhaps you should let me be the judge of that." Maggie's heart lurched as she realized he had advanced around the end of the sofa and even then was coming toward her. "In any case, it hardly signifies. You will marry me, Miss Willoughby. You have no other choice in the matter."

Maggie uttered a gasp of outrage. How dared he presume so much! He was arrogant and overbearing, and she had not asked to be made his wife. Indeed, she had only been trying to save him from a similar fate with Lady Gwendolyn. Suddenly it seemed to her that disgrace could not be any worse than to live a lifetime with a man who could not love her, indeed, with a man who must inevitably come to despise her for having entrapped him into such a marriage.

"You are wrong, Lord Charlesworth. I will not marry you. Not even if it means living in utter disgrace for the rest of my life."

"Why, Miss Willoughby?" he demanded, seeming to gauge the distance between them. "If I am to bear the infamy of having ruined an innocent female, I deserve at least to know why you will not marry me."

"Be-because I could never trust a man who has lied to me almost from the very moment we had the misfortune to meet," she declared, grasping at straws as she backed uncertainly before his advance. "How can I be certain even now that you are not lying to me, that you are not Charlesworth but Oliver Crandall?"

"I could show you the birthmark on my left hip, Miss Willoughby, if it will make you feel any better," he suggested and, to her horror, began peeling off his coat as though he meant to disrobe right then before her.

"You wouldn't dare!" Hastily Maggie turned her back on him. Only then, having understandably forgotten her ankle in the circumstances, she cried out as she felt it give way beneath her.

"Dammit, Maggie!" The next instant she found herself swept up for the fifth time in less than twenty-four hours into a strong pair of masculine arms. "How am I to get it through that hard head of yours that I love you and want to marry you if you will not hold still long enough for me to prove it?"

Instantly Maggie froze, her heart beating erratically beneath her breast.

"You-you what?" she gasped, unable to believe she had heard correctly.

"Love you," he repeated obligingly. "Can you truly think I should have let Ollie talk me into what can only be described as an extremely troublesome charade had it been otherwise? It was the only way I could rid myself of Lady Gwendolyn long enough to insinuate myself into your affections. Perhaps I did not lose my heart to that little girl I encountered at Brierly, but you may be sure I fell head over ears in love with the haughty young beauty at the skating pond."

Maggie dropped her eyes, unable or unwilling yet to snatch at the happiness which seemed tantalizingly within her grasp.

"And how do I know that was you?" she demanded. "You might be Oliver for all I know."

"And, you, my dear, sound perilously like Lady Gwendolyn. Is making sure you are to become a countess so very important to you?"

"No, how can you say so?" she countered, hurt that he could believe her so conniving. "On the other hand, I have every right to know which man I am marrying. And a birthmark cannot tell me, of that you may be certain. I am afraid, sir, that you have no choice but-but to kiss me."

Tilting her head back and puckering her lips, she waited, her eyes open to see what he would do.

She did not have long to wait. A blue fire in his eyes, he covered her mouth with his.

Not even the most lurid of romances could have prepared her for the fiery tumult of emotions that coursed through her then. Passionately tender, he aroused a sweet conflagration within her which left her breathless and dazed. Her head spinning, she blinked up at him when no little time later he released her.

"Well?" he murmured, his voice husky with barely controlled passion. "Are you satisfied as to who I am?"

It was perhaps little wonder that neither of them heard the click of the key in the lock or knew when the door was thrust open.

"Er—Milt, old boy," interrupted Oliver Crandall, poking his head in. A heavy sigh was heard to emanate from his lordship. "Sorry to intrude. I came to let you out as soon as I could. Er—there was something I wanted to ask you."

"Don't tell me," growled Charlesworth, apparently not in the least pleased at having been rescued. "You somehow let the lady escape you, in which case you wish to retain the title for just a little while longer."

"Well, not exactly. As it happens, we have fortunately been discovered by the duchess herself in what can only be construed as compromising circumstances. We are to be wed by special license with the greatest dispatch possible. The thing is, I hadn't the heart to tell the old dragon her daughter was getting a fortune but not a title. It occurred to me, old boy, that perhaps you wouldn't mind putting it off till Gwen and I have sailed to Greece for the honeymoon. After all, what can it hurt? By the time we get back, everything will have blown over, and . . . Er—Milt. Milt. Don't you do it, Milt!"

His lordship, the Earl of Charlesworth, after carefully depositing his love in her wheelchair, had already straightened and was advancing purposefully toward his scapegrace younger brother, younger, that is, by a mere four minutes. Maggie saw his arm go back and heard the crunch of a fist coming in contact with what gave every indication of being a very hard chin. Then he had turned, and, rubbing the knuckles of his good right in the palm of his left, he bent to retrieve Maggie once more from her chair.

131

"Now," he said with every appearance of immense satisfaction, "where were we?"

Maggie grinned, twin imps peeping out in her cheeks. "You, my dear Lord of Misrule, were about to return me to my room *before* we are discovered in similar circumstances to your brother's."

"Somehow that is not quite what I had in mind," he replied reflectively. "Still, no doubt you are in the right of it. Not, however, before I have your answer."

"I begin to believe, Lord Charlesworth, that you are something of a tyrant. I warn you I am not at all good at taking orders. Very likely I should prove a most unconformable wife."

"And I, my dear, shall prove a most accommodating husband — *after* we are wed. You will promise to marry me, Maggie Willoughby, or I swear I shall lock the door and throw away the key."

"You would not dare."

"Oh, would I not?" he answered, taking a determined step toward the doorway. "Either you give me your answer now, or we wait until someone thinks to come looking for us."

"Well then, since you would appear to leave me no choice," she said before he could kick the door shut, "I think it only fair to tell you that I am not in the least good at waiting."

An exceedingly dangerous glint ignited in his eyes. "And neither, I warn you, am I," he said in tones that left her little doubt that he would not be put off a second longer. "Tell me, Maggie. And don't say you have any doubts as to who I am, for I promise I shan't believe you."

"Oh, but I haven't the least doubt who you are." Laying her head against the broad shoulder conveniently placed for that very purpose, she gazed up at him with shining eyes. "My dearest Milton Crandall, Lord Charlesworth, you are undeniably the man I fell in love

132

with at first sight beside the skating pond. And, yes. Oh, yes, I *will* marry you—just as soon as I can walk again. The breaking of the withes, notwithstanding, nothing, absolutely *nothing,* will persuade me to proceed down the aisles in that odious wheelchair!"

The Christmas Knight
by Anthea Malcolm

Amanda was standing at the windows that looked out toward the drive when she saw the carriage arrive and discharge its single passenger, a slender fair-haired man wrapped in a greatcoat who ran quickly up the long shallow stairway toward the house. The leaded-glass panes, a relic of the original fifteenth-century building, turned the wavering shapes of the rain-drenched garden into something seen underwater, while the rain-drenched man, whose outlines were also blurred, seemed by his purposeful movement an alien presence, an explorer perhaps, a figure bent on adventure and discovery. Amanda smiled at this conceit and opened the door to the man who now stood on the threshold, dripping rain and clutching a packet wrapped in oilskin.

He had been an age in getting to Ludlow. In the ordinary course of things there was no one Amanda would rather see than Owen, and now, with so much to tell him, she could barely conceal her excitement and relief. "Take Mr. Thorn's coat," she said to the young footman who had made a hasty entrance into the hall, "he's quite thoroughly wet. And tell Lord or Lady Windham he's arrived. We'll be in the library."

Owen surrendered his greatcoat but refused to part with the packet, and Amanda, knowing that the packet was at the heart of the puzzle that had disturbed her all the morning, held her tongue until they were in the privacy of the dark-paneled library, a room so far shunned by the other guests. "The most extraordinary thing has happened," she said, drawing him toward the fireplace where the burning logs were giving off a welcome scent of pine, "and you must tell me what it means, for I'm sure I have no idea myself. Senhor Ribeiro has gone, and in the most peculiar way, before seven this morning and with nothing but the hastiest of notes to Charles, and he only arrived yesterday, and I quite understood that he had come expressly to meet you." She looked up into Owen's eyes, hoping to find the explanation there, but he was clearly as startled as she. "Why would he refuse to meet you?" Amanda went on. "He came all the way from Portugal so you could return his book because he didn't want it entrusted to the mails, and he left just on the day you're expected to arrive. I call that distinctly odd. If he'd taken you in dislike, he wouldn't have agreed to meet you in the first place, though he had to, didn't he, if he wanted to collect his book."

"It's not his book." Owen's smile, so sweet-tempered she could hardly take offense, told her she had got the story rather muddled. "It belongs to his nephew, Eugenio Ribeiro, who inherited it from his grandfather who was a collector of sorts and had a really splendid library. Has, I should say, for the library passed intact to his son and then to *his* son, Eugenio. If I make myself clear."

Amanda frowned. "That part's clear enough. But who is our Senhor Ribeiro?"

"One of the brothers. The father's brothers, that is. I believe it's a large family. And therefore an uncle of Eugenio, *my* Senhor Ribeiro."

"Owen, you're being difficult."

"Not at all. I was given an introduction to the family when I went to Lisbon last year. Eugenio was the only one at home, and we quite hit it off. We're much of an

138

age, and though he doesn't share my passion for books, he quite respects what he owns. I was struck absolutely dumb when he showed me the Caxton book"—Owen glanced at the packet which he was still holding—"and he insisted that I borrow it, but naturally he wants it back. He wrote that his uncle, Raimundo Ribeiro, was coming to England on business and would I meet him, which of course I would. The thing was, I was promised here at Ludlow for Christmas, so I asked Charles if I could bring another guest. Charles had met Eugenio when he was stationed in Lisbon, and he said by all means Uncle Raimundo must come as well, and so he did, and no, Amanda, I have no idea why he left." Owen's eyes, serious and not a little worried, belied the lightness of his words.

"Then you don't actually know him."

"That's right. Whyever he left—and I can think of a dozen reasons, none of which are any of our business—it was not for fear of meeting me."

"Still, he was our guest, and one can't but help feel . . ." Amanda shrugged, not sure how to continue.

"That one should do something. Of course, and we will, though there's precious little we can do. I'd like to see the note he left for Charles, and then I want to talk to any of the servants who saw him before he left." His hand flicked lightly against her cheek. "Don't worry, Amanda, I daresay we'll hear from the man himself before too many days have passed."

His words were reassuring, as was his touch, and Amanda, who accounted Owen her very dearest friend, forced herself to smile. "Is that the notorious book?" She indicated the packet.

"Notorious? I should hope not, though it was French originally. Caxton had it translated for English tastes." He laid the packet on the writing table which stood against the wall and was beginning to unwrap it when his eye was caught by a nearby object. "What an exquisite piece of work. Is it yours?"

Amanda nodded, feeling pleased and embarrassed all at once. Owen was looking at a silver inkstand, a closed box with a hinged central handle, very plain save for a design of shells on the borders and feet and an engraving of a great seabird on the top.

"May I?" Owen asked. He opened the front compartment which contained a silver inkpot and a sand-caster, each with a shell and bird design, and a small compartment at one end for wafers. The rear half of the box was a single compartment and contained an assortment of quills and a knife. "It's quite the best thing you've done," he said with obvious sincerity.

"It is rather good, isn't it? Much better than the first one I tried, which I gave to Papa. I made this one for Charles."

"Fortunate brother. I'd say it's much to his taste. Did you bring anything else with you?"

"No," Amanda said, too quickly, and then, "that is, just one small piece. I'll show it to you later." Perhaps, she added to herself. She was not a proper apprentice, but she had haunted Mr. McIver's workshop since she was thirteen, and McIver, a well-known silversmith in Edinburgh and a friend of her father's, had finally agreed to teach her what he knew. Unlike her parents, Owen thoroughly approved of her efforts. He was a discriminating critic, and she owed much to his observations, but for a reason she could not name, she was reluctant to put her latest work before him.

Owen must have sensed her discomfort, for he suddenly changed the subject. "What was he like, Raimundo Ribeiro?"

It took Amanda a moment to call up the man's face. "Quite charming," she said, "though rather somber, as though he'd had a great sorrow or perhaps as though he

140

took the matter of sin rather too literally. But very handsome, with dark liquid eyes and thick black hair and a quite splendid moustache." She grinned. "An exotic flower for an English garden, particularly in the dead of winter. Though no more, I suppose, than the Arnquists, who are tall and incredibly fair. Charles knew them in Sweden. Nor Baron von Frisch, who's Austrian and round and funny and the most good-natured man imaginable. He's stationed in England now, as are the Arnquists, and Charles is returning their hospitality."

Owen turned round. "Good Lord. Who else is here?"

"Family mostly. Aunt Isabel and Aunt Fidella, and Nicola's brother Jeremy and her sister Helena and their broods. Then there's Lord Mulgrave, an uncle of Helena's husband who lost his wife last year and had no place else to go. And the Lambton-Hills. They're the young couple Nicola and Charles helped get married against their parents' wishes, which means that they're still estranged from their respective families and had no place to go either."

"Quite a gathering of lost lambs."

"Christmas is the time to do it," she answered, a note of tartness in her voice. "That's the lot, I think, if you don't count the children. Nearly everyone has brought some. Lady Duffield was to come as well—she's a friend of Aunt Isabel's—but she cried off at the last moment."

"Throwing Nicola's table sadly out."

"Senhor Ribeiro threw it in again." Amanda looked sharply at Owen who had given a near imperceptible start at Lady Duffield's name. "Not that Nicola has ever cared whether her table is in or out."

"Which is why your brother, who had the good sense to marry her, is one of my most cherished friends."

They looked at each other in a moment of perfect accord until Amanda, surprised by a sudden access of self-consciousness, turned to the writing table. "Owen, aren't you ever going to let me see that book?"

Owen looked down at the table where the book lay in its half-opened oilskin wrapping. Quickly removing the last of the covering, he lifted out the volume, which was bound in leather that had darkened with use and age to a warm umber, and held it out to her. The binding had dried and begun to crack, and Amanda took the volume carefully. It must have been over three hundred years old, and it was a wonder that it had survived these many years. "May I open it?"

"My dear girl, of course." Owen's smile was quick. "It won't crumble under your hands or anything of the sort. In fact, it's in remarkably good condition."

Amanda moved to a chair where she could get the light from the window. Owen followed. She was aware of his presence, just behind her chair, and knew that his eyes were following the movement of her hands as she opened the book on her lap. " 'The Most Pleasant History of Blanchardyn,' " she read, stumbling a little over the unfamiliar form of the letters, " 'Son to the King of Fries; and the fair Lady Eglantine Queen of Tormaday, surnamed The Proud Lady in Love.' Why, it's a romance," she said, looking up in delight.

"Did you expect sermons? All very well in their place, but not at all the sort of thing to take my fancy."

"I suppose not," Amanda said, dismissing the matter as irrelevant, which it certainly was. "Did Caxton write it?" she continued.

"No, the story's far older than that. It goes back at least to the thirteenth century. It appeared first in France, in verse and then in prose. Caxton's translation probably dates from 1489, and I assure you it was read as avidly then as it will be by you if I give you the chance."

"You can't possibly know that."

"What? Readers of the past or this particular reader in the present?"

"Both." She stood up, turned to face him, and held out the book, trying to keep her face stern.

"Oh, Amanda, I know you. You would never turn down a good story."

"What story?" Neither of them had heard the door open, but they turned now to face the intruders. "We heard you were here," said Verity, advancing into the room. Nicola and Charles's foster child had grown rapidly these past few months and was now tall for her ten years. She was followed by Jeremy's stepson David who liked the company of girls and did not mind that he was only eight.

"What story?" David echoed, coming to stand before Owen. "Is it in that book?"

"It is, though it's a very long story so I don't think I'll be able to read it to you."

"You could tell it to us," Verity said.

"I could," Owen admitted, "though I rather think it's time I paid my respects to your mother and father. Have you any idea where they are?"

The children regarded him blankly. "Then I think I'd better find them." Owen tucked the book firmly under his arm and prepared to leave the room.

David, not to be put aside, was in his way. "What's the story about?"

"It's about a prince," Owen said with what Amanda considered admirable patience. "A prince who wants to be a knight. Unfortunately, his father has seen to it that he's been taught everything but how to joust and bear arms."

"How very sensible," Amanda murmured.

Owen raised his brows but kept his eyes on the child. "So he has to leave home to do so."

David frowned. "What's his name?"

"Blanchardyn."

"Blanch—that means white, doesn't it?" Verity said. "Is he a white knight?"

Owen looked thoughtful. "In a manner of speaking, I suppose. Heroes usually are."

"Is there a princess?"

"There's a queen. Her name is Eglantine."

"The proud lady in love," Amanda contributed.

"How funny. What does that mean?" Verity asked.

Amanda looked at Owen, but he indicated that she should continue. "I rather imagine," she said after a moment, "that she doesn't want to settle for just any man, but only one who is very very special."

"Like Blanchardyn," David said.

"Exactly. And that's all we're going to talk about for now." Owen put his arm on David's shoulder, led him round the leather sofa which faced the fireplace, and urged him to the door. Verity followed, but as they left the room they became entangled with Nicola who was about to enter it, and with the ensuing questions and explanations it was several minutes before Nicola was able to send the children on their way and attend to her new guest.

"You've been telling them stories," Nicola said, advancing into the room and offering her hands to Owen, "and it's on your own head—they'll never let you be."

Owen took her hands. "I like stories."

"So do I," said Amanda.

Nicola's normally lively manner vanished. "I, too, but the one I have to tell you is more than a little odd. Charles is in the drawing room, talking to Senhor Ribeiro."

"He came back," Amanda said with heartfelt relief. "I'm so glad."

"You'd best restrain your joy and set your wits to

144

work." A faint frown marred Nicola's expressive face. "The Senhor Ribeiro who arrived today and is now drinking our very best sherry is not the Senhor Ribeiro who came and went yesterday." Amanda and Owen made sounds of disbelief. "I'd swear to it," Nicola insisted, "though there is a distinct resemblance."

"Black hair?" Amanda asked. "Soulful eyes?"

Nicola nodded. "And a luxuriant moustache."

"You can hide a lot of things under a moustache." Amanda was thoughtful. "It's an interesting problem, though I can't imagine why one would want to impersonate the other . . . Oh! Owen, the book."

"Yes, it's awkward, that." Owen cast a vague glance around the book-lined walls, then walked purposefully to the darkest corner of the room and inserted the pleasant history of Blanchardyn into one of the upper shelves where, to Amanda's eye, it disappeared. "If you don't mind," he said, addressing Nicola. "At least until we know where we are."

"You'd better come into the drawing room," Nicola said. "You'll have to meet him sooner or later, and perhaps you can tell us if he seems at all plausible. Amanda, come too and tell us what you think."

Owen moved to the door and held it open for the ladies. "I don't suppose you've put the question to him directly."

Nicola's hazel eyes gleamed with mischief. "It hardly seemed good form. And to tell you the truth, he left us both quite breathless."

They said no more until they reached the drawing room, a large low-ceilinged chamber furnished with an eye to comfort and conversation. The rain had stopped and a wintry sun shone through the bank of windows that nearly filled one wall. Bars of light fell across the two men who stood there, one dark, one fair. Charles appeared to be pointing out some feature of the landscape to his guest.

Nicola crossed the room quickly, her bright voice announcing to all that this was no more than the happiest of social gatherings. "Charles," she said to her husband, "here's Owen come at last. Senhor Ribeiro, may I present Owen Thorn, one of our dearest friends. He's acquainted with your nephew, Eugenio Ribeiro, and has been quite longing to meet you. And my husband's sister, Amanda Berwick." Nicola did not choose to explain that Amanda was only a half sister, and Amanda was grateful for this tact. She had not known Charles well during her childhood, but since his marriage she had begun to make long visits to the Windhams, both in London and in Devon, and she now felt closer to Charles than to her brothers in Edinburgh.

"What a charming surprise." Senhor Ribeiro bowed over Amanda's hand, holding it a good deal longer than she thought necessary. This second Ribeiro was very like the first, a little taller, perhaps, and a little broader of shoulder, though not, Amanda considered, quite so sober or so correct. But perhaps that had something to do with the hand. She professed herself delighted to meet him, and did not add, "again."

The visitor was far more straightforward with Owen, though he greeted him with equal enthusiasm. Owen inquired after Eugenio's health and the state of his horses and his garden and asked about several of the servants by name. "Your nephew was kind enough to put his carriage at my disposal," Owen said, almost as an afterthought. "His coachman, Jorge, had the lightest hand with the ribbons I've ever seen."

"I know Eugenio's stable well," Senhor Ribeiro said gravely. "There is no one there by the name of Jorge."

"Is there not?" Owen made a creditable show of surprise. "I must have mistaken the name, I have the most shocking memory."

Ribeiro waved the lapse aside, but Amanda knew that Owen had given the other man a test and that he had passed it. She saw Owen meet her brother's eyes and saw the message that passed between them. Ribeiro raised his brows in polite inquiry.

"I'm sure you'd like to see your room," Nicola said hurriedly, "and I'd like to introduce you to your fellow guests, though I'm afraid they're scattered all about the house and grounds just now, but—"

"But there's something awkward that has occurred," Charles put in smoothly, "and I think you'd best hear about it before you find yourself in a crowd."

"Only do sit down." Nicola indicated a grouping of sofas and chairs near the fireplace which, like its smaller companion in the library, boasted a vigorous fire. "Sit down, everyone. I don't know whether it's a prank or something rather worse, but we may as well be comfortable while we consider it."

Ribeiro indicated that he was desolated that his arrival had caused any problems and that he was quite willing to listen to whatever Lord and Lady Windham had to say.

"It's not your arrival," Charles said when they were all seated, "it's the other man's." There was a moment of silence so intense Amanda heard it as a kind of ringing sound. Ribeiro was perfectly quiet, and he had no expression at all. Though, she admitted, it was hard to tell behind the moustache. "He arrived yesterday," Charles went on, "and announced himself as Raimundo Ribeiro, and I had no reason to doubt that that was who he was. He stayed the night but left early this morning, which surprised us as he had come expressly to meet Mr. Thorn who was not expected until this afternoon. We were given a note saying that he'd been called away on some private matter, and we learned later that one of the grooms drove him into Honiton

147

where I imagine he caught a coach."

Charles said no more, but let the silence develop. He was watching Ribeiro with care—indeed, they were all watching this second Raimundo Ribeiro—but the object of their combined gaze seemed unaware of their interest. He had been attentive while Charles was speaking, but now that Charles had done, Ribeiro turned thoughtful. Thoughtful, and then—yes, amused. A smile was barely visible beneath the overhanging moustache, a smile which grew and erupted at last in a shout of laughter. "Forgive me," he said, aware now of the puzzled faces turned toward him. "It is Henrique. It must be." He drew out a handkerchief and mopped his eyes which had begun to water with mirth. "My brother," he explained. "We are very much alike."

"There is a distinct resemblance," Charles acknowledged. He was courteous but clearly not satisfied with this explanation. "The man may well have been your brother, and I am glad to have a name to put to him. But what I do not understand is—"

"Why?" Nicola broke in impatiently. "Why would he do such a harebrained thing? What would he have to gain by passing himself off as you?"

Owen stirred in his chair, but it was Amanda who answered the question. "He wanted Eugenio Ribeiro's book."

Ribeiro threw up his hands. "No, that I cannot believe. At least—You may be right, Miss Berwick, but I assure you it would be nothing more than what you call a—a prank. There is nothing vicious in Henrique." He turned back to Nicola, his face now thoughtful. "I see I must tell you about my brother, Lady Windham, though it pains me to do so. He is younger than I by no more than a year, and we have always been close, though less so, alas, in recent years. But there has always been a—a certain rivalry between us. You understand, this is common between brothers. I have not seen Henrique for many months. He has been in Paris, where our sister lives with her husband, a Frenchman. I will travel there when my business in your country is concluded—I have not seen my sister in several years—and I will speak harshly to Henrique for imposing himself so outrageously on my English friends." Ribeiro gave an expressive shrug. "Not that he is likely to take me seriously. Henrique, I fear, has a levity of manner that has often brought disgrace upon our family."

He said no more. Indeed there was no more any of them could say, short of accusing him of fabricating the entire story, and that seemed unlikely. Charles, with a suitable air of gravity, thanked Ribeiro for his frankness and assured him that no more would be said about the character of his brother. "We'll have to explain who he is, of course, lest the other guests ask awkward questions. Fortunately, he was introduced only by his surname."

Ribeiro murmured that this was indeed fortunate.

It was Owen who raised the matter of the book. He had brought it with him and was eager to consign it to Senhor Ribeiro's care, but in view of the appearance of the other man who might have had designs on his nephew's property and who just might be lurking in the neighborhood seeking for an opportunity to lay his hands on it, wouldn't it be wise to place it in Lord Windham's care, at least until Senhor Ribeiro left Ludlow.

Amanda thought it very well done. Owen had at once acknowledged Ribeiro's right to the book and made it impossible for him to claim it. When Nicola had taken their Portuguese visitor off to his room, she turned to Owen and Charles and asked the question that had been on her lips since Ribeiro had told them about his scapegrace brother. "Do you believe him?"

"I have no reason not to," Charles said. "I met the nephew when I was in Lisbon but not the uncles. But there certainly is an Henrique, and his reputation is much as Ribeiro has sketched it. You can't deny the resemblance between the two men. And the disappearance of the first argues for the legitimacy of the second. Owen?"

"I don't know." Owen rose and moved to the fireplace, his expression thoughtful. "It seems only prudent to keep the book under lock and key for the time being. Perhaps Henrique will turn up and tell us his version of the story."

His smile told Amanda that he expected nothing of the kind. "I suppose the book is worth a great deal of money," she said.

"A matter of two or three hundred pounds, I would guess. More perhaps to someone who coveted it for its own sake. It's said to be the copy owned by Jane Shore, Edward IV's mistress, and if true that would raise its value, though not, I would guess, to more than a few hundred pounds. That might be a fortune to a schoolmaster, but the Ribeiros are a wealthy family."

"Henrique may be short of the ready," Charles suggested. "Or perhaps he simply wants to make mischief."

"He's certainly made a puzzle. And I hate puzzles I can't solve," Amanda added with feeling.

The men laughed and they went on to talk of other things until Nicola returned, bearing with her the Countess Arnquist, a tall slender woman with white-gold hair who did not look at all as though she had two half-grown daughters, and another woman whom Amanda had not yet met. She proved to be one more surprise on this day when people came and went without reason or apparent thought for the trouble they might cause. It was Lady Duffield, who had sent Nicola a pretty letter of apology saying she would not be able to come to Ludlow and then had come after all.

Amanda, who had heard Lady Duffield described as a woman of great charm, decided at once that she had entirely too much charm for a person to be quite comfortable in her presence. She must be nearly fifty, but age seemed an irrelevant attribute for Pamela Duffield. Masses of fair hair, wide-spaced blue eyes, the color of the sea on a summer day, and a smile so inviting one could not help but smile in return. Her smile was now directed at Owen, who was bending over her as though she were some fragile flower that had to be protected from the wind.

Jealousy, Amanda reminded herself, was an unbecoming emotion and ought to be relegated to the nursery, which was where she could last remember feeling it. Owen may have been her friend for the past three years, but he had other friends as well. Or perhaps Lady Duffield, with whom Owen was obviously well-acquainted, was something more than a friend, or had been in the past. Young men, in their inexperience, frequently sought out older women, and women like Lady Duffield, all admiration and warm acceptance, no doubt played a useful role in their training. Amanda watched the two of them critically. No, there was certainly nothing like that between them now, and, if there once had been, it should be no concern of hers.

Her thoughts were interrupted by the arrival of Nicola's sister, Helena Lydgate, along with her sister-in-law, Elizabeth Crawford, Verity, and the two Arnquist girls. They had been cooped up all the day, Helena said, and the rain had stopped, and did anyone want to take the air? They might walk as far as the home farm and meet up with the men who, heedless of the weather, had abandoned their company some two hours before. The countess, who looked a vigorous woman, assented readily, but Lady Duffield said she would retire to her bedchamber to recover from the rigors of her journey. Owen escorted her from the room, leaving Amanda to decide that the company of the other women was preferable to her own wayward thoughts.

Amanda had no wish to dwell on her absurd burst of jealousy. Nor on the strange self-consciousness she had felt with Owen when they were in the library nor the stirrings of feelings that seemed quite at odds with their sturdy friendship. She mounted the stairs to her room to make ready for the walk, uncomfortably aware that there were things that could get in the way of friendship, especially between men and women. She would have to be very careful. She could not bear it if she lost Owen as a friend.

The cold brisk air restored Amanda's spirits. She concluded she had been suffering from an attack of the megrims, and she put Owen and Lady Duffield and all those attendant thoughts from her mind. But the problem of the Portuguese imposter remained, and a quarter-mile beyond the stable Amanda excused herself and turned back to the house, thinking to stop at the stable and question whomever had driven the first Senhor Ribeiro to Honiton. It proved to be Dickon, one of the grooms, but he was able to tell her nothing but that Senhor Ribeiro had appeared eager to dust off and that he had tipped him handsomely when they arrived in Honiton.

"Where did you take him?" Amanda asked, frustrated by this meager information. "Did he say anything about hiring a post chaise? Do you know which way he was going?"

"The Golden Lion," the groom said quickly. "And no, and no. I swear, I've told you all I can."

Amanda beat her hands in impatience, then apologized to Dickon for suggesting otherwise. The groom tipped his hat and returned to his work, but Amanda stood irresolute, feeling unreasonably disappointed and not sure what line to take next. When she raised her eyes, she found Owen standing in front of her. "You heard?" she asked.

"I heard." He put one long finger under her chin and raised it gently. "Be not perturbed, fair maid. I, Owen Thorn, have information."

"What? Owen, don't tease. I shall die if you don't tell me."

Owen stepped back, reached into his pocket, and drew out a sheet of paper, the broken wax clinging to its edges. "Delivered by hand, not a quarter of an hour ago. Read it."

Amanda took the sheet and perused it quickly, looked up at Owen in wonder, then lowered her eyes and read the letter again. It was brief and much blotted. The author wrote a flowing hand but had struggled with an inadequate pen. He signed himself Raimundo Ribeiro, and he apologized to Mr. Thorn for his precipitate departure from Ludlow. If Mr. Thorn would be so good as to come to the Golden Lion in Honiton, where he would remain for the next day or two before moving on to London, he would be happy to give him an explanation. Mr. Thorn might also think to bring along the book belonging to his nephew Eugenio, and he remained his obedient servant.

"So the second Senhor Ribeiro may be right," Amanda said thoughtfully. "Henrique is persisting in his masquerade. He must be desperate to get his hands on the book. Unless—"

"Unless," Owen said, "the second Ribeiro is the imposter, and the real Raimundo is waiting in Honiton with a thumping good story. Would you like to go for a drive?"

"You're going to see him now?"

Owen grinned. " 'The goodness that thou mayst do

this day, do it.' And I confess I'll be in a fidge till I hear what the man has to say. Your cloak is warm, isn't it? Good. It's not yet three. We'll be back before dark. Do come, I'd like the company."

Nothing would have kept Amanda at home. She followed him farther into the warmth of the stable where he gave orders for his carriage to be made ready. "Owen," she said while they were waiting, "you haven't brought the book?"

"Never fear. At this moment it's being viewed reverentially by Ribeiro—the Ribeiro currently in residence, who is most likely the real Raimundo—but Charles will see that it's returned to his keeping the moment Ribeiro is through."

"What if Ribeiro takes the book and tries to make a run for it?"

"On foot? In foul and dismal weather? Unlikely, and Charles is to be told if anyone asks for a carriage or horse."

Amanda sighed. The mystery might soon be solved, but it might well be only deepened. What if the first Ribeiro, whom she had rather liked, proved just as plausible as the second, who had been entirely too familiar? Not that her own feelings should enter into it, but it did seem difficult to know how to judge between them. Owen seemed not at all concerned about how the matter might be resolved. For him the chase was all.

Which was not quite fair. Owen had a very healthy concern for the disposition of the book, for which he felt responsible, and he wanted to give it to someone who would take it back to Eugenio Ribeiro and not appropriate it for his own use. Still, it was a whacking great problem, and problems were things he enjoyed.

They were soon in the carriage with Owen's coachman on the box. Amanda had wrapped her cloak tightly around her, for the day had turned cold, but her hair was free, the bright gold curls tumbling about her face and neck in reckless abandon. Owen studied her profile, the small straight nose, the full mouth, the short rounded chin. Her eyes, dark-lashed, were hidden, but he knew them well, an intense dark blue in color, large and rounded as though she looked on the world in perpetual wonder and surprise. Amanda had been seventeen when he first met her, and a child. Or nearly so. She had had none of the coquetry of her age, but she had had wit and an audacity of mind that had quite charmed him. Through the succeeding years of their friendship it had never occurred to Owen to think of her as other than Charles's younger sister. But here, in the confines of the carriage, with an unaccustomed silence between them, he was forced to recognize that Amanda was a devastatingly pretty girl.

It was a surprising observation, for Owen was not used to thinking of Amanda in terms he would apply to ordinary women. Amanda was far from ordinary, but she was, he had to admit, a woman. Why, she must be all of twenty. Old enough to be thinking of marriage, old enough to interest men who would not be put off by what was probably a modest dowry. Nor by her parentage. Amanda might be half sister to Lord Windham, but her mother had been divorced, and though she had been respectably married to Amanda's father, an obscure Scottish baronet, long before Amanda's birth, the taint of her past had touched her daughter. Owen winced in sympathy. He knew well the feeling of being set apart from one's peers, of inhabiting a world that was in some unspoken way askew.

Still, Amanda was an adorable creature, and a man who really loved her would not care a whit for what her mother had done. This set Owen to thinking of the unmarried men of his acquaintance and which of them would appreciate Amanda's rarity and would be ready to give her the freedom she needed and deserved. Owen frowned. There was not one he would care to see as Amanda's husband. If he did not look sharp—and by thunder, he intended to do just that—she would find herself leg-shackled to a thoroughly unsuitable fellow who would not understand her at all.

Having settled Amanda's future to his satisfaction, Owen felt it was time to bring her out of her silence. Since the Ribeiros were much on her mind, he entertained her by talking of his journey to Lisbon and everything he had learned of Portugal and the Portuguese. Amanda responded with enthusiasm. By the time she had no more questions to ask, they were climbing the hill that led into Honiton, and, as if by agreement, they turned to their respective windows, for the view was quite their favorite in Devon. The Otter valley opened out below, its abundant hedgerows struggling to impose some order on the luxuriant hills and pasture land—greener now in the rain which was falling once more—the Otter River bisecting the whole.

The rain lasted through their arrival in Honiton and their dash across the yard of the Golden Lion to the shelter of the inn, but once they were inside, it stopped abruptly and a welcome beam of sun forced its way through the window, turning the raindrops on Amanda's hair into glittering points of light. Lost in admiration, Owen was startled to hear the voice of the innkeeper, to whom he had spoken on their arrival, informing Mr. Thorn that the gentleman was in and would be pleased to receive him.

Senhor Ribeiro had taken the best private parlor that the inn afforded. He was waiting for them with every evidence of impatience, his muscles tense with expectation, his florid moustache quivering as he spoke. He had clearly not expected Amanda, but he greeted her courteously and allowed her to make the introduction, after which he begged his guests to be seated and offered them some wine. Amanda took a chair by the fire which was burning reluctantly on the stone hearth but refused the wine. Owen, who had no objection to drinking with imposters, said he would be pleased to join Senhor Ribeiro in a glass.

"Your health, sir," Owen said, raising his glass.

"And yours, Mr. Thorn. And Miss Berwick's," he added with a glance at Amanda.

They sat and looked at each other. Ribeiro seemed uncomfortable under their scrutiny but unable to resent it. Owen drank, smiled, and lowered his glass, not taking his eyes from the other man. They were remarkably alike, the Ribeiro now at Ludlow and the Ribeiro here in Honiton, almost of a height, with the same heaviness of face and the same dark hair and eyes. The man before him had perhaps a less florid complexion and something less of flesh than the man he had met earlier that afternoon, but the greatest difference was in their manner. The second Ribeiro exuded confidence and good humor and the awareness that he would be welcome wherever he chose to go, while this man, even allowing for the difference in his situation, was almost diffident.

Ribeiro cleared his throat. "I regret I was called so suddenly away. I had brought you messages of good will from my nephew, and I am happy to convey them now."

Owen continued smiling but said nothing, knowing Ribeiro would not be comfortable with silence. Amanda, bless her, knew when to be silent as well.

Ribeiro wavered under their combined gaze. "You will understand that it was only the most urgent business that called me away. A private matter," he added hastily, to make it clear that he could not divulge its particulars. "I received a letter yesterday afternoon that made

157

it imperative for me to take my departure."

Owen had already heard of the letter, which had been delivered by a boy from the Dolphin, Honiton's other inn, and received by one of the younger Ludlow footmen who had in turn carried it to Senhor Ribeiro. The footman, who was an observant lad, had said that the letter was addressed in a fearful scrawl, as though the writer had been in a great hurry or had taken care to disguise his hand. "You are bound for London, I believe," Owen remarked.

"That is correct," Ribeiro said eagerly. "Yes, that is where I must go."

Owen raised his brows. "Yet you linger in Honiton."

"To see you, my dear sir. To fulfill my commission from my nephew." He leaned forward eagerly. "You have brought the book, have you not?"

Amanda made a sound, something between a snort and a sniff, that echoed Owen's own surprise at the crudeness of Ribeiro's approach. It seemed unlike the man, but perhaps he was growing desperate. "No, I have not," Owen told him. "The book is still at Ludlow."

"But I must have it," Ribeiro insisted. "I cannot stay in this place, and I have promised Eugenio. Please, Mr. Thorn, you have no cause to refuse to give it to me, it is my nephew's book and you have promised to return it to him."

"Which I am more than happy to do, Senhor Ribeiro. But I'm in something of a quandary." Owen set his glass on the table which stood between Ribeiro's chair and his own. "A man arrived this afternoon at Ludlow who also calls himself Ribeiro and who expects me to give the book to him. You see my problem. Who is the real Raimundo Ribeiro?"

"But I am Raimundo," said the other man who had gone quite white. "Miss Berwick, tell him. I arrived yesterday at Lord Windham's house. How was I announced?"

"In the same way as the man who arrived this afternoon. Of course, we have only his word that he is Raimundo Ribeiro." Amanda cocked her head and looked at him thoughtfully. "And we only have yours that you are Raimundo."

Ribeiro's face became suffused with color. He leapt out of his chair, making inarticulate sounds, then turned away and began striding back and forth across the room, beating his hands together and muttering imprecations in Portuguese. Owen recognized the language and its general intent, but the subtlety of the cursing was beyond his command. After several minutes of this activity, Ribeiro came to a halt, withdrew a folded sheet of paper from his pocket, and perused it slowly, the frown on his face deepening. Then he uttered one great oath, crumpled the paper in his hand, threw it on the floor, wiped his hand over his forehead, and faced his guests once more. "You must forgive me," he said, speaking now in English. He was breathing hard, and his face was moist from his exertions. "You must forgive me," he said again. "I am very angry. It must be Henrique. My brother. It must be he who is at Ludlow."

Owen exhaled in a small sigh of delight. It was exquisitely symmetrical, each brother accusing the other. And virtually nothing to choose between them. "I'm afraid I don't understand," he said, his face showing nothing but polite incomprehension.

Ribeiro drew an enormous breath and threw himself into his chair. "I see I must tell you the whole. I have a younger brother, Mr. Thorn. As children we were close, but as we came of age our interests and way of life pulled us apart. Henrique is in Paris. That is, I thought he was in Paris, but it appears he is now in Devonshire. I think he would like to cause me mischief and embarrassment. No, I do not know what he is about. The book may be part of it, or perhaps he wishes to cause a rift between me and my nephew. We are both of a serious turn of mind, Eugenio and I, and we have always been good companions. Not so Henrique, who has a levity of manner of which Eugenio has often complained. Henrique, I fear, is inclined to be jealous. He can be vengeful—not vicious, you understand—his vengeance is only intended to make his victim look the fool." Ribeiro sighed and shook his head. "It is an absurdity. I do not know what my brother thinks he is doing."

The descriptions tallied. Whichever of the two was Raimundo, they were agreed on the character of Henrique. "I don't suppose," Owen said, "that there is a third brother lurking about?"

"A third? No, no, we were once three, but Eugenio's father, God rest his soul, is dead these ten years. May I repeat, Mr. Thorn, I am Raimundo, and this man who says he is me is an imposter. Perhaps he is not even Henrique, but if he is not, then I am at a loss."

"The resemblance is very striking," Amanda said.

"Yes, I think we must assume that one of you is Henrique. But which? Indeed, which?" Owen watched Ribeiro carefully and saw his color rise.

"You doubt what I have told you, sir?"

"Not at all. We heard much the same story earlier this afternoon from the other Senhor Ribeiro. I do beg your pardon," Owen added quickly as the import of his words struck the man before him. "It was necessary to hear the story from you independently. But you see what a dilemma it puts me in. I am much inclined to believe everything you say, but three hours ago I was much inclined to believe the other fellow. If you were Henrique and heard that Raimundo was coming, wouldn't you do precisely what you have done, invent a

160

reason for a quick departure, then remain in the neighborhood in the hope of obtaining your nephew's book."

Ribeiro was trembling with indignation. "I invent nothing, Mr. Thorn. I will show you. Yes, I will show you." He rose unsteadily and crossed the room to retrieve the crumpled paper he had tossed there, then returned to his chair. He was on the point of handing it to Owen when his eyes went to Amanda. He hesitated.

"Miss Berwick," Owen assured him, "is the soul of discretion. And I'll tell her about it in any case."

Ribeiro nodded reluctantly, but he kept the paper, smoothing it out on his lap. "I did get a message, Mr. Thorn. The hand did not appear familiar, but now that I know Henrique is involved, it is plausible that it is his. The writer claimed to be the friend of a lady. A lady, you understand, with whom I was once acquainted."

"Intimately acquainted?" Owen thought he knew what was coming.

"Yes," Ribeiro said, his manner grown a little stiff. He glanced again at Amanda, then shrugged and turned back to Owen. "The lady was coming to Ludlow and would find my presence—what is the word he uses?" He picked up the paper. "Ah, yes. 'She would find your presence inconvenient. I am sure in view of your past friendship that you would not wish to embarrass—' The lady," he concluded. "It is a delicate matter. I could do no other but what I did."

Owen regarded Ribeiro with sympathy. The lady, he knew, was Pamela Duffield, for she had confided her concern to Owen shortly after her arrival, and had, in fact, been inclined to leave the house at once when she learned that Ribeiro was also staying there. It was with some difficulty that Owen persuaded her that the party was large and the light in the evening dim, and she would have no difficulty in avoiding an encounter with

Senhor Ribeiro, whom by her own admission she had not seen in twenty years. "It was a considerate action, sir, and lends credence to your claim."

"But it doesn't prove it, you know." Amanda said, as though fearing Owen might turn credulous. "If the letter is from Henrique, then Henrique knows about Lady—There's no use going about the bush, it's Lady Duffield, isn't it? It couldn't be anyone else." She took Owen's silence for assent and turned to Ribeiro. "So if Henrique knows about Lady Duffield's friendship with Raimundo, and Raimundo obviously knows about it too, then you could be either one. Raimundo, I mean, or Henrique. I don't see that we're any more forward than we were, though I must say, Senhor Ribeiro, that I rank your claim the higher."

Ribeiro made her a small bow. "I must be grateful for that small amount of trust."

Amanda smarted under the implied rebuke, which she had the grace to see was deserved. Her chin went up. "I'm sorry, but we must be objective about this. The ownership of the book is at stake, and if you're really Raimundo and have your nephew's interests at heart, you should not want to see Mr. Thorn make a mistake."

Ribeiro spread his hands wide in a gesture of resignation. "What more can I do? I know who I am. How am I to prove it?"

"That is a facer, isn't it?" Amanda said cheerfully. Then her eyes widened. "But of course. There's only one person at Ludlow who knows who Raimundo Ribeiro is. We'll have to put the two of you side by side, and Lady Duffield can tell us which of you he is."

"No," said Owen, leaning forward in his chair.

"No," said Ribeiro, looking immensely shocked at the suggestion. "It would cause her untold distress."

"Men," Amanda muttered, a frown of displeasure on her face. "I don't mean to embarrass the lady, but in heaven's name, how else are we to know the truth? I'm not suggesting we make a great show of it, though considering the trouble the two of you have put us to, it might be a jolly good thing to do. We can handle it all very quietly, and Lady Duffield can give us the answer in a matter of minutes. Unless," she went on, an unexpected gleam in her eye, "you think that she won't be able to recognize you."

"It's possible, you know," Owen said. "I understand it's been something like twenty years." Ribeiro raised his brows, and Amanda stared at Owen in surprise. Owen saw that an explanation was called for. "I'm in the lady's confidence," he murmured.

Ribeiro waved the matter aside. "The lady will know me," he said with great dignity. "But I do not see how I may without risk return to Ludlow. If Henrique and I are seen together, it will cause comment, and I will not—no, I will not cause Lady Duffield any mortification. Mr. Thorn, you will have to find another way out of your dilemma." He rose, as though to indicate the interview was at an end.

"I have it," Amanda said, jumping up and turning to Owen. "The mumming." She turned to Ribeiro. "It's a custom we have at Ludlow," she explained. "Christmas night everyone dresses up—not absolutely everyone, but most of the younger people—and we have a kind of parade and dance and—you know the kind of thing."

Ribeiro nodded.

"I'll send you a costume. There's a great long gray robe up in the attic. You can be Friar Tuck."

"I beg your pardon?"

"Oh, one of our—he was a follower of Robin Hood." Amanda frowned. "Your moustache will be a problem, it's a dead giveaway. I know, I'll contrive a hood with holes for the eyes. You may look rather like someone out of the Inquisition—" She stopped, as though she

163

had made an indelicate reference, and then remembered happily that Portugal was not the same as Spain.

Ribeiro took her embarrassment in good part. "An unhappy moment in our neighbor's history, Miss Berwick. I will contrive to look like your Friar Tuck."

"Splendid. Mr. Thorn will bring it to you tomorrow. You will do that, won't you, Owen? And then you must arrange to arrive at Ludlow at seven o'clock, Senhor Ribeiro. We'll send a carriage for you. Go round to the right side of the house and you'll see a door. Someone will meet you there, and you can join our parade."

"And Lady Duffield?"

"There'll be dancing afterward," Owen said. "I'll warn Lady Duffield what we're about, and she'll be prepared for you to approach her. And then I'm afraid you're on your own."

"I understand," Ribeiro said. "If you assure me of the lady's compliance, I will do what is required."

They parted from him amicably and returned to the entrance hall where Owen ordered the carriage brought round. Amanda was in high spirits. "It will be such fun," she said when they were underway. "I adore masquerades."

Owen could not feel that what they had agreed to qualified in the least as fun, especially now that it was clear Pamela Duffield must be part of it. "I don't know how else we might have managed it," he said, aware of the grudging quality in his voice, "but it's an awkward matter at best."

"For one of them," Amanda acknowledged, "but whichever it is, he'll deserve it."

"I was thinking of the lady."

Amanda made a sound of impatience. Owen had begun the afternoon's adventure as a great lark, and she knew just the point at which he had gone all serious. "Why do men think women are such poor creatures? I

164

don't know Lady Duffield at all, but I'd swear, Owen Thorn, that she's learned all kinds of ways to protect herself from the winds of fortune and that she's not nearly as fragile as she appears."

Owen grinned. "Not everyone is like you, Amanda."

She gave him a sudden sidewise glance. "Oh," she said, aware that she was in danger of going all serious herself, "I'm much more like other people than you think."

Amanda was not particularly fond of dancing, but that evening it occurred to her that there were a number of advantages in an activity which allowed a gentleman to place his arm, however lightly, around one's waist. After playing several lively country dances, Nicola had acceded to Baron von Frisch's request for a waltz. Though the dance was rendered less dashing and elegant than usual by the dogs and toddlers who were eager to join in the fun, there was a quality to it which had been quite lacking at the London balls Amanda had attended.

She must have waltzed with Owen at least half a dozen times before, and he was certainly not holding her more closely than usual. Whatever it was that set this moment apart, it was far more intangible. Amanda could not have put it into words, but she knew it had something in common with the delicacy of finely wrought metal and the sheen of highly polished silver and that magical moment when one's creation first begins to take shape. She had long ago decided that if she ever married, which she was not at all sure she wished to do, only Owen could tempt her. But that had been a matter-of-fact, logical thought, and there was nothing logical or matter-of-fact about the way she felt now.

Reluctant to break the spell and made strangely awkward by her own feelings, Amanda said little and only once or twice risked a glance at Owen's face. His eyes were strangely pensive with none of the teasing glint to which she was accustomed. That might be a good sign, but Amanda had a lowering feeling that it simply meant he was thinking of something else.

Nicola brought the dance to an end with a flourish. Just as Owen released Amanda, a determined young spaniel pushed its way between their feet, tail wagging vigorously. Amanda looked up, her awkwardness momentarily forgotten, and saw Owen smiling down at her. Her thin poplin dress suddenly felt unusually warm, and she was honest enough to admit it was due to more than the exertion of the dance, just as her light head could not entirely be accounted for by the mulled wine. Then Owen's expression altered, and Amanda knew he was gazing past her, toward the petit-point settee where Lady Duffield was sitting in unusual isolation. His eyes were filled with what could only be called concern. More concern, surely, than was warranted by the problem of Senhor Ribeiro.

An insistent tug at her skirt ended Amanda's reflections. She automatically bent down and extended her arms, and Susanna, Nicola and Charles's small daughter, ran into them. Any annoyance Amanda might have felt at the interruption was banished as the child planted a sticky kiss on her cheek. Amanda straightened up, Susanna in her arms, just as Verity, David, and the older Lydgate children fell upon Owen.

"You promised to tell us the story," Verity informed him.

"I did?" Owen raised his brows. "Well, 'pon my soul, I think you're right. Come along then." He led them to the fireplace, followed by some of the younger members of the party who toddled after their older cousins, their hands on his coat tails. One would never have guessed

166

Owen had anything but holiday festivities on his mind.

Nicola had risen from the piano, putting a temporary end to the music and dancing, but voices and laughter still filled the room. Owen selected an armchair to one side of the fire, and the children clustered on the floor around him. Amanda joined them, Susanna on her lap.

"Now," said Owen, frowning in recollection, "how far had we gone?"

"We hadn't gone anywhere at all." Verity's voice held a touch of asperity. "Except that Blanchardyn had left home to be a knight."

"Yes, so he had. And he comes upon a wounded knight whose lady has been carried off by a great villain, and Blanchardyn begs the wounded man to dub him knight so he—Blanchardyn, that is—can go off and avenge him."

"How do you dub a knight?" David asked, his eyes serious with concentration.

"You hit him on the shoulder with your sword," Verity said with the superiority of two years.

"Something like that." Owen went hastily over this first adventure, which had an unhappy ending, and came to Blanchardyn's encounter with the Knight of the Ferry.

"When does he meet Eglantine?" The younger Arnquist girl, who had heard of the story from Verity, had decided to join them.

"Very soon. The Knight of the Ferry thinks Blanchardyn would make a very good husband for the Queen. Eglantine has refused to marry anyone, including King Alymodes of Cassidonie. The King has sworn to have her and is now besieging Tormaday, her capital city. The Knight tells Blanchardyn the Queen is out riding, and he should go after her and kiss her."

David made a face. "That's stupid," Verity said. "He hasn't even seen Eglantine."

"It would make her notice him," said the Arnquist girl who was thirteen and had some understanding of these things, "but I think she'd be very angry."

"So she is. She swears to have him killed, but she changes her mind when Blanchardyn decides to defend her city and she sees what a very good fighter he is. She says it would be too cruel to kill a knight for only a kiss."

David grew impatient. "When does he fight the King?"

"Right now." Owen embarked on an enthusiastic description of Blanchardyn's feats in battle, passing rather quickly, Amanda thought, over the slaughter that these entailed.

"What about Eglantine?" Verity asked.

"She is, I fear, more in love with him than ever. In those days, being gallant in battle was the way to a lady's heart. Unfortunately Blanchardyn is taken prisoner. King Alymodes refuses to ransom him and sends him off to Cassidonie."

"And then?" said several voices when it was clear that Owen was going to say no more.

Owen raised his hands. "Enough. We'll have the rest tomorrow."

"Couldn't you tell us just a little more?" five-year-old Bella Lydgate asked wistfully.

Owen looked at the circle of young faces and gave a reluctant smile. "Well, perhaps another quarter-hour," he said and proceeded to take up the thread of the story again.

The children listened with rapt attention, but Amanda found it difficult to focus her thoughts on Blanchardyn and Eglantine's adventures. The yule log blazed in the huge Tudor fireplace with comforting, familiar warmth, and the scent of pine blended with the spices from the bowl of mulled wine on the sofa table, but for a number of reasons, tonight was unlike any Christmas Eve in her memory. Though Amanda's mother had tried to preserve the traditions she remembered from childhood, Christmas at home had never been as lively and boisterous as it was at Ludlow. Amanda secretly suspected that her mother was depressed by the holiday. Christmas was a time for families, and the divorce had separated Ione Berwick from her own family and from her firstborn child.

Feeling a twinge of guilt because she was not more homesick, Amanda glanced at the piquet table where Senhor Ribeiro was playing a hand with Countess Arnquist. The lamps were intentionally low tonight, allowing the fire and Christmas candles to cast a holiday glow over the room, and Amanda was not at all sure she could have said whether the man playing cards was the first Raimundo Ribeiro or the second. Even if he were an imposter, she doubted if Lady Duffield, who had not gone within a dozen paces of him all evening, would have noticed the difference.

Lady Duffield herself was still seated on the settee, and Aunt Isabel, no doubt having noticed her friend's isolation, was approaching on Lord Mulgrave's arm. Amanda was watching them when her attention was suddenly drawn back to Owen, not by the story, but by the change in his manner of telling it. He did nothing as obvious as falter or break off, but his voice became curiously flat. His attention had been diverted and Amanda knew where.

Lord Mulgrave was now seated beside Lady Duffield, and Isabel had taken herself off and joined a group clustered about the pianoforte. Amanda was disposed to smile. Her aunt had tried her hand at matchmaking more than once in the past, though to Amanda's mind the kindly but rather staid Lord Mulgrave would be quite out of his depth with Lady Duffield. Still, it

169

hardly seemed cause for Owen's obvious concern.

Really, the two Senhor Ribeiros were the least of the mysteries at Ludlow this Christmas. Perhaps, Amanda thought, absently shifting Susanna on her lap to make room for David's younger brother, that was the real cause of her jealousy. Not Lady Duffield herself but the realization that Owen had a life of which she knew nothing, a life she could not share. It occurred to her that despite their friendship, she knew remarkably little about Owen Thorn. He was an engaging companion and much sought after by hostesses, but he took his work very seriously. Though he probably wouldn't admit it, Amanda knew he was viewed with respect by scholars at both Oxford and Cambridge. He had an independent income which allowed him to live in apparent comfort but seemingly no property. He lodged in the Albany, which was how he had met Charles, who had had rooms there before his marriage. He never spoke of his family.

When the party at last drifted upstairs, Amanda found herself in a curiously pensive mood. The magic of the waltz had not gone, but there was a bittersweet quality to the feeling, and she could not have said whether the ache in her chest came more from sorrow or from joy.

She awoke on Christmas morning to the sound of rain tumbling off the eaves and spattering against her window, and found her spirits much improved. There was a great deal to be done and no time for moping about. Steeling herself against the cold, Amanda splashed icy water on her face, pulled on a warm wool gown and worsted shawl, and ran a brush through her tangled hair. Then she opened a drawer in her dressing table, took out the hood she had put together yesterday in the short time between their return from Honiton and the dinner bell, and slipped into the hall. She had little more than half an hour before the maids would begin making their rounds with hot water. Even now there was a risk of encountering an early riser, but the first-floor corridors proved empty, and she was able to climb the narrow spiral stairs to the attic in peace.

Amanda knew precisely what she was looking for: a long, loose, crudely made garment of rough fabric. She had come across it when she and Nicola were going through the trunks in the attic the week before, pulling out clothes which might do for the mumming. Nicola had laughed at the sight of the garment and said it had been thrown together for the character of Friar Tuck in a long-ago theatrical.

Bundling the garment up in her arms, Amanda ran lightly down the stairs and pulled her shawl about her for her dash across the gardens and stable yard. True to his word, Owen was waiting in the stable, a sleepy-looking horse already saddled. "I'm sorry," Amanda told him, rain-soaked and breathless. "I'm afraid you'll have a wet ride."

"That," Owen assured her, "can be nothing to rising at such an ungodly hour. Do you know I haven't even had a cup of tea, let alone coffee?"

Amanda grinned. "I thought knights thrived on privation."

"Very likely," said Owen, taking the monk's habit and hood from her and wrapping them in a carriage rug he had ready. "I can't recall ever having had the smallest desire to be a knight."

"Maybe not, but in the past twenty-four hours you've gone questing for the real Senhor Ribeiro and saved the local lord and lady from having their Christmas court disrupted by a blood feud between brothers. And, of course, through all this you've made sure the fair Lady Duffield doesn't suffer any embarrassment."

Even as she spoke, Amanda knew this last was a mistake. If she ever learned more about Owen, it would be because he decided to tell her himself, not because she went fishing for information. Owen, who had been smiling until the reference to Lady Duffield, turned away and carefully fastened the rug-wrapped bundle behind the saddle. "Right," he said briskly, taking the horse by the reins and coaxing it toward the door. "If anyone asks where I am, say I wanted a bit of exercise before breakfast. No one who knows me will believe a word of it, but they're all too well-bred to ask questions."

As it happened, Owen's absence was scarcely remarked. Most of the party went to church in the village, and when Amanda returned, she found Owen stretched out before the library fire, warm and dry and reading the latest news about the Lavalette affair in the London papers. The children were with her, so it was impossible to ask how his meeting with the first Senhor Ribeiro had gone, but he gave her a brief, warming smile which indicated all was well and asked if it was time to choose costumes for the mumming.

Nicola, now busy with the preparations for Christmas dinner, had reluctantly turned the mumming over to Amanda. The garments they had selected last week, all sturdy enough to do withstand the vigors of holiday merrymaking or worn enough that it didn't matter, were assembled in the largest of the attic rooms. Leading the cavalcade, Amanda opened the door onto the smell of camphor and lavender, and set the lamp she had brought, to supplement the gray light from the windows, on a scarred table.

Costumes from theatricals lay side by side with relics of long-ago Windhams: a crimson farthingale, a slashed doublet, a periwig in want of curling. The mummers—the young people and older children and one or two like Nicola's brother Jeremy who refused to let adulthood take the fun out of things—fell to with enthusiasm. Most were inclined to try on whatever was nearest at hand, but Verity moved about the room with customary precision, then carefully selected a sacque of dark green damask and a Tudor hood of even darker velvet. "I'm going to be Maid Marian," she explained, holding out these garments for Amanda's inspection.

"Not Queen Eglantine?" David asked, tipping back a tricorn hat which hung down to his ears.

Verity shook her head. "Amanda's going to be Eglantine," she said, as if this was quite decided.

"Who?" asked Caroline Lambton-Hill, fastening an embroidered stomacher over her striped sarcenet gown.

"Eglantine," said Verity matter-of-factly. "And Owen's going to be Blanchardyn. We don't have a proper suit of armor, but there's a helmet somewhere. And he can have the doublet. It's almost old enough."

To argue, Amanda decided, would only be to draw unnecessary attention to the suggestion. Owen was kneeling beside Bella Lydgate, trying to disentangle her from a voluminous wrapping gown, and he did not seem to have heard Verity's remark. Amanda resolutely turned away to see what the older Lydgates were up to, but as she threaded her way between the chests, her eye fell upon a white satin kirtle, yellowed and stained, with only a fragment of lace remaining at the square-cut neck. It would do admirably for Eglantine, Amanda thought, running her fingers over the delicate fabric.

"There!" Verity's excited voice rang out suddenly over the whisper of fabric and creak of hinges and cries of discovery. With an air of great satisfaction, she dropped an ancient helmet, which looked far too ornamental ever to have seen battle, over Owen's carefully combed hair. "You're going to be Blanchardyn," she informed him.

Owen pushed back the rusty visor and grinned at her.

173

"Whatever my lady commands."

Verity grinned back and didn't say anything about Eglantine. Amanda wasn't sure whether she was glad or sorry, but when they left the attic, she carefully gathered up the white kirtle. After all, she had as much right to be Eglantine as anyone else did.

Verity's mention of Blanchardyn brought more requests for the story, and once the costumes had been safely stowed in bedrooms, they gathered in the library for the last installment.

"Right," said Owen as the Arnquist girls slipped into the room. "Everyone attending? It's not the sort of thing one can tell twice." And it wasn't. There was the trip to Cassidonie and the great storm at sea which no one but Blanchardyn survived and Blanchardyn's walk to Prussia where he took service with the Prussian King and became good friends with his son Sadoyne and their fight against the King of Poland. "And in the meantime," Owen said, "King Alymodes's son—"

"I say," David interrupted, "there are a lot of kings in this story."

"There are," Owen conceded. "Alymodes is the king who's besieging Eglantine. His son is driven by a storm to Friesland where he takes another king, who is Blanchardyn's father, captive and carries him to a dark dungeon in Cassidonie."

The elder Lydgate boy frowned. "I don't see why Blanchardyn is fighting the Poles when he should be rescuing his father."

"And Eglantine," Verity added.

"Ah, you have a point. The thing is," Owen continued, "Blanchardyn is a very great warrior, but he can't do it all on his own, and he has to get the King of Prussia to give him ships and arms and men to help him. But there's another storm, and they end up back in Cassidonie, where Blanchardyn finds his father and sets him free. And then, at last, off they go to Torma-day."

Verity let out a huge sigh. "It's about time. I would think Eglantine would have given him up."

"I'm afraid she's still desperately in love. There's a great battle which Blanchardyn wins, but his friend Sadoyne is taken prisoner by King Alymodes, and Blanchardyn has to go off and rescue *him,* so he says goodbye to Eglantine once more. He leaves her in the care of Subyon, a knight who proves to be a dreadful rascal, for he vows to wed the Queen and take control of her kingdom. But Eglantine escapes to a castle and sends word to Blanchardyn to come rescue her. Which he does. There's another great battle and Subyon is killed and then—" He looked about him expectantly. "How do all stories end?"

"They get married and live happily ever after," Verity said promptly. "But I don't see why Blanchardyn had to put the bad knight in charge of Eglantine. She could have been in charge of herself. Queen Elizabeth was."

"And she was a very good queen. But I'm afraid for all his adventures Blanchardyn was a rather conventional young man."

"What's 'ventnal?" David's little brother asked.

"Stuffy," Verity told him. "If you loved a queen, you wouldn't put someone else to rule in her place, would you, Owen?"

"I wouldn't dream of doing anything so presumptuous." Owen was grinning, but Amanda knew that he spoke the truth. Owen would not be the sort of husband to object if his wife had interests beyond her home and children. Such as silversmithing, for instance. It would really be a tragedy if such a paragon remained a lifelong bachelor.

The rain continued all afternoon, but the wind was only sporadically violent, and the road from Honiton

175

should have been quite passable. If the first Senhor Ribeiro did not put in an appearance tonight, Amanda decided, pausing to glance out the landing window as she climbed the stairs to dress for dinner, they would have to assume it was from fear of being exposed as an imposter.

Completely innocent of what lay in store for him, the second Senhor Ribeiro was at his most charming at dinner, exclaiming over the charm of English customs and complimenting Nicola on the roast goose and mince pie with a smile which seemed to have as much to do with her person as with her table. This, Amanda acknowledged, was all to his credit, for he had been taken aback by the presence of small children at the meal.

In truth, the sheer size of the gathering was enough to daunt anyone. Earlier in the afternoon, the party had been supplemented by the Tarrington family, who were cousins of the Windhams and lived but a quarter-mile from Ludlow. In addition, the Harewoods, a neighboring family with two grown sons and a recently married daughter, had been invited to Christmas dinner, as had the vicar, Mr. Sedgwick, and his wife and children. To accommodate such a crowd, Nicola had thrown open the double doors between the dining room and breakfast parlor, using sprays of holly and ivy on walls and table to blend the gleaming dark paneling of the one with the bright white-painted walls of the other.

Lady Duffield was seated beside Lord Mulgrave, far away from Senhor Ribeiro. Aunt Isabel, Amanda suspected, had enlisted Nicola's aid in her matchmaking scheme, and it seemed to be working. Mulgrave and Lady Duffield had been awkward with each other in the drawing room last night, but now they were laughing together like old friends. Amanda wondered if Mulgrave knew about Senhor Ribeiro, and if not, what would happen if he found out. The evening was seeming more

MORE PASSION AND ADVENTURE AWAIT... YOUR TRIP TO A BIG ADVENTUROUS WORLD BEGINS WHEN YOU ACCEPT YOUR FIRST 4 NOVELS ABSOLUTELY *FREE*
(AN $18.00 VALUE)

Accept your Free gift and start to experience more of the passion and adventure you like in a historical romance novel. Each Zebra novel is filled with proud men, spirited women and tempestuous love that you'll remember long after you turn the last page.

Zebra Historical Romances are the finest novels of their kind. They are written by authors who really know how to weave tales of romance and adventure in the historical settings you love. You'll feel like you've actually gone back in time with the thrilling stories that each Zebra novel offers.

GET YOUR FREE GIFT WITH THE START OF YOUR HOME SUBSCRIPTION

Our readers tell us that these books sell out very fast in book stores and often they miss the newest titles. So Zebra has made arrangements for you to receive the four newest novels published each month.

You'll be guaranteed that you'll never miss a title, and home delivery is so convenient. And to show you just how easy it is to get Zebra Historical Romances, we'll send you your first 4 books absolutely FREE! Our gift to you just for trying our home subscription service.

BIG SAVINGS AND FREE HOME DELIVERY

Each month, you'll receive the four newest titles as soon as they are published. You'll probably receive them even before the bookstores do. What's more, you may preview these exciting novels free for 10 days. If you like them as much as we think you will, just pay the low preferred subscriber's price of just $3.75 each. *You'll save $3.00 each month off the publisher's price.* AND, your savings are even greater because there are never any shipping, handling or other hidden charges—FREE Home Delivery. Of course you can return any shipment within 10 days for full credit, no questions asked. There is no minimum number of books you must buy.

4 FREE BOOKS

TO GET YOUR 4 FREE BOOKS WORTH $18.00 — MAIL IN THE FREE BOOK CERTIFICATE T O D A Y

Fill in the Free Book Certificate below, and we'll send your FREE BOOKS to you as soon as we receive it.

If the certificate is missing below, write to: Zebra Home Subscription Service, Inc., P.O. Box 5214, 120 Brighton Road, Clifton, New Jersey 07015-5214.

FREE BOOK CERTIFICATE

4 FREE BOOKS

ZEBRA HOME SUBSCRIPTION SERVICE, INC.

YES! Please start my subscription to Zebra Historical Romances and send me my first 4 books absolutely FREE. I understand that each month I may preview four new Zebra Historical Romances free for 10 days. If I'm not satisfied with them, I may return the four books within 10 days and owe nothing. Otherwise, I will pay the low preferred subscriber's price of just $3.75 each; a total of $15.00, *a savings off the publisher's price of $3.00.* I may return any shipment and I may cancel this subscription at any time. There is no obligation to buy any shipment and there are no shipping, handling or other hidden charges. Regardless of what I decide, the four free books are mine to keep.

NAME

ADDRESS   APT

CITY   STATE   ZIP

TELEPHONE
(   )

SIGNATURE   (if under 18, parent or guardian must sign)

Terms, offer and prices subject to change without notice. Subscription subject to acceptance by Zebra Books. Zebra Books reserves the right to reject any order or cancel any subscription.

GET
FOUR
FREE
BOOKS
(AN $18.00 VALUE)

ZEBRA HOME SUBSCRIPTION
SERVICE, INC.
P.O. Box 5214
120 BRIGHTON ROAD
CLIFTON, NEW JERSEY 07015-5214

and more beset by pitfalls. Amanda turned to Owen who was seated beside her. She was beginning to understand some of his concerns.

"A little more mince pie, Amanda?" Owen asked blandly.

Amanda, who had a healthy appetite, decided that more pie would not be at all amiss, but she was not to be so easily fobbed off. "Don't you think," she asked him, adroitly maneuvering a slice of pie onto her plate, "that if someone is helping someone else solve a problem, she—or he, of course—has a right to know anything that might have a bearing on that problem?"

Owen returned the pie to the table, which had been left uncovered in all its Jacobean splendor in honor of the holiday. "Anything," he agreed, "which has a bearing on the problem."

"Suppose," said Amanda, cutting into the flaky pie crust, "that the second person didn't realize it did."

"Then the second person would be making a sad mistake. But it would be his—or her—responsibility."

Amanda sighed. "I might have known you'd say that."

"Yes, I rather think you might. Ah, the wassail bowl. Aren't they going to pass it round?"

"No, we're modern at Ludlow, we drink it out of cups," said Amanda as the steaming, fragrant drink was handed around. "I thought you detested wassail punch, and I should think that the second person would at least credit the first person with enough sense to see what was under her nose."

"If the second person failed to do that, he most humbly apologizes," Owen returned. It was no more than the truth. He did not find it surprising that Amanda, far too acute for anyone's comfort, had grown suspicious about his relationship to Pamela Duffield. What did surprise him was his strong impulse to tell her the whole. It was not a story he had shared with anyone, even a close friend like Charles, yet it suddenly seemed important that Amanda understand. The reasons for this were as yet unfocused — perhaps because he would not put them into words, even to himself — but they undoubtedly had something to with the way he had felt when he held Amanda in his arms last night.

Owen took a sip of the wassail punch. Amanda was right, he had never been particularly fond of the drink, which was entirely too sweet for his taste. But perhaps it was less the taste than the fact that it symbolized a holiday which always brought to the fore his sense of not belonging. Those feelings, of course, were merely remnants of nursery and schoolroom days, but it was amazing how much they stayed with one. Holidays brought them out with a vengeance.

Amanda's attention had been claimed by Rob Newfield, Lady Tarrington's younger brother, who was seated on her other side. The party being an informal one, the younger Mr. Harewood, who was seated across the table, had been drawn into the conversation as well. Both he and Newfield were looking at Amanda with open admiration, and Amanda, instead of treating them with her customary practical manner, seemed to be positively reveling in their attentions.

Owen's fingers tightened around his punch cup. Rob and young Harewood might be five or so years Amanda's senior, but they were both far too young for her. Not that their admiration was surprising. With the bright gold of her hair gleaming in the candlelight and the soft green stuff of her gown revealing an enticing bit of neck and shoulder, Amanda was unquestionably lovely. Of course, she was not at all in his usual style, Owen told himself, and then wondered, with a rueful smile, what his usual style was. Amanda was certainly not like any of his mistresses, but though he had been very fond of all these women, they had been no more interested in a permanent entanglement than he. He was still not interested in one, Owen reminded himself, replying quite at random to a comment from Jeremy's wife, Elizabeth, who was seated on his other side. The wassail punch cast a dangerous spell.

"I'm glad to see Lord Mulgrave enjoying himself," Elizabeth murmured, her eyes straying to the far end of the table. "He's been lonely since his wife's death."

Owen glanced at Mulgrave, who was laughing with uncharacteristic abandon at something Pamela had just said. Elizabeth was right. Mulgrave's marriage had not been a love match, but his wife's death had deprived him of companionship.

"I expect Lady Duffield welcomes the company as well. It isn't always amusing to be a widow," said Elizabeth, whose first husband had been killed in the Peninsula.

Owen nodded absently, then caught the full drift of Elizabeth's remark. He looked sharply at Mulgrave and Pamela. Was it possible—? Well, of course, with Pamela anything was possible, he'd learned that years ago. But was it at all likely? And if so, how did he feel about it?

The sound of Senhor Ribeiro's deep laugh reminded Owen that he had more immediate concerns. If all had gone according to schedule, Owen's valet had already admitted the first Senhor Ribeiro to the house. In another hour or so the brothers would be in the same room and then it might be necessary to do a good deal of improvising.

In keeping with the spirit of informality, the gentlemen did not linger at table but accompanied the ladies to the drawing room. The nurses brought the youngest children in, so that the company now stretched from Susanna, who was not yet two, to Mrs. Harewood's mother, who was well past seventy. The yule log still burned brightly in the fireplace, and the Arnquist girls entertained the company with Christmas songs from their own country. Finally, when the children were beginning to grow restless, Nicola nodded at Amanda, and Amanda slipped from the room, a signal for all the mummers to follow her and make ready.

Owen donned the doublet and helmet without his valet's assistance, then joined the others who were congregating at the stairhead. Nothing at Ludlow was ever done along strictly conventional lines. Instead of dressing as traditional holiday figures, the company had chosen to portray characters from history or literature: Verity as Maid Marian; David as King Arthur; the Lambton-Hills as Romeo and Juliet; Jeremy as a druid. Owen could not place the others. He couldn't see Amanda at all, though that was probably the fault of the bloody visor. Owen pushed it up, decided to leave it that way, and caught sight of Amanda, coming down the corridor from her room. She was wearing a white dress and jewels in her hair and at this distance, in this light, the illusion was complete. Suddenly, Owen knew precisely who Amanda was meant to be, and with that knowledge came an irresistible impulse. Not giving himself time to reconsider, Owen made his way through the increasing throng, took Amanda by the shoulders, and lightly brushed her lips with his own.

It was the briefest of kisses, and he released her at once, aware of a strong desire to do just the opposite. Amanda looked at him in utter bewilderment. "What was that about?" she demanded.

"Blanchardyn greeting his Eglantine. I say," he added, with a show of concern, "you are Eglantine, aren't you? If you aren't, I'm most fearfully sorry."

Amanda attempted to gather her wits. She greatly feared she was staring up at him like a complete cab-

180

bage-head, and if she were not careful, she would find herself admitting the lowering truth, which was that this was the first time she had ever been kissed. "Of course I am Queen Eglantine," she said, with an assumption of regal authority. "And I would most certainly be angry, save that I fear I am going to need your help in the evening ahead."

Owen grinned. "I rather think it may be the other way round. Shall we join your courtiers, Your Majesty?"

Despite the grin, there was a look in his eyes which made Amanda feel a little shy. She took Owen's arm with an elaborate formality which helped mask her feelings. At least she had the satisfaction of knowing that the white kirtle fit very well. With Nicola's borrowed tiara atop her unbound hair, she almost felt she looked the part.

"I do hope," Owen murmured, "that you saved the first dance for me."

"I couldn't," Amanda reminded him, "I'm already promised to Friar Tuck. Is he here yet?" she asked, anxiously scanning the crowd on the landing.

"I sincerely hope not. He's to wait until the last possible minute. It's safer that way."

Just as Owen and Amanda joined the others, Nicola ran down the corridor, breathless and laughing, a brocade mantle thrown over her velvet dress. "I couldn't resist," she said apologetically, going to stand beside Jeremy. "Lead on, Amanda. You're the closest thing we have to a Lord of Misrule."

It was a large party which trooped down the stairs with mock solemnity. The younger Harewoods and Sedgwicks, attired in finery brought from their respective homes, joined in, and no one remarked on the addition of a tall figure in a monk's habit whose face was concealed by a hood. Amanda allowed herself one glance over her shoulder to make sure that Senhor Ribeiro had indeed joined the party, then resolutely ignored him. When they reached the high-ceilinged hall on the ground floor, she signaled for quiet, without complete success, and Verity and David began to beat vigorously on a pair of ancient drums. Amanda exchanged glances with Owen, then flung open the drawing-room door.

Exclamations of delight and mock surprise greeted the mummers as they erupted into the room. As Amanda and Owen led a stately promenade about the chamber, Verity and David kept up a steady beat on the drums, punctuated by laughter from the onlookers and giggles from more than a few of the mummers. As with the dancing on the previous night, the dogs and younger children were eager to join in the fun. Nicola caught Susanna by the hand, and Jeremy swung his son onto his shoulders.

The hilarity was all to the good, Amanda decided, for it kept Senhor Ribeiro from attracting undue attention. Even so, she was relieved when the promenade broke up and Nicola moved to the piano. "The plot begins," Owen said softly, giving Amanda's arm a comforting squeeze. "Have a care, fair Eglantine."

"This is the easiest part," Amanda muttered, detaching herself and hurrying toward the hooded Senhor Ribeiro. It would look odd if he did not dance, and there was no one else to partner him. The first dance, which belonged exclusively to the mummers, was an old-fashioned minuet, a dance Senhor Ribeiro performed with skill and grace. He might lack his brother's dash, but he was not without his own brand of charm, and Amanda began to see how he could have attracted Lady Duffield.

A waltz followed the minuet, and the line between the mummers and the rest of the company blurred. Jeremy seized hold of Elizabeth, Verity dragged Charles onto the dance floor, and others of the audience joined in the dancing. Some of the mummers temporarily retired to the sidelines, breathless and laughing, and it was easy enough for Amanda and Senhor Ribeiro to follow their example. They stood on the edge of the dance floor, well removed from the chandelier and as far away from any candles or lamps as Amanda could contrive. A few moments later, Owen made his way toward them, Lady Duffield on his arm. She looked, Amanda thought, rather pale, but she smiled very prettily when Senhor Ribeiro inclined his head.

It was Ribeiro who spoke first. "Madam, allow me to express my gratitude—"

"Oh, don't be stuffy, Raimundo," Lady Duffield said with a light laugh. "You always refined too much upon the forms. That is, you did if you are who you say you are. But that's what we're here to find out, isn't it?" She smiled again and extended a delicate gloved hand to him. Despite the season, she wore a short-sleeved frock of French gauze, striped in silver, over a slip of crimson satin. Amanda suddenly felt ridiculous in the ancient white kirtle.

"So far so good," Owen murmured as Lady Duffield and Senhor Ribeiro moved onto the dance floor.

"Yes." Amanda summoned up a bright smile. "Have you thought what we're going to do when she tells us which is the imposter?"

"I rather thought we'd confront him. But not, I think, until the house has quieted down."

Amanda studied the dancers swirling before them, holiday finery beside bits of costuming, the soft swish of merino and sarcenet blending with the stiff rustling of brocade and the jangle of ornamental swords. "And have you thought what we're going to do if she can't make up her mind?"

183

"Don't be difficult, Amanda."

"I was only trying to consider every eventuality. That's what Charles says to do. By the way, I rather think we should warn him and Nicola before we accuse one of their guests of being here under false pretenses. Oh, dear."

"What?" Owen asked sharply.

"I don't think Lord Mulgrave is at all happy." Mulgrave was seated on a sofa near the fireplace, listening politely to Mrs. Harewood's mother, but his eyes kept straying to Lady Duffield and the man in the monk's habit.

Owen grimaced. "It can't be helped."

"But suppose he tries to find out who his rival is? Then we'll really be in a pickle."

"I doubt Mulgrave will do anything. He's a man of great self-control."

"Yes, he's always struck me that way. Except when he's around Lady Duffield." Amanda glanced at Owen. The helmet made it difficult to see much of his face. "Are they very well-acquainted?"

"I believe they met before this house party, if that's what you mean. If you want further details, you'll have to ask them. Don't you think it's time you danced with your Blanchardyn, Queen Eglantine?"

The waltz had come to an end, and Nicola was beginning an écossaise, but it was still very pleasant to be partnered by Owen. Amanda could not see Friar Tuck, but the second Senhor Ribeiro was in conversation with Charles by the far end of the fireplace, and Lady Duffield was gracefully making her way in his direction. Lord Mulgrave stopped her as she passed him. After a brief exchange, Lady Duffield moved on. Mulgrave stared after her for a long moment, then turned abruptly and walked off in the opposite direction.

Amanda glanced up at Owen. "Problems?"

"A side complication. It can be dealt with later."

"You don't think," she asked, "that this might be a good time to change your mind about what does and doesn't have a bearing on this particular problem?"

"I never change my mind in the midst of an adventure," Owen returned, just before the movement of the dance separated them.

They did not risk further conversation during the dance, and the music had barely come to an end when Rob Newfield appeared and reminded Amanda that she had promised to dance with him. "I say," he added as they waited for the new sets to form, "who is that fellow in the monk's habit? You were dancing with him earlier."

"I assumed he was one of the Harewoods. He hardly said a word." Amanda exchanged a meaningful glance with Owen, then took Rob by the hand and drew him onto the dance floor.

"Don't think so," said Rob. "They all seem to be accounted for."

Amanda shrugged. "Maybe he's one of the Sedgwicks then. He wasn't a very interesting man, Rob. I'd much rather talk about your new horse."

When the dance came to an end, Amanda quickly scanned all four corners of the drawing room. There was no sign of Friar Tuck, but Owen, still wearing the doublet and helmet, was sitting on a low stool, peacefully scratching one of the dogs behind the ears. Amanda made her way to his side. "Well?" she asked, pulling up a chair and dropping down beside him.

"Crisis averted. Friar Tuck is hiding in my room until we've sorted out who's who."

"I don't know what's taking Lady Duffield so long." The last Amanda had seen, Lady Duffield was still conversing with the second Senhor Ribeiro.

"Patience, my child. You wouldn't want her to make

185

a mistake." Owen pulled the helmet from his head and ran a hand through his matted hair. "Armor is clearly not meant to be worn in well-heated houses." Then suddenly he froze. "Don't say anything, Amanda, but Lady Duffield is walking toward us."

Owen and Amanda met her in front of the fireplace, on the edge of the dance floor, in the midst of a crowd, which probably made it the best place in which to exchange a private confidence. With another pretty smile, Lady Duffield took Owen's arm, leaned toward him, and said three words, softly but distinctly enough for Amanda to hear as well. "It's Friar Tuck."

Owen threw back his head and laughed, as if Lady Duffield had just told them a particularly clever joke. Amanda joined in the laughter as did Lady Duffield who, Amanda was forced to admit, was certainly not a fool. After a decent interval, Lady Duffield moved off, and Owen and Amanda walked in the opposite direction, passing within a few feet of the man they now knew was Henrique Ribeiro as he led Caroline Lambton-Hill to the dance floor.

"Right," said Owen, when they could reasonably consider themselves out of earshot. "Are we clear on the next move?"

"I'll talk to Nicola. It won't look odd if I pull her away from the piano. You can explain to Charles. Then at the appropriate moment we'll produce the real Raimundo Ribeiro. What could be simpler?"

"If I had the time, I could give you quite a list." He started to move off, then turned and grinned at her. "Has anyone ever told you you're a splendid conspirator, Amanda?"

"That," said Amanda seriously, "is the nicest compliment I've ever received."

"Gammon, my girl," Owen said and went off in search of Charles.

* * *

The past two hours had been a great test of Amanda's patience, but somehow she had managed to join in the caroling, though her off-key voice drew a curious look from Verity, and to sip tea and sample holiday delicacies, though she could not claim to have tasted any of them. Now, at last, the gathering in the drawing room had broken up and all the pertinent people were gathered in the library. Or almost all. Nicola had brought Lady Duffield and Charles had just followed with Henrique Ribeiro, but there was no sign of Owen and Raimundo.

One could not precisely say that Henrique looked nervous, but he certainly appeared less comfortable than Amanda had ever seen him. "Is this another of your charming English customs?" he inquired, leaning against the mantel in a pose of studied unconcern. "Do we await more holiday revelry?"

"You could say that." As always in moments of high drama, Charles was a model of composure. He was at the table where the decanters were set out, calmly pouring drinks as if this were indeed simply an extension of the day's festivities. Amanda accepted a glass of sherry from her brother and settled back into the soft leather of the sofa. Nicola was seated beside her, and Lady Duffield was settled in an enormous wing chair, looking more fragile and delicate than ever.

"Do sit down, Senhor Ribeiro," Nicola said with her most charming smile. "I'm afraid the others are late."

Even as she spoke, there was a faint whoosh, and the light from the lamp by the door wavered for a moment. "So sorry to have kept you waiting," Owen said, strolling into the room. "I do thank you for your patience, Senhor Ribeiro. I'm afraid we have been dreadfully remiss, but you must note that we did not allow all of

Christmas day to pass without reuniting you with your family."

Before the startled Henrique could respond, Owen stepped aside, and Raimundo Ribeiro, neatly attired in the clothes he had worn beneath Friar Tuck's habit, followed him into the room.

Henrique Ribeiro regarded his brother for a long moment, his face devoid of expression. Then he gave a reluctant smile and stepped forward, his hand extended. "Henrique," he said, shaking his head sorrowfully. "So you have returned to confess your subterfuge. It was really too bad of you."

Raimundo stood very straight and did not take his brother's proffered hand. He fairly bristled with indignation. "You." A long phrase in Portuguese followed, which Amanda greatly regretted she was unable to translate.

Owen tactfully waited until Raimundo had done, then addressed Henrique. "Better give over, Ribeiro. I'm afraid Lady Duffield has identified your brother quite conclusively."

Henrique whirled round to stare at Lady Duffield. "My dear Pamela," he exclaimed, "can it be that you doubt me?"

Lady Duffield gave a tinkling, appreciative laugh. "Very well done, Senhor. For a moment in the drawing room I almost wondered if I had been mistaken. Twenty years is a great time after all, and you and your brother are very like. But there are certain things about Raimundo that I will never forget." She cast a charming smile at Raimundo, who lowered his gaze to the floor in acute embarrassment.

Henrique looked from Lady Duffield to Raimundo, started to speak, thought better of it, and at last gave a philosophical shrug. "You have caught me. Well and fairly. I hope you will accept my apologies for so trespassing on your hospitality," he added with a smile which included Amanda as well as Nicola and Charles. "You must believe that I would not have done so had the temptation not been great."

"Yes," said Amanda, "about the temptation. I rather think you owe us an explanation."

"My thoughts exactly," said Owen, advancing into the room.

"But of course." Henrique waited until everyone—including, after a few well-chosen words from Owen, Raimundo—was seated. "As I believe you all know, I currently reside in Paris. From time to time, I pay a visit to our sister Carlota, who married a Frenchman long before all the unpleasantness on the Continent. Carlota has always been fond of me, despite my scapegrace ways." He smiled apologetically. Raimundo scowled furiously.

"Carlota informed me," Henrique continued, "that Raimundo would be visiting her in Paris shortly after the New Year, but that first he had to attend to some business in England for our nephew Eugenio. Raimundo, she told me, was invited to spend the Christmas holidays in Devonshire at a house called Ludlow. I would scarcely have given the matter a second thought had it not happened that at that same time I had formed a most agreeable connection with an English lady—you English have been quite overrunning Paris since the peace, you know. This estimable lady had, I think, best remain nameless, but she has long been a friend of Lady Duffield. When I told her that my brother would be staying at Ludlow, she said it was the greatest coincidence, for she had just had a letter—"

"Lucinda Carlow," Lady Duffield exclaimed. "She's always had a shockingly loose tongue."

"I fear I must bow to Lady Duffield's powers of deduction," Henrique said, inclining his head in Lady

189

Duffield's direction. "My dear friend Mrs. Carlow informed me that Lady Duffield was also to be a guest at Ludlow over the holidays, and knowing the relation in which my brother had once stood to Lady Duffield, I was"—he paused, hesitating carefully over his choice of words—"shall we say, I was much struck by the dilemma in which Raimundo would be placed, for I knew he would not wish to cause Lady Duffield any embarrassment."

"So you decided to save him such embarrassment by taking his place?" Nicola inquired.

"Oh, no, Lady Windham. It was not until Mrs. Carlow informed me that she had received another letter from her friend and that Lady Duffield, learning that a certain gentleman, whom she did not wish to meet, was to be among the guests at Ludlow, meant to cry off from her engagement—"

"I could wring Lucinda's neck," Lady Duffield said with feeling.

"It was not until I learned this that my plan began to take shape. Lady Duffield was not to put in an appearance at Ludlow, but she would be expected. Knowing my brother's chivalrous nature, I was confident that an appeal on Lady Duffield's behalf would cause him to quit the house party. I could then take his place, secure in the knowledge that Lady Duffield would not arrive and denounce me as an imposter." He sighed. "It was an excellent plan. I was very nearly successful."

"But why?" Amanda could not contain her curiosity. "What did you hope to gain?"

Henrique turned his melting brown eyes upon her. "Need you ask, Miss Berwick? The book, of course."

Raimundo started to speak, then threw up his hands in disgust and reached for the brandy Charles had given him. Owen leaned back in his chair and crossed his legs. "A great deal of trouble, surely, for something

190

worth only a few hundred pounds."

Henrique smiled. "A few hundred pounds may be a mere trifle to you, Mr. Thorn, but to a man such as I, leading a quite hand-to-mouth existence, it is nothing to be sneezed at. And now," he continued, getting to his feet, "I believe it is past time I made my departure. You must allow me to thank you for your hospitality, Lady Windham. I apologize for accepting it under false pretenses. I will take my leave before I cause you further embarrassment."

"Nonsense," Nicola said in a warm voice which held more than a trace of amusement. "We wouldn't turn anyone out of the house at this hour, especially with the weather so dismal. And I certainly wouldn't ask any of the servants to drive you into Honiton on Christmas night in the middle of a storm." The wind had come up during the evening and even indoors they could feel its constant buffets. "I daresay your brother can tolerate your presence under the same roof for one night. After all," Nicola concluded, a smile playing about her lips, "the book is safely under lock and key."

Henrique returned the smile appreciatively. "Just so, Lady Windham. My greatest thanks. I will be gone before breakfast."

Henrique's exit was followed by silence, broken at last by a gust of acrid smoke from the fireplace. Charles rose to poke up the smoldering fire. "I would not have believed it of him," Raimundo said suddenly. "I do apologize. My brother's behavior has been unpardonable."

"It's not your fault," Nicola assured him. "And you must admit he was very enterprising about it."

"Yes," said Amanda thoughtfully, "and all for—I mean, I know a few hundred pounds would be the absolute earth to some people, but for all his talk about a hand-to-mouth existence, he doesn't look like one of them. Or am I wrong?" she asked, turning to Raimundo.

Raimundo, who had fallen to staring at his hands, as if in contemplation of his brother's sins, looked up at her and shook his head. "Henrique has always lived extravagantly, Miss Berwick. I would not have thought a few hundred pounds would be a sufficient sum to arouse his interest. Indeed, I would have thought he could borrow that much from Carlota easily enough, but perhaps he found he had asked her for money once too often."

"I must say," Lady Duffield observed, "he took it remarkably well."

"There was very little else he could do," Charles said, returning to his chair.

"That doesn't necessarily mean—Oh, Lord." Amanda looked at her brother. "You *do* quite definitely have the book, don't you?"

Owen and Charles exchanged glances. "It's been locked up since yesterday," said Charles, but he rose and crossed to a tall mahogany cabinet which stood between two glass-fronted bookcases. As he pulled a key from his pocket and unlocked a lower drawer, Amanda was aware of how very quiet the room had become. Charles pulled the drawer open, and Amanda was quite certain she heard him breathe a sigh of relief.

"All accounted for," he said, turning back to the others, the book held carefully in both hands. "Care to have a look at it, Owen, just to be on the safe side? Although," he added, exchanging glances with Nicola, "it would be a bit much if it turned out to be counterfeit."

Unlike the others, who were all looking at Charles, Owen was staring fixedly at the amber liquid in his glass, a frown on his face. But at Charles's words he roused himself, set down the glass, and crossed to the sofa table where Charles had placed the book. Amanda leaned over the back of the sofa and watched with interest as Owen studied the worn volume.

"It's genuine," he said after a moment, but his face still wore a faint frown.

"What is it?" Amanda asked.

"I'm not sure. Except that I suspect you're right. I don't think Henrique was after the book at all."

"Oh, dear, do you think we ought to count the silver?" Nicola asked.

"No," said Raimundo firmly. "Even Henrique would not stoop to such a common crime."

Amanda did not see precisely what made stealing silver worse than stealing a book, but it did not seem politic to say so. "Owen," she said slowly, turning possibilities over in her mind, "is it possible that the book is more valuable than we realize? I mean this particular book. Could there be something which sets it apart from other first editions of *Blanchardyn and Eglantine?* Or could—"

She broke off because of the marked change in Owen's expression. The frown was gone, and he looked at once appalled and strangely excited. "Good God," he said softly. Then he turned up the lamp that stood on the table, opened the front cover of the book, and ran his finger down the spine.

A slow, satisfied smile crossing his face, Owen closed the book. "Children," he said, surveying the company, "I'm afraid the drama isn't quite over. Might I suggest we adjourn to Henrique's chamber? I do not think it would be wise to let this wait until morning."

Raimundo bounded out of his chair. "Are you saying—" he began.

"I think," said Owen, moving to the door, "that we had best let your brother tell us about it."

To Amanda's relief, no one suggested that the ladies

remain in the library. Nicola and Lady Duffield were not about to be left out of things, and Owen and Charles were not foolish enough to try to exclude them. As for Senhor Ribeiro, he appeared entirely preoccupied with the question of what further mischief his brother was up to.

Henrique, who had removed his coat but otherwise was still fully dressed, took the arrival of such a deputation in his bedchamber remarkably well. "You have thought of further questions you wish to ask me?" he said politely, ushering the ladies toward the settee and chairs before the fireplace.

"You could say that," said Owen cheerfully, taking up a stance beside the settee. "We've come to ask you for something quite specific. Being a fair man, you will have to agree that it cannot possibly be called yours."

Henrique regarded him with a very creditable look of surprise. "But Lord Windham locked the book in the cabinet after I looked at it yesterday. Indeed, even before my brother arrived I had begun to wonder how I would manage to recover it."

"Oh, but you didn't need the book." Owen's expression was intent, but Amanda could tell he was enjoying himself hugely. "By yesterday afternoon you were already in possession of the object which had brought you to Ludlow. I don't wonder you admitted to your charade so easily. We hadn't really disrupted your plans at all."

"My dear Mr. Thorn, I must beg leave to differ with you."

"You may beg whatever you wish, Senhor Ribeiro. If you do not produce the object in question, Lord Windham and I are prepared to search your room."

Charles nodded in confirmation of this last, quite as if he knew exactly what Owen was talking about.

"Henrique," said Raimundo, when his brother did not

immediately answer, "I don't know what it is you have stolen, but I demand that you return it at once."

At this, Henrique gave a shout of laughter. Then, as he had done in the library when he admitted he was not Raimundo, he gave a shrug of resignation. "If it were not for Lady Windham's generous insistence that I stay the night, I would be long gone by now. Ah, well, you cannot deny that it was an excellent plan."

Without further protest, he walked to his bedside table, picked up a slim volume which had been lying there and carried it to a Pembroke table near the fireplace. Opening the book, he carefully abstracted a fragile sheet of paper from between its pages. "Is this what you are looking for, Mr. Thorn?"

Owen stared at the paper for a long interval with amazement, reverence, and delight. Amanda came to stand beside him, but a view of the paper told her little. It was covered with a faded and quite indecipherable writing. The paper itself looked old, as old as the pages of *Blanchardyn and Eglantine*. Amanda glanced quickly at Owen. "This was hidden inside the book?"

"Beneath the inside cover, unless I'm very much mistaken. When I looked at it in the library just now, it seemed to have been recently resealed."

"But what is it? And why did someone go to such trouble to hide it?"

"It is a letter from a lover to his mistress, quite an ordinary love letter, save that it mentions, almost in passing, the existence of a child. And I imagine the lady went to such pains to hide it because she was Jane Shore and her lover was Edward IV."

Dead silence greeted Owen's announcement, followed by a medley of questions and exclamations. It was Charles who went to the heart of the matter. "Edward IV died in 1483. Didn't you say the book probably dated from 1489?"

Owen nodded. "The letter undoubtedly predates the book. One can never know exactly what happened, but I suspect Jane Shore kept it as a keepsake and only decided to hide it later, sometime after Bosworth. By 1489 a relationship to a Yorkist was as much a liability as an asset. She must have felt her child's safety was best guaranteed by anonymity, yet she couldn't bring herself to destroy the letter." He turned to Henrique. "How in God's name did you know it was there?"

"I was not at all certain that it would be, Mr. Thorn. But I knew from my father that this book had once been the property of a woman called Jane Shore. I never gave the matter much thought, but when I learned Raimundo was on his way to England to collect the book, I asked some English friends who this Jane Shore was. I learned that there was a story—probably apocryphal, my friends told me—that she bore Edward a child and that he referred to the child in a letter he wrote to her. The letter had never come to light. I began to wonder about Jane Shore's book. I had already realized it would be easy enough for me to lure Raimundo away and take his place. He smiled apologetically at the whole company. "It seemed too good an opportunity to miss."

"Honestly, Bella," Amanda said sharply. "I said the gingerbread wasn't for us to eat."

Abashed, Bella Lydgate put the half-eaten gingerbread back on one of the plates of holiday treats and favors which were crowded on the breakfast-parlor table, waiting to be placed in Christmas baskets.

"Now that you've taken a bite you might as well finish it," Amanda said with a sigh, surveying the filled baskets which were strewn on the sideboard and windows seats, and wondering how many more would be required to accommodate all the children who were to visit Ludlow this afternoon. It was a Windham family custom to hold open house for their tenants on Boxing Day. Each family was given a Christmas box when they departed, and all the children received baskets of favors.

Bella took the gingerbread back and ate it with such a subdued expression that Amanda regretted her sharpness. "I'm sorry," she said, ruffling the little girl's hair. "I didn't mean to snap at you. I'm feeling a bit out of sorts this morning."

"I suppose it's because you got to bed so late last night." Verity was tying lengths of satin ribbon around the finished baskets with practiced fingers. "I think I like the Senhor Ribeiro we have now better than the other one."

"I wish he hadn't left so early this morning," said David, adding an orange to a basket. "The other one, I mean. We missed all the fun parts."

"I thought there was something rum about the friar last night," said the elder Lydgate boy thoughtfully.

"You didn't!" His younger brother rounded on him indignantly. "You're just saying that now you know the story."

A spirited quarrel ensued which Amanda did her best to ignore. Verity was right, she hadn't got much sleep last night, but that wasn't the reason for her uncertain temper this morning. No, the problem was that, in spite of the real Senhor Ribeiro being identified and the book safe and the valuable letter recovered, the entire episode had left her with more questions than answers.

The opening of the door interrupted her reflections. Amanda looked up, expecting Nicola or Elizabeth or Helena, and instead saw Lady Duffield standing in the doorway, a charming look of apology on her face. "I'm so sorry." Lady Duffield smiled at the company in a way that reminded Amanda that, however much unlike a mother Pamela Duffield might look, she had five children of her own. "I was hoping I might have a word with Miss Berwick, but I didn't realize you were engaged in such serious business. May I help?"

Amanda hadn't the least idea what Lady Duffield wanted to say to her, but an extra pair of hands was a great help, and Lady Duffield proved surprisingly successful at diverting the children. Amanda was both grateful and annoyed. It seemed a bit unfair that a woman as beautiful as Lady Duffield and as adept at charming grown men should be equally popular with children. Still, they managed to finish filling the baskets with no more quarrels or stolen gingerbread. When the children had gone off in search of other amusements, Amanda faced Lady Duffield across the basket-strewn room and waited for her to speak.

Lady Duffield was staring at her hands and Amanda could have sworn the woman was nervous. "I asked to speak to you, Miss Berwick, because I think it is important that you understand Owen, and I don't believe this is something he would ever tell you himself."

"I don't," said Amanda, treading carefully, "see how Owen is any concern of mine."

Lady Duffield looked up and gave a faintly mischievous smile. "You know the answer to that better than I, Miss Berwick. As to my own interest in the matter, it is very simple. Owen is my son."

It was an astonishing revelation, and yet it so exactly made sense of all that had happened in the past two days that Amanda did not think to question it. She sat in silence for a moment, the words repeating themselves in her head. Then she looked at Lady Duffield, uncertain how much she could ask, unwilling to let the matter end there.

"You are very young, Miss Berwick," Lady Duffield said, "but I do not think you shock easily."

"No," Amanda agreed, "I most certainly do not."

"I'm so glad, for Owen could not—But never mind about that. You want to know about Owen. It's a simple enough story." Lady Duffield had regained her customary composure. "Not long after my marriage, I suffered a miscarriage and went abroad to recuperate. My sister accompanied me, but my husband remained in England. He was some twenty years my senior and ours was not a love match, so I parted from him without regret. In Rome, I met a young Englishman and—" She smiled and gave an expressive shrug. "I was twenty, he was twenty-three. There was a girl at home to whom he was to be betrothed, and his parents were very eager for the match. But he was young and impetuous and ready to abandon all for love. In some ways, I was a great deal older than he. When he asked me to run off with him I knew it was impossible. We quarreled, quite bitterly." To Amanda's surprise, a shadow of pain crossed Lady Duffield's face. "It was only after I returned to England that I realized I was with child. Not a pleasant predicament for a young woman whose husband could not possibly be the father. Eventually I had no choice but to tell my husband and he agreed to stand by me. There was no question, of course, of the child being accepted into our household."

Amanda heard the note of genuine regret in Lady Duffield's voice and for the first time fully understood that this woman had had to give up her child. And that Owen had had to grow up without his mother. Amanda was not sure precisely what Lady Duffield could have done differently, but it seemed shockingly unfair that Owen had in effect been abandoned by both his parents. "What happened?" she asked bluntly, her compassion for Lady Duffield diminished by her concern for Owen. "To Owen, I mean."

Lady Duffield smoothed a crease from her flounced

jaconet skirt with great care. "I went to Ireland for the birth, and then an aunt of mine agreed to take him in. She was a kind woman, but her health was not good and Owen was left to the care of nursemaids. I saw him occasionally, though of course he did not know who I was. My aunt died when he was five, but fortunately one of my cousins said she could look after him. She and her husband were charming people, but they had three sons of their own, and though Owen was always treated well, I'm afraid he never quite felt he *belonged*. When he was twelve, I finally told him the truth about our relationship. I must say he took it remarkably well, especially as I would not tell him anything about his father."

Lady Duffield sighed, as if acknowledging that perhaps she had been in the wrong. "We had quarreled so *very* badly, you see—Owen's father and I—and he was married by this time and had a family of his own. But it was time for Owen to go to school, and while I'd been able to give my cousin a little now and then to help with the housekeeping, school fees were quite beyond me. I'm afraid I'd rather put off thinking about it and finally my cousin's husband sought out Owen's father and told him the whole. He was—he was not pleased with me for having kept the truth from him. But he had a large income and he was able to put Owen through Eton and Cambridge, and eventually he told Owen he was his father. I'm afraid," said Lady Duffield with a faint frown, as if only just realizing how true her words were, "that it hasn't been at all easy for Owen. And this house party has been exceptionally difficult."

"Because of Senhor Ribeiro?" Amanda asked. "I can see why you decided not to come when you learned he would be here, but what made you change your mind?"

"Senhor Ribeiro? Raimundo?" Lady Duffield gave a

light, silvery laugh. "Oh, no. I own his presence was a bit awkward—especially when he turned out not to be Raimundo at all—but I decided not to come to the house party because I did not wish to meet Owen's father."

Amanda's eyes widened. "Owen's father? You don't mean Lord Mul—" She bit the words back, for if she were wrong they were quite unpardonable.

"I very much mean John Mulgrave," Lady Duffield said with another mischievous smile. "You've no notion how ardent he was at twenty-three."

"Oh." Amanda digested this information with difficulty.

"When I learned he was to be among the guests at Ludlow—it was quite bad of Isabel not to warn me, though I imagine she had her reasons—my first instinct was to avoid a meeting that would be painful for both of us. But then I began to think about the fact that we were both now free, and I wondered if there was any chance—I never really got over John, you see."

"So at the last minute you decided to come to Ludlow after all."

"I did. And," Lady Duffield said, her mouth curving into a smile of pure girlish delight, "the wonder of it is that he was glad to see me. I thought it might all come to nought when he found out about Raimundo, but I told him everything this morning, and I think that gave John the push he needed. So you see, after twenty-seven years Owen is finally going to have parents who are properly married."

Amanda, whose feelings toward Lady Duffield had improved steadily in the course of the interview, gave her wholehearted congratulations, but Lady Duffield waved them aside. "I did not come here to talk about myself. I hope you understand Owen better now, Miss Berwick. What you decide to do with the

201

information is, of course, entirely up to you."

Amanda left the room in a thoughtful frame of mind. Owen's mother had made two things very clear: Owen was interested in Amanda, but if Amanda wanted that interest to lead to anything more than their present friendship, she was going to have to do something about it herself.

Owen walked slowly down the Bath-stone steps which led to the lower terrace of the back garden, mulling over the interview he had just had with his father. When he realized John and Pamela were going to spend Christmas under the same roof, he had been prepared for fireworks. Instead, they had become betrothed. His parents never ceased to surprise him.

A rattle of glass diverted his attention, and he turned round to see Amanda emerge through one of the French windows from the summer parlor. She wore a cloak of scarlet wool, but the hood was thrown back, and her bright hair streamed over her shoulders and down her back as she ran toward him. "It's all right," he called, amused by her precipitate dash, "I'm waiting."

Amanda descended the stairs at a more moderate pace, which was a mercy, for though the day was fine and crisp, the stone was still damp and slippery from yesterday's rain. "May I walk with you?"

Owen grinned at the sudden formality. "I gathered that was the general idea. Are the baskets finished?"

"Yes, and I think the best thing we can all do for Nicola now is to stay out of her way. Really, I don't know how anyone manages to enjoy the holidays after they have a family of their own, especially women."

"I expect the answer is that a lot of them don't," Owen replied, "especially women."

Amanda pulled a face at him. "What's going to happen to the letter?" she asked as they started down a winding gravel walk bordered by tall hedges.

"That's up to Eugenio Ribeiro, but I expect he'll give it to a museum, which is really where it belongs. I don't know its monetary value, but to a scholar it's priceless."

"Poor Jane Shore. It must have been beastly for her. I hope she wasn't separated from her child." Amanda paused, then added in the same conversational tone, "Speaking of children, I just had a talk with your mother."

Owen stopped and stared at her, not sure whether to laugh or to curse. Amanda stared back at him, perfectly matter-of-fact. "Look," she said, "I can understand if you don't want to talk about it. But I want you to know that I understand, at least a bit. Parents who break the rules can make things rather awkward for their children."

Owen felt a flash of anger at Ione Berwick. "I'm sorry," he said gently.

"I wasn't asking for sympathy," Amanda assured him. "I don't really blame them—parents I mean—for I'm a firm believer in breaking the rules. But the sad thing about my mother is that it didn't seem to make her very happy, at least, not any happier than she was before she left Charles's father, so it seems rather a waste to have gone through all that fuss, only of course I'm glad she did because if she hadn't I wouldn't be here. But that doesn't alter the principle of the thing. Ever since I was old enough to understand at all, I've been determined not to marry until I was sure I'd found exactly the right person."

"A proud lady in love," Owen said lightly.

"Well, yes, I suppose you could put it that way." Amanda had been walking briskly, her eyes fixed on the path ahead. Now she stopped, withdrew her hands from the folds of her cloak and held out a bunched-up silk scarf. "I know at Ludlow they exchange gifts on New

203

Year's Day," she said, speaking very quickly, her eyes lowered to her hands, "but I thought perhaps today would be a good time to give you this."

Owen took the scarf which proved to be wrapped, rather hastily by the look of it, around a small object. Aware of Amanda's anxious eyes upon him, he carefully unwound the scarf and caught his breath. He was holding a small silver figure: a knight in full armor, drawn sword in one hand, as exquisitely fashioned as anything he had seen Amanda do.

Seeking for words which would properly acknowledge such a gift, Owen looked into Amanda's eyes and realized she had offered him far more than the silver knight. And for the first time he knew, with complete, blinding certainty, that he had every intention of taking it. If only he could find the right words. "It's beautiful," he told her. "The finest gift I've ever received. Amanda—"

"Yes?"

Owen hesitated, conscious of the bright sun and the hint of freshness in the cold air. It was a good time for beginnings. "I never felt I had a family," he said slowly. "There were always people about who were kind to me, but I knew I didn't really belong to them. I had quite decent parents, but they weren't on speaking terms with each other. Lots of people's parents aren't, of course, but mine weren't married either, which rather complicated things." He smiled. "Now that I come to think of it, each of them asked me about the other suspiciously often. I should have realized where the wind lay. But you see," he continued, sobering, "I've always been disgustingly self-sufficient. I thought I liked it that way. I never thought about beginning a family of my own. At least, not until recently."

"Until you learned your parents are getting married?" Amanda's blue eyes were at once grave and expectant.

204

Owen shook his head and grinned suddenly. "Until I saw you flirting with Newfield and young Harewood last night. I felt the strongest desire to knock their teeth in. You can't possibly marry either of them, Amanda. They aren't remotely good enough for you."

He heard Amanda expel her breath, as if a great weight had just been lifted from her shoulders. Owen wasn't sure which of them moved first, but the next thing he knew she was locked closely in his arms and he was kissing her, gently at first, then with a hunger he had scarcely known he felt until he allowed himself to admit that he wanted her. He raised his head at last, because it was still necessary to breathe, and looked down at her, dazed, shaken, and happier than he could ever remember being.

Amanda smiled at him. Her cheeks were flushed with color, but her gaze was steady, and she managed to speak in her customary direct way, though she, too, was more than a little breathless. "If you have decided to start a family, Owen, I do hope you will consider me. I love you quite desperately, and I'm convinced there isn't anyone else who's remotely good enough for *you*."

Owen looked down into Amanda's upturned face, conscious of a growing wonder and delight. Amanda seemed quite content to do nothing but return his gaze. Neither of them heard the footsteps that must have been quite audible to anyone in his right mind. The hedges hid the rest of the walk from view, and they did not turn round until they heard Charles's voice.

"Nicola wants you for something or other," Amanda's brother told her, "but I think I shall tell her you couldn't be found. If you want privacy, I recommend the summerhouse. Nicola and I found it remarkably convenient when we were betrothed."

Amanda grinned. "You really are a capital brother, Charles."

"I do my best. By the way," Charles added, looking from his sister to Owen, his expression grave but his eyes lit with humor, "I trust this is some sort of declaration. Amanda's an extraordinarily sensible girl, but I feel I ought to stand in for her father."

"Oh, quite," Owen assured him. "Though frankly, old fellow, I have every intention of marrying her whether you approve or not."

"And I have every intention of marrying him." Amanda looked at her brother with a smile of pure happiness. "You see," she said, snuggling against Owen and feeling his arms slide securely around her, "once we proud ladies in love make up our minds, there's no stopping us."

Historical Note

Jane Shore and Edward IV's child is a figment of the author's imagination. Though Jane Shore was literate, there is no evidence that she owned a copy of *Blanchardyn and Eglantine*.

Eugenia's Miracle
by *Elizabeth Morgan*

The Honorable Charles Foxworth eyed his younger sister with a degree of misgiving, not unmixed with a certain resignation. Eugenia was in particularly high spirits tonight, and in his long-suffering experience, this was an ill omen for her anticipated behavior at Lady Wellthorpe's soirée.

It was not that Miss Eugenia Foxworth was lacking in good manners. On the contrary, her charm was widely renowned, and it was commonly held that no gathering could truly be considered a success unless the sparkling Miss Foxworth had appeared. Nor was she a flirt, despite her popularity; several astute hostesses had remarked upon the fact that she was just as likely to be found chatting among the dowagers as to be seen dancing with one of the many eligible gentlemen who frequently professed their admiration.

The problem, thought Charles, was simply that Miss Foxworth was not what most mamas would consider prettily behaved. She was a shade too outspoken for the demands of decorum, and she showed a most regrettable tendency to disregard the strictures of her elder brother. She tended to espouse views that made his conservative soul shudder, such as her frequent declarations that women should enjoy the same legal and social rights as men, or that they should be allowed to practice professions. Try as he might to warn her that most gentlemen would be put off by such views, she merely declared that eccentricity was in vogue and that she preferred to remain unwedded so that she could enjoy the independence of a widow without having to suffer the inconvenience of marriage. Perhaps if their mother had been alive and Eugenia had not been left to his own uncertain guardianship, she might have been a more biddable miss, but Eugenia had attained her majority several months ago, inheriting a considerable independence, and as she frequently reminded him, Charles had little choice but to accept her as she chose to be.

It was also apparent that this evening she was seemingly inclined to startle the world with her dress, as she had done on more than one previous occasion. Miss Foxworth, who was presently scrutinizing her image in the drawing-room mirror, was attired in a long-sleeved gown of gold-hued silk, accented at its high throat and wrists with emerald ribbons. Another ribbon was threaded through her flame-colored hair, accentuating the paleness of her skin. Fortunately for Miss Foxworth, she did not suffer from the freckles that so often plagued the true redhead; instead, she was blessed with a near translucent complexion that made her golden hazel eyes appear even more striking. She always wore strong colors, as opposed to the muslin pastels commonly deemed suitable for unmarried maidens, but Eugenia insisted upon her own style, and as several ladies of the Ton had recently taken to imitating her quirks of fashion, Charles had had to admit defeat on that point.

He would have been quite surprised, however, had he been able to fathom her thoughts at that moment, because Eugenia was giving her image in the mirror a good talking-to. It was a week before Christmas, and the nearer that date approached, the more difficult it was to ignore the pain of a very special anniversary. Two years before, at Christmas, she and Will Stanfield had exchanged a vow that had inscribed itself indelibly upon her heart, and

210

time had done nothing to ease the heartache of knowing that that vow could never be fulfilled. Over the course of time, she had learned to hide her feelings with a show of high spirits and ready humor, and she had found a certain solace in the bluestocking interests so deplored by Charles. Yet the sadness still lingered whenever her thoughts grew quiet, and the image of her lost love would rise before her, making a mockery of her efforts to forget.

Before that notion could once more fill her eyes with tears, she turned to Charles with a smile that trembled almost imperceptibly. "I am in the mood for a party tonight," she declared brightly. "December is such a dreary month, and I think everyone could use a bit of revelry."

Charles groaned audibly. Lady Wellthorpe's genteel gathering was scarcely to be considered a risky venture, but where his sister was concerned, anything was a possibility.

"Jen, I beg of you, do not do anything rash," he pleaded. "I suppose it is my own fault for telling you that the Reverend Pankhurst had asked my permission to pay you his addresses; I should have known that you would try to kick up a dust."

Her smile was genuine now as she reached out to tweak a fold of his neckcloth, a gesture that would have appalled his meticulous valet. The two of them were both of the same moderate height, and although his coloring was more subdued than hers, his hair being more brown than red, no one could ever have mistaken their relationship.

"You have to admit, Charles, that there is method in my madness. You know very well that if I ever did wish to marry, which I do not, the Reverend Pankhurst would be the last man suitable for that honor. I'd have him in Bedlam before a month was out!"

Charles coughed, reluctant to agree. "I simply feel that if you insist upon refusing this latest in your string of eligible offers, you could do it more discreetly than by kicking up a lark in public!"

"Don't worry, Charles," she reassured him. "Much though the idea tempts me, I will do nothing to embarrass the House of Foxworth. But neither will I be the wife of the Reverend Pankhurst, and the sooner he realizes it, the sooner I pray he will leave me in peace. And much as I love you, Charles, I rather wish that you would do the same and stop pushing the poor man in my direction."

"It would be a suitable match," he defended. "The Reverend Pankhurst is of good family, comfortably situated, and of admirable character, and if you were to treat him with the least degree of consideration it is likely he would cherish a lasting *tendre* for you."

She uttered a laugh that to his sensitive ears sounded rather rude. "I will grant that he is a paragon, but for that very reason, I would think you should find him completely unsuited to me! You are forever harping upon the failings of my own character. Besides, I do not consider you to be a particularly good judge of such matters in view of your own betrothal to Priscilla Preston-Smythe. I will never comprehend how you could do such a thing and without the least warning to me beforehand!"

His color heightened slightly. "Miss Preston-Smythe is a young woman of excellent character, and I am of the age when it is my responsibility to marry and settle down."

"Settle down?" Eugenia riposted, the green ribbon in her hair glinting as she shook her head. "Charles, you have been settled down all of your life. What you need is to be shaken up and taught to enjoy yourself, which you will never do if you are leg-shackled to Miss Preston-Smythe."

"Eugenia, you are going beyond the line of what I can allow!"

She sighed. "I loathe it when you call me 'Eugenia' in that tone. Very well, Charles, I apologize to the estimable Priscilla and beg that you will forgive me. But quite frankly, she is not the right woman for you, just as none of the men you keep foisting

212

upon me could ever be right for me."

Charles looked away from her, letting his gaze fall upon the portrait of their deceased parents that hung over the marble mantelpiece. Their somber visages often served him as a reminder of the heavy responsibility he now bore as head of the household. "I am sorry, Jen. I suppose I do rather push things a bit in that regard, but it is for your own good. I want you to be happy."

Eugenia touched his hand in quick sympathy. Before Capt. William Stanfield had gone off to fight in the war against the French tyrant, he and Charles Foxworth had been the closest of friends. That was of course how Eugenia had first met him. Then, after Will was reported missing in action from a distant Portuguese battlefield, it was Charles who had borne to her that terrible news. He had shared her suffering later as well, when the final word came that Will was dead. It was not surprising that he hoped his sister had forgotten her love of long ago; judging by her outward behavior, Eugenia had long ago cast aside any appearance of mourning. He could not know the painful truth, that Will's image still burned so brightly in her heart that the faces of living men were faded by comparison. As she could never admit to that, however, she hid once more behind her mask of eccentricity.

"Your apology is accepted, Charles. And trust me, if I ever meet a man who truly believes that he and I are the equals of one another and who agrees that females should be permitted to hold political office, I will march him right up the steps of St. George's. Now, let us be off to Lady Wellthorpe's. I declare, the evening beckons me with a siren's call!"

The carriage was summoned, and moments later they were rumbling the short distance from their home in Brook Street to Lady Wellthorpe's elegant mansion in Grosvenor Square. It had been a mild winter so far, but the gray chill of a London December discouraged all but

213

the most hardy souls from strolling more than a few blocks. As she listened to the horses' clattering hooves, Eugenia struggled once more against the lowness of spirit which drove her in search of outrageous distractions. To-night she would as ever be the ebullient character she played in public until the time came to return home to her heartache.

The memory of that fateful Christmas Eve two years before rose vividly to her imagination, and for a brief moment she allowed herself to linger over it. Eugenia had fallen in love with Charles's tall dark-haired friend almost from the first moment of meeting those deep brown eyes smiling down at her. For many months, whenever they met at the Foxworth home, Eugenia concealed her infatuation behind teasing and jokes, and it was obvious that Will enjoyed his relationship with Charles's "little" sister, despite the fact that she had already turned nineteen and had made her debut into society. Suddenly, however, it seemed as though the easy laughter had stopped, and the humorous glint in Will's eyes had disappeared. Eugenia was ready to despair, wondering how she had offended him, until the night that the three of them prepared to depart together for a Christmas party. Will had stepped forward to help her into the carriage, taking hold of her hand, but instead of moving to assist her, he had simply stood and looked down upon her, all the while clasping her gloved hand in his own. For a moment her heart had pounded wildly, and she was terrified that her feelings must surely show on her face, but she could not look away.

And that night everything changed. They danced together as if for the first time, and every look, every brief touch was magical. Eugenia could never remember after-wards whom she saw or what she said at that party, be-cause after her dance with Will, nothing and no one else existed for her. It was upon their return that night, when Charles had excused himself briefly, that Will had closed

214

the door of the study and taken her into his arms with a passion she would never forget. A few moments later he had released her abruptly, murmuring apologies: he was sorry, it was his fault, she was too young, he should never have lost his head, it would never happen again. And it was then that Eugenia flung herself into his arms and drew his head down, her hands buried in his hair, bringing his lips back to hers.

But the happiness was short-lived. They exchanged words of love when at last they could speak, but Will steadfastly refused to become formally betrothed. Some months before, he had purchased a captaincy in a line regiment and would be leaving all too soon; furthermore, he believed that Eugenia was too young to know her heart, especially since he had practically swept her off her feet. When he returned from his tour of service, he promised that if her feelings were unchanged, as he knew his own would be, then he would announce their love for all the world to know.

No amount of Eugenia's pleading could sway him, and for that, she knew herself to be partly to blame. Anyone who knew her in the lighthearted guise she had affected could be forgiven for believing that it reflected her true character. The serious side of her nature had been well-hidden for fear that her deeper feelings would be revealed in an unguarded moment. Moreover, her orphaned status gave further weight to Will's reluctance to take the slightest advantage of her vulnerability. Because she lacked the protection of a parent, having only the guardianship of a brother not much older than she, a hasty engagement might give rise to unpleasant gossip.

So Eugenia agreed, albeit reluctantly, to keep their betrothal a secret. But on one point she had remained adamant: the small ring of gold and seed pearls which Will gave her as a token of their bond would never be removed from her hand. Like the other vows they had made, that promise had not come true in the strictest sense; a year after his death, she had taken it from her finger in response to the pleadings of her brother that she should not waste her youth in mourning. No one knew that she wore it still, upon a slender golden chain around her neck.

The carriage drew to a halt before Eugenia realized that her brother had been as silent as she on the brief journey and that a small frown was creasing his brow.

"What is the matter, Charles?" she teased lightly. "Are you still afraid of how I intend to frighten away the good reverend?"

"No, no," he shrugged a shade uncomfortably. "I was thinking of something else, that's all. Just a rumor that I heard; nothing to concern you."

Eugenia eyed him suspiciously as he handed her down from the carriage. "Whenever you say that, you tend to be plotting something that is 'for my own good.'"

"I wish I knew whether it was or not," he replied cryptically, but then the door was opened to them, and the chance for further conversation was lost as their cloaks were taken from them and their arrival was announced to their hostess.

Lady Serena Wellthorpe had been close friends with Mrs. Foxworth for many years until that lady's unfortunate demise, and she had been happy to sponsor her goddaughter's debut into society. It had always been a source of regret to her that Eugenia had not "taken"; in fact, at times she harbored the suspicion that Eugenia had deliberately resisted all her efforts to arrange a suitable match. It was all the more vexing because her daughter Frances had recently made her own debut, and some of Eugenia's ridiculous ideas about female emancipation seemed to be rubbing off upon the younger girl, who had begun to show a marked lack of enthusiasm for her own potential suitors. Nevertheless, Lady Wellthorpe greeted her two young guests with genuine pleasure, although she could not resist making rapid mental calculations about the various eligible men in atten-

216

dance with whom Eugenia might be partnered.

"Hello, my dears," she breathed, bestowing lavender-scented kisses upon their cheeks. "I am so delighted to see you. And if I am not mistaken," she added, glancing significantly at Eugenia, "my sentiments are shared by someone else here tonight."

"Aunt Serena, you are incorrigible," Eugenia laughed, using the fond nickname by which she and Charles both addressed her ladyship. "I wish that you would give up trying to foist me off upon some poor man whose life I should undoubtedly make into a misery."

Lady Wellthorpe could not help but be struck by the likelihood of such an outcome, but her strictly conventional nature prevailed. "My dear, it's a good thing I know you so well, else I might not realize you were making a jest."

At that moment, Charles uttered a muffled laugh, earning a look of reproach from her ladyship which soon softened into a beam of pride. The Honorable Charles was turning into just such a young man as she would have wished to have as a son, and she viewed his recent engagement with favor. Not that one could be precisely fond of Miss Preston-Smythe, his intended, but Charles was assuming his social responsibilities in an admirable fashion. If only Eugenia could be induced to follow his example!

Further reflections in that direction were interrupted by the arrival of her daughter, Frances. With a quiet word of greeting, she accorded Charles a shy smile as they shook hands and then was promptly borne away by Eugenia, who recognized an escape route when she saw one. The two girls strolled away arm in arm, and Lady Wellthorpe, even while she conversed politely with Charles about his approaching nuptials, mused once more upon the contrast between Eugenia's striking vivacity and Frances's more subdued charms. Attired charmingly in a pale pink gown, Frances had her mother's own soft brown hair and gentle blue eyes, although at the moment, unseen by her fond

217

parent, those eyes were lit with laughter.

"You cannot mean it, Eugenia," she breathed, caught between amusement and dismay. "Why would you want to shock the Reverend Pankhurst?"

"Because if I do not, I'm afraid he means to make me an offer," Eugenia replied.

"Oh, I see," Miss Wellthorpe said, and she did, at least in part. As Eugenia's dearest friend, she knew better than anyone else the sorrow that Eugenia had learned to hide, and she understood more than even Eugenia herself supposed. "But he is such a worthy gentleman."

"Worthy be damned," Eugenia said calmly, prompting Miss Wellthorpe to utter a gasp of shocked protest. "Besides which, Fanny, I have a reputation to live up to!"

"Live down to, rather," her friend replied drily. "What have you got planned, dare I ask?"

"I am not certain yet; I am waiting for, shall I say, divine inspiration. Oh, dear, here comes Miss Priss; no doubt she has something edifying to say to me, as usual. How do you do, Miss Preston-Smythe?"

"I am very well, thank you, Eugenia," replied the tall blond woman whose rather sharp features were arranged into a polite smile. She and Eugenia maintained a mutual dislike that was couched in the utmost cordiality; in Miss Preston-Smythe's opinion, her future sister-in-law was little short of a hoyden and in need of a firm rein.

"I scarcely need any assistance identifying you, my dear," Miss Preston-Smythe added with a touch of condescension. "One should never dream of wearing colors that make one's hair stand out like a beacon, but then, you have always had your own quaint notions, haven't you?"

"Good evening, Miss Preston-Smythe," Miss Wellthorpe hastened to intervene, correctly interpreting the martial light in her friend's eye. "I see that you have guessed Eugenia's scheme: Christmas colors of red, gold, and green. You yourself look like a veritable goddess this evening."

The diversionary tactic succeeded, as Miss Preston-

218

Smythe preened ever so slightly. It was one of her private conceits that she bore a resemblance to Aphrodite, and she had a penchant for wearing white gowns in the Grecian mode.

"How charming," Eugenia smiled. "You look like a girl in the first flush of youth."

As Miss Preston-Smythe was older than Eugenia by several years, this compliment met with less favor, but its recipient prided herself upon her diplomacy. "That is very kind of you to say, Eugenia. Perhaps when Charles and I are married, I will be able to persuade you to follow my lead in matters of fashion."

Charles approached as she spoke, and the three ladies' facial expressions were very different. Miss Preston-Smythe came as close to a simper as her very proper upbringing would allow; Miss Foxworth eyed her brother with fresh irritation at his stupidity in choosing such a bride; and Miss Wellthorpe went slightly pink before dropping her eyes in shyness.

"Good evening, Priscilla, good evening, Fanny," he said, bowing over the ladies' hands with the brisk ease of familiarity. "You are both in exceptional looks tonight."

Miss Wellthorpe's color deepened, but before she could utter a reply, a new diversion was created at the doorway by the arrival of a portly figure, whose short stature was more than compensated for by the booming voice with which he greeted his hostess.

"Reverend Pankhurst!" Miss Preston-Smythe exclaimed archly, recognizing the suitor of her soon-to-be sister-in-law. "No doubt he has come here tonight expressly to see our Eugenia, hmm?"

But Miss Foxworth had spied deliverance in the shape of her old friend Henry Talbot and was engaging in a bit of discreet hand-signaling. Mr. Talbot, a lanky blond young man with mild pretentions to dandyism, responded by approaching Charles and the ladies with a bow and a suave greeting, and showed admirably little surprise when

219

Eugenia seized his arm and, with a hasty apology to the others, propelled him toward the dancing area.

"You were heaven-sent, Henry," Eugenia exclaimed as soon as they were safely out of earshot. "I'm afraid I was on the verge of saying something quite unladylike to Miss Preston-Smythe."

Mr. Talbot was unimpressed. "When have you ever done otherwise?"

"Not at all! I am studiously polite, as well you know, but that creature has a way of vexing me beyond what is tolerable."

"In my experience, the words *vexatious* and *female* are one and the same. Why any man would consider leg-shackling himself to one of your sex is beyond my comprehension."

"Don't be so ungallant, Henry! I know you tire of having all the ambitious mamas chasing after you, but that is the cost of being such a prize on the marriage mart. If only you could gamble away your fortune, you would have no more cause for complaint!"

Mr. Talbot's faintly aloof expression was warmed by a slight smile. "Speak for yourself, Eugenia. A rich young lady with no overbearing mama is quite a catch, especially when she is not precisely ill-favored."

"Oh, you!" Eugenia cast him a teasing smile that, in a man not sworn to preserve his bachelor freedoms, might have stirred some degree of amorous interest. As it was, however, Mr. Talbot and Miss Foxworth got on well simply because neither one was interested in forming any serious connection. They could flirt with each other at ease and in so doing keep other matrimonial prospects at a distance.

None of this was apparent to curious onlookers, however, and as they danced, familiar speculations arose. They made a striking couple, given his blond handsomeness and her red-headed beauty, and no one watching them would have guessed that Miss Foxworth and Mr.

Talbot were now discussing nothing more exciting than the composition of poultices most effective for a hunter's strained fetlock.

It was not until some time later, as Eugenia was seated beside Mr. Talbot in the supper room, that she glanced across the room and saw a man seated, his back to her, with coal black hair cropped fashionably close to a well-shaped head. He turned his head in response to a question, and she saw the outline of a long, straight nose balanced by high cheekbones and a strong chin. In a most uncharacteristic moment of weakness, Eugenia dropped her glass of ratafia.

It was fortunate for Eugenia that Lady Wellthorpe had just indulged herself with the purchase of several Aubusson carpets, so that the consequence of her faux pas was merely a dull thud and not a mortifying crash. It was also fortunate for Lady Wellthorpe's carpet that the glass was nearly empty, not full. But Eugenia was in a state of shock. She had spent too many months torturing herself with imagined glimpses of darkhaired men with laughing eyes, berating herself for her own folly; nonetheless, her gaze was riveted upon the unknown stranger's head as he nodded in a movement that was somehow familiar.

There was a roaring in her ears, not entirely due to the noise in the room, although that served to mask her sudden silence. Mr. Talbot, who was engaged in recounting a humorous anecdote, did not immediately find anything amiss until he glanced her way and noted her sudden pallor.

"I say, Eugenia, are you all right?" he inquired solicitously. "You look as though you've seen a ghost!"

"No. I don't know, perhaps I have. Henry, who is that man over there, the dark-headed one speaking to Colonel Taggart?"

Mr. Talbot obediently looked. "I do not know, but I can inquire."

"I shall come with you." Eugenia moved to her feet,

almost as though in a trance. "It looks like someone I once . . . knew."

Together they approached the table where two men were seated, the elder of whom Eugenia recognized as an old friend of the family.

"My dear Miss Foxworth, you're looking splendid as usual," Colonel Taggart blustered affectionately, rising to his feet and taking her hand in his usual firm grip. "Evening, Talbot. I see you've snared our charmer for this evening, lucky dog. Here, here, there's someone I would like to present to both of you."

Feeling as though she were in a daze, Eugenia slowly turned her head and stared at the other man, who stood looking down at her. The man's features were shockingly familiar, but his brown eyes were icy cold with no warmth of recognition.

"Miss Foxworth, I would like you to meet Major Stanfield; Major, I present Miss Foxworth, and this young rascal here is Henry Talbot."

Eugenia could feel the blood rushing back into her pale cheeks. "Major Stanfield." A whisper was all she could manage.

"You will forgive me if I do not shake hands." The man's voice was deep and crisp as Mr. Talbot instinctively gestured forward, and it was not until that moment that Eugenia registered the fact that the major's right sleeve was pinned shut, hanging empty below the elbow. A shocked, involuntary gasp escaped her, drawing his cold gaze back upon her.

"Miss Foxworth and I have met," he drawled, "though I doubt if she remembers me."

Colonel Taggart laughed. "Since you've been away awhile, my boy, I doubt that she does; Miss Foxworth here has quite a reputation as our local breaker of hearts." It was the colonel's little joke, and he patted Eugenia's hand fondly as he spoke, but it was the sense of the words that registered upon his listener, drawing forth a sardonic expression that was not quite a smile.

"How long have you been in town, sir?" Mr. Talbot inquired politely, but Eugenia could not hear him, nor was she aware of the reply. Will was alive! Or was he? This man bore the same name and looked alike enough to be his twin, but his manner was so very different, almost disapproving. And how could he be alive when Charles had told her of his death more than a year before?

She forced her jumbled thoughts aside when she heard herself being addressed.

"Miss Foxworth, we should not keep you from your supper," Major Stanfield was saying. "This military talk cannot be of any interest to you."

"Oh, it is," she stammered. "But I—" There was only one way to find out his identity, and she cast her manners to the winds. "Forgive me, Major, but may I ask, what is your Christian name?"

He lifted one dark brow. "I was right, then; you do not remember me."

"Please, sir, your name?" she insisted.

"My name, Miss Foxworth, is William Arthur Stanfield."

It was he! Will was alive! She felt faint. Never before in her life had she felt so constrained by social convention, when her every instinct was to fling herself into this man's arms.

"It *is* you, Will," she breathed, and she actually took a step forward before she recollected herself. "I thought you were dead!"

"Indeed, that's what we all thought," Colonel Taggart interrupted, oblivious to any undercurrents of emotion. "But Stanfield here outsmarted his doctors, and here he is, promoted to Major and back in one piece."

"Slightly less than one piece, Colonel," Major Stanfield amended. "After all, Boney managed to keep my arm as a souvenir."

Eugenia could not prevent the shocked exclamation that

223

rose to her lips or the look of horror that leapt into her eyes as she comprehended the magnitude of what he must have endured. But Major Stanfield's mouth curved into a bitter smile of comprehension at her apparent disgust.

"Pray forgive my blunt way of speaking, Miss Foxworth. I am afraid I am unaccustomed to the delicate sensibilities of a lady. My only regret is that I cannot add myself to the ranks of those competing for your favors upon the dance floor." His tone, however, implied not so much regret as disdain, and Eugenia could feel the enormity of the distance that her thoughtless reaction had created between them.

"Would you instead call upon me, Major Stanfield?" she implored, paying no heed to Colonel Taggart's harrumph of disapproval at her boldness. "I will be at home tomorrow, and there is much that I—I mean, my brother and I—would like to ask you."

"I make very few social calls, Miss Foxworth. But I am of course honored by your request."

At that moment, the noise of the musicians striking up anew came as an unwelcome interruption, and Eugenia was left with no more than that politely ambiguous reply before she was approached by another gentleman for the next dance and was obliged to make her adieu. The next time she was able to look back in Major Stanfield's direction, he was gone.

As Eugenia danced and chatted politely with one partner after another, her inner thoughts were in turmoil. Will Stanfield was alive, and yet he was not the same man he had been before. It was indeed a stranger whom she had encountered. Oh yes, he had been matured by time and experience, and heaven only knew what he must have endured with such a grievous injury and many slow months of recuperation.

But why, if the report of his death were false, would he have made no effort to contact her in all this time? And why the cynicism in his present manner toward her? She knew that her reputation was that of a social butterfly, and Colonel Taggart's lighthearted words had certainly not aided much in that regard, but there was nothing of which she knew that could have earned Major Stanfield's apparent censure. And was there nothing at all left of his regard for her?

It was at that moment that she saw Charles and Miss Preston-Smythe dancing together, and as she observed her brother's rather preoccupied expression, something clicked in her memory: that "rumor" that had nothing to do with her. As soon as the dance was ended, she excused herself and headed straight for the settee where Charles and his betrothed were taking a moment's respite.

"Charles, I have something particular to discuss with you. Would you excuse us for a moment, Miss Preston-Smythe?" Eugenia asked, the unsettled state of her emotions making her tone more peremptory than she would have wished.

Unfortunately, Miss Preston-Smythe did not care to be dictated to by her future sister-in-law. "Charles and I have no secrets from each other, my dear Eugenia. Whatever you have to say to him may be said to me."

"Very well, then," Eugenia responded. "Damn you, Charles!"

Miss Preston-Smythe gasped, but Eugenia's glittering gold eyes were fixed upon her brother's face.

"You knew that Will Stanfield was alive, didn't you?"

Charles's suddenly heightened color was a dead giveaway. "I had heard that he was, yes, and I knew it was possible he would come back to London. But I did not wish to upset you with the news when it could have proved to be false."

"Upset me!" she exclaimed. "Did it not upset you to learn that he was alive when you had known for a year that he was dead?"

Charles cleared his throat. "Well, in point of fact, I did not ever know it for certain."

"You told me he was dead, Charles." Her voice dropped to scarcely above a whisper. "How could you do that?"

"I am sorry, Jen, but it was Will himself who begged me to do it. His batman sent me a letter telling me that Will had lost an arm, and, according to the doctors, the risk of infection meant that he had virtually no chance of surviving beyond six months. His last wish, he said, was to spare you the agony of waiting for the inevitable. He wanted you to move on with your life, and because you were so young, he was convinced that you would fall in love again quickly. Frankly, I had to agree with him."

"How *dared* you do such a thing, Charles!" Eugenia dashed away a tear with the back of her hand.

"You must not presume to criticize your brother," interposed Miss Preston-Smythe. "He was your guardian and knew what was best for you. And we *all* know how flighty you are."

Eugenia clenched her fists, and only the recollection that they were at a public gathering prevented her from making a most impolite retort. She turned back toward her brother.

"Perhaps you felt you were right at the time, Charles. But you must admit that things are different now."

"That is true enough," he agreed, more cheerfully. "You are not in love with him anymore."

And as he spoke, that notion was being shared by Major Stanfield as he stared into the fire of his bedroom in Berkeley Square. Throughout the long, agonizing months of his recovery, as he had fought against the horrors of infection and bloodletting, he had clung to his memories of Eugenia as a laughing young girl. He could not remember precisely when his fondness for Charles's sister had grown into something more profound; it was simply as though one day he had truly looked at her for the first time and seen the radiant beauty of her face. He, who was naturally of a serious bent, had felt his heart soaring

226

in a giddy spiral, and when he had finally taken her in his arms that Christmas Eve, he had felt a passion for her that was almost frightening in its intensity.

But Eugenia had been young, not just in years but in the lightheartedness of her temperament. Her professions of love could have been the outpourings of a transient infatuation, and with acute consciousness of the five years' difference between them, Will's innate caution had prevailed. No formal betrothal would be announced until his return, so that Eugenia could have the opportunity to meet other men and to decide whether or not her feelings for him were real. Later, when he had believed himself to be dying, he had been comforted by the thought that she would quickly find a new life for herself.

Now, as Will sipped from the brandy snifter held in his left hand, it seemed that his suspicions had been justified. It surprised him that Eugenia was still unwedded; moreover, he had assumed that she would be sobered and matured by the intervening years, much as he himself had been. Miss Foxworth, however, had not truly grown up after all but had remained the superficial creature he had always suspected her of being.

She had grown even more beautiful with time, of course, but by all reports she treated no man seriously, least of all those who were ensnared by her flirtatiousness. It was said that she had refused a number of offers and that she had declared herself to be uninterested in marriage. He was fortunate, he supposed, not to be bound by any formal vows to such a shallow creature!

But his expression was grim as he continued to watch the flames, long into the night.

"I simply cannot understand men," Eugenia declared as she paced back and forth across the Wellthorpes' morning parlor. The gown of fine merino swishing about her was a deep sapphire blue that made her golden eyes seem to sparkle even more furiously. Miss Frances Wellthorpe watched in sympathy with a slight frown knitting her fine brows. She herself was the picture of a gently bred young lady, a panel of embroidery resting in the lap of her cream-colored muslin frock. The edifying volume that the two ladies had intended to discuss as part of their weekly reading circle, a treatise on female suffrage, lay forgotten upon the sewing table.

"I do not know what is worse," Eugenia continued, "to be told a lie or to be told nothing at all. In both cases, I was being kept from the truth."

"It was a hurtful truth," her companion interjected. "Major Stanfield supposed that he would die, and you would have suffered, knowing that he was in terrible pain and being able to do nothing about it. You cannot blame him for wishing to shield you from that torture."

"Oh, Fanny, I know. But had I known that Will was alive, I could have found the camp where he was and helped nurse him back to recovery. I would have gone to any lengths to be with him."

"Perhaps that was precisely what Major Stanfield feared," Fanny replied. "You mustn't forget how dangerous it would have been for you to attempt any such thing. He knew that you were impulsive and headstrong, and could not let you put your own life at risk."

"But I am *not* like that!" She paused at her friend's skeptical expression. "At least, I am not the flibbertigibbet that Miss Priss and Charles seem to think I am. And speaking of Charles, his crime is really the worst of all."

Miss Wellthorpe went a delicate shade of pink. "You cannot blame your brother for carrying out what he thought was his friend's last wish."

"No, that is not what I meant. It is rather the fact that he failed to tell me as soon as he heard that Will might be alive."

"I am certain that he meant only to protect your feelings."

"Well, that was carrying his protectiveness a bit too far! And I do not know why you should try so hard to defend him!"

Eugenia glanced petulantly at Miss Wellthorpe, but her expression altered as she noticed her friend's flushed cheeks and tightly clasped hands. All of a sudden, the oddest notion dawned upon her. "Fanny, do you have a *tendre* for my brother?"

"No, no, do not say such a thing," Miss Wellthorpe stammered, looking away. "I did not wish—I would not for the world—"

"Forgive me, my dear, I did not mean to pry." Eugenia sank into the chair beside Miss Wellthorpe's and leaned forward to take hold of her hands. "Your secret is safe. But why did you not tell me?"

"He is engaged to Miss Preston-Smythe," was the simple reply. "Whatever feelings I—I might imagine myself to harbor would be wrong to have."

"But are you so certain that he could not return your regard?"

"Oh, pray do not say such things, Eugenia. I have accepted that there is no hope for me, and you must do the same."

A gleam entered Eugenia's eyes. Fanny and Charles? No, it would never work—he was too priggish, too formal. But then again, it was easy to overlook the attractive qualities in one's own brother, and presumably there was reason enough for Fanny to have fallen in love with him. He was, after all, a very eligible young man and good-looking in his own way. What was more, her friend would be just the sort of good wife Charles wished to have, while her gentle humor would temper his stubbornness and bring out the lighter side of his nature. Yes, Fanny and Charles! Of course, one could not forget his regrettable connection with Miss Preston-Smythe, but the date of the wedding would not be announced until Christmas, and that was still a week away. Many things might happen in the interim!

"But, Eugenia, we were speaking of you, not of me," Miss Wellthorpe said, interrupting that train of thought. "You must accept that Major Stanfield did what he thought was best for you at the time."

"How I loathe those words! 'What was best for you'; 'for your own good'! I shall never understand why men think that females are so witless, when most often quite the reverse is true. But Fanny, why would he be so cold to me now? How could he have treated me as though I were a stranger?"

"You must admit, Eugenia, that two years is a long time and that Major Stanfield must have been changed by his experiences. It is only natural to expect some distance of feeling."

Eugenia felt her heart constrict. "Not on my part. When I saw him, I thought that I—" She paused, biting her lip. "But Fanny, he was scarcely even polite to me. It was almost as though he—he disapproved of me."

"Perhaps he wished to appear aloof to save his pride in the event that you no longer cared for him. My mother has often said that gentlemen are sensitive about their vanity and that sometimes a show of coolness means that they fear to be rejected. Or perhaps he was afraid that you would be repelled by his wound. Many injured people are sensitive in that regard, you know."

"But I would never—oh, no!" She clapped her hand to her mouth. "Fanny, when I saw his arm, I was so shocked that I gasped aloud!"

"Oh, Eugenia, surely you did not!" Miss Wellthorpe reproved.

"I did. He must have thought I was disgusted by it, when all I could think of was how much he must have suffered. All those months after he left, I had nightmares about the horrors of the battlefield and those terrible infirmaries we all pretended not to know about. I still cannot bear to imagine it!"

"One cannot wonder at his chill reaction, then."

"I see now that it was no more than I deserved. When I see him, Fanny, I will explain to him the nature of our misunderstanding, and I will tell him that his injury makes not the least bit of difference to my feelings for him. Then, surely, this will all come right."

It was not until the day had passed, however, that Eugenia was forced to give up hope that Major Stanfield would respond to her invitation to pay a call at the Foxworth residence. Casting aside the proprieties in her impatience, she had gone so far as to send him a note, in response to which his valet had returned a brief billet stating that numerous engagements prevented Major Stanfield from sparing the time to visit at any time in the near future.

It was equally useless for her to seek to enlist Charles's aid on her behalf for he was nowhere to be found. In fact, had Eugenia been less preoccupied by her own concerns, she would have noticed that her brother was suffering from an unusual degree of moodiness. With the approach of Christmas, when the date of his impending nuptials would be announced, Charles was experiencing a marked lowering of spirits.

Miss Preston-Smythe, in the meantime, was becoming more forthright about the changes she intended to make at the Foxworth residence once she took up the reins as its mistress, as she liked to say. Miss Foxworth needed discipline as everyone knew, but there were many other faults to be found in any establishment governed by a mere bachelor. Slovenly habits were to be eradicated, and such lapses as the presence of disgusting animals would not be tolerated. Charles, who was quite comfortable with his bachelor habits and who enjoyed nothing more than a quiet evening with his dogs sleeping at his feet, was beginning to view the prospect of his future life with Miss Preston-Smythe with a feeling akin to apprehension. He therefore spent a great deal of time at his club, out of the

231

reaches of any female whatsoever.

Eugenia was therefore forced to conclude that if Major Stanfield would not come to her, she would go to him, and the only question that remained was how. She could not go alone, and Frances, albeit her dearest friend, would be agog with horror at the thought of going to a gentleman's lodgings. Eugenia thought too much of her friend to beg for her escort under any sort of false pretenses; there were others, however, for whom Eugenia had fewer scruples.

Thus it was that Miss Foxworth and Miss Preston-Smythe found themselves in a closed carriage at an early hour the following morning headed toward Berkeley Square. Both ladies were well bundled against the cold, and Miss Preston-Smythe thought privately that although she deplored Eugenia's taste for strong colors, she had to admit that the emerald lambswool cape Miss Foxworth wore was particularly becoming. It did not occur to her that there might be another reason for the special glow in her companion's cheeks.

"I am so grateful for your escort on this errand of mercy, Priscilla," Eugenia sighed. "Accustomed as you are to acts of charity, I knew that you could not refuse me."

Miss Preston-Smythe smiled coolly. Delivering baskets of fruit to the ailing was exactly the sort of role in which she fancied herself as a model of upright behavior. "What exactly is the nature of the complaint from which your friend suffers?"

"It is a condition which results in a certain, how shall I say, disfigurement. That is the reason why my friend prefers to remain unidentified to all but the closest friends and family."

Miss Preston-Smythe concealed a shudder.

"However," Eugenia continued, "I am assured that this condition is by no means contagious, but I shall not risk exposing you personally. It will be best for you to wait downstairs while I pay my visit."

232

As she spoke, the carriage drew to a halt in front of an elegant townhouse, and Eugenia leapt nimbly down without waiting for the groom's assistance. "Please wait here for a moment, Priscilla, so that I may be assured that my friend is feeling well enough to receive me."

She rang the bell, and when the door was opened, she uttered a cheery "Good morning," stepped past the startled, middle-aged man who stood there, and closed the door smartly behind herself before he could recover from his surprise.

"Do not be alarmed," she smiled at him. "I am really quite sane. I presume that you are Major Stanfield's valet?"

"My name is Rogers, Madam. I was the major's batman in the the war." He bowed slightly.

"How do you do, Rogers. I am Miss Eugenia Foxworth."

"You are Eugenia?" he exclaimed. "Begging your pardon, Miss Foxworth, but the major used to call that name when he—" Rogers cleared his throat. "What are you doing here, miss?"

"I must speak with the major in private, and he has refused to come to see me. So, I had to come myself."

"But miss, he will not receive you, and besides, you should not have come alone!"

"A lady is with me, Rogers, but this is where I need to ask for your assistance. I do not wish for her to know where we are. I have told her that we are visiting an ill friend of mine who does not wish to be identified. If you could keep her in the foyer and refuse to tell her the name of your employer, I will find a way to make Major Stanfield see me for half an hour."

Rogers frowned. "I do not see any reason why I should go against the major's wishes, miss."

Eugenia looked at him soberly, and her voice was very serious. "If I fail in my intent, Rogers, your master will be no more or less unhappy than he is now. If I succeed,

233

his life will be changed for the better."

"And what is your intent, miss?"

"To become Mrs. Stanfield."

The valet's eyebrows shot upwards and stayed there, even as his mouth slowly curved into a smile. "I see, miss. If you will be so kind as to bring your friend to the door, I will endeavor to do my part."

Eugenia sent him a warm look of gratitude on her way out, and a few minutes later the carriage had been sent round to the stables, and the two ladies had been shown into the front parlor. Miss Preston-Smythe had somewhat nervously accepted an offer of tea, and Miss Foxworth, carrying the basket of fruit, excused herself in order to pay her charitable visit.

It took a while for her to locate the major's whereabouts, but she finally opened the correct door, discovering him in his bedchamber. He sat in an armchair near the window, and she was relieved to see that he was decently clad, though he was still in shirtsleeves. Her eyes adored him silently, sweeping over the familiar lines of his handsome face and the broad set of his shoulders; he was more muscular than she had recalled, and the gravity of his expression was more pronounced.

He did not hear her entrance over the rustle of the newspaper which he was attempting to fold with his one hand, and it was not until she moved forward into the room that he became aware of her presence.

The major leapt to his feet with a startled oath, which Eugenia discreetly ignored. "Eugenia! What the devil are you doing here?" His face was very pale, a fact of which she might have taken notice had it not been for the pounding of her own heart.

"I came to see you, Will," she said softly. "I had to talk to you."

"You should not be here! Where's Rogers? I'll have his hide for this!" The major was finding it difficult to regain his bearings with the very woman he had sought to put out of his mind standing before him, her red hair glinting in the morning light.

"Pray keep your voice low; Priscilla Preston-Smythe is downstairs, and I do not want her to hear you. She does not know where we are, but her presence serves to mind the proprieties, so you need not concern yourself about that. And do not blame poor Rogers, because I gave him no choice but to cooperate.

"But none of that matters. Will, I had to tell you why I was so shocked to see you two days ago. I had mourned your death for so long, and even now, as I look at you, I can scarcely believe that you are still alive." Without being fully aware of her actions, she stepped closer and raised her hand in an involuntary gesture. But when she would have touched his chest, he moved aside, and the small rejection wounded her. "Why did you not tell me you were alive, Will?" she persisted. "How could you have been so cruel?"

The major's reply was curt in tone. "I did not think that I would survive my injury. It was best for you to go back to the pleasant life for which you were suited by nature and which I see you have been enjoying in my absence. I knew it would not be long before you had forgotten me."

"Will, you cannot mean what you are saying. I loved you so much, and when I thought that you were dead, I—" Tears blocked her throat for a moment. "I did not think that I could go on living. I had to pretend, so that no one knew. But Will, I—oh, please, let me hold you!"

Major Stanfield had no time to protest before Eugenia hurled herself against his chest. His arm tightened around her for a brief instant but then he recollected himself and released her, standing very still as she quietly sobbed against his shirt.

It took a moment for her to realize that her embrace was not being returned. The feel of his warm strength overwhelmed her senses at first, along with the reality

235

that he was truly alive; but then she gradually became aware that he was simply standing motionless before the storm of her own emotion. She forced her fingers to release the folds of his shirt, fighting a sharp stab of humiliation.

"You must compose yourself, Eugenia," Major Stanfield said coolly. "You are overwrought."

"I beg your pardon." She stepped away from him, fumbling for a handkerchief and averting her eyes. "I will endeavor not to embarrass you further."

"You do not . . . embarrass me." His voice was more gruff than he would have liked. "I simply do not wish for you to distress yourself further on my account. The past is over and done with; you have your own life, and I have mine."

Eugenia raised her head sharply at that, looking at him through eyes that were still moist. "What do you mean, Will? Are you married?"

He turned and walked toward the window, so that his features were harshly etched in the bright light. "No. I am scarcely a likely prospect for that now."

"What on earth do you mean?"

Major Stanfield laughed mockingly. "Oh, come now, Eugenia, you needn't pretend. I know that my infirmity renders me an object of disgust or pity in the eyes of most women; you yourself were repelled by it."

"No! I was shocked, which is not at all the same thing!"

"Forgive me if I fail to perceive the distinction. In any case, I cannot pretend to be the same man I was before, and no woman wishes to be chained to a cripple."

"You are being nonsensical!" Eugenia exclaimed indignantly. "A cripple indeed! Here you are, hale and handsome, and yet you speak as though you were prostrate upon your bed!"

"None the less, Eugenia, I am unfit to be a husband."

She narrowed her eyes. "Oh? Do you mean that there

236

were other parts of you shot off that you have failed to mention?"

"Eugenia!" He struggled against a smile and lost. "I meant that I cannot manage the simplest tasks. I cannot write a letter, I cannot ride, I cannot—"

"None of that counts for aught! You may learn to write with your left hand and I daresay other things besides. But even though you should be missing a dozen limbs, it would not matter to a woman who loved you. It does not matter to me!"

"You do not know what you are saying, my dear," Major Stanfield replied a shade too calmly. "You do not love me; what you feel is mere sympathy. And I can no longer be part of the active, sociable life that is so much a part of you. Riding to hounds, playing cards, dancing, all that is lost to me forever. We no longer suit, even if we thought we once did."

Eugenia could not bear to see the dreams that had quickened in her heart be crushed again without a struggle. "Will Stanfield, listen to me. I do love you. I never stopped loving you, and I never shall. Now I shall ask you a question, and I want a truthful answer: have you stopped loving me?"

Time had stopped for a long moment before he made his reply. "That is not the point."

"You cannot say no! Oh, Will!" Upon which exclamation she launched herself once more into his uncooperative embrace, this time flinging her arms about his neck and planting a kiss upon his cheek before letting go.

She faced him squarely, and what she glimpsed in his eyes gave her hope and the courage to continue. "You promised me a betrothal when you returned, Will, and I shall hold you to that promise."

The major frowned at her remark, but she was already whisking herself out the door.

When she came downstairs, Rogers was standing behind Miss Preston-Smythe's chair, and he cast her an enquiring look which changed to one of puzzlement when he perceived her red-rimmed eyes. Eugenia responded with a brief, rueful smile. No victory, but as yet no surrender!

Miss Preston-Smythe rose to her feet. "Why, Eugenia, have you been weeping?"

Miss Foxworth dabbed delicately at her eyes. "I'm afraid so, Priscilla. You see, I have just learned that my friend's ailment is . . . irreversible."

"What?" Priscilla exclaimed. "There is no hope of a cure?"

"Alas, no. Indeed, if what has been lost should somehow be restored, it would be nothing short of a medical miracle."

A loud snort from Rogers was turned hastily into a cough. Eugenia turned to him with only the faintest twinkle in her eye. "Would you be so kind as to summon our carriage?" she requested gravely.

"Of course, madam," Rogers replied with a bow. "And might I say, madam, I am assured that despite any contrariness of mood you may have encountered, the invalid was most grateful for the call."

The two ladies departed soon afterwards, much to the relief of Miss Preston-Smythe, who had no wish to linger in the presence of any mysterious diseases. And Eugenia, while not precisely cheered by her encounter with Major Stanfield, was nonetheless hopeful. It was perhaps enough of a miracle that he should be restored to her alive; the rest would depend upon her own ingenuity.

When she returned home, after depositing Miss Preston-Smythe at her own residence, she was surprised to find Charles in the library, going through a stack of accounts with apparent ill temper.

"These damned bills are all in confusion!" he exclaimed. "I must hire a man of business one of these days; I cannot make heads or tails of this!"

"Charles, is everything all right?" Eugenia inquired solicitously; normally, her levelheaded brother took great pride in managing the household accounts with his usual efficiency.

"No, it is not. Well, I suppose it is, but I have something of a headache. And where have you been this morning?"

Eugenia paused to remove her gloves. "Well . . ." she drawled, "I do not believe you would like it if I told you."

"What have you been up to now, Jen?" he sighed.

"'I have been paying a morning call upon Major Stanfield."

"*What* did you say?"

"I said, I have been—"

"I *heard* you say that! I meant, have you taken leave of your senses? You know better than to visit a gentleman's lodgings!"

"Oh, but I was not unescorted, Charles. Priscilla came with me."

"*Priscilla?* Oh, now I know you are funning. Miss Preston-Smythe is all that is proper, and I cannot imagine her engaging in such hoydenish behavior."

"Indeed? Well, all I shall say is that you may ask her yourself whether she accompanied me this morning and whether she waited in the front parlor for half an hour while I paid my call."

"My God!" Charles exclaimed. "Miss Preston-Smythe has always droned on about how undisciplined you are—which is, by the bye, absolutely *true,*—but I thought for certain that she herself would set a better example. In fact, her uprightness of character was the principal reason why I offered for her, even though personally I—"

"You what, Charles?"

"Never mind! I simply can scarce believe what I am hearing!"

"Do not exaggerate the crime, Charles," Eugenia said with a twinge of remorse. "No real harm was done."

"No harm, indeed! Your reputation, and hers, could

239

have been blasted forever. What if one of his male acquaintances had stopped by and found you there? You would have found yourself in a terribly compromising situation. This kind of thing is no more than I would have expected from you, Eugenia, but coming from Priscilla, this is rather a shock."

And with the supposedly perfect image of his betrothed thus further tainted in his mind, Charles went off to brood in solitude. Females were a pesky lot, indeed; in fact, the only ones of his acquaintance whom he actually liked were his sister, at times, and her friend, Frances Wellthorpe. Fanny was rather a taking little thing, come to think of it. But as for the rest of them, they were undoubtedly more trouble than they were worth.

Mr. Talbot toyed with his quizzing-glass, one elegantly booted foot crossed over the other as he lounged in the most comfortable chair of the Foxworth drawing room. He rather liked the new yellow color scheme; Eugenia, with her unerring eye, had chosen a bright shade that set off the room's dark wood and brass to perfection. It also set off her own coloring, and Mr. Talbot enjoyed the pretty picture she made as she perched upon the sofa in an amber-hued gown. His mood was guarded, nonetheless, as it had been ever since he had received her missive earlier that day, inviting him to pay a call.

"I may as well get straight to the point," Eugenia declared. "Henry, I need to ask you for some advice regarding the male sex."

Mr. Talbot sat up sharply. "I *beg* your pardon?"

"You heard me perfectly, I have no doubt. I have a question which I cannot very well ask of my own brother, and as you are my best acquaintance of the masculine gender, I will have to ask it of you."

A frisson went up Mr. Talbot's spine. "Eugenia, for the Lord's sake, surely there is some married female—Lady Wellthorpe, perhaps—who can help you. Not, I beg you, my humble self!"

"Oh, *dear!*" Eugenia clapped one hand to her laughing mouth. "How very improper you must think me! No, no, it is not *that* sort of question. What I need to know is simply this: what are the ways in which a girl can force a man to marry her?"

"Eugenia!" Mr. Talbot exclaimed, horrified. "What girl and what man? Surely you do not mean me, do you?"

"No, of course not. Well, perhaps yes, but only in the most hypothetical sense. And I am not speaking of the sort of conduct that leads to a hasty marriage over the anvil in Gretna Green. I am asking, what circumstances would make you, or any honorable gentleman, feel obliged to wed a particular female, even if you did not wish to do so?"

"I will only answer if you promise that it is some other poor devil you have in mind."

"Yes, of course, it is another poor devil entirely," she assured.

"Very well, then." At this point, Mr. Talbot chose to fortify himself with a long sip of tea, wishing that it was brandy instead. "There are a variety of situations, I suppose. The easiest would be for the chap, let us call him the P.D., to be penniless and for the lady to have a huge fortune. Will that do?"

"No, I am afraid it will not," Eugenia shook her head. "The P.D. has a healthy fortune himself, and besides, he would not marry for such a reason as that."

"A noble sort, eh? Well, let me think. There could have been a promise made among the parents and the young lady raised to think that she was betrothed to him all along. That would make it devilish difficult to draw back."

"No, that could not work here."

"Confound it, Eugenia!" Mr. Talbot exclaimed irritably. "If you don't like any of my ideas, you may think of your own! You are the one who reads novels, not I!"

241

"Do forgive me," Eugenia begged contritely. "Your ideas are very good indeed, but please think on. There has to be another possibility."

He frowned for a moment. "I suppose that if the P.D. found himself with the lady in a compromising situation, he would be obliged to offer for her."

Eugenia perked up visibly. "What kind of compromising situation?"

"You know—being alone in her bedchamber, that sort of thing."

"Or in his bedchamber?"

"Yes, of course."

"Oh, *dash* it all, Henry!" Eugenia declared. "I could have been compromised already, if only I'd had the sense!"

Mr. Talbot lifted an eyebrow but went on, ignoring the interruption. "It would be important, though not strictly necessary, to have someone discover the P.D. and the lady together, preferably her father."

"Or another male relative!" said Eugenia, brightening.

"I see that you have a grasp of the essentials," Mr. Talbot remarked drily.

"Thank you, Henry; I shall forever be in your debt for this!"

"I do not want your gratitude, thank you very much. What I want, Eugenia, is your solemn promise that whatever scheme you may hatch, you will keep me completely out of it!"

The next day, Christmas Eve, dawned brightly, and though the sky was slightly overcast, the temperature was warmer than expected. That was good news to many, including Eugenia, as she prepared for the social highlight of the holiday season to be held that night: the Earl and Countess of Claverton's masquerade. She had slept little the night before as her mind turned over various plans of strategy, but as the time for departure neared, her qualms were gradually replaced by a feeling of calm. No doubts could be permitted to interrupt her concentration now: tonight was the night for action!

Charles, on the other hand, was anticipating the evening with something more like dread. The more he reflected upon the behavior and character of Miss Preston-Smythe, the clearer it became that he had made a serious error of judgment. What had appeared to him to be refinement of taste now seemed mere snobbishness, and her staunch moral values now smacked of self-righteousness. He had never really wondered before why a lady possessed of blond beauty, good family, and secure fortune should have remained unwed; perhaps if he himself had not been so priggishly detached from the gossip at his club, he might have been warned off in advance. Now, the prospect of committing himself to the lady for life was daunting in the extreme.

And Major Stanfield, in his turn, was looking forward to the evening with mixed emotions. He had his own memories of that Christmas Eve past, and it seemed as though fate were determined to torture him in that regard. To have seen Eugenia again and to have virtually held her in his embrace had stirred up emotions he had thought to be long since controlled. In practical terms, of course, nothing had changed; as he was now, physically incapacitated and somber in disposition, he was the last man who could be compatible with the social butterfly Eugenia had always been and obviously still was. Her declarations of feeling were surely due to a combination of pity and misguided loyalty, and would soon fade. It was simply an unfortunate circumstance that the deep regard he cherished for her still burned as hotly as ever, for it would have to remain unrevealed.

The masquerade was too frivolous an entertainment to have drawn him out under most circumstances, but the long-standing friendship between his late father and the Earl of Claverton mandated his appearance. It was a gala affair, and when he arrived at nine, it was already threatening to turn into a crush. All the fires were lit, and many ladies, beneath their masks and satin dominos, were wishing they had brought their fans.

Major Stanfield stood to one side watching the gaily colored swirl of the dancers. As usual, it was easy to spot Eugenia in the crowd; not only did her coppery red hair gleam unmistakably bright, but she wore a domino of bright red that ought to have clashed but somehow did not.

"Major Stanfield?" a gentle voice inquired, and he turned to find Miss Frances Wellthorpe at his side. She was appealingly attired in a domino and mask of pale blue satin that enhanced the blue of her eyes, with silver-and-pearl eardrops dangling from her delicately shaped ears.

"Miss Wellthorpe." He bowed to her with his customary grace. "It seems a long time since I have seen you last; you were still in the schoolroom, I believe."

"Yes, Major. We used to meet in passing at the Foxworths. May I tell you, Major, how happy we all are that you are returned safely?"

He smiled his thanks down at her.

"And may I add that one lady in particular is not merely happy but is quite over the moon?"

The major's smile faded. "I am afraid that you are mistaken there, Miss Wellthorpe. It is only natural that in the initial shock of seeing someone thought to be lost, one may be deceived by one's emotions. Such reactions are not to be taken seriously, as you will someday learn from experience."

"Indeed?" Miss Wellthorpe's gaze sharpened as did her tone. "I already know a great deal more about such emotions than you may think, Major. And if you believe that Eugenia's feelings for you are shallow or transient, it is you who are sadly mistaken."

The suddenly frank turn of the conversation took Major Stanfield aback. "Miss Wellthorpe, I know that you mean well, but whatever may have existed between Miss Foxworth and myself is hardly of your concern."

Miss Wellthorpe drew in an indignant breath. "I beg to differ, Major. You know nothing of what has happened here in the last two years, whereas I have been a witness to Eugenia's own suffering."

"Suffering? I think not." Major Stanfield uttered a short laugh. "The admired and courted Miss Foxworth has enjoyed every minute of my absence. It is not that I wish to attach any blame, mind you; it is simply not in her nature to be serious or steadfast."

"I would not normally dream of saying this to a gentleman, Major Stanfield, but you are a damned fool." Miss Wellthorpe's cheeks were very pink, but she did not waver. "Eugenia Foxworth is the most courageous person I know. When Charles told us that you were killed, she was utterly devastated to the point where I knew that she was contemplating suicide. No, no," she shook her head in response to the major's agitated expression, "she did not attempt anything of the sort. But it took all of her strength to carry on normally and not give way to despair. She put on a bold front in order to spare the feelings of my mama and Charles, so that they would not know how deeply she was affected, but there were many times when she and I were alone, and the look in her eyes would make me want to weep. I still see that look, Major."

Major Stanfield was visibly shaken. "I still do not see how what you say can be true, considering her many amorous conquests."

"She has had many suitors, yes, because she is beautiful, charming, and possessed of a healthy fortune. What else would you expect? But she has never been a flirt, and she has always made it clear that she does not intend to marry. If others choose not to believe that she is sincere in that opinion, it is scarcely her fault."

Major Stanfield nodded in the direction of the dancers.

"Even so, Miss Wellthorpe, you must confess that Miss Foxworth and I are of two completely different temperaments. She spends all of her time in pursuit of the frivolous pleasures that I once enjoyed but can enjoy no more, even should I have any interest in doing so."

"Not all of her time is thus spent," Miss Wellthorpe contradicted him. "Eugenia is dedicated to a number of social causes, including female literacy, and she donates a good deal of her time and money to a school for indigent young women. She attends lectures on political topics and holds discussion meetings in her home. I know that such things are viewed askance in our world and that she is often held to be an eccentric, but I have no doubts about the sincerity or depth of her beliefs."

"Forgive me, Miss Wellthorpe, but why are you telling me this?"

She paused for a moment. "Perhaps it is because I am her friend, and I cannot stand to see her hopes dashed where you are concerned. Or perhaps it is because love is a very precious thing, and when it is shared by two people it is nothing short of a miracle. If you care for someone, and you are lucky enough to have them care for you, you must not throw such a miracle away."

Major Stanfield looked at her sharply. "Do you speak again from experience, Miss Wellthorpe?"

"No, no, of course not," she stammered, and this time it was not indignation which reddened her cheeks. "I see my mama waving at me, Major, so I can speak no further. But please, I beg of you, do not dismiss what I have told you. And when you see Eugenia, ask her what it is that she wears around her neck." Upon those words, Miss Wellthorpe vanished into the crowd, leaving Major Stanfield alone with the tumult of his thoughts.

The lady under discussion, meanwhile, was preparing to put a plan into motion that was about to tarnish the portrait of virtue just painted by her friend. She had located a small sitting room curtained off from the hallway

246

upstairs and was busily arranging herself upon the sofa. Her domino was at hand, ready to be donned at a moment's notice if needed, but Eugenia was engaged in loosening the bodice of her gown to expose one creamy shoulder, mussing her hair, and otherwise creating an image of dishevelment.

Mr. Henry Talbot, who remained blissfully ignorant of his role in the plan, was scanning the crowd. Eugenia had asked him to summon Major Stanfield to the first room on the right, upstairs; then, she said, he was to wait a few minutes and give the same message to her brother, adding that she was in need of assistance. Mr. Talbot had no wish to know what this was all about, but he accepted his orders gracefully. The only inconvenience was that neither Major Stanfield nor Mr. Foxworth was in sight.

He did recognize Miss Wellthorpe moving near him in the crowd, however, and decided to ask for her assistance.

"I say, Miss Wellthorpe," he hailed her. "Have you seen Stanfield tonight? Eugenia wants to see him upstairs, straight away."

"Yes, he is in the blue salon. But why would Eugenia ask to see him privately? Is she in some sort of difficulty?"

Mr. Talbot shrugged. "Haven't the foggiest and don't want to. I just do as I am told." Upon which, he moved away.

Miss Wellthorpe, however, was disconcerted. Eugenia could not know what had just been said about her; what if she were to play the flirt and thus unknowingly undermine all of Frances's good intentions? Miss Wellthorpe rushed towards the stairwell.

When she reached the first room, she threw back the curtain and was met with a shocking sight. Eugenia lay on the couch in an apparent state of disarray, one arm dangling listlessly while the other was flung dramatically across her brow.

"Eugenia!" Miss Wellthorpe exclaimed, running forward in her anxious haste. "Are you all—" Unfortunately, she failed to see a small footstool and tripped over it, falling hard.

"Fanny!" Eugenia sat bolt upright. "For pity's sake, what are you doing?" In a moment, however, irritation at her friend's unwelcome appearance gave way to concern. "Fanny, are you hurt? Speak to me!" Eugenia jumped from the couch and ran to kneel at Miss Wellthorpe's side.

"Oh, my head," Miss Wellthorpe murmured. "I must have struck it against something, it hurts so. And it feels so hot in here, I can scarcely breathe."

"Here, let me assist you." Eugenia tried to raise her but could not; instead, she had to content herself with removing Miss Wellthorpe's mask and loosening the ribbons at the neck of her gown to give her more air.

"What is going on here?" At that moment, Charles strode into the room. "Henry Talbot told me you were looking for me, Jen, but—Miss Wellthorpe, why are you on the floor?"

"Fanny has struck her head, Charles. Henry got it all wrong, but oh, I *am* glad to see you. Can you help me move Fanny to the couch? I am not strong enough to lift her."

Charles bent and lifted Miss Wellthorpe in his strong arms, and at that moment, her blue eyes flickered open, and she uttered a soft gasp. He stood without moving, an expression of dawning surprise upon his face.

Eugenia, meanwhile, had rushed into the hall in search of help, only to encounter Miss Preston-Smythe. "Where is your brother, Eugenia?" the lady demanded in peremptory fashion. "I heard Mr. Talbot ask him to come up here, and I wish to know what is going on!"

"Wait a moment," Eugenia cried, but Miss Preston-Smythe had already swept forward into the room and emitted a shriek at the sight she beheld. Miss Wellthorpe, herself in a becoming state of disarray, was being held aloft in the arms of Mr. Foxworth, and neither one showed any signs of dissatisfaction with the situation.

Upon hearing the shriek, however, both their heads turned, and a similar look of guilty consternation came over their faces.

"Well, what have we here?" exclaimed Miss Preston-Smythe angrily. "I never dreamt that I should ever see *you*, Miss Wellthorpe, showing such a reprehensible want of conduct! And as for you, Charles, I see that I have been sadly taken in by your gentlemanly veneer. For you to engage in dalliance on the very eve of announcing our wedding date is the outside of enough!"

"Priscilla, this is not what you —" Charles began.

"Not another word from you, sir! Our engagement is at an end!" And with a flounce of her skirts, Miss Preston-Smythe swept out of the door.

Eugenia stared after her with lips parted in astonishment. A compromising situation had indeed occurred but not the one she had so artfully planned! Her trepidation was soothed, however, by the smiling look now being exchanged by the two culprits as Eugenia walked back inside the room.

"You had better put her down now, Charles," Eugenia chided fondly. "You will have plenty of opportunity for that sort of thing later on, I daresay."

"Eugenia!" Miss Wellthorpe exclaimed, blushing. She showed no inclination to unwind her arms from around Mr. Foxworth's neck, however, as he set her gently upon the sofa. "Thank you, Charles, I feel much better now," she added demurely.

It was at that moment that Major Stanfield arrived with Mr. Talbot following close behind. "Will someone tell me what is going on here?" the major commanded, taking rapid note of the fact that Mr. Foxworth and Miss Wellthorpe were apparently cuddling each other upon the sofa.

"I can explain, Will," Mr. Foxworth said, rising to his

feet. "It cannot be announced right away, but Miss Wellthorpe is going to become my wife."

"So I see," the major commented. "You seem to have been practicing for the honeymoon."

"Not at all!" Charles blushed. "Miss Wellthorpe appears this way only because she suffered a fall."

"That is true," Miss Wellthorpe agreed. "You see, when I found Eugenia lying on the sofa in such a shocking state, I ran toward her and tripped, striking my head."

Major Stanfield turned toward Eugenia, and his dark eyes swept over her, missing nothing of her exposed shoulder and disheveled hair. "And what was Miss Foxworth doing in this room to begin with, pray?"

"Well, you see," Mr. Talbot spoke up helpfully. "Eugenia and I—"

Before he could finish his sentence, however, Major Stanfield strode forward and delivered a left-handed punch to the jaw that sent Mr. Talbot reeling backwards, landing heavily upon the floor.

"You filthy bounder," the major ground out. "You dared—"

"No, I did not!" Mr. Talbot defended. "Eugenia, tell him! And will you please also tell him that Boxing Day is the day *after* Christmas, not the day before!"

Eugenia's attention, however, was distracted. "William Stanfield, I do believe you are jealous!"

The major turned the full force of his angry gaze upon her. "No, I am not!"

"Yes, you are! You claim to have no feelings for me, but here you are, engaging in a jealous brawl. And what is more," Eugenia continued, warming to her subject, "you, who despise and reject all frivolous pursuits, are exposing two ladies to a display of fisticuffs!"

"You always did have a punishing left, Will," Charles murmured slyly.

"Your one-two combination was better," the major allowed, his features softening into a smile.

250

"There, you see, Fanny? Now he is using that horrid boxing cant in front of us. You are all witnesses to Major Stanfield's shockingly improper behavior!"

The major's attention, meanwhile, was captured by the slender chain that lay against the pale column of Eugenia's throat. He reached for it, tugging gently until the seed-pearl ring came into view.

"You have worn this all along?" he murmured incredulously.

"Next to my heart," she whispered.

The major looked deeply into her eyes, and then slowly he smiled, and her heart turned over. "I see that I have been well and truly outflanked on all counts," he said gravely. "How may I atone for my breach of conduct, Miss Foxworth?"

Eugenia turned toward her audience. "Well?"

Charles shook his head. "You'll have to marry her, old man."

Miss Wellthorpe nodded mournfully. "Nothing less than marriage will serve."

Mr. Talbot opened one eye. "If you want my opinion, a glass of brandy would do the trick. But if you are going to marry her, you had better do so straight away, before anyone else gets hurt!"

Major Stanfield bowed solemnly toward Eugenia, and only the laughing glint in his eyes gave him away. "Well, Miss Foxworth? Will you give me a happy Christmas by doing me the honor of becoming my wife?"

"I will," Eugenia replied, moving into the warmth of his embrace, "if you would only be so good as to compromise me a bit further, just to make sure . . ."

And so he did.

The Yuletide Wish
by Dawn Aldridge Poore

"I wish you wouldn't try to make me feel guilty, Mama. I do not intend to present myself when Ryven and Miss Darcy arrive. That's all there is to it." Miss Anthea Thorne's blue eyes snapped with irritation. "Ryven means nothing to me one way or the other."

"And I suppose Mr. Wolcott does?" her mother suggested, moving her footstool so that her feet were closer to the fire. "Don't try to cozen me, Anthea. I know exactly why you refused Vincent Wolcott's offer. For the four years past, you've been comparing every man you meet with Ryven and, although you won't admit it to me or to yourself, you've found every other man sadly lacking."

Anthea's cheeks burned and she turned to the window to keep her mother from seeing her. "Chatwin says it's going to snow," she said finally, idly watching the heavy black clouds pile up in the sky. "It would be nice to have snow for Christmas."

"I agree, however, Christmas is two weeks away and, besides, Chatwin's always predicting snow. I'd almost believe he'd predict snow in July. It might serve to keep him from tending the garden properly."

"Chatwin's a wonderful gardener, Mama." Anthea turned to look at her mother in surprise. "Thornedene's gardens are the pride of the county."

"I know," Lady Lynden said complacently, "and that's all because of my doing, I assure you. If I weren't here to nudge

Chatwin at every opportunity, the gardens would be a weedy mess."

"You're very good at nudging, Mama," Anthea said with a laugh, turning away from the window.

"Thank you, my dear. One of the lessons every lady should learn is how to manage people properly. Of course, I assure you that I nudge only when necessary. I believe," she added with a smile, "that your father calls it meddling, but even he must admit that I always get results." There was a short pause as she waited for Anthea to cross the room. "Sit here by me, Anthea." She patted the cushion beside her. "We need to talk."

"Don't try to nudge me, Mama." Anthea sat, but there was a stubborn set to her mouth. "It's no use to discuss Ryven. I do not wish to see him while he's here. His letter said he and Miss Darcy were only going to stop by on their way to Morven Hall so they could drop Dickon off to spend Christmas with us. At most, they should be here perhaps an hour or so."

Lady Lynden rolled her eyes toward the ceiling. "And to think my own flesh and blood is such a coward. You should be down here, Anthea, dressed to the nines, reminding Ryven what he could have had."

"If not having to look at that odious creature is cowardly, then so be it," Anthea said. "Besides, rumor has it that he's going to offer for Miss Darcy at Christmas. I heard that they'll announce their engagement at the New Year's ball at Morven."

"I see you've kept up with that 'odious creature' enough to know about his comings and goings, not to mention impending engagements." Lady Lynden's tone was dry.

"Not really." Anthea wouldn't meet her mother's eyes. "Lizzie Bowen just happened to mention it in her last letter to me." She paused. "I couldn't believe it, Mama. Judith Darcy! 'Look like the innocent flower, but be the serpent under't.' That's Judith Darcy. Ryven doesn't know what he's getting."

"You could do something about that if you wished, Anthea."

"No, Mama." Anthea's tone was final. "I can't. Ryven made it perfectly plain that he doesn't care at all for me, and now I refuse to have anything to do with him. I despise the man." She stood up and shook her skirts.

"Anthea, please sit back down." Lady Lynden's voice was mild, but there was a hint of steel under it. Anthea sat. "There. That's better." There was another pause while Lady Lynden thought. "We've needed to have this talk for a while, and I do admit to being remiss. I thought the problem would take care of itself, that you would develop a *tendre* for someone and settle down. But since you refused Wolcott's offer . . ."

"Mama, this isn't at all necessary. I do not choose to be married."

"Of course you choose to be married, Anthea. It's the only thing to do. When Ryven asked you to break your engagement to him four years ago, I didn't like it above half, but I could understand his reasons."

"What?" Anthea's voice was bitter. "That he 'wasn't ready' to get married. Not ready at one and twenty?"

Lady Lynden frowned a little, then patted Anthea's hand. "He wasn't ready, even though he was one and twenty. You, at seventeen, were more ready than he was. Yes, Anthea, it was the best thing that he asked you to break the engagement then."

"And I suppose, Mama, that now he's quite ready to marry Miss Darcy." Try as she might, Anthea could not keep her voice from shaking. Lady Lynden glanced at her but did not remark it.

"Yes, I think now that Ryven's ready for marriage," Lady Lynden said placidly. "Hold up your hands." She began winding her wools around Anthea's upraised hands, straightening the strands as she worked. "My point is, Anthea, that you've allowed this . . . this contretemps between you and Ryven to displace your whole life. You were but seventeen, but you insisted on returning to Thornedene. I

257

was busy seeing your father off to Portugal, or I would have made sure you stayed in London and enjoyed yourself. As it was, you came to Thornedene and you've practically made a vocation of languishing on the vine."

"I've done no such thing!" Anthea exclaimed. She tried to move her hands but had to keep them still to keep the wool taut. "Really, Mama! Languishing on the vine, indeed."

"It's true, Anthea. You've all but retired from society and you're but one and twenty. Your brother's only twelve years old, but I believe he goes out more than you do."

"At least Ned isn't thrown in the way of every single man in England," Anthea said heatedly. "It's embarrassing. The last time I visited Cousin Margaret, she had a different bachelor to supper every night."

"I thought as much. If I recall, you feigned illness and came back to Thornedene."

"I wasn't feigning. I was sick to death of being paraded in front of everyone like some calf up at auction." Anthea giggled at the recollection. "Mama, it was terrible. After the first fortnight, Margaret was reduced to bringing in whomever she could find—the only requirement was eligibility. When she brought in poor Hazelwood—the one with the terrible squint—I thought it best to put her out of her misery and return to Thornedene."

"Then you aren't comparing all men to Ryven?" Lady Lynden rolled the wool into a ball, put it into her basket, and Anthea dropped her hands to her lap.

"Of course not!"

"Well, then am I to conclude that you may reconsider and look favorably on Mr. Wolcott?"

Anthea was visibly alarmed. "Mama! Really! Mr. Wolcott is very nice, unexceptionable even, but . . ." She let her words trail off.

"I believe I understand, my dear." After a moment Lady Lynden patted Anthea's hand. "Yes, I understand—perfectly. Will you hand me my embroidery?"

The door was flung open, and Ned ran headlong into the room. "How much longer, Annie?" he asked, hopping from first one foot to the other.

"Not long. I can't believe you're this excited about Dickon coming to spend Christmas with you."

Ned sprawled on the floor in front of the fire. "I am. I haven't seen him since he had to go to Italy with his aunt. I can't wait!" With that, he was on his feet again, running to the window.

"Chatwin says it's going to snow," Anthea told him with a laugh, crossing to the window. She put her arm around her brother's shoulders, and they looked out. "You and Dickon can make snow angels and a snow fort."

"Will you help us? You make the best snow forts of anybody, Annie." He looked at her, then back out the window. "Maybe it'll snow ten feet."

"I certainly hope not," Lady Lynden said, putting aside her workbasket and looking fondly at the heir. "Don't get your hopes up, Ned. It probably won't snow at all—you know how Chatwin's predictions are." She stood. "Now run along, dears. Anthea, think about what I said, and perhaps you'll want to come down and meet Ryven and Miss Darcy, after all."

"Of course she will," Ned said. "It would break Nicholas's heart if he doesn't get to see you, Annie. I'd wager he would."

Anthea ruffled Ned's hair, a fine, silky blond like her own. "You're too young to wager, you imp, and don't you dare address Ryven as Nicholas. You're to call him by his style."

"Why? He once told me to call him Nicholas. I remember that."

"That was a long time ago," Anthea said, turning away.

"Will we be expecting you down?" Lady Lynden asked.

Anthea paused, thinking of an excuse. "I don't think so."

Ned ran over and took her hand. "Of course she'll come down to see Nicholas—Ryven, I mean. Dickon told me that Nic—Ryven was looking forward to seeing you, Annie, and Dickon knows everything there is to know about Nicholas."

"Brothers always know more than they should," Anthea

259

said with a laugh. "If you promise to hush, I'll think about coming down." She went out, Ned dragging her along as he chattered on about plans for a snow fort and, if the gods of the weather proved benevolent, weather cold enough to freeze the pond so he, Dickon, and Annie could go skating.

As a door shut behind them, Lady Lynden leaned back in her chair and thought a while. Finally, she wiggled her warm toes and sighed in satisfaction. "Just a little nudge in the right direction," she said aloud to herself. "I think that will do nicely." She smiled and rang for tea, quite pleased with herself.

Outside, the first flakes began to float lazily down to the ground.

After settling Ned down with chocolate and biscuits and placing him where he could see the drive, Anthea went to her room. Maybe, just maybe, Mama was right—perhaps she was taking the cowardly way out. She glanced in the mirror. She hadn't even seen Nicholas Moreland, Viscount Ryven, since the day he had asked her to break their engagement four years ago. Except once, she hastily reminded herself—once when she had been with Margaret and had seen him driving in the park with the Season's current lovely by his side. Anthea had moved away, and he hadn't seen her, but the sight of him had been so painful that she left London and hurried back to Thornedene. That had been two years ago. Since then, she had been careful to plan her visits to London. The world of the Ton was so small that it was almost impossible to avoid someone.

"I am being a coward," she said to her reflection in the mirror. "Mama's right—I should show that odious man what he missed." She made a face at her reflection and rang for Parrish, her maid and dresser, a pearl beyond price when it came to working wizardry with the rouge pot and hairbrush. Parrish had had several offers better than service with Anthea, but she preferred to stay at Thornedene. She said it was because she couldn't trust her dear Miss Thorne to anyone else, but Anthea knew the real reason: Parrish and Chatwin had an "understanding."

By the time Parrish had finished, Anthea felt she looked better than she had ever looked in her life. She hadn't told Parrish why she wanted to look good, it wasn't necessary— Parrish *knew*.

Anthea went down, only to be met by an excited Ned. "Annie, its snowing! Did you see? If it keeps this up, we'll have enough snow for a little snow fort." He grabbed her hand and dragged her over to the front window so she could see for herself.

Ned was right. Two or three inches of fluffy snow covered the ground, and it was still coming down from a gray sky, although slowly and lazily.

"Will they get here before it gets too bad to travel?" Ned asked anxiously.

Anthea patted his head and hugged him. "Certainly. They should be here any time. Parrish told me that Chatwin had told her that their baggage wagon had already dropped off Dickon's trunk. Dickon should be along presently."

"Look, Annie, is that something?" Ned pointed to a smudge on the horizon, barely visible through the snow. Anthea peered out the window. "I don't know, Ned." They stood for a few minutes until they were able to see for sure that a carriage was coming up the driveway. Ned remained by the door, while Anthea went to the drawing room so she could be reclining prettily on the sofa when Ryven and Miss Darcy arrived. She would be the picture of someone without a care in the world.

Anthea heard the voices in the hall and carefully placed herself to advantage on the sofa, holding a novel to read. In just a moment the door was flung open and two females rushed in. A very large, wet, bushy cat leapt from the older lady's arms and jumped right on Anthea's stomach, leaving the imprint of two muddy, snow-encrusted paws.

"Oh, Puffy, you bad little baby!" Mrs. Darcy shrieked, snatching up the cat as it yowled and spat right in Anthea's face. "Mama's little baby shouldn't be bad!"

Anthea leapt to her feet, trying to keep her temper as Puffy jumped to the floor and began arching its back and

261

hissing while it clawed at Anthea's ankles. Anthea jumped back to avoid a second vicious swipe of its claws against her stockings and fell backward over Lady Lynden's footstool, landing with her legs on the footstool, her derrière on the floor between the chair and stool, and the rest of her propped inelegantly up against the front of the chair.

"An interesting pose, Miss Thorne," a familiar, lazy voice drawled. "I did not recall that you were particularly afraid of wild animals."

"Nicky, how can you malign Mama's poor little Puffy?" Miss Judith Darcy asked, a pretty, practiced pout on her face. She placed a hand on Ryven's arm, unmistakably signifying her claim, and smiled down at Anthea.

Anthea did not smile back. Instead, she looked straight up from the floor right into Ryven's green eyes and quite caught her breath. Four years ago she had thought Ryven one of the handsomest men around, but now . . . He had grown a trifle taller and filled out. His shoulders were broad under his bottle green coat and his brown hair was cut to frame his face. It took Anthea a second to realize the difference—four years ago he had been a good-looking boy, now he was the handsomest man she had ever seen.

Ned and Dickon rushed in and saved Anthea from having to reply to him. "Annie, isn't this famous—Dickon has brought along his pet mouse." Ned set a cage containing a frantic mouse on the table. "Good Heavens, Annie," he said, staring at her as she tried to get in a more presentable position, "What happened to you? Your dress is all muddy, and you really shouldn't be sitting on the floor. Not with company here, anyway."

Anthea's answer was drowned out as Puffy escaped his mistress once again and landed on the mouse cage, snarling, hissing, and yowling. Ryven took advantage of the confusion to offer his hand to Anthea and help her up. Anthea thought for a second about refusing but decided that would be churlish, so she took his hand. It was almost a jolt when they touched, rather like Mama's description of her electrical treatments at Bath. Anthea didn't dare look at Ryven.

Instead, she busied herself with brushing off her gown as best she could and trying to fight down the blazing heat in her cheeks. "You're looking particularly fine, Annie," he said softly, close to her ear so she could hear him in the din.

"Thank you," she answered stiffly, pulling away. She didn't want to say more. This had been a terrible mistake— she should have stayed in her chambers as she had planned. Instead of making Ryven realize what he had missed, the tables were turned. She glanced up to find Miss Darcy looking at the two of them. Miss Darcy stepped forward, neatly placing herself between Ryven and Anthea.

"Nicky dear, I do hate to be impolite, but don't you think we need to leave soon? The weather looks so forbidding."

"Judith, I simply cannot travel again until I have refreshed myself," Mrs. Darcy said, collapsing on the sofa. "Puffy is so out of sorts, and I need a pot of tea and something to eat."

Anthea, glad for a diversion, took charge, sending Ned and Dickon upstairs with the offending mouse, sending to the kitchen for cream and a treat for Puffy, ringing for tea and cakes, and having a footman fetch her mother. Lady Lynden came in just as everyone finally got quiet and settled down in front of the fire.

"My dear Ryven, Mrs. and Miss Darcy. How wonderful to see you." Lady Lynden advanced into the room and glanced at Anthea. Her eyes widened as she saw the muddy pawprints on Anthea's gown, but, practiced hostess that she was, she ignored it and sat down beside Mrs. Darcy. "I have so wished to meet you and your charming daughter, Mrs. Darcy," she said, pouring tea and passing it around. "I know you must be fatigued from your journey."

"It's been terrible, just terrible," Mrs. Darcy said as Puffy finished his cream and jumped up on his mistress's lap. "Look, my little darling is so tired and journeyworn."

Lady Lynden glanced in sympathy at Miss Darcy. "I'm sorry to hear that, Mrs. Darcy. I wouldn't think of letting your charming daughter leave Thornedene in such a state.

263

My dear, would you like to go upstairs and rest for a short while?"

"I think Mrs. Darcy is speaking of Puffy being tired and worn, Mama," Anthea said, enjoying the sight of Ryven squirming as Puffy hopped onto his lap and began shedding long, white hairs all over the front of his coat.

"Oh, I'm sorry." Lady Lynden stifled a smile.

"If Judith isn't fagged, she should be. We cracked a wheel and had to stop to get it repaired. That's why we're late, and to tell the truth, Lady Lynden," Mrs. Darcy leaned forward to get her cup refilled and have another cake placed on her plate, "the accommodations were not of the best."

Lady Lynden plied her with extra cakes. "In that case, Mrs. Darcy, could I offer you the opportunity to rest and refresh yourself a few minutes upstairs? You do look quite tired."

"Really, Mama, I don't think we have time, and what with the weather—" Judith Darcy began, but Ryven interrupted her.

"I do believe a little rest would help you make it through the rest of the journey, Mrs. Darcy. The snow seems to be tapering off. If you wish to rest for an hour, we can still be at Morven before dark."

Anthea glanced out the window. It seemed to her that the snow had increased, but surely Ryven had noticed that. She turned her attention to what her mother was saying. "It's settled then," Lady Lynden said briskly as she rang for the servants. "I wouldn't dream of allowing you to continue your journey as fatigued as you are, my dear Mrs. Darcy. Ryven, I'll send a footman on horseback to Morven to tell them you'll be there later."

Recognizing a natural commander, Ryven nodded. "That will give me time to make sure Dickon is settled in with his mouse and baggage." He looked around the room as Anthea avoided his eyes.

"By all means, make sure the mouse is settled." There was an acid edge to Miss Darcy's voice, but Ryven smiled blandly at her.

264

"Boys do get attached to pets," Lady Lynden said. "I'm sure you care a great deal for your pet, Mrs. Darcy."

"Oh, my, yes! I couldn't live without my Puffy." Puffy answered to this by jumping across Lady Lynden's lap and making a halfhearted lunge at Ryven's boots, but Ryven merely picked him up and handed him to Mrs. Darcy. "In an hour or so then, ladies?" He turned to leave, and Anthea could have sworn he winked at her.

As soon as Mrs. and Miss Darcy were settled in behind closed bedroom doors to rest, Anthea turned to her mother. "How could you?" she demanded.

"Anthea, really! Have we ever turned a weary traveler away from Thornedene?" Lady Lynden paused a second. "I do believe you should have Parrish look at that gown before the stain sets." With that she was off down the stairs, leaving Anthea standing there. Anthea heard Ryven's voice at the foot of the stairs and did the only thing she felt she could do in the circumstances — she fled to her room and rang for Parrish.

An hour later, dressed to Parrish's satisfaction in another gown, Anthea started down the stairs. Ned and Dickon came running up the steps, whispering loudly. "Annie," Ned gasped excitedly, "do you want to come on up and see Bertram?"

"Who is Bertram, and why are you whispering?" She put her arm around both Ned's and Dickon's shoulders as they stood next to her.

"We have to whisper — Mama said so. She said she'd banish us to the nursery forever if we woke Mrs. Darcy," Ned said, looking around the corner toward Mrs. Darcy's room. "Mama said Mrs. Darcy needed to rest as long as possible."

"And Bertram is my mouse," Dickon added, getting to the most important part before Anthea could ask why Mrs. Darcy shouldn't be disturbed. "Nicholas bought Bertram for me so I could have a little pet of my very own to carry with me when I had to go to Italy. I had wanted a bird, but I'm glad Nicholas got me a mouse. Bertram's ever so much nicer than a bird."

"Yes," Ned agreed. "Annie, you can take him right out of his cage and put him in your pocket—if you want to—as long as you're careful to keep your hand on him."

"You have to keep your hand on him?"

"Nicholas said Bertram might run away if I didn't hold him," Dickon said gravely, "but he likes to be held and petted."

"Do you want to see him, Annie?" Ned asked enthusiastically, tugging eagerly on her hand.

One of the last things—if not *the* last thing—she wanted to do was hold and pet a mouse, but there was no resisting the appeal in Ned's and Dickon's eyes. "I'd love to," Anthea said. She walked to the nursery between the two of them as they chattered without stopping. Inside, she saw Bertram's cage held the place of honor on a table in front of the window. "So Bertram could watch the snow," Dickon explained gravely, taking Bertram out and carefully handing him to Anthea. "Nicholas says I must be careful and not let Bertram get lost. I watch him every minute he's out of his cage."

"A good idea," Anthea agreed, holding Bertram carefully and scratching him behind one pinkish, almost translucent ear. "I imagine you've grown quite attached to Bertram."

Dickon nodded. "I love him almost as much as I love Nicholas."

"I certainly hope I should rank above a mouse." Anthea turned toward the sound and started as she saw Nicholas lounging in the nursery doorway. "Careful there, Annie," he said, coming across to the window and clasping her hands in his to make a safer bed for Bertram. "We mustn't allow Bertram to escape," he said with a chuckle, "or I think Dickon would have both our heads." He took the mouse from her palms and placed it back in the cage, carefully snapping the latch. "There, Dickon, Bertram's all safe and sound."

"Good." Dickon looked at his big brother with affection. "I wish you could stay for Christmas. When do you have to leave?"

Nicholas ruffled Dickon's hair. "I can't stay until Christmas, but I may be here for a few days—look at that snow."

Anthea felt herself go pale, and she bent over the cage to look out the window. There were several inches of fluffy snow on the ground, and more was coming down fast and thick.

"Oh good!" Ned said joyously. "You can stay and help us build a snow fort. Annie's already promised."

"Ned, I really don't think Ryven would want to build snow forts with us," Anthea said, while at the same time, Nicholas said, "I'd like nothing better! Dickon and I haven't built a snow fort in ages."

"Our fort against yours!" Dickon said to Ned as the two of them danced around in excitement. "We can beat you, I know it!"

Caught up in their enthusiasm, Anthea laughed. "You won't have a chance, Dickon. I warn you that Ned and I are unsurpassed in building snow forts!" She turned, eyes sparkling, to see Nicholas staring at her in an odd way. Quickly she turned away and looked back out the window to hide her confusion. "At any rate, we can't begin to build one until the snow stops."

"Are you sure you're going to stay, Nicholas?" Dickon asked. It was plain that nothing would please him more.

Ryven nodded. "I just came from talking to Lady Lynden. There's plenty of room here, so we'll stay until the road is passable. How long depends on the weather."

Ned and Dickon were ecstatic, planning snow forts, snow men, snow angels, sleigh rides, and skating if the pond froze. Anthea, however, felt the blood drain from her face as she stared numbly at the falling snow outside. Days in the same house with Ryven and Judith Darcy! She didn't know how she would endure it. With a mumbled excuse, she left, leaving Ned, Dickon, and Ryven making plans together.

Anthea evidently found the enforced visit no more disagreeable than did Miss Darcy, who was so overset at the news that she began berating her mother in front of everyone. Miss Darcy felt that if Mrs. Darcy had gone on as planned, the party could have made it to Morven Hall before the snow worsened.

"On the contrary," Lady Lynden said mildly. "You were absolutely correct to stay here, Mrs. Darcy. Only think what could have happened if you and Miss Darcy had been stranded in the snow."

"So true." Mrs. Darcy sat and fanned herself vigorously. "I don't believe my health would have withstood the shock. I'm rather delicate, you know."

"I can see that," Lady Lynden observed, her glance taking in Mrs. Darcy's robust, buxom form. "One should never take chances with delicate health."

Defeated, Miss Darcy flounced to a chair and sat. "Fustian!" she said, glaring at her mother. She didn't dare glare at Lady Lynden.

By the next morning, the snow had stopped, and the sky was a hard, clear blue. The temperature had turned bitterly cold, so there was no chance of the snow melting for several days. "Aye, it'll be on the ground for a long spell," Chatwin said gloomily. Ned and Dickon were in alt. Anthea was not.

"Perhaps," she said to Ryven as she buttered her breakfast muffin, "you and Miss Darcy should ride on to Morven on horseback. I'm sure they're anxious about you."

"On the contrary." He reached for the jam at the same time she did and touched her hand. There was the barest hint of a smile on his face as she jerked her hand back. He picked up the jam and spooned some out. "I couldn't possibly let a delicate soul like Miss Darcy get out in this weather. I'm afraid she'd be quite overset to have to go floundering through snowdrifts while she was trying to look fashionably elegant. It wouldn't do at all. Jam?" He placed the jam pot in front of her plate.

"I merely thought someone at Morven Hall might be worried." Anthea tried to keep her voice level.

"I thought that as well and sent a footman on horseback over this morning to tell them we'd be here for a few days." He looked at her in mock dismay. "Don't tell me you've for-

268

gotten that Ned, Dickon, you, and I are to build snow forts today? Will you do me the honor of being my partner?"

"I've already promised Ned," Anthea said, "and it would seem to me that you and Miss Darcy should work together."

"Ah, perhaps, but Miss Darcy isn't promised to me."

Was he saying more than just words? Anthea glanced at him sharply, then rose. "I'm not promised to you either, Ryven."

"No, not any more." He gave her a half smile. "I was young then, Annie. Younger than my years. Perhaps—"

"There's no changing things, Ryven. That's all over and done. Both of us have gone on to other things." She turned and started for the door, but his voice stopped her.

"*Both* of us? I really hadn't heard that, Annie. Who is the lucky gentleman, and are congratulations in order yet?"

Anthea turned and looked at him, ready to deny any entanglement, but then she thought, why not? Ryven didn't know anything about her life and didn't care. He was merely toying with her, much the way a cat would play with a catnip mouse. She had refused Vincent Wolcott, but at least the mention of his name might let Ryven know that she had forgotten the past. "His name is Vincent Wolcott," she found herself saying, "and I doubt you know him. He's a most exemplary gentleman."

"And by implication, I'm not." He laughed softly, then frowned and bit his lip as he thought. "Wolcott. Vincent Wolcott. I don't believe . . ." He snapped his fingers together and broke into laughter. "Woolie. Good Lord, Annie, you can't mean Woolie—that is, Vincent Wolcott—the secretary to Lord Kilcannon. We were in school together."

"Yes, that's exactly who I mean." She kept her voice neutral. "I'm surprised you know of him. I didn't think the two of you would run in the same circles."

"To tell the truth, Annie, we don't. Wolcott's a damn queer fish. What in the world would you want with him, anyway?"

She *didn't* want Wolcott, but it was too late to turn back. "I'm shocked at your lack of manners, Ryven," she snapped, trying to cover up her feelings. Actually the term "a damn queer fish" described Vincent perfectly, but she wasn't going to let Ryven know that.

"My manners haven't changed a bit, Annie." He smiled lazily at her.

"No, they're as bad as ever," she said before she could stop herself. "For your information, Vincent is worth two of you on any day." With that, she turned and stalked out the door. Her exit, however, was marred by the sound of Ryven's laughter. "Vincent Wolcott, indeed," she heard him say, and she knew exactly the way he was smiling to himself and shaking his head.

She met Miss Darcy on the stairs. "Is Nicky at breakfast?" Miss Darcy asked. She looked rather frowsy this morning. "My dear Miss Thorne, I simply cannot go on without my baggage and my maid. I must talk to dear Nicky about leaving."

Anthea suspected the "dear Nicky" reference was for her benefit, but she ignored it. "You'll find him at the breakfast table," she said shortly, going by Miss Darcy.

"Miss Thorne." Judith Darcy's voice was ice. "This is a most unpleasant situation for both of us, but I think we should have something of an understanding between us. I know you were once engaged to Nicky—a youthful infatuation, if you will—and I want you to know that I intend to marry him."

"What either you or Ryven do or don't do is of no consequence to me, Miss Darcy." Anthea tried to make her voice as cold as Miss Darcy's. "As far as I'm concerned, you may have him, and I wish you well."

"Oh, I fully intend to have him." Miss Darcy's smile could only be termed mercenary. For a moment, Anthea almost felt sorry for Ryven—almost. He deserved whatever he got.

"Good luck to you, Miss Darcy," Anthea said, walking on up the stairs. She didn't look around until she had safely closed her chamber door behind her. Parrish was in the room going through her clothespress.

"Lady Lynden wishes me to attend to Miss Darcy," Parrish said, "She also said I was to select some of your things for Miss Darcy to wear since her baggage was sent on to Morven Hall." Parrish pulled one of Anthea's least favorite dresses from the clothespress, one made in a particularly vile shade of bright blue. "I thought perhaps this," Parrish said, her face perfectly straight.

"Parrish, surely you don't intend to do that to Miss Darcy? I've always hated that dress."

Parrish held the dress up and looked at it critically. "That's because it doesn't suit you, Miss Thorne. I think it will do very nicely on Miss Darcy, as will those." She gestured toward the bed where several dresses were piled. Anthea glanced at them, then back at Parrish. "Parrish, take the sprig muslin I had made in London. If I must share, I intend to share the best as well."

With a grimace, Parrish pulled the muslin from the clothespress and added it to the dresses on the bed. "Take some underwear, as well," Anthea instructed.

A while later, Anthea felt she had gathered several of her nicest things to send, and there was nothing of which Miss Darcy might complain. Parrish gathered everything up in her arms. "If you don't need me now, I'll go attend Miss Darcy."

"You may not need to attend her past this morning," Anthea said. "Miss Darcy was going to talk to Ryven about leaving, although he did say he planned to stay here until the road was passable.

"That'll be a while. Chatwin says this'll be on the ground for days." Parrish walked stiffly out the door. She didn't relish the prospect of sharing her dear Miss Thorne's best dresses and underthings with anyone.

By midmorning Ned and Dickon were to be put off no longer. Anthea left the fire in the drawing room, had to make an obligatory visit to the nursery to see how well Bertram was getting along, then went to her room to bundle up in boots, a pelisse, a scarf, and mittens. It was time to build the snow forts.

To Anthea's amusement, Miss Darcy planned to help them. She originally had declined, saying the cold weather always ruined her complexion, but when she discovered Ryven would be building a snow fort, she decided to join them. It was to be Anthea and Ned against Ryven, Dickon, and Miss Darcy. Ned wasn't in the least worried about the imbalance in the numbers. "I have a plan," he told Anthea.

As they were going out, Miss Darcy met them at the door. She looked as if she were going riding in the park, dressed in Anthea's blue wool, wearing a hat of blue with a white plume, and carrying Lady Lynden's white fur muff. Her feet were daintily shod in Lady Lynden's blue kid slippers that looked to be at least a size, or perhaps two, too small. Ryven looked at her sharply but said nothing. She smiled archly at Anthea, took Ryven's arm, and they waded out into the fresh snow, Anthea following them. Ned and Dickon ran ahead, shouting and throwing snowballs at each other. "Here, Annie," Ned yelled, throwing a snowball her way. The snowball hit Miss Darcy's forehead and splattered, right below the white plume. She stood stock still for a moment, then began to scream, "You horrid, horrid brat! Look what you've done!"

"I apologize, Miss Darcy," Ned said, dashing up to her. "Here, let me help you." He reached up to try to get the snow off her face but only managed to knock the blue hat into the snow.

"Now look what you've done!" she shrieked again. She tried to stamp her foot in anger but succeeded only in shoving her foot deep into a pile of snow. "Oohhh! Ryven, you should send this . . . this *urchin* to his room! He should be birched! Soundly!"

"But I apologized," Ned said quickly, looking at Ryven in appeal. "I meant to hit Annie in the face."

"And what would Annie have done at that?" Ryven asked, trying to keep from grinning at Ned. He wasn't successful.

"She'd probably have landed me a facer if she could have gotten to me," Ned admitted.

"Enough of this," Anthea said. "Ned, I've told you to watch your language. And you," she looked at Ryven, "shouldn't encourage such slang." Before Ryven could answer, she turned to Miss Darcy. "Miss Darcy, let me help you." Anthea wiped Miss Darcy's face with the corner of her scarf, picked up the hat, dusted the snow from it, and placed it on Miss Darcy's head. "Do you want to go back inside? Ned would be glad to take you in, I'm sure."

Miss Darcy shoved the hat firmly on her head. "I'm sure he would," she said shortly, "but no, I do *not* wish to go inside." Her mouth was a straight, angry line, and her cheeks were blazing.

They followed Ned and Dickon without speaking to a level part of the side yard and began building their forts. Anthea and Ned made big solid snow bricks to use for walls and then began making snowballs to stockpile behind the walls. Dickon and Ryven did the same while Miss Darcy stood there, her hands in Lady Lynden's muff, shifting from first one foot to the other. "Poor Miss Darcy has to be freezing," Anthea said to Ned as they worked. "I can't imagine why she doesn't go inside. She could watch from the window."

"She's out here because she's a ninnyhammer," Ned said, "and, besides, she doesn't want to leave you alone with Nicholas."

Anthea's head jerked up, then she felt herself blush. "That's ridiculous! There's nothing at all between Ryven and me. Furthermore, I certainly wouldn't be alone with him. You and Dickon would be more than adequate chaperones. Besides," she added, trying to change the subject, "didn't I tell you to call him by his style?"

"Yes, you did." Ned stopped forming his snowball and sat down beside the pile he had made. "Do you still like him—Nicholas, I mean? It's important that I know."

Anthea refused to look at him, concentrating instead on making her snowball perfectly round in her mittened hand. "Of course I like Ryven, Ned. I like Dickon very much, too."

"But would you like to *marry* him—Nicholas I mean, not Dickon, of course. I should like Nicholas for a brother."

"That's not a possibility," Anthea said shortly. "Get busy making snowballs. Dickon seems to have a huge pile of them." She gathered up an armload of snow and dumped it in Ned's lap. Ned laughed and threw some snow back at her. They wasted several snowballs throwing them at each other while Ryven and Dickon yelled encouragement at one or the other. Finally they called a truce so they could replenish their snowball pile. "I had hoped," Ryven called out, "that you'd use all your snowballs and be forced to surrender your snow fort."

"Unfortunately for you, we have plenty of raw material," Anthea said, laughing.

"Nicky," Miss Darcy said, pouting, "I'm cold." She was ignored as everyone else went back to work. "I think I'll go in," she said plaintively, shoving her hands up to the elbows into the muff.

"You should do that," Ryven said with a smile. "I'm sure you need to get warm."

"Would you mind helping me?" Miss Darcy's voice was small and weak. "I'm so afraid I'll fall in this terrible snow."

Ryven dusted off his mittens and took Miss Darcy's elbow. "While you're inside," Anthea called out, not looking up from her work, "could you ask that hot chocolate and cakes be put out? We'll be in as soon as we finish."

"I'll be back to help you, Dickon," Ryven said, lifting Miss Darcy as she faltered. They made their way through the snow, Miss Darcy periodically sagging against Ryven so that he almost carried her the last part of the way. Dickon and Ned looked at each other, grimaced, then nodded knowingly.

Ryven returned and in a short while, the snow forts were finished. The group decided to go inside for the promised chocolate and cakes, then return in midafternoon for the big snow battle. They all went inside, shaking snow from their clothes, and went on into the drawing room where a good fire was blazing. Miss Darcy was in front of the fire, a blanket around her shoulders. Her nose was very red. Lady Lynden and Mrs. Darcy flanked the fireplace, Lady Lynden engaged in her embroidery, Mrs. Darcy engaged in stuffing Puffy with bits of cake.

"I did not realize," Mrs. Darcy said pointedly, "that young ladies built snow forts and gamboled out of doors in the weather. It will ruin your complexion, my dear."

Anthea pulled off her mittens and put them on the hearth to dry. Standing up, she glanced at herself in the mirror above the mantel. True, her face was pink, but her eyes sparkled.

"I think Annie looks just fine," Dickon said. "Annie, do you want to go with us to see Bertram?"

"I'd love to, but I'll do that later," she said. "Right now the two of you get upstairs and take off those wet clothes. I'll send you up some chocolate."

"And cakes?" Ned asked, hope in his voice.

"Yes, cakes, too. Now go on." She put her hands on their shoulders and propelled them out the door.

"They've dripped all over," Miss Darcy said disapprovingly. "They should have been sent straight upstairs." She turned to Ryven with her prettiest pout. "And as for you, I need to take you to task, sir, for deserting me. I insist you stay indoors this afternoon and play cards with Mama and me."

"A splendid idea," Lady Lynden said before Ryven could protest. "I'll play with you so we can make four. Anthea really doesn't care for cards."

"A wise choice," Ryven commented, stretching out his hands to the fire. He looked rather glum, and Anthea remembered that Ryven had never cared for card games. Gambling on a boxing match or a horse race was one thing, but he had always berated card games as an insipid waste of time.

"Then it's settled," Mrs. Darcy said. "Anyone sane would much prefer a good game of cards to that weather."

Ryven turned and leaned against the mantel. "I wish I could oblige you, but I promised Dickon and Ned to join in their snowball fight this afternoon."

Miss Darcy looked at him critically and tossed her blond curls. "Really, Nicky, how ridiculous. A promise to a child doesn't count. The boys can play their little games by themselves." She glanced at Anthea. "I'm sure Miss Thorne will be available to play with them."

Ryven answered before Anthea could say anything. "She'll be there, I'm sure, and so will I, Judith." Ryven's voice was hard. "I try never to break a promise to anyone and would *never* break a promise to Dickon. I'll join you for a game or two of cards, but my midafternoon belongs to Dickon." He smiled briefly to take the edge off his words. "Now if you'll excuse me, I need to change these wet clothes." He sketched a small bow and left.

"Well, I've never!" Mrs. Darcy gasped. "Such rudeness!"

"True, but understandable when you realize how attached Ryven is to Dickon," Lady Lynden observed mildly. "Do you know the story?" She paused a moment, then, at Mrs. Darcy's blank look, continued. "Their mother died when Dickon was born and poor Grenfell was so devastated he couldn't really be a father. He wouldn't even look at Dickon for two or three years, even going so far as moving to London and refusing to return to Morven. It was left to Ryven, a mere stripling at the time, to be both father and mother to Dickon. As a result, he's always been very protective of Dickon, even after Grenfell remarried."

There was a small silence, then Miss Darcy spoke. "Such an attitude toward a child is still ridiculous," she said, shaking her head. "Nicky's going to have to forget all that. What Dickon needs is a good boarding school. After Nicky and I are married, I certainly don't intend to devote my entire life to children."

"A very wise attitude," Lady Lynden said absently, reaching for her basket of wools. "Anthea, dear, do you realize your boots are dripping?"

Anthea went upstairs to change. Parrish was there with hot bricks for her feet and warm, dry clothes. "Put my clothes where they'll dry, Parrish. I promised to go back out this afternoon."

"I know, Miss Thorne. Master Ned told me to make sure you looked better than you did this morning." Parrish chuckled. "I told him it was hard to gild the lily."

Anthea laughed but did go to her mirror and take a long look at herself. She looked well enough, but she would never have the town bronze of a Judith Darcy. Still, perhaps it was time to quit being the country miss and get out. Maybe she would go visit Margaret in London after all.

The afternoon snowball battle was fierce, three against two even though everyone tried to convince Miss Darcy not to come out. She was determined to come outside and even took a quilt on which to sit. In the spirit of things, she borrowed a pair of mittens and threw a few snowballs, although they all seemed to land in the bushes to the left of Anthea and Ned's snow fort. However, just as Anthea thought all was well, Miss Darcy almost had a fit of hysterics when both Anthea and Ned hit her squarely on the head when she looked over the top of her snow fort. They had to call a halt to the snow battle until Ryven could wipe the snow from Miss Darcy's head and convince her to calm herself. "You did that on purpose," she said finally, glaring at Anthea with dislike. "I *know* you did."

"Of course she did," Ryven said cheerfully. "That's the object of a snowball battle. Would you like to go inside now?"

"No," Miss Darcy snapped. "Never."

After dozens of snowballs and much ado, the snowball battle was declared a draw and everyone went back indoors, agreeing to meet and fight again another day. Ned and Dickon were in high spirits, although Miss Darcy was quite obviously drooping.

That night after supper, Anthea slipped off to the nursery to say good night to the boys. They were there in the dark, looking out and showing Bertram the moon and stars shining in the cold, clear sky. "We're talking about our yuletide wishes," Ned said to her, whispering in the dark.

"Ah, Ned, you shouldn't do that. Remember that your yuletide wish isn't supposed to be told until Christmas Eve," Anthea said, her voice sounding unnaturally loud in the dark, still room.

"And just what is a yuletide wish?" Ryven asked, coming into the room, the doorway a rectangle of light behind him.

Anthea turned to look at the shadow filling the room. For a moment, he looked larger than he was. "What are you doing here?" she demanded.

"I saw you slipping up the stairs and decided you and these two were probably up to no good, so I followed."

She smiled at the laughter in his voice. "It appears you were wrong this time."

"I've been wrong before. I apologize." He hesitated as though he wished to say something else, then gave a slight shrug of his shoulders and came over to stand at the window with them. "Now tell me about yuletide wishes."

"Yuletide wishes are always supposed to come true," Dickon said, "or at least that's what Ned says."

"Always?" Nicholas ruffled Dickon's hair with his fingers, then put his hand on the boy's shoulder. "I didn't know there were wishes that always came true."

"Do they? Always?" Dickon asked, peering around Nicholas to look at Ned.

Anthea chuckled. "No, not always." She found herself whispering because it seemed to be the way to speak in the dark. For a second, she tried to speak in a normal tone, but it seemed too loud in the night. "A yuletide wish is supposed to be something you want to happen to you during the next year, but it's also supposed to be something you're willing to make happen. You just can't sit around and wait for whatever it is."

"I see. It's the same way I wished for a pet, but instead of just waiting around, I told Nicholas, and he got me one." Dickon frowned as he thought about it.

"Sort of." Anthea and Nicholas exchanged smiles. "I suppose that would be doing something about your wish. Usually, though, you're supposed to work in

278

some way to make it happen."

Dickon turned around and looked at them. "Can anyone make a yuletide wish, and does it have to be done at a special time?"

"It's time now, isn't it, Anthea?" Ned asked. "You always told me that I needed to wish on the moon and then I get to tell you about my wish on Christmas Eve."

Nicholas put his other hand on Ned's shoulder. "I have a question about this—does your wish come true at Christmas Eve when you tell it?"

"Not always," Anthea admitted. "Sometimes you need to work on it all year, then it's supposed to have come true by the next Christmas.

"Could we make wishes now?" Dickon asked. "The moon looks fine to me tonight."

Anthea peered out into the sky. "I don't see why not, but remember, you have to be careful about your wish—it must be something you're willing to work at, and perhaps wait on, all year."

Dickon grabbed Ned's hand. "I think we need to talk about this." They went outside the door, and Ryven and Anthea could hear them whispering excitedly.

Ryven glanced out the window again. "I've never heard of yuletide wishes. Tell me, Anthea, is this a custom passed down from generation to generation?"

She laughed. "Do you promise you won't tell on me?" At his nod, she continued. "Once when Ned was younger, Mama and Papa were in Portugal, and he wanted them to come home and he also wanted a pony. I convinced him to make a yuletide wish, knowing that Mama and Papa would be home by March and that I could manage to get him a pony by summer. I concocted the whole thing to see him through that Christmas, but I haven't had the heart to tell him any differently. Since that time, every year he looks forward to making his yuletide wish."

He moved close to her, so close she was acutely aware of him—the smell of him, the slightly rough texture of his coat sleeve against her bare arm, the touch of tenseness she felt whenever he was around. "I think it's quite wonderful that you should care enough about him to create yuletide wishes."

Anthea fought down the impulse to move away from him. Instead, she concentrated on looking at the stars outside. "I meant only for it to see him through that one Christmas, but it's become something of a Christmas tradition at Thornedene. I'd have to say it's worked out well — every year Ned makes a wish, then works all year for something he wants."

"And you? Do you ever make yuletide wishes?"

"Of course. Doesn't everyone?" She laughed and turned to look up at him. It was a mistake.

He moved even closer, put his hand on her arm, and Anthea trembled with the effort of standing still. "Anthea," he whispered huskily, "there's something I need —" He was interrupted by Ned and Dickon rushing into the room. "We're ready to make our yuletide wishes," Ned announced.

Anthea was almost giddy with relief. She stepped back away from Nicholas, drew Ned to her, and put her arm around his shoulder. "Are you ready right now?"

Ned nodded. "Dickon and I have discussed something, and we'd like to wish together. That's all right, isn't it?"

"Of course," Anthea told him, moving to stand behind him. He and Dickon stood by Bertram's cage and looked out at the moon. Anthea could see their lips moving as they whispered their wishes to themselves, both of them frowning with concentration. They held hands as they wished. "There," Dickon said, taking a breath. He and Ned looked at each other with satisfaction.

"I'd like to make a yuletide wish too," Nicholas said, "but I don't know about telling it at Christmas Eve. Is that a necessary part of yuletide wishes?"

Ned looked at Anthea with a question. She thought for a moment, then smiled at Nicholas. It was easier with some distance between them. "I think telling it would be entirely up to you. Ned and I find that sharing our wishes makes us work harder to make them come true, but I wouldn't think

280

you'd have to tell if you didn't want to."

"Oh, I intend to work quite hard on mine," Nicholas said with a chuckle. "Ned, Dickon, tell me how to do this."

"Annie, why don't you make your wish now, too?" Ned said to Anthea. Before she could protest, Nicholas had clasped her hand in his. "A good idea. Let's wish together." He smiled at her. Anthea looked at the moon and the edges of it blurred as tears filled her eyes. Nicholas was probably wishing that Miss Darcy would accept his offer while her wish . . . a wish came involuntarily to her mind, but she dismissed it . . . her wish was going to be to try to survive until Nicholas and the Darcys would leave. "Please, please help me get through this," she wished to the moon.

"There," Nicholas said, looking down at her. "Did you wish?" She nodded and pulled her hand from his. One way to get through this was to keep as far away from Nicholas as possible. Her wish was already working. "I need to go help Mama entertain Mrs. Darcy," she said. "You two boys get ready for bed."

"I'll stay a few minutes and make sure they do," Nicholas said. "Will you play and sing when I get downstairs?"

"I think Miss Darcy is planning to sing," Anthea said hastily and hurried from the room. Thank goodness for the dark so Nicholas couldn't see her expression until she composed herself. With any luck, she could get down to the drawing room and be involved in a card game with Mrs. Darcy before Nicholas got out of the nursery.

For the next few days Anthea worked hard to make her Yuletide wish come true. She was careful never to be alone with Nicholas; she made suggestions to ensure that Nicholas and Miss Darcy were always together; and she spent as much time away from them as she could without seeming inhospitable. Unfortunately, Nicholas seemed intent on spending as much time with Dickon, Ned, and Anthea as possible. There was no escaping his presence.

Most of Anthea's time seemed to be taken up by Ned, Dickon, and Bertram. Dickon she loved—he was almost a copy of Nicholas—and Bertram turned out to be a mouse with quite a personality. All in all, considering Nicholas was in the house, Anthea was as content as she could be.

Miss Darcy, however, was another story. Anthea was afraid the silly chit would completely alienate Nicholas. No matter what Nicholas, Anthea, and the boys did, Miss Darcy whined and complained. She didn't like to repair snow forts, she didn't like to make snow angels, she didn't like to have treasure searches, she didn't like to play any games at all, and, most particularly, she didn't like Bertram. She even went so far as to suggest that the best use for poor Bertram would be as a between-meal snack for Puffy. Ned and Dickon were horrified. It took Anthea the better part of an hour to calm them and assure them that Bertram would be quite safe as long as he was at Thornedene.

"I hate her," Dickon said fiercely, "and she doesn't like me either."

"I'm sure she likes you," Anthea said, "and, Dickon, you really shouldn't hate anyone. Give Miss Darcy a chance, and I'm sure you'll find she's really . . ." Anthea faltered. There was nothing she could find to praise in Miss Darcy. "Perhaps Miss Darcy has never had a pet and doesn't understand your feelings for Bertram," she finally said.

"She doesn't understand anyone's feelings," Dickon said with heat. "Even Nicholas thinks—"

"Dickon!" Ned interrupted with a warning look.

The two boys looked at each other and nodded. "Would you like to go ice skating, Annie?" Ned said, changing the subject almost too casually. "Chatwin says the ice on the pond's just right."

"I'd love that," Anthea said, "but first, I want to know what's going on with you two."

They looked up at her, their faces as innocent as those of two cherubs. "Annie," Ned said, "I'm really surprised at you. We just wanted to ask you to go with us. You don't have to if you don't want to. You're the one who's always telling me not to go to the pond to swim or skate unless I take someone grown-up with me." He paused. "If you don't want to go, we can ask Chatwin."

"The two of you are up to something, I just know it." She paused to let them say something, but they merely looked at her blandly. "All right." She gave it up. "I can see I'm not going to get anything out of you two. We'll go skating. This afternoon?" They nodded and ran to get Chatwin to sharpen the skates.

Anthea was rather surprised when everyone gathered to go to the pond since both Nicholas and Miss Darcy were standing there. She was rather annoyed; she had managed to avoid them for the most part for the last few days and didn't care to be in any proximity with Nicholas. However, she hid her feelings and smiled broadly at them. "What a good surprise to see you're going with us! Have you ever skated before, Miss Darcy?"

"No, but dear Nicky has promised to teach me." Miss Darcy put her hand on Ryven's arm and looked up at him. She was dressed, quite unsuitably as usual, in blue velvet, again carried Lady Lynden's white fur muff for her hands, and now had on a bonnet trimmed with white fur. She looked more like a model for a pattern card than someone going out for an afternoon in cold weather.

Ned, Dickon, and Chatwin came in with the skates. "Chatwin's going with us, Annie," Ned announced. "I don't think he trusts you to watch us. He does say the ice is thin at the edge next to the fence."

"There's no need . . ." Anthea began at the same time that Ryven said, "I think that's an excellent idea, Chatwin." She frowned at Ryven, but he merely smiled sunnily at her, and they all headed out toward the pond, Chatwin carrying the skates and leading the way as his heavy, hobnailed boots broke through the crusty snow, making a path for them. "Start warming up tomorrow," he said, pausing to sniff the air and hold a thumb up to feel the wind.

"I hope not," Dickon said, turning to look at Nicholas. "You'll have to leave if it warms and the snow melts."

"It can't be too soon for me," Miss Darcy said, leaning heavily on Ryven as she picked up her skirts in a futile attempt to keep them out of the snow. "Nicky, I'm getting all

283

wet in this awful stuff. I *hate* snow."

Anthea glanced at Nicholas, and he looked back at her, rolling his eyes upward. Before they left, they had all tried again to convince Miss Darcy to stay indoors, but nothing would do her except go with them so, as she had said, her dear Nicky could teach her to skate. Dear Nicky didn't seem to care for the idea, but Miss Darcy was adamant.

At the pond, Chatwin walked out to test the ice and sweep the snow from it with a broom. Ned and Dickon immediately put on their skates and followed him out. The ice was perfect — clear, smooth, and slick.

Miss Darcy sat on the bench beside the pond's edge as Ryven bent to strap her skates onto her elegantly shod feet. Anthea reached for her skates that Chatwin had left in the snow. "If you'll wait a minute, Annie, I'll do that for you," Nicholas said.

"Thank you, but I can manage," Anthea said stiffly. She didn't want him that close. Evidently Miss Darcy didn't either. As soon as her skates were strapped on, she clung to Ryven's shoulders. "Oh, Nicky, I do believe I'm going to fall." She sagged heavily into him, almost knocking him backward. As he struggled to regain his footing and support Miss Darcy at the same time, Anthea stood and skated by them, waving.

Nicholas was forced to spend his time with Miss Darcy as she clung to him relentlessly, crying all the while that she was going to fall and begging him not to leave her alone. In the meantime, Dickon, Ned, and Anthea skated around them, tossing a snowball or two at each other, and finally making figure eights and circles around each other. Chatwin sat on the bench at the edge of the pond, smoking his pipe, and calling out periodic warnings for them not to get too close to the far edge where the ice was thin.

"Look, Nicholas," Dickon called, doing a particularly fine turn around Anthea. "Come join us!"

Nicholas looked at them for a moment, then back down at Miss Darcy. "Nicky, don't leave me," she whimpered, clutching his coat, "I'll fall."

"Come on, Nicholas!" Dickon shouted as he and Ned made some circles.

"Make a circle with me, Annie!" Ned yelled as he and Dickon grabbed Anthea's hand and turned her around. She spun, and when they let her go, she bumped into Nicholas. He caught her by the waist and spun her around again to be caught by Ned and Dickon as she laughed.

"Don't let me go!" Miss Darcy screeched. "I'll fall if you do!" She waved her arms and tottered on her skates.

"Don't worry, Miss Darcy," Ned called out, "Dickon and I will take care of you." The two boys skated toward Miss Darcy.

"No, no!" Miss Darcy waved her arms and tried to move toward Ryven and Anthea but forgot she was on skates and slick ice. She went crashing to the ice with a loud thump. Ned couldn't stop in time and tripped over her, falling flat on his face. Anthea rushed to him and sat him up. His nose was pouring blood.

Miss Darcy sat up, her hat all askew. "Nicky, help me," she moaned. "That horrid child has killed me."

"I wish," Ned muttered to Anthea through the blood and his rapidly swelling nose.

"Hush," Anthea said, mopping at Ned's face with her scarf. She felt along his nose. "I don't think it's broken, but I really can't say." She turned for Nicholas, but he and Chatwin were busy picking up a sobbing Miss Darcy. Chatwin hoisted her to her feet, gave her a disgusted look, then left her sobbing on Ryven's chest while he came over to check on Ned. He glided his work-roughened fingers along the sides of Ned's nose. "Not broken, but we'd better go back. That's going to swell."

"Why are you so worried about him?" Miss Darcy said, sobbing. "He should be punished! Birched thoroughly or at least sent to bed without supper. I *insist* on it—he did that on purpose!"

Anthea had had enough. "Of course he did," she snapped. "I'm sure he waited around all afternoon for you to fall just so he could sprawl over you and break his nose!

285

That's the silliest thing I've ever heard of." She turned and swabbed at Ned's nose. "Come on, Ned, let's go home."

They skated for the edge of the pond where Dickon and Chatwin joined them. As they sat on the bench taking off their skates, Miss Darcy kept sobbing into Ryven's coat. "That's right, take up for him," she cried, looking at Ned with a red, splotchy face. "Both of those little heathens should be flogged. That might teach them some manners."

"I could suggest the same for you," Anthea snapped, taking Ned and Dickon by the hand and stalking away, leaving Ryven to deal with Miss Darcy. She could have sworn she heard Chatwin chuckle as he fell in behind them.

"Wadn' on purpose, Annie, I swear," Ned said as they walked, his voice muffled through the scarf he held to his nose.

"I'm glad you did it," Dickon said fiercely, "and I would have done it if I'd thought of it. I hate her."

Anthea forced herself not to agree with them. "Hush, Dickon. Remember that I told you that you shouldn't hate anyone. If you gave Miss Darcy a chance, I'm sure you'd find that she has many good qualities." Her disclaimer sounded insincere even to her ears. Chatwin managed a "humph," and Anthea glared at him. "Miss Darcy simply isn't accustomed to dealing with boys," she finished lamely.

"No, that's not it." Dickon shook his head. "She doesn't like me at all. If she and Nicholas get married, I'll probably never see him again." He sounded unutterably sad.

Anthea gave him a quick hug. "Nicholas would never allow that to happen." They reached the door. "Let's get Ned's nose attended to, then go share some crackers and cheese with Bertram, shall we?"

Anthea had Dickon bring Bertram's cage to her room where she and the boys sat in front of the fire and ate. Ned was going to have a fine bruise, but no other damage had been done. He was quite proud of his injury, and he and Dickon took turns admiring it in Anthea's mirror. She had asked that they come to her room, because she was afraid Nicholas would come to the nursery once he had calmed

Miss Darcy. She really didn't want to talk to him right now, and she was chagrined at the thought of facing Miss Darcy after being so rude to her. Besides, Anthea decided, it was time to talk in private to the boys about all of them being more polite to and considerate of Miss Darcy.

There was a tapping at her door, and Anthea was sure it would be Nicholas, but when the door opened, it was Judith Darcy. She stood for a moment in the doorway and coldly looked at the three of them gathered around in front of the fire with Bertram's cage sitting on a footstool and Dickon holding Bertram in his lap. "I should have known I'd find the three of you sitting here plotting." She slammed the door behind her. "Well, I'm here to tell you it won't work. Ryven, Mama, and I are going to leave tomorrow, and that'll be the end of it." She crossed the room and stood in front of Dickon. "And as for you, brat, you might as well decide to make a vocation of school, because that's where you'll be staying."

Dickon turned pale and squeezed Bertram until he squeaked. Only then did Miss Darcy notice the mouse in his hands. "Put that filthy animal back in his cage!" She stepped back, close to the footstool, blocking Dickon's access to the cage. He held the mouse out in his hands. "I can't . . ." he began.

"What do you mean, you can't? Put that filthy rodent back before I get Mama's cat in here. That's what should be done with it anyway."

"But, Miss Darcy . . ." Dickon, the mouse in his hands, came close to her and held Bertram in front of her. Bertram, evidently tired of being squeezed, squeaked again and leapt from Dickon's hands right onto Miss Darcy's bodice. He found footing in the lace on her gown and scampered up to her shoulder. Miss Darcy screamed and flailed at Bertram with her hands. She tried to step backward but fell over the footstool, knocking Bertram's cage into the blazing fireplace. Bertram tried to climb up her hair, but she knocked him off, and he went flying across the room while Miss Darcy fell on the floor shrieking. Dickon leapt over Miss

Darcy and ran across the room, screaming for Bertram.

Bertram was nowhere to be seen, but the rest of the household had managed to congregate in Anthea's doorway where they were treated to a splendid view of Miss Darcy in the throes of hysterics. Mrs. Darcy ran into the room. "Oh, my poor darling," she said, "whatever have they done to you?"

Puffy, ever alert, leapt from Mrs. Darcy's arms and went crashing across Anthea's dressing table, dislodging Bertram from his hiding place behind Anthea's hairbrush. Bertram fled, mere steps in front of the cat. Dickon gave chase, sliding across the table after Puffy, catching him by the tail. Puffy dangled off the edge of the dressing table as Bertram dashed under the bed. Immediately, Puffy splayed all four feet and let out a howl that matched Miss Darcy's in intensity. Terrified, Bertram left the safety of the bed and ran under the clothespress while Ned slid across the floor in a futile effort to catch him.

It took several maids to get Mrs. and Miss Darcy to their rooms and calm. As it was, Miss Darcy had to drink Lady Lynden's special soothing tea before she was able to rest. She spent the remainder of the night lying in bed with a maid putting lavender-water towels across her forehead. Puffy was locked in Mrs. Darcy's room with a special meal until Bertram could be located, a task that occupied Anthea, Ned, Dickon, and Nicholas for the rest of the evening. By bedtime, Bertram was still missing, and it took all of Anthea's persuasive powers to make Dickon go to bed. Even at that, he cried himself to sleep while Anthea and Nicholas stood by, promising to do everything they could to find Bertram.

"It looks hopeless," Nicholas said with a sigh as they left the nursery after Dickon had finally gone to sleep.

Anthea had to agree. She knew of no other place to search. "Perhaps Bertram will appear once you've taken Mrs. Darcy and Puffy on to Morven," she suggested. "They tell me you're leaving tomorrow."

"Yes."

Was it her imagination, or did he sound disappointed, Anthea wouldn't let herself think on it. He was probably only sad to leave Dickon in such a state.

"Anthea," he began.

"I know what you're going to say," she answered, "and I promise I'll do everything I can for Dickon. Good night." With that, she fled and closed her chamber door behind her with relief.

By midmorning the next day, Bertram was still missing, and worse, Miss Darcy was in the hall having conniptions when Anthea came downstairs. "It isn't as if the child is going to die," she snapped to Nicholas as she stood there ready to leave. "This shows me clearly that your regard for me isn't what I thought it was."

"My regard for you is exactly the same," Nicholas said mildly. "Dickon is my brother, and I do not intend to abandon him."

"He'd hardly be abandoned here in this house full of people," Miss Darcy insisted. "You're actually abandoning Mama and me. No *gentleman* would allow us to travel alone on these roads."

Nicholas was undecided for a moment. "You're absolutely right," he said at last. "It's my duty to escort you and your mother to Morven, and I shall do so. Then I intend to return here and take care of Dickon."

This was too much for Anthea's curiosity. "Whatever is wrong?" she asked, coming down the stairs.

"The bra—*child* has the measles," Miss Darcy said shortly.

It took Anthea a moment. "Dickon? Good heavens, this is sudden. I thought he had had the measles before. I'll have to go see him and reassure him that we're still searching for Bertram."

"Oh, my dear, I'm afraid I can't allow that." Lady Lynden came in from the drawing room carrying Puffy. She seemed all too glad to hand the wriggling cat to a footman with instructions to take him out to the carriage—immediately. "You haven't had the measles, Anthea, and I simply

289

cannot allow you to be exposed. It would ruin your complexion."

"I'll probably catch them anyway," Anthea pointed out. "I know Ned will come down with them and I'll just have them then."

"No matter. I won't allow you to go near Dickon. Ned has already had the measles, as have I, and Nicholas tells me he had them as a child. So, my dear, there will be enough to see to Dickon without you endangering yourself." Lady Lynden turned toward Miss Darcy. "I'm so sorry your stay here has been fraught with accidents, but I assure you that you and your mother are welcome any time. I do hope you'll return." She turned to smile at Mrs. Darcy in the doorway. "Dear Mrs. Darcy, please say you'll be back. You did promise to give me some advice on planning my water garden."

Anthea stared in amazement. Her mother was usually cordial, but this was entirely beyond what was called for. She watched as her mother supervised the loading of the carriage and managed to get Mrs. and Miss Darcy seated with fur robes on their laps and hot bricks to their feet to keep them warm, then hurried Ryven out the door to escort them, telling him she would personally see to Dickon until he returned.

At last they were away, Miss Darcy unable to resist giving Anthea a triumphant smile and a wave as the carriage started down the drive. "Well, thank goodness they're gone," Lady Lynden said, wiping her hands as though getting rid of them. "Come, Anthea, help me gather my embroidery. I plan to spend the entire afternoon with Dickon since I doubt Ryven will return until tomorrow."

Anthea paused in the hallway and looked hard at her mother. "Mama, just what are you up to? If you have some scheme to throw me on Ryven, I can tell you right now that it won't work."

Lady Lynden looked at Anthea with clear blue eyes. "Really, Anthea, I can't imagine where you get such a streak of imagination. It must come from your father's family, since I'm sure no one in my family was ever so gothic." She turned to go into the drawing room. "I do expect you to be courteous to Ryven, since he'll be here until Dickon is well again. The man is quite worried—you know how attached he is to Dickon."

Anthea could get nothing else from her except chatter as they spent the morning gathering up Lady Lynden's wools and embroidery. Outside, the sun was shining brightly and, aside from the hiss of the fire, the only sound was the steady drip of the melting snow. In the afternoon, Lady Lynden went upstairs to see to Dickon and Ned. She had decreed that Ned should be confined as well, since Dickon needed company. Anthea spent the entire afternoon searching for Bertram. She had not realized there were so many places in a large house where a small mouse could hide.

As Lady Lynden had predicted, Ryven didn't return until the next day. By then, the roads were perfectly clear, although muddy, and the weather was warm. Anthea had put on her boots and had gone outside so she could wave up to Dickon and Ned as they stood at the nursery window. Ned called down that Dickon was too sick to come to the window, and Anthea was worried about him. She called up that she was still looking for Bertram and then started walking around the outside of the house, looking for any place a small mouse could have escaped. It seemed hopeless.

Ryven drove up just as Anthea was going inside. He walked her in, and Anthea had to own to herself that he looked perfectly splendid in a greatcoat and boots. She quickly curbed her imagination, but it was too late—there was a telltale blush creeping up her face. Quickly, she began a conversation just to put some distance between them. "I'm worried about Dickon," she told him. "Mama's been up there all afternoon, and that's not like her at all. Before, when either Ned or I were sick, she only stuck her head into the room and inquired about us. Dickon must have a terrible fever if she feels the need to stay with him constantly. Ned said he was too sick to come to the window when I went outside to wave to them."

Ryven looked grave. "Thank you for telling me. I'll go

291

right up." He took the stairs two at a time, then stopped and looked back at her when he reached the landing. "Have you found Bertram?"

She shook her head. "I've looked everywhere, but he's so small he could be hiding in anything. Tell Dickon I'm still looking."

"I will, and," he smiled warmly at her, "thank you."

Lady Lynden and Nicholas spent the next several days taking turns staying in the nursery, at times even staying together in there with Ned and Dickon. They refused to allow Anthea to come near the door, giving her reports daily on Dickon's condition. According to Nicholas, Dickon had a very high fever. Anthea asked if they should not call a doctor, and after some discussion with Lady Lynden, the family doctor was called in for a consultation. Nicholas came downstairs to the drawing room where Anthea was waiting and reported that the doctor felt Dickon would be fine with a great deal of care and rest but that there was really nothing to be done medically. Nicholas sat and leaned back in his chair. "I'm glad Dickon was here when he came down with the measles. He's really quite attached to you."

"I like him very much," Anthea admitted. She walked away from Nicholas to look out the window. She had tried to avoid him, but he seemed to be always somewhere around.

She heard Nicholas get up and walk across the room to stand behind her. "Your mother tells me that you . . ." he paused, searching for words, "you have something of an attachment for Vincent Wolcott. I'm sorry I laughed when you mentioned him."

Anthea turned to look at him. Feeling suddenly giddy, she turned back to look out the window, seeing nothing. "I don't have an attachment for Vincent. It's true he's offered for me, but . . ." she paused, "I'm not sure I wish to marry right now."

"I understand that problem completely," Nicholas said, a touch of bitter laughter in his voice. He hesitated for a moment. "Do you truly care for him?"

Anthea took a deep breath. Much as she would like to in this instance, she had never been able to lie. "He's a dear friend, and I care for him very much." That was true as far as it went.

"Ah." Nicholas moved to stand where he could lean against the window frame and look at her.

"What do you mean, 'ah'?"

He laughed softly. "That means that I know what you're saying to me, Annie. Do you remember that I usually knew what you were thinking?"

"I remember many things, Nicholas, not the least of which was the way you asked me to break our engagement. Now, if you don't mind, I have several things to do." She walked away from him and caught her breath. Something about him being close to her always brought on an attack of breathlessness.

"I apologize for that, Annie." His voice was low. "It was because I was thinking of you that I did it."

"Thinking of me!" She turned to face him. "That's ridiculous! You were thinking of your own selfish person, not of me."

He crossed the room and took her hand. "That's not true, Annie. I knew myself well enough to realize that I hadn't seen enough of the world, and, if we had married then, I would have been like all the other young bucks in London — chasing around to sample a taste of every vice in town. I couldn't do that to you."

"So you decided to get rid of me, then sample every vice in town."

He let go of her hand. "Annie, it wasn't that way at all."

"Don't try to cozen me, Nicholas, it won't work anymore. Now if you'll excuse me . . ." She fled out the door and up to her room before he could say anything else to her.

She successfully avoided Nicholas for the rest of the day. Lady Lynden took her to task at supper for not being sociable and suggested that perhaps she was coming down with something. Anthea did protest a headache and left Lady Lynden and Nicholas talking together, telling them she

293

wished to go to bed early.

Anthea did go to bed and slept for an hour or so, then woke up. She lit her candle, tried to read a novel for a while to make her sleepy, then blew the candle out and lay there in the dark, thinking. Around midnight, she thought she heard a noise and, after listening intently, decided it was someone giggling. She got up, put on her dressing gown, and went out in the hall just in time to see Ned and Dickon, barefooted, running toward the nursery, carrying some cakes and laughing. Anthea followed to the nursery door and was just about to open it when she heard a voice behind her. "Surely you don't want to catch the measles for Christmas." She turned to face Nicholas.

"I saw Dickon and Ned running down the hall, laughing and eating. Dickon certainly didn't look sick." Her voice was sharp.

"You must have been dreaming. Let me look." Nicholas moved her away from the door and opened it, peering inside. "They're both in bed, sound asleep," he said, closing the door carefully.

"I'm telling you I saw them, and what's more, Dickon didn't have a spot on him."

"Annie, did you take anything for your headache? Let me get you some milk or tea." Nicholas took her arm and walked her back down the hall toward her room. "You must have been having nightmares." He propelled her through the open door of her room. "Go on to bed, and I'll be right back with something for you to drink. Would you like some laudanum? The doctor left some for me to give Dickon when he was feverish."

Anthea whirled on him. "Don't patronize me, Nicholas. No, I do not want anything to drink or any laudanum. Furthermore, I know what I saw. I saw Dickon and Ned carrying cakes to the nursery. They were giggling, and there wasn't a thing wrong with either of them."

Nicholas looked injured. "If they were out, they shouldn't have been, I assure you. They were in bed when I looked in on them. Believe me, I'll talk to them tomorrow.

Dickon could expose the whole household to catastrophe if he doesn't stay in the nursery." He smiled sweetly at her and took her hand in his. "Go back to bed, Annie, you do look tired. If I can't get you something to drink, I can tell you good night and sleep well." He smiled at her, and before she knew what he was doing, he leaned over and kissed her softly. "Good night, sweet," he said, smiling at her again as he closed the door.

Anthea stood there in shock for a moment before she walked over to the bed and sat down on the edge of it. She closed her eyes and ran the tip of her tongue over her lips. They were tingling where Nicholas had touched her. Would these feelings for him never go away? Just when she had thought she had forgotten, he had reappeared. She couldn't—wouldn't—allow herself to be hurt a second time.

The next morning was Christmas Eve, and Lady Lynden reported that Dickon was worse. She suspected he had been out of bed and had suffered a backset. Anthea told her she had seen the boys and mentioned that Dickon didn't have any spots. "I know," Lady Lynden said, frowning. "He won't get better until the spots appear. I hope it's soon."

"Oh," Anthea said, "I thought the spots appeared immediately."

Lady Lynden smiled indulgently. "No, dear, they're the last thing to happen. Tell me, have you seen Nicholas?"

"No, and I don't intend to." Anthea got up and left. She thought she heard her mother chuckle as she went out the door but decided she must have been mistaken.

That night Anthea went to bed early and slept soundly until the middle of the night. Something woke her up, a slight scratching, scrabbling sound. There was a red glow from the fireplace where the last log was still burning slowly. She sat up in bed and looked around. There, sitting on the hearth, was a familiar figure. She peered again, just to make sure. It certainly looked like Bertram—she was positive it was Bertram. Quickly she got out of bed, but as soon as she moved, Bertram scurried away, running for safety under the clothespress. Anthea quickly lit a candle and got down on her hands and knees but could see nothing in the darkness. She was going to have to lure Bertram back out where she could see him.

If she managed to capture Bertram, she thought, where would she keep him? Nicholas had taken his cage for Chatwin to repair. There was only one thing she could do — go to the kitchen and get some cheese, try to capture Bertram, then keep him in a hatbox until morning when she could give him to Nicholas. Quickly she stirred up the fire and put on her slippers and dressing gown. She took her candle out into the hall and went down to the kitchen. She came back upstairs with a chunk of cheddar and a cup of tea to drink while she sat and waited for Bertram to take the bait. She had gotten as far as her door when Nicholas opened his door and stepped into the hall dressed in breeches and a shirt, his cravat untied and dangling.

"Unable to sleep, Annie?"

She hesitated a moment, then decided she might need help. "I've found Bertram, but he won't come out from under the clothespress. I've got some cheese to lure him out."

"I've got his cage. Just a minute." Nicholas went back into his room, reappearing with Bertram's cage, newly repaired. "Let's see if we can get him. Dickon would like to have Bertram back better than anything else."

They went in her room, and Nicholas put another stick of wood on the fire, then placed some cheddar in Bertram's cage and a trail of small bits leading to the clothespress. "There, that should do it. All we can do is wait."

They waited in a comfortable, familiar silence for the better part of an hour, sitting quietly together on the hearth. Finally, Nicholas spoke. "I love you, Annie."

She looked up at him sharply. The light from the fire illuminated his face. "I love you," he said again. "I know I hurt you four years ago, and I'm sorry, but I want you to know that I never once stopped loving you."

"A strange way you showed it, Nicholas." She paused a

moment. "Judith Darcy plans to marry you," she said abruptly. "Surely you're aware of that."

"I wondered when you would mention her." He closed his eyes and grimaced. "Yes, I'm more than aware that Judith Darcy has plans to marry me. She's made that abundantly clear." He touched Anthea's arm and leaned toward her. "Annie, I promise you that I never gave her the least encouragement. From the time I first met her in London, she's been everywhere I've been and has managed to trap me more than once into taking her places or driving out with her. And, worse, calling me 'dear Nicky' in public." He ran his fingers through his hair in exasperation. "Annie, you know what kind of person she is: she lets nothing get in the way of what she wants. She and her mother invited themselves to Morven for Christmas, and I was more than rude about it, but nothing stopped either of them." He took her hand in his. "I've never cared in the least for Judith Darcy. Do you believe me?"

She smiled at him in the firelight. "I believe you, Nicholas."

He leaned back against the woodwork of the mantel. "Did you ever wonder why there was never really anyone else for me, Annie? It was because I was always comparing others to you, and they were never what you were. I think I've loved you always." He paused a moment, listening to the hall clock chime. "It's after midnight, Annie, and that means it's Christmas. You said we could tell our yuletide wishes on Christmas Eve, and since I didn't tell you then, I'm going to tell you now." He reached over and took her hands in his. "I wish you would marry me, Annie. That's all I've ever wanted, I just didn't know it before." He drew her to him and kissed her. "Annie, please," he whispered, "I promise you I'll spend the rest of my life making you happy."

"Nicholas," she whispered. Her head told her to say no, but she found herself murmuring his name again. It was all she could say before he kissed her again.

"I love you, Annie," he whispered again, his lips against

her neck.

"I love you, Nicholas." She pulled away shakily, but he still held her hands.

"Then you will marry me—you'll make my yuletide wish come true?"

"Nicholas," she began, trying to listen to her head, but she looked into his eyes in the firelight, and that was her undoing. He kissed her again, thoroughly. "Yes," she finally murmured against his ear. She never wanted this to end.

Nicholas shifted his weight so he could move her closer to him. There was a noisy chatter and a screech. Bertram had crawled between them and was being squeezed. "Grab him," Nicholas said, reaching for the elusive mouse.

Bertram dodged him and leapt up on Anthea's dressing gown, his claws scrabbling in the lace edging so he wouldn't fall. Anthea laughed and picked him up. "Bertram, do you know the problems you've caused?" she asked, picking up a chunk of cheese for him to nibble.

She placed Bertram and the cheese in the cage, and Nicholas fastened it. "Look at him eat," Nicholas remarked as Bertram fell on the cheese voraciously. "I think that must have been his yuletide wish."

Nicholas was afraid to stay longer for fear someone would discover them, so he took Bertram and started back to his room. At her door he paused and kissed Anthea again, lingering over the touch. "You didn't tell me your yuletide wish," he murmured. "Do you want to?"

"No," she said with a smile, "but I will. I didn't want to wish it, but it was my first wish and just popped right into my mind. I wished . . ." She stopped and took a deep breath. "I wished you would fall in love with me again."

"That came true," he said with a smile. "I never stopped loving you, but I did fall in love with you all over again. I don't know which is better." He touched her face with his fingers, and Bertram's cage clanged against the door where he held it with his other hand. "I'd better say good night," he whispered, closing the door reluctantly.

Anthea leaned against the closed door and looked out at the Christmas stars. "Thank you," she murmured.

The next morning, Lady Lynden came into Anthea's room before she got up. "I understand from Ryven that the two of you have cause for celebration this Christmas," she said. "I'm delighted."

"So am I," Anthea said, smiling and stretching luxuriously in the bed. "Merry Christmas, Mother."

"Come down for breakfast. We have a surprise for you." Lady Lynden smiled at Anthea. "Merry Christmas, my dear."

Anthea went downstairs to the breakfast parlor and was certainly surprised. Dickon, Ned, Nicholas, and Lady Lynden all sat there, looking quite pleased with themselves. Nicholas came over and put his arm around her. "It's time to tell yuletide wishes," he said. "My yuletide wish was that Anthea accept my offer to be my wife," he told them, "and this Christmas, my wish came true."

"Mine—ours," Dickon looked at Ned, "came true. We both wished that you and Anthea would get married, didn't we, Ned?" He smiled happily. "All this and Bertram back, too."

Anthea sat down, too surprised to stand any longer. "I thought you were deathly ill, Dickon. Did you have a miraculous recovery?"

"Yuletide wishes, Anthea," Lady Lynden said cryptically.

"Yuletide wishes? Good heavens, Mama, whatever—" She stopped suddenly and looked at the boys. "All right, out with it. Why are you two looking like the cats that ate the cream?"

"It was our yuletide wishes," Ned began, looking to Nicholas for support.

"You told us that we were supposed to work to make our yuletide wishes come true," Nicholas said, smiling." So we did."

"Yes." Ned grinned in satisfaction. "And work it was. It was certainly no easy job getting rid of Miss Darcy, and it was touch and go there for a while because we couldn't figure out a reason for Nicholas to stay here. Then Mama had the brilliant idea of having Dickon come down with the measles."

"You never had the measles?" Anthea was aghast.

Dickon laughed and shook his head. "No, but I think staying in the nursery was worse. I do want to tell you, Anthea, that I wouldn't have stayed shut up in there for anyone else except you."

"We had to do something in a hurry so that I had an excuse to stay here," Nicholas said. "I thought it worked rather well." He leaned over and kissed her on the forehead. "We're going to have to leave shortly for Morven Hall so we can announce our engagement at the New Year's ball. This time, I don't want to wait."

Anthea smiled back at him. "Nor do I. My only question is how we're going to fit Bertram into the wedding party."

"Mama will think of a way," Ned said serenely, "won't you, Mama?"

"Of course. I always do." Lady Lynden smiled beatifically at them. "I knew the two of you were still in love with each other. All it took was a small nudge for you to discover it." She rose and went to the door, turning to smile at them. "Merry Christmas, my dears, and I wish you many more."

A Holiday Betrothal

by Lois Stewart

"Ride a cockhorse to Banbury Cross."

Startled, Charlotte Kinley lifted her head and stared blankly at her abigail. "What did you say, Sarah?"

"It's the old nursery rhyme, ma'am. We're jist leaving the town of Banbury, and I was wondering why I didn't see no cross."

Charlotte glanced out the window of the carriage at the handsome stone houses lining the street. She'd been so lost in thought that she hadn't noticed they'd arrived in this old market town of northern Oxfordshire on the banks of the Cherwell River.

"Actually, I believe the cross was destroyed long ago by the Puritans," she informed the abigail with a smile. Then, as the carriage rattled across a stone bridge and headed westward out of the town, she began to shiver. Not that it was especially cold, even though it was past the middle of December. She shivered because her heart felt like a lump of ice. During the journey from her home in Lancashire, the passing miles had served as a kind of insulation against her apprehensions. Now, suddenly, she realized she was only a few miles away from destiny. Eight miles, to be exact. Cortona, the estate of the Marquess of Sherborne, lay eight miles to the west of Banbury. There, on Christmas Eve, at a grand gathering of the county, her betrothal to Lord Sherborne would be announced.

Yielding to a momentary panic, she lifted her hand to knock at the window glass and order the coachman to stop the carriage, to turn it around and head back to Bury, the mill town in Lancashire where she'd spent most of her life. There was still time to change her mind. She needn't fulfill her promise to marry a stranger. But before she could rap on the glass, reason and common sense took over. Her hand dropped. It *was* too late to change her mind. She was committed to marrying a man she'd met only three times in her life.

She thought back to that first meeting, less than three months ago, feeling again the shock of utter surprise and grief at the revelation that had preceded it . . .

Phineas Kinley put down his glass of claret and said abruptly to his daughter, Charlotte, "I've been keeping something from ye, love, something ye ought to know. Dr. Lyall's given me notice to quit."

"Papa!" Charlotte gasped. She and her father were sitting in the snug parlor of the house off the High Street of Bury, enjoying a companionable half-hour at the end of the day, as they'd grown accustomed to doing in the years since the death of her mother. Charlotte looked at Phineas closely. Gray haired and ruddy of face, he was much heavier now than he'd been in his youth, but he didn't look ill. "I don't believe it," she said firmly. "You're not dying, or anything close to it."

"Yes, lovey, believe it. My old father, he had the same spasms of chest pain I've been having. One day a terrible bad spasm left him paralyzed on his left side, and next day, he was gone. Dr. Lyall says I'll go the same way."

"Papa, just because Grandfer died that way . . . You've been working too hard, that's your problem. You need to rest more. You should take a nap after lunch every day and leave the mill early, instead of staying there until all hours."

Ordinarily a very reserved man, Phineas reached over to clasp Charlotte's hand, blinking his eyes against a sudden film of moisture. "My dear, ye mustn't fight this. What will be, will be. What we must do now is plan for the future. Now, then, it's long been worriting me that I'd be leaving ye all alone when I die. I've decided ye should have a husband. And I've found ye one."

Charlotte gaped at her father, forgetting for the moment the dreadful news he'd just given her about his health. "Papa! You're funning. You *must* be funning."

"Nay, that I'm not. I'm dead serious. I've found ye a lord o' the realm. Ye'll be a grand lady, a marchioness, no less!"

Charlotte had a sinking feeling. Never much inclined to jokes or humorous small talk, her father did, indeed, look dead serious.

"It was this way," Phineas continued. "I had my banker in London, Mr. Cotton, looking out for a swell, someone from an aristocratic family, a lord, if possible, mayhap even a duke! I wasn't about to give my only daughter to a nobody, that I'll tell ye! Well, Mr. Cotton couldn't find any dukes. I reckon they're in short supply. However, he did come up with this here Marquess of Sherborne, who seemed just right. According to Mr. Cotton, his lordship's a widower, young and presentable. Not a wastrel, I was pertickler about that. No, he served in the Blues and later sat for his home borough in Parliament. Mr. Cotton says his title is an old one, and he has a large estate in Oxfordshire. It will be a fine match for ye, the best that ever was or ever could be."

By this time Charlotte had begun to recover her composure. She said tartly, "The marquess sounds like a paragon, Papa, a real Go among the Goers. I daresay he'll be a fine match for someone but not for me. Just to name one objection, why would he be interested in marrying a mill owner's daughter from Lancashire, when he could have the pick of the young ladies of the Ton?"

"Because his lordship's pockets are to let, that's why, and ye're a great heiress, my girl, or so ye'll be one day. A few months ago, y'see, when he inherited the title, the marquess discovered that his father had nigh sunk the estate in a sea of debts. The old gentleman was a gambler, both on 'Change and at the tracks. But worst of all—" Here Phineas, a shrewd businessman to the core, allowed himself a smug smile. "Worst of all, the marquess's father had the bad judgment to sell off his holdings in the Funds at a huge loss only hours before the news o' Wellington's victory at Waterloo reached London. So now, to make a recover, Lord Sherborne needs a rich wife."

"I wish him luck," said Charlotte dryly.

"Now, now, lovey." Phineas shifted uncomfortably in his chair. "The fact is, with Mr. Cotton's help, I've already made the match between ye and the marquess. Provided, that is, that the pair o' ye suit. I wouldn't wish ye to marry a man ye couldn't abide. I've arranged for Lord Sherborne to pay us a visit, so's the pair o' ye can get acquainted, ye might say."

Aghast, Charlotte exclaimed, "Then you can just *un*arrange the visit! Papa, I know you think you're doing this for my own good. I know you don't like the thought of my being alone in the world, except for Great-uncle Jeremiah, and he, poor old thing, is getting touched in his upper works. But you must consider that Dr. Lyall may simply be wrong in his diagnosis. You'll probably live to be a hundred."

"Nay, my love, that's wishful thinking."

Charlotte swallowed hard. "Well, then, be as it may, I don't wish to marry this man. I don't wish to marry *anybody,* not for a long time, anyway. As for Lord Sherborne, he and I are complete strangers. We have nothing in common. Why, except for attending school in Tunbridge Wells, I've never been farther away from Bury than Manchester or Liverpool! I've never even been to London. I wouldn't know how to talk to Lord Sherborne's fashionable friends."

"Now, wait one moment, my girl," said Phineas curtly. "Ye're as much a lady as this here marquess is likely to meet, I've seen to that with yer fine schooling and all."

"You're prejudiced, Papa. Think about who you and I really are. Your father was a yeoman farmer. You've become a wealthy mill owner, true enough, but to the county gentry you're still a farmer. They're so prejudiced that they won't even consider you for the post of justice of the peace. Why should Lord Sherborne look on you and me any differently? What kind of a marriage could he and I have, coming from such unequal stations? No, Papa, it won't do. Write to Lord Sherborne and tell him not to come."

"I fancy it's too late for that, my girl," said Phineas, looking past her to their housekeeper, Mrs. Graves, who stood in the doorway of the parlor.

"Sir, ma'am," said the housekeeper in a flustered voice. "It's Lord Sherborne."

"I invited his lordship to have supper with us, and he's dead on time," murmured Phineas approvingly.

Charlotte rose slowly to her feet as Lord Sherborne strolled into the room. He was everything her father had described, and more. Tall, handsome, dark haired and dark eyed, with a well-shaped, sensual mouth and a cleft in his chin. He looked to be in his late twenties or early thirties. The superb tailoring of his black evening coat and breeches would have sent any aspiring dandy in Bury into a fit of teeth-gnashing envy. But it was the polished perfection of his address, the confident, unconsciously arrogant air of the aristocrat who has always known his place in the world, that would have set him apart in any Lancashire gathering.

If he had any qualms, however, about either his company or his surroundings, he showed no signs of them. He bowed with an easy grace, saying, "Mr. Kinley? Miss Kinley? I'm very pleased to meet you."

The dark eyes met Charlotte's, and he smiled, and her defenses crumbled in the face of that cool, faintly aloof charm. Reason, logic, and common sense alike disintegrated. In the first few seconds of her meeting with Jeffrey Weston, Marquess of Sherborne, Charlotte Kinley fell madly and irretrievably in love.

She spent the rest of the evening fighting the attraction. This proved difficult, because the marquess was the perfect guest. There was no indication that he felt out of place. He sent his compliments to the cook on her excellent dinner. He said politely to Charlotte, "I understand you attended Miss Porter's female academy in Tunbridge Wells. A very fine school, I believe."

Charlotte caught the glimmer of a smug smile on Phineas's lips. What other revelations had her father made about her in order to display her qualifications to be a marchioness? "Yes," she replied, concealing her irritation, "I think Miss Porter's academy is an excellent school." Before she quite realized how it came about, she and Jeffrey were deep into a discussion of

Lord Byron's poems. She reflected later that it was quite the most literary conversation she could remember having at her father's dinner table.

Then it was Phineas's turn. Jeffrey asked him a polite question about the cotton spinning industry, which sent her flattered father off on a long and involved description of the processes of carding, drawing, and roving, ending with an account of throttle spinning effected by the use of a flyer revolving around the bobbin. Jeffrey listened with what appeared to be absorbed interest.

Throughout the evening, Charlotte was conscious of Jeffrey's close, guarded gaze, but she couldn't read the expression in those dark eyes. Had he arrived in Bury without having definitely decided on the marriage? And was he now carefully studying her in an effort to make up his mind whether she would suit? Whatever his thoughts, he didn't bring up the matter of their betrothal, to her vast relief.

"Well?" Phineas demanded, when the marquess had departed for his lodgings at a nearby inn. "D'ye like the man?"

Charlotte glared at her father. "You're a conniving wretch, Papa, but you'll not connive me to the altar. In the event, like as not, now that the marquess has met me"—she looked down with a disparaging glance at the very plain muslin dress she'd donned for a quiet meal with her father—"now that he's met me, I daresay he won't come back to the house, let alone make me an offer!"

But the marquess proved her wrong the very next afternoon, when Phineas, with his characteristic bluntness and efficiency, had contrived to get Charlotte and the marquess alone on a drive about the town and its surroundings.

She dressed very carefully for the excursion, in a becoming walking dress and a brand-new pelisse and bonnet. She greeted him with what she hoped was a cool, poised friendliness, only to have the afternoon turn into the most excruciatingly uncomfortable experience of her life. Because she was so intensely conscious of the marquess's physical presence in the narrow confines of the carriage, she found it impossible to concentrate on what he was saying. She had to keep repressing

308

an unruly urge to move closer to him, to slide her fingers through the crisp black curls of his fashionable coiffure, to place the tip of her finger into the deep cleft in his chin. . . . "No!" she exclaimed aloud.

"I beg your pardon?" The marquess was staring at her in well-bred surprise.

Charlotte flushed a deep red. What was the matter with her? She was twenty years old, she'd met scores — well, a good many, anyway — of young men, both in the mill-owning circles of Bury and at assemblies in Manchester, and none of them had ever affected her in this way. In fact, the thought of marriage hadn't seriously occurred to her before. An only child and motherless since the age of six, she'd been happy in her close companionship with her father.

"I was thinking how different this part of Lancashire must be from your home in Oxfordshire," she said, inventing hastily. "We're on the edge of the Black Country here, you know."

The marquess glanced out the window of the carriage at the blackened buildings of the town. "It does seem a little — er — grimy."

"It's the smoke from literally hundreds of furnaces in the area," Charlotte explained. "Sometimes at night, when I look out over the valley, I think the whole area must be on fire, with flames belching from all those furnaces and every window of every factory blazing with light. The soot clings to everything, you know, even the trees and shrubbery and the grass. It creeps inside the houses. Our housekeeper complains bitterly about having to dust several times a day."

She knew she was babbling and wondered what he could possibly be thinking of her. Well, what did it matter? she thought grimly. After today, she'd probably never see him again. Even if he made an offer, which she considered unlikely, she was going to reject it. She said aloud, "Papa thought you might like to see the mill. Shall we go there now?"

"*You'll* show me the premises?" The marquess sounded surprised.

"Why, yes. I know all about the mill. Papa's seen to that." Did Lord Sherborne think it ill-bred for a lady to know about the workings of a business from which her family derived its livelihood? She mentally tossed her head, taking a perverse enjoyment in showing Jeffrey every detail of the mill, a vast structure, nine stories high, containing, she pointed out with relish, 90,000 spindles. She also showed him the neat rows of workmen's cottages and the new school her father had recently constructed for the child apprentices in the mill.

"Your father's employees look contented and hard-working," the marquess observed as they were riding back to Bury.

"Yes, I think they are. For instance, Papa doesn't believe children should work more than ten hours a day, though most mills require them to work as many as fifteen hours a day. Papa also insists that the children and their families have clean, decent places in which to live. You see, Papa feels very close to his workers; he was one of them not so long ago, so what hurts them, hurts him." She gave him a level look. For some reason she didn't wholly understand, it was important for her to make the marquess realize that she and her father were proud, rather than ashamed, of their origins.

Lord Sherborne gazed at her thoughtfully. "You seem to know a great deal about your father's business."

"Well, I'll inherit the mill one day. Papa thinks I should know how to manage it."

"I see." The marquess was very quiet for the remainder of their drive. Charlotte wondered what he was thinking about. Was he making up his mind about the marriage? At the house, after the housekeeper had served them tea and cakes in the parlor, she quickly found out. He went straight to the point, saying, "I believe you know why I'm here, Miss Kinley."

"Yes." Charlotte turned her head to hide the quick flush that suffused her cheeks.

"Your father, quite wisely, I think, wanted us to meet before we made a final decision about marrying. After spending time in your company last night and today, I must tell you that I'm quite willing to go forward in this matter, if you are equally agreeable." He smiled faintly. "We're both too sensible, I think, to speak in terms of undying devotion. The mutual advantages of the match are obvious without the need for false

310

romantic declarations." He paused, waiting politely for Charlotte's reply.

She wanted to scream, "No, I'm not willing to go forward! I don't wish to get married for mutual advantages!" From the first moment she'd heard of her father's scheme to marry her into the nobility, she'd had every intention of refusing the marquess's offer, supposing he were to make one. Now she looked down the years and saw herself growing old in a civil, bloodless relationship with a man who'd married her only for her money and who would probably go to his grave regretting it, and her resolve hardened. So when she heard herself saying, "I'm quite agreeable to the match, Lord Sherborne," she was convinced for one hideous, confused second that someone had stolen her voice.

"That's settled, then." The marquess sounded relieved. He rose and came over to her chair, putting out his hand to draw her to her feet. Smiling, he said, "Come, now. I think it's time to be a little less formal, don't you? Won't you call me Jeffrey?" Bending his head, he kissed her lightly on her brow.

In that moment, Charlotte made up her mind that she would never, under any circumstances, allow Lord Sherborne to realize what her feelings for him were. That much she owed to her pride, in a marriage of unequal affections. She moved pointedly away from him, saying, "Papa will be delighted. He's always wanted to see me creditably established, and now I'll be a marchioness." Out of the corner of her eye, she was pleased to observe a faint expression of disapproval settling over the marquess's handsome mouth.

As the carriage paused to allow the gatehouse keeper to throw open the great wrought-iron gates of Cortona, Charlotte began to shiver again with nervous tension. In minutes at most, she'd be face to face with her stranger-betrothed.

She'd seen Jeffrey only once since their engagement, and that was on the day of her father's funeral when he'd come to Bury on a brief visit of condolence. Phineas had died a short month after his daughter's betrothal, quickly and quietly, as he would have wished. Charlotte knew that Jeffrey's presence at the funeral was no more than a gesture of propriety. She was very conscious of the wall of constraint between them. However, during his few hours in Bury, they had come to an important agreement, the setting of their wedding date. In Phineas's will, he'd left instructions for Charlotte that she was not to delay her wedding in order to observe a formal mourning period. So here she was, six weeks later, about to visit Jeffrey and his family for the Christmas holidays. One week from today, on Christmas Eve, her engagement would be formally announced. Two months after that, at the beginning of March, she would be married. Sitting in the carriage as it entered the driveway of Cortona, Charlotte again had to fight back the impulse to rap on the glass and order the coachman to turn around.

"Great heavens, ma'am, this here park must be nigh as big as a whole county," murmured Charlotte's impressed abigail, looking round-eyed out the window of the carriage at the seemingly endless winding drive through a well-wooded park. Off in the distance a herd of fallow deer was grazing, and away to the right an alley led up a gentle slope to a small domed structure that looked vaguely like a temple.

After what seemed like miles, the driveway finally terminated in a sweeping curve in front of an enormous building, the central block of which, to Charlotte's stunned gaze, appeared to be modeled on a gigantic Roman triumphal arch. Curving colonnaded curtain walls led off on either side to twin pavilions. She later learned there were two matching pavilions in the rear. As the carriage slowed and came to a halt, a swarm of liveried servants swept out of the great central door to let down the steps of the carriage, take charge of Charlotte's baggage, give her coachman directions to the stables, and escort her up the steps and into an immense hallway, where Jeffrey was waiting to greet her.

"Welcome to Cortona," he said, smiling, as he walked toward her to take her hand. "You've had a pleasant journey?"

"Oh, yes. Quite. Thank you." She knew she must sound like a nervous schoolgirl. She resisted the urge to snatch her hand away, although the touch of his long, strong fingers had caused a peculiar tingling sensation to run through her body. He looked fully as handsome as she remembered. It wasn't fair, she thought resentfully. If only he'd developed a squint or a wart, it would be so much easier to make her galloping heartbeat settle down.

She jerked her gaze away from him, glancing around the great hallway paved in black and white marble; tall alabaster pillars marched down the sides of the room, interspersed with niches containing statuary. Her eyes widened.

Jeffrey laughed. "Ridiculous, isn't it? This hallway is modeled after the atrium in the Baths of Titus in Rome. My grandfather returned from his Grand Tour of the Continent bound and determined to build a Palladian villa. This house is as close as he could come to a villa he visited in Northern Italy. But come," he added, motioning to a doorway on the left of the hallway. "My mother is eager to welcome you."

The handsome, elegantly gowned woman waiting in an equally elegant drawing room extended a limp hand to her guest, saying languidly, "So nice to meet you, Miss Kinley. I trust you'll have a pleasant visit with us."

Manner and voice were transparent, telling Charlotte without words that Drucilla, Lady Sherborne, was *not* eager to welcome her son's future wife.

A servant came into the room with a whispered message for Jeffrey, who rose, saying vexedly, "Will you excuse me, Charlotte? My bailiff wishes to see me." He smiled. "Perhaps it's for the best. This will give you and Mama an opportunity to get acquainted."

"Do sit down, Miss Kinley," said the dowager when Jeffrey had left the room. "Will you have some tea? And then you must tell me about your journey from Derbyshire."

"Lancashire."

"Oh, yes. My memory, I fear, is not what it was." Handing Charlotte a cup of tea, Lady Sherborne said abruptly, "Far be it for me to interfere, Miss Kinley, but I feel I must give you my opinion. My son informs me that you and he plan to marry in the early spring. In view of your father's very recent death, would it not be more seemly to postpone the wedding—and yes, the announcement of it, too—to a later date? One would not wish to offend public opinion, I'm sure you'll agree."

"I'd rather offend public opinion than go against my father's wishes," said Charlotte quietly. "Papa didn't want me to be alone in the world after his death. He wanted me to be married as soon as possible."

"Oh. I believe Jeffrey did say something of the sort . . ." Lady Sherborne's voice trailed away, leaving a distinct impression that, while she didn't agree with Phineas's position, she was too well-bred to say so. She noticed that Charlotte's eyes were fixed on a large portrait over the mantel. "That's Cicely," she said.

"Cicely?"

"Why, yes. Jeffrey's wife." The dowager sounded mildly surprised.

"Oh." Charlotte stared at the spun gold hair, the violet eyes, the soft rosy lips of the beautiful girl in the portrait, feeling a little stupid. Somehow, in the turmoil of the past few months, distracted by her grief for her father and the necessity to keep the mill running smoothly, she'd completely forgotten that Jeffrey was a widower. Oh, Phineas had informed her of it; Charlotte could even vaguely remember Papa saying that Jeffrey was the son-in-law of a duke. But certainly, on the few occasions they'd met during their brief courtship, Jeffrey had never spoken of his wife or even mentioned her name. Was there any significance to the omission? Well no, probably not. It would, she supposed, have been awkward for both her and Jeffrey if he'd talked at length about his wife to her successor.

"She was so lovely," sighed the dowager. "You know, I daresay, that she was Lady Cicely Layton, the daughter of the Duke of Sandridge. She and I were distant cousins. Our branches of the family have always been very close. Would you believe it, Cicely's mother and I schemed from our children's cradles that they should marry, and they did!" Lady Sherborne gave a tinkling little laugh. Then, sobering, she added, "Cicely and Jeffrey were married for such a short time. The wedding was four years ago at Christmastide. And then, little more than two years later, she was gone. Congestion of the lungs. Jeffrey was so prostrated with grief, we feared he'd never get over his loss."

The dowager sighed again. "Last year, for example, he simply refused to come here for Christmas, even though his father hadn't been well for some time. I think now that my husband suspected he would die soon and wanted to have all his family around him for his last Christmas. As you probably know, he did die some six months later. Jeffrey must have regretted not coming here last year during the holidays, but I expect he simply didn't want to be reminded of past Christmases."

Lady Sherborne raised her eyes to the portrait again. "You see, dear Cicely had always taken such delight in the yuletide, as she liked to call it. She loved all the holiday customs, the yule log, the holly and the ivy and the mistletoe, the suckling pigs and the roasted chestnuts, the wassail bowl and the carolers. She especially loved our annual Christmas Eve party here at Cortona, when she could visit with all the friends and neighbors she hadn't been able to see while she and Jeffrey were living in London."

Charlotte set down her cup so suddenly that the cup rattled against the saucer. She didn't doubt that the mention of the annual Christmas Eve party had been deliberate. Lady Sherborne had meant to contrast the happiness of previous such celebrations with an unspoken disapproval of the announcement that would be made on this Christmas Eve. But, of course, Charlotte had already realized that the dowager's reminiscences had had a very unsubtle purpose, to convey to Charlotte how unfavorably she compared to the beautiful Cicely.

"My dear Miss Kinley, I'm keeping you here with my babbling," said the dowager with a totally unconvincing display of solicitude, "when you must be anxious to retire to your bedchamber and rest after your long journey."

Helping Charlotte dress for dinner several hours later, her abigail murmured in a voice filled with misgiving, "Oh,

315

ma'am, your gown does look so very plain."

Charlotte knew quite well why a dress that had seemed perfectly presentable to her abigail in Lancashire now appeared to be so inadequate. Since their arrival at Cortona, Sarah had grown steadily more impressed with the magnificence of Jeffrey's home. It wasn't hard to understand. The entire Kinley house in Bury could have fitted comfortably into two or three of the public rooms at Cortona.

"I'm in mourning, Sarah," Charlotte said shortly. "I'm not aspiring to be a fashion plate."

Nevertheless, she moved to the cheval glass to check her appearance. It was true. The gown *was* very plain, the handwork of a seamstress in Bury. Charlotte had stubbornly insisted on wearing mourning for Phineas for at least a few weeks until after her engagement was announced. Unfortunately, black didn't become her. It made her fresh complexion look sallow and dulled the blueness of her eyes. She studied herself critically. She had masses of curling brown hair, even features and good teeth, and a slender erect figure. She was far from being plain. She was also far from being a beauty like the golden-haired young girl in the portrait in the drawing room.

Absently Charlotte pulled on her gloves and picked up her reticule. Obviously Lady Sherborne had adored Cicely and would have preferred someone like her to be her next daughter-in-law, instead of a mill owner's daughter. Well, there was nothing Charlotte could do about the dowager's feelings. But Lady Sherborne had also indicated that Jeffrey had been very slow to recover from the loss of his wife. Charlotte paused on her way to the door of the bedchamber. Was it possible that Jeffrey still hadn't recovered from Cicely's death? Would he remember her and mourn for her this Christmas Eve while he announced his coming marriage to a woman who so little resembled her?

Straightening her shoulders, Charlotte left the bedchamber and started down the stairs. She was borrowing trouble. It was two years, after all, since Cicely's death. Time enough for Jeffrey's grief to fade. In any case, he'd never pretended that his marriage to Charlotte was a love match.

He came forward to meet her when she entered the drawing room, and her heart skipped a beat. He looked so handsome in his severely elegant evening clothes. With the slightly formal air that was beginning to be so familiar, he asked, "You're rested, I trust, from the effects of your journey?"

"Yes, thank you—" Charlotte broke off, staring in bewilderment over Jeffrey's shoulder at a young woman in a gown of lavender-colored gros de Naples. For a startled moment, Charlotte thought that the portrait over the mantel had suddenly come to life.

Jeffrey took her arm. "Charlotte, I'd like to make known to you my sister-in-law, Arabella Layton. Oh, and my brother-in-law also, Thomas Layton."

Charlotte mumbled something in answer to the introduction. Something she couldn't afterwards remember. Her mind was in a whirl. Arabella—no, it must be *Lady* Arabella Layton. If she was Cicely's sister, she was the daughter of a duke. And her brother, a slender blond youth of about eighteen, must be *Lord* Thomas. Lady Arabella could almost have been the twin of her—older?—sister Cicely. The same spun gold hair, the same huge violet eyes, the same delicately perfect features. Lord Thomas resembled both his sisters.

Lady Arabella curtsied gracefully. "I'm happy to make your acquaintance, Miss Kinley," she said. Her brother ducked his head in a bow.

"Come now, Bella, you mustn't stand on ceremony with Charlotte," said Jeffrey firmly. "I've told you she'll soon be a member of the family."

With a sweet smile that didn't quite reach her eyes, Arabella said, "But of course. I'm so glad you've come, Charlotte."

Lady Sherborne motioned Charlotte to a seat beside her. "Such charming creatures, both of them, don't you think?" she murmured, gazing at Arabella and Thomas. "I'm delighted that their father allowed them to come to us this Christmas. As I was telling you, I've always felt so close to all of dear Cicely's family. Why, I vow I think of Arabella practically as my niece!"

As the evening progressed, Charlotte began to wonder if

317

Arabella and Thomas had consciously decided to bombard Jeffrey with memories of Cicely. Even when a comment or a question was directed at Charlotte, the conversation seemed inevitably to turn back to Cicely.

"Do you ride, Miss Kinley—I mean, Charlotte?" asked Thomas.

"No, I never learned."

"Oh. Cicely was a bruising rider, you know. A pretty whip, too. Arabella also handles the ribbons very well, eh, Jeffrey?"

The marquess smiled at Arabella, saying teasingly, "Indeed, our Bella is on the way to being a first-rate fiddler."

She made a little face at him. "Oh, you, Jeffrey."

"It's getting much colder," Thomas remarked a little later at the dinner table. "Today one of the gamekeepers allowed as how he smelled snow in the air. By Jove, that would be capital, snow at Christmas."

"I love snow and the cold," said Arabella, her face lighting up. "Remember, Jeffrey, how you taught me to skate several winters ago when there was ice on the pond in the village? Oh, and the Frost Fair, the year the Thames froze over. That was so much fun. I'll never forget the skating, the swings, and the skittle alleys, and the oysters and the brandy-balls and the gingerbread! We literally had to drag Cicely away, she was enjoying herself so much." She stopped short, looking suddenly stricken.

"Yes, I remember," said Jeffrey briefly. He turned to Charlotte, saying, "Perhaps you'd like to have a tour of the estate tomorrow?"

"Thank you, I'd enjoy that."

Flushing a deep red, Arabella reached blindly for her wine glass and upset it. While the servants were rushing to mop up the spill, Lady Sherborne launched into a detailed account of the number of guests expected at the Christmas Eve party. Under the cover of the dowager's small talk, Arabella gradually recovered from her embarrassment, although, when the ladies retired to the drawing room a little later, leaving the gentlemen to their port, she still appeared somewhat subdued. She went to the pianoforte, where she sat, playing softly to herself.

Gazing at Arabella, Lady Sherborne said to Charlotte in a low voice, "Poor darling Bella, I'm sure she never meant to remind Jeffrey of hurtful memories. She simply forgot for a moment that Cicely caught a chill at the Frost Fair. It eventually went to her lungs, and several weeks later she was dead."

Was it always going to be like this, Charlotte wondered? When she became mistress of Cortona, would she hear echoes of Cicely in every conversation?

Arabella left the pianoforte when Jeffrey and Thomas entered the drawing room. Her eyes sparkling, she said, "Dear Lady Sherborne, I've the greatest favor to ask of you."

"Why, of course, my dear."

"Will you play for us to dance? With Miss Kinley—I mean, Charlotte—we have two whole couples!"

The dowager smiled indulgently. "Well, why not? Jeffrey, Thomas, will you move those two settees? There, now you'll have enough room." She seated herself at the pianoforte. "What shall I play?"

"I don't remember the name of the piece, but it goes like this . . ." Arabella hummed several bars of a song.

Lady Sherborne looked dubious. "Yes, I know the tune, but, my dear Bella, isn't that song a—a waltz?"

Arabella smiled. "Oh, dear, have I shocked you? So many people think the waltz isn't quite the thing, because the patronesses at Almack's won't allow it to be performed there. But Maurice Ventnor—he's my great friend Susan's brother—was an aide to Lord Wellington at the Congress of Vienna, and Maurice swears that before long the waltz will be danced everywhere. In any case, we're quite private here. Nobody will see us."

"Minx," said Lady Sherborne fondly. "You could charm the birds from the trees." She made no further objection but began playing a lively waltz tune.

Making it quite clear, Charlotte thought, who would be dancing with whom, Arabella put her hand on the marquess's arm. She said roguishly, "Jeffrey, I won't believe you if you tell me you don't know how to dance the waltz."

The marquess's eyes crinkled with amusement. "Bella, you little wretch, are you insinuating I spend my leisure hours in questionable haunts? You'll have Charlotte thinking me a frippery fellow with no regard for the *convenances!*" But he put his arm around Arabella's slender waist and led her out into the cleared space in the middle of the floor. With a catch in her throat, Charlotte had to admit that they were as graceful as drifting thistledown as they moved through the patterns of the dance.

"Miss Kinley? I mean, Charlotte?" Thomas Layton stepped in front of Charlotte with a jerky bow.

"I'm sorry. I don't know how to waltz. I fear we're much behind the times in Lancashire."

Thomas held out his hand. "I'll show you. The steps aren't difficult."

The steps were indeed simple enough, Charlotte thought after several agonizing minutes in Thomas's wooden embrace, during which he stomped on the toes of her delicate silken slippers, but Cicely's brother was no dabster on the dance floor. Heaven help the young ladies at Almack's when he was unleashed against them! "Could we stop, Thomas?" she said with a smile. "You're an excellent teacher, but I'm quite tired after my long journey."

She sat down to watch Jeffrey and Arabella, thinking how perfectly they moved together. At the end of the dance, they happened to pause beneath the cut-glass luster from which was suspended an arrangement of holly and mistletoe.

"Watch out, Bella, you're right under the kissing bush," Thomas chortled.

Her startled expression fading into a smile, Arabella looked up at Jeffrey. "My dear Bella, I'm not such a ninnyhammer that I'd neglect such a golden opportunity," he said with a laugh. He put his arms around her in an enveloping hug and kissed her on the lips. Then, still laughing, he walked over to Charlotte, extending his hand as Lady Sherborne began playing another waltz tune. "May I have the pleasure?"

He is so obviously being dutiful, making sure I don't feel left out, thought Charlotte with a pang. *If I should dance with*

320

him, right after he's danced with Arabella, he'll compare the two of us and come to the conclusion that I have two left feet. And I don't want to get too close to him. If we should stop anywhere near the kissing bush, with everyone looking at us . . . She suppressed her disjointed thoughts, saying coolly, "Thank you, but, as I was just telling Thomas, the waltz hasn't yet penetrated to the wilds of Lancashire. Another time, perhaps? After I've learned the steps? I collect you wouldn't wish me to make a cake of myself!"

Jeffrey raised an eyebrow. "You're being much too modest."

"No, not at all. Simply realistic. But do go on dancing with Arabella. It's a pleasure to watch you."

He gave her a long look. Did he suspect the welter of emotions behind her calm facade? Could he have any idea of the wave of jealousy that had swept over her when he embraced Arabella under the kissing bush?

"Oh, I think we've had enough of dancing for tonight," he said easily. "What about a game of whist? Or perhaps you'd prefer backgammon? But I must warn you, my mother is so devoted to her whist game that she might become violent if we thwart her!"

Fortunately for Charlotte's self-esteem, she was a very fair whist player. At the end of the evening, the dowager bestowed on her new partner a few words of faintly grudging praise. "Very well done, my dear Charlotte. Of course, we must admit that we held excellent cards."

As the party was about to separate for the night, Jeffrey said casually, "If you're not too tired, Charlotte, may I suggest a stroll to the conservatory?"

Arabella opened her mouth and closed it again without speaking. Lady Sherborne said with an air of faint disapproval, "I would have thought the conservatory could wait until tomorrow. . . . But there, I'll say good night, my dear Charlotte. Don't let Jeffrey keep you from your bed too late."

Charlotte walked out of the great central hall with Jeffrey and down a long glass-enclosed corridor lit by hanging lamps. They were quite alone, but Charlotte had a sudden vision of hordes of servants lurking in all corners of the great house, waiting to extinguish the lights after the family had retired for the night. She wanted to laugh at the contrast between her home in Bury—where, more often than not, she, not a servant, was the one who made the last rounds at night, snuffing out the candles and lamps—and this vast establishment. Then her amusement faded as she reflected that one day soon she'd be the mistress of Cortona, and the servants would be waiting for *her* to retire for the night.

The conservatory was very large, dimly lit by hanging lamps and pervaded by the moist earthy smell of growing things. There was a palm tree in the corner, and Charlotte could see slips of pineapple and ripening grapes on a trellis, but mainly the greenhouse seemed to be devoted to flowers and shrubs.

"My mother likes fresh flowers in the house all year around," Jeffrey observed. He motioned to some bright red, funnel-shaped flowers. "She's locally famous for her fuchsias."

"Lovely," murmured Charlotte. The sweet, beguiling scent of mignonette filled the air, making her feel lightheaded. Or was it Jeffrey? He was standing several feet away from her, and in the dim light she couldn't really see his face clearly, but she was so acutely aware of him physically that she might have been touching him.

"Mama is right, you know. We could have waited until tomorrow to come here," Jeffrey said coolly, "but I wanted us to have a chance to talk away from the others. We've seen so little of each other. The other day I counted it up, and we've met just three times since that first meeting in Bury. And here we are, practically married! I think it's important for us to become better acquainted, and soon, don't you agree? We wouldn't wish to meet at the altar as strangers, after all."

"Oh, no." What was the matter with her? She had the curious sensation that she and Jeffrey were drifting closer and closer together, when, in point of fact, neither of them had moved an inch.

"Unfortunately, we won't have many opportunities to be alone until the New Year," Jeffrey continued. "The house will soon be full of neighbors paying calls and guests arriving for the Christmas Eve party. So I thought tomorrow we might go for a drive so that I can show you the estate. We'd have a little privacy, too. There's a folly in the park you might like to see—"

"Folly? Oh, do you mean the little classical-style building we drove past on the way to the house?"

"That's the one. The village is also considered very pretty. It's a pity we're in the middle of winter. The countryside in this part of Oxfordshire is lovely in the warmer months."

"Oh, well, I can see the scenery later, can't I? Summer always comes eventually." Charlotte bit her lip. She was babbling again. Never in all her life had she sounded so inane. To hide her confusion, she bent over a rose bush, murmuring, "What a heavenly scent."

"Here, allow me." Jeffrey leaned down to twist a half-opened rose from the bush, muttering a stifled exclamation as his thumb jammed on a thorn. He held the rose out to her, and then, when she didn't take it immediately, he tucked the bloom into the cluster of curls on the crown of her head. Cocking his head to study the effect, he smiled, saying, "It looks very chic. You have beautiful hair, Charlotte."

Putting out his hand, he slowly ran his fingers through the springy masses of her hair. Mesmerized, scarcely breathing, Charlotte stood motionless as those long capable fingers moved down to stroke her face and throat caressingly before settling on her shoulders. Slipping his arms around her waist, he brushed her mouth in a featherlight kiss, his lips fluttering against hers as he murmured, with a shadow of a laugh in his voice, "I can't think of a better, easier, more enjoyable way to get acquainted, can you?"

Her heart was thudding, and her bones had turned to jelly, and Charlotte wanted nothing more than to surrender to the sweet, unfamiliar, enticing feelings sweeping through her body as Jeffrey's arms tightened and the pressure of his warm, clinging lips became more demanding. Instead, she pushed so hard against his chest that, caught by surprise, he nearly lost his balance and fell.

He exclaimed incredulously, "Good God, Charlotte, what's the matter with you?"

Her back half turned to him, she stood silently, fighting for calm. She'd so nearly made a fool of herself. She knew that Jeffrey hadn't simply given in to his emotions when he kissed her. He'd never given her any reason to believe that he had any personal feelings for her. From the very beginning, the arrangement between them had been purely business. His lovemaking a moment ago had been just as premeditated, just as practical as his original proposal of marriage had been. He'd probably reasoned that, even in a marriage of convenience, their relationship might progress a little more smoothly if he injected a bit of romance into it. Perhaps he even thought she was expecting, wanting, him to kiss her. Perhaps her face had given her away when she'd observed the affectionate spontaneity of his kiss to Arabella.

She turned back to Jeffrey. "Nothing's the matter with *me*."

"Well, but . . ." He stared at her in bewilderment. Suddenly he said, "You're not — you can't be offended with me for kissing you, surely?"

Charlotte said coolly, "Offended? No, not really. However, I do think you were — what's that hunting expression some of my friends use? Oh, yes, I have it. I think you may have been rushing your fences. As you pointed out a few minutes ago, we're still practically strangers."

Even in the dim light, she could see his lips hardening. "I'll also point out that we're strangers who are about to be married. Let's understand each other, Charlotte. You say I've been 'rushing my fences.' Does that mean I'm not to touch you in any way during the course of our engagement?"

Charlotte swallowed hard. "I merely meant to say that I think it's hypocritical to pretend to — to romantic urges that neither of us feels."

"I see. So something like a chaste peck on the cheek might be permitted?"

Goaded by the cool irony in his tone, Charlotte snapped, "I have no objections to that."

"Splendid. For a moment, I feared you were implying that our courtship *and* our marriage would be of the mind only."

Charlotte's voice matched his in coolness. "Indeed, not. I'm quite aware that you must have an heir to your estate, and I've long since ceased to believe that babies are found in the cabbage patch."

"You relieve my anxieties no end," he said dryly. He paused, studying her in the dim light. After a moment, he said, "Well, Charlotte, I'm glad we had this little talk. It's cleared the air as far as I'm concerned. And now, my dear, I daresay I should heed my mother's advice and not keep you from your bed until all hours."

He extended his arm politely, and Charlotte, without speaking, placed her hand on his sleeve. In silence, they walked out of the conservatory and up the stairway to her bedchamber. Charlotte's thoughts were chaotic. She'd mismanaged the scene in the greenhouse. She'd merely intended to prevent Jeffrey from realizing how vulnerable she was to his lovemaking. Instead, she might have damaged their relationship beyond repair. Stealing a glance at his polite, impassive features, she had no idea what he was thinking about.

At the door of her bedchamber, he swung around to face her. Bending his head, he brushed her cheek with his lips. "It's permissible?" he asked. If he was angry, if he was mocking her, the expression in his dark eyes was unreadable.

"Yes, of course. Good night, Jeffrey."

"Good night. Shall we meet in the morning room about ten o'clock for our drive?"

The next morning, Charlotte stood hesitating in the great marble hallway. A footman appeared out of nowhere and said politely, "May I help you, ma'am?"

"I'm to meet Lord Sherborne in the morning room."

"This way, ma'am."

Charlotte felt, rather than saw, the inquisitive glance of the footman as he walked along beside her. Had the servants, by some mysterious process of mind reading, already grasped the fact that she was to be the new mistress of Cortona? Or—lowering thought—was she so obviously a guest from a different order of society that it had occasioned the servants' curiosity?

The morning room was a pleasant room with comfortable, well-used furniture, a distinct contrast to the magnificence of the rest of the house, but Charlotte walked into it with a dragging reluctance. She hadn't slept well. Her eyelids felt grainy, and her stomach was still churning nervously at the memory of the scene in the conservatory last night. She dreaded being alone with Jeffrey on their drive.

Lady Arabella was already seated in the room, reading a book, when Charlotte entered. Cicely's younger sister looked even more impossibly beautiful in the full light of day, her aureole of blond curls set off by pale blue ribbons that matched her gown of sprigged muslin. Being in the same room with her made Charlotte feel like a bedraggled jackdaw in her simple black dress and pelisse.

Arabella put down her book. "Oh, good morning, Miss Kin—Charlotte. Are you exploring the house?"

"No, I'm to meet Jeffrey here at ten. We're going for a drive around the estate."

Arabella consulted the little jeweled watch pinned to her bodice. "You're very early. It's only a quarter of the hour. Come, let me show you some of the rooms on the ground floor before Jeffrey joins you."

Having eaten a meal the evening before in the cavernous dining room literally walled with silver plate, Charlotte wasn't surprised to find that the state bedrooms, the music room, and the chapel were on a similar scale. However, she was unprepared for the Grand Saloon opening directly off the entrance hall. It was a vast circular room with a soaring dome, floored in marble, with a gilded, coffered ceiling and a ring of antique paintings encircling the upper walls of the rotunda.

"This is where the Christmas Eve ball will take place," said Arabella. Her face glowed with reminiscent pleasure. "It's always such a splendid affair. I've heard people say that no other yuletide celebration in England can match it. Next year, of course, now that Jeffrey's succeeded his father, you'll be the official hostess of the ball." She giggled. "Lady Sherborne will no doubt tell you she'll be happy to be relieved of all the preparations for the ball, but don't you believe her. She's always complaining that being the mistress of Cortona is a great deal of work, but secretly she loves it."

Charlotte privately agreed that, after their marriage, she and Jeffrey would probably have to remove the dowager bodily from the premises and pack her off to the dower house, but she merely smiled politely at Arabella's facetious remark.

Her eyes sparkling, Arabella added, "There's the most delicious rumor circulating in the county. The present Lord Lieutenant, Lord Ilworth, isn't expected to live very long, and the *on dit* is that the Regent will appoint Jeffrey to the post." Arabella's forehead furrowed in a thoughtful frown. "The appointment would mean that you and Jeffrey would be doing a great deal of official entertaining. And then there's the town house in London. Jeffrey's father was quite ill the past few years and rarely went up to Town. But I know that Jeffrey intends to be active in the House of Lords and will certainly open the town house for the Season. You'll be a very busy hostess."

Arabella paused, looking even more thoughtful. "Have you considered how different your life will be, Charlotte? Jeffrey told us that you and your papa lived in quite a tiny house in Lancashire. I daresay you never sat down to more than a dozen at most at table? It would have been so much easier for Cicely. . . . Ah, well, I do hope you won't feel overwhelmed by all your new duties."

Voice and expression reflected only a kindly concern, but Charlotte wasn't deceived. Lady Sherborne and Arabella had already displayed their lack of enthusiasm for Jeffrey's choice of a bride. Every word of Arabella's transparent little speech had been intended as a barb, to point out Charlotte's lack of qualifications to be Marchioness of Sherborne.

Well, I won't let her see that she's drawn blood, Charlotte decided, lifting her chin. She said composedly, "I'll do my very best, Arabella, that's all I can say. If I need advice, I'm sure I can come to Lady Sherborne—or to you."

"Oh. Certainly." Arabella sounded startled.

"There you are, Charlotte. The servants told me you and Bella were taking the grand tour." Charlotte turned to see Jeffrey standing in the doorway of the saloon. He glanced up at the rotunda, grimacing. "Did Bella tell you the saloon is modeled on the Pantheon in Rome? Thank God my grandfather ran out of funds before he could make it as large! Are you ready to go for our drive?"

When they reached the carriage, which was waiting in front of the house, Jeffrey handed her up the steps, tucked a warm robe around her legs, and placed some hot bricks at her feet. "Comfortable?" he asked solicitously as the carriage rolled down the driveway.

"Very much so. Thank you." Charlotte stole a sideways glance at him. He looked and sounded very much as he had when she arrived yesterday, pleasant and friendly. Perhaps he'd put the scene in the conservatory out of his mind. In the course of a sleepless night, perhaps she'd been magnifying how disastrous the encounter had been. Charlotte began to relax. Soon she was enjoying the drive.

They visited the little classical folly in the park. "Every person who ever made the Grand Tour of the Continent returned home bent on building one of these follies," Jeffrey said with a deprecating shrug that didn't quite hide a pride of ownership. The building, graceful with its columns and miniature dome, looked chilly and unwelcoming and out of place in the depths of winter, but, as Jeffrey remarked, it was a pleasant place in which to while away a hot summer afternoon. "My mother and my—" He caught himself. "Mama and Cicely were fond of taking tea here."

To her horror, Charlotte found herself saying, "Do you miss her very much? Cicely, I mean?"

He looked away. For a moment, Charlotte thought he wasn't going to answer. Then he said evenly, "Time has a way of taking the edge off sorrow. Cicely's been gone for two years."

Charlotte wanted to sink through the ground. She'd resented the frequent references to Cicely on the part of Lady Sherborne and Arabella, and here she was, doing the same thing herself. Jeffrey probably thought her very forward or insensitive or both.

Catching sight of a group of fallow deer quietly grazing near the folly, she hastily changed the subject. "What beautiful little creatures," she exclaimed, walking slowly toward them for a better look. She expected them to dart away at her approach, but they seemed quite tame, merely moving back a few feet to continue their grazing.

Coming up to her, Jeffrey said, "Would you like to feed them? They're very fond of horse chestnuts." He took a small bag out of the pocket of his greatcoat and handed it to her. She looked down at the bag in her hand and then shifted her gaze rather apprehensively to the deer. "Go ahead," Jeffrey said reassuringly. "I swear they're not the least bit ferocious."

To Charlotte's delight, several of the little creatures came slowly up to her to take the glossy brown seeds from her hand. Living in a town all her life in the midst of a grimy and congested milling district, she'd never had any contact with animals, save for a pet dog or cat. At one point, she glanced up to observe Jeffrey watching her, a smile of appreciative amusement on his lips.

"Did you use to feed the deer when you were a boy, Jeffrey?"

He laughed. "Indeed I did. Watching you brings it all back."

For a fleeting moment, she felt a warm glow suffusing her heart. It was as if there was a sort of communion between them as they shared what was to her a unique experience.

"Here, now, wot's this?" A sturdy man in gaiters and low-crowned hat, with a musket over his shoulder, suddenly appeared from behind a screen of trees.

"Beggin' yer pardon, my lord," said the man in some confusion, touching his cap. "Didn't realize it was you. Them poachers, they've been mighty bad of late."

"That's all right," Jeffrey told the gamekeeper. "I'd rather you were overly vigilant than not." He nodded a dismissal, and the man moved off.

"You can't mean that anyone would want to kill these beautiful little things," said Charlotte indignantly. "They're so tame, it would be like slaughtering a friend."

Jeffrey shrugged. "Poaching game is on the increase. I've been told it's mainly the work of ex-soldiers and sailors discharged after Waterloo and unable to find jobs yet." He glanced at the empty bag in her hand. "I see those greedy creatures have consumed your offering. Shall we continue our drive?"

Outside the park, they drove through a country of low hills, undulating meadows, meandering streams now half frozen over, and stretches of orderly fields edged by luxuriant hedgerows, which Charlotte thought would be quite lovely in the spring, starred with the white blossoms of the hawthorn.

"All of this land belongs to you?" she asked at one point in awe after they had driven for what seemed like miles.

Jeffrey nodded. "For about as far as you can see. I understand it looked much different years ago, before my father enclosed the estate. When he was young, the members of the hunt could sweep across the commons and the open fields without having to open a gate or jump a hedge."

"Did the enclosure cause a great deal of hardship?"

"Hardship?" Jeffrey looked at her blankly.

My grandfather lost his farm when the landowner terminated his lease and enclosed the property," Charlotte explained. "Fortunately for him, Grandfer had saved a bit of money from the weaving he'd done in his own home. He opened a small shop in Manchester, and Papa eventually founded a mill with the nest egg he inherited from my grandfather. But most of Grandfer's fellow tenants were left destitute. No land, no cottage, no employment."

Jeffrey shrugged. "I really don't know what happened at the time of enclosure here at Cortona. It was many years before my time. I believe my father was satisfied with the results. He often spoke of higher crop yields and healthier livestock."

Jeffrey sounded almost indifferent, and Charlotte felt rather shocked. She was so accustomed to Phineas' absorbed interest, not only in all aspects of his business and the milling industry in general, but in every detail of his workers' living conditions.

Leaning forward to peer out the window, Jeffrey said, "We're coming into the village. As I was telling you, it's considered very pretty. Most of the cottages are

330

built of the local stone."

The village of Westbridge was tiny, consisting of a single short street lined with small cottages constructed of mellow, rosy stone. The street was deserted except for a group of children playing at hopscotch, who glanced up curiously at the sound of the carriage wheels and then returned to their play.

"I wonder why the children aren't in school at this time of day," Charlotte observed.

"I'm not sure there is a school in Westbridge," said Jeffrey. "It's one of those things that I—"

Charlotte interrupted him. "You're not sure if there's a school?" she asked indignantly. "But how can that be? This village is on your property. These people are your tenants. You certainly ought to know if the village has a school, and if there isn't one, you ought to provide it! Why, when Papa discovered that the mill children couldn't read and write, he promptly built a school for them and hired a teacher!"

"I have no doubt that your father was a paragon."

Charlotte heard the throb of anger in his voice and looked at the set expression of his mouth and realized she'd allowed her impulsive tongue to run away with her manners. "I'm sorry," she said stiffly. "I had no right to tell you how to manage your affairs."

He quickly recovered his composure. "As I was about to say, I have a great deal to learn about the management of the estate. Until very recently, I never expected to inherit, and since my school days I've spent little time at Cortona. Perhaps you didn't know that I'm the child of my father's second marriage. He was quite elderly when he married my mother, and he already had a son, my brother Robert, twenty years older than myself, who of course was the heir and whom my father groomed to succeed him. There was no need for me to know anything about estate management. In any case, both my father and Robert tended to leave the day-to-day details of running the estate in the hands of our bailiff, Silas Adams. Silas would almost certainly have resented any interest I might have shown, on the grounds, and quite rightly so, that it was none of my affair. I've come to the conclusion that my father probably allowed Silas too much of a free rein over the years. To this day, months after I succeeded to the estate, Silas is all too inclined to say in answer to any question, 'Now, now, my lord, you just leave these matters to me.' "

Jeffrey paused for a moment and then said coolly, "I trust this explains why I seem so ignorant about my own property. You were right, you know. I *should* know whether the village has a school. I assure you that I intend to look into the matter immediately.".

He didn't sound angry or resentful, even though she'd falsely accused him of being a neglectful landlord. Moreover, it had been an impertinence on her part even to raise the issue. She had no standing in his life. They weren't even officially engaged as yet. He had every right to be angry, but instead he'd retreated behind a mask of impersonal politeness. With a sinking heart, Charlotte thought back to the small beginnings of closeness she'd felt with Jeffrey earlier in their drive. The closeness was gone, and it was her fault.

"Ye should have let me pack yer pattens, ma'am," said Sarah. "Mine, too," added the abigail. "My toes are fair freezing, that they are."

"We'd certainly both be more comfortable if we were wearing pattens," Charlotte replied ruefully, looking down at her feet. There'd been a light dusting of snow during the night, and she could feel the cold dampness through her thin slippers. She hadn't thought to bring her serviceable pattens with her to a fashionable place like Cortona. But then, of course, it hadn't occurred to her that she might feel the need to flee from Jeffrey's house to take a long cold walk with Sarah in the park.

She'd spent most of the evening last night trying to hide her low spirits over the depressing end to her afternoon drive with Jeffrey. He hadn't given any outward sign that he was annoyed with her. In fact, he'd been courteous and attentive, everything a considerate host should be. But she was well aware of the little gulf that had opened up between them after their visit to the village. There hadn't been even a trace of the warmth and companionship she'd felt earlier, during their encounter with

332

the deer.

Arabella and her brother Thomas hadn't made the evening any easier. They had a seemingly inexhaustible supply of anecdotes about Cicely's beauty and perfections. At one point, Arabella had looked up at Cicely's portrait over the mantel in the drawing room and said anxiously, "Charlotte, it just occurred to me—you're not thinking of taking Cicely's portrait down, are you?" Then she'd looked away in pretty confusion, but to Charlotte, Arabella's spitefulness was perfectly transparent.

And Thomas had chimed in, "By Jove, Charlotte, if you take the portrait down, I know my mother will be happy to have it."

Jeffrey had said curtly, "There's been no talk of removing Cicely's portrait," and quickly changed the subject.

Sarah interrupted Charlotte's musings as they plodded along through the trees of the park. "Do ye have the headache, ma'am? Ye're very quiet this morning."

"No, I'm very well. I just needed some fresh air." Certainly it would be understandable if she had the headache, Charlotte reflected. Thus far, her stay at Cortona had been unsettling. Take, for example, her latest encounter with her future mother-in-law.

As Charlotte was completing her toilet that morning, Lady Sherborne had come to the bedchamber, ostensibly to inquire if her guest had everything she needed. It soon became obvious that the dowager had other concerns on her mind. "My dear Charlotte," she began with a sweet smile, "I haven't been able to stop thinking about something you said last night at dinner. Am I mistaken, or did I hear you say that your mother was a Dunston from northern Lancashire?"

"Why, yes, my mother's name was Mary Dunston."

"Was she related, by any chance, to George Dunston of Highcliffe Hall? A very old family, not titled, of course, but much respected."

"No, there's no connection. Mama's family kept a sweet shop in a little town near Lancaster."

" 'Oh. I'd hoped . . . It would have been of so much interest to all our friends . . .'' Lady Sherborne's voice trailed off into disappointment. In a moment, however, she came back to the attack. Glancing at Charlotte's simple black sarcenet gown, she said, "My dear, might I make a suggestion? I appreciate your desire to remain in mourning for your father, but I do think it might be more appropriate if you were to go into colors for the Christmas Eve ball. I'm sure you wish to look your best, in view of the important announcement that's to be made at the ball."

When Charlotte didn't reply immediately, Lady Sherborne said quickly, "Naturally, no one would expect you to wear anything bright or gaudy. One of the quiet shades of second mourning would be the very thing." She looked down complacently at her own dress of light purple silk. "I've taken my own advice, as you've noticed. My dear husband has been gone for only six months, but I know he wouldn't wish me to look like a black scarecrow during the holidays! Now then, I realize there's not enough time to have a new ball gown made for you, even supposing there was a modiste in Banbury who was capable of it. So I'd be very happy if you would wear one of my own dresses. We're much of a size. Only the slightest alteration would be necessary." The dowager paused to look at Charlotte with an expectant smile.

Charlotte felt a sudden sharp stab of resentment. Apparently Lady Sherborne had resigned herself to her son's unfortunate marriage and was now attempting to put the best face on the situation by making sure Charlotte at least looked presentable in front of her friends. That it would never occur to the dowager that she was being condescending was even more hurtful and humiliating than her offer of a ball gown.

Repressing an urge to seize Lady Sherborne by her exquisite neck and strangle her, Charlotte replied, "That's very kind of you. If you really think I could wear your gown, I'd be happy to do so."

But after the gratified dowager left, Charlotte had vented her feelings by picking up a small mirror from the dressing table and throwing it against the wall. Immediately she knelt down to pick up the pieces. There was no need for her outburst to create additional work for the chambermaids. Was she overreacting? After all, she'd always planned to come out of mourning after her engagement was announced. Papa would have wanted it that way. And agreeing to wear the dowager's gown was a very small concession to make, surely, if it meant an improvement in her relations with Lady Sherborne. But Charlotte hadn't been able to convince herself. Still seething, she'd grabbed her bonnet and pelisse and called for her abigail, and had gone for a walk in the park.

"Oh, look, ma'am, there's one of them tiny deer we saw from the carriage the other day."

At the abigail's words, Charlotte looked up to find that she and Sarah were approaching the little domed folly. Several fallow deer were grazing beside it. Charlotte checked her steps at the sound of a shrill scream coming from the direction of a nearby copse of trees. She ran behind the trees, pausing in horror at the sight of a small child collapsed on the ground and writhing in pain. The child, a girl of perhaps ten, clothed inadequately in a cotton dress and a tattered shawl, was shoeless. Apparently she had stepped on a jagged bit of fallen branch that had pierced her bare foot. Beside her on the ground was a leather snare encircling the neck of a dead rabbit.

A man burst through the underbrush, exclaiming, "Caught ye red-handed, by God!" At the sight of Charlotte and her abigail, he stopped in midstride. Charlotte recognized the gamekeeper whom she and Jeffrey had met the day before. He raised a finger to his cap. "Good day, ma'am. If ye'll excuse me, I'll jist attend to this here poacher." He reached down a rough hand to pull the child to her feet. Sobbing with pain and terror, the girl collapsed against him. Blood was streaming from her foot.

"What will happen to her?" Charlotte asked apprehensively.

The man shrugged. "Cain't say, ma'am. A whipping, surely. Mayhap a spell in gaol. She's lucky, she is, that she warn't carrying a gun. That'd mean fourteen years transportation. If she'd shot at me and wounded me, she'd be for the nubbing cheat. Hanged from a gibbet, if I make meself clear," he added with relish.

"Hanged?" Charlotte repeated in horror. "For catching a rabbit?" She looked again at the weeping, bedraggled child and said firmly, "I can't believe Lord Sherborne would wish to imprison a child for snaring a rabbit. Release her, please. I'll take all responsibility."

"But ma'am, it's my job ter pertect his lordship's property from poachers," began the keeper uneasily, still retaining his grasp on the child. "If'n it gets about that I've let some'un off—"

"Your job will be quite safe," Charlotte assured him. "You can go. No, wait. The child's foot is bleeding badly. If you'll carry her to the house, I'll see that the wound is attended to."

The little girl began to struggle. "Please, ma'am, don't make me go ter his lordship's grand house," she sobbed. "There'd be no hiding who I am or what I've done. Everyone'd know I'd been caught poaching."

The girl's terror was quite real and understandable. If Charlotte appeared in the servants' quarters of the house with a wounded child in tow, the news would be all over Cortona in minutes. Although Charlotte was quite certain she could persuade Jeffrey not to prosecute, it might be much better for all concerned if the incident never became public. She said to the gamekeeper, "Go to the stables and tell my coachman to bring the carriage here immediately. I'll take the child to her home. Don't tell the coachman why I want the carriage. In fact, don't speak of this to anyone, including your fellow gamekeepers, do you understand?"

Visibly relieved, the gamekeeper replied, "Yes, ma'am, I understands perfickly. I'll jist be off, then." He lowered the little girl to the ground and walked off through the trees.

Sinking down on her knees beside the child, ignoring the damp cold that penetrated through her clothing, Charlotte said gently, "Let me look at your foot."

Slowly, hesitantly, as if she was still afraid to trust her newly found benefactor, the girl pushed her foot forward. Charlotte examined it carefully. The wound had ceased to bleed profusely, but the sharp stick had pierced completely through the

336

foot, leaving a deep, jagged wound. Rising, Charlotte glanced around her and then lifted her skirts, quickly unfastening her petticoat and pulling it off. She knelt down again and gently swathed the injured foot in the petticoat. "There, that'll do until we can get you home. Where do you live?"

"In the village, ma'am, right next ter the church."

"And what's your name?"

"Jessie. Jessie Reeves." The child was shivering with cold in her worn shawl, but she seemed somewhat less fearful.

"That's a pretty name. Jessie, why — ?" Charlotte broke off. She'd been about to ask why the girl had been setting snares for Jeffrey's rabbits when she must have known the stringent penalties against poaching. It was a stupid question. From the child's extreme thinness of body, her ragged clothes, and her lack of shoes, it was obvious that Jessie had been poaching to provide food for her family.

Charlotte looked up with relief as her carriage rolled to a stop in the driveway. The coachman jumped down from the box and walked toward her, his face deeply puzzled.

"We're taking the little girl to her home in the village," Charlotte told the coachman. "Will you carry her to the carriage, please?" After Jessie was settled on the seat, Charlotte picked up the dead rabbit and deposited it on the floorboards of the carriage. The child's eyes widened.

The carriage passed the church at the end of the village street and halted in front of one of the small stone cottages. Several children watched curiously as the coachman carried Jessie through the garden gate of the cottage. Instructing Sarah to remain in the carriage, Charlotte grasped the snare with the rabbit dangling from it and jumped out to follow the coachman up the path.

The door of the cottage opened before the coachman reached it. A frightened-looking woman appeared in the doorway. She wore a mob cap and a voluminous calico apron, and she was obviously in an advanced stage of pregnancy. She stared in dismay at the bloodstained linen wrapped around Jessie's foot and stammered, "I saw all o' ye coming from the window — what's wrong with my Jessie?"

337

The child lifted her wan face from the coachman's shoulder. "I've hurt me foot, Mum. This kind lady brought me home. She's visiting at his lordships's house."

Stepping around the coachman, Charlotte said, "Good day, Mrs. Reeves. I'm Charlotte Kinley."

The woman's eyes were fixed on the rabbit hanging from Charlotte's hand. Her face twisted with apprehension.

"Mrs. Reeves, I really think we should get Jessie into the house so we can attend to her wound."

"Oh. Yes. Please ter come in, ma'am." The woman stood aside. The coachman carried Jessie into the cottage and placed her carefully on a wooden chair, one of the few articles of furniture in the painfully neat but scantily furnished room. A little boy of two or three sat on the floor next to a meager fire of twigs and sticks burning on the hearth.

Dismissing the coachman, Charlotte said to Mrs. Reeves, "Please don't worry about Jessie. I'm sure she'll be quite all right once the wound is cleaned, although she'll be uncomfortable when she walks for a few days. Will you be able to manage? You have some clean cloths for bandages?"

"Yes, thank ye." But the woman stood as if rooted to the floor, seemingly unable to take her eyes from the dead rabbit. "Did Jessie—?"

Charlotte nodded. "Yes, she snared the rabbit, Mrs. Reeves, but don't be concerned. I promise you she won't be punished. And as long as the creature is dead, you may as well have the use of it." She hesitated a moment. Then, opening her reticule, she took out a handful of coins. "I'd like you to have these. Perhaps you could buy a treat for the children."

The woman's face crumbled. She groped her way blindly to a chair and sat down, rocking herself back and forth while the tears gushed down her cheeks in a steady stream.

Stricken, Charlotte turned to Jessie. "I'm so sorry. I never meant to offend your mother."

"She's not offended, ma'am," said Jessie, her thin little face glowing beneath the tear stains and the lines of pain. "She's happy, if ye can believe it. Ye have no idea how much that"— she pointed to the coins in Charlotte's hand—"how much that will mean ter us. Things 'ave been right bad of late."

"I'm glad I could help. Jessie, did your father die recently? Is that why matters have been so difficult for your family?"

"Oh, no, ma'am. Pap ain't dead. Fact is, until last spring, he was working as a laborer on his lordship's home farm, and we was doing very well. But then he got hurt and lost his leg and couldn't work, and since then we've been livin' on the rates, and we jist ain't been able ter manage on eight shillings a week, not in the winter, anyways. Summers we kin grow a few vegetables in the garden, and we don't need no fire then, neither."

Charlotte was so shocked that she couldn't speak for a moment. Then she said incredulously, "Your total income is eight shillings a week? But no family could possibly live on eight shillings a week."

"It's been hard, ma'am, and that's the truth. Pap always says we'd have been better off in the old days, before the Enclosures, y'know. Back then, we could have grazed some chickens or a pig on the commons, and gathered firewood in the waste, too. But o'course, we ain't allowed ter do that now."

After a pause, Jessie added in a small voice, "I know it was wrong ter poach his lordship's rabbits, ma'am, but y'see, we didn't have no food in the house. I couldn't let Billy starve" — she motioned to the silent little boy near the fireplace — "could I? And Mum, ye may 'ave noticed, she's increasing. She needs extra food now."

Charlotte drew a deep breath. She opened her reticule again and drew out several banknotes, which, together with the coins, she pressed into Jessie's hands. "There, that should help for a while. Look, Jessie, I told your mother my name, but I'm not sure she took any notice. Can you remember it? It's Kinley, Charlotte Kinley. Now, if there's any further trouble about that wretched rabbit, or if you should need help of any kind, send me a message at Cortona. Ask for Sarah, my abigail." She patted the little girl's shoulder. "I'll be going now."

"God bless ye, ma'am. I think ye must be an angel in disguise."

Charlotte laughed. "I never yet met an angel dressed in black. Goodbye, Jessie."

* * *

"My dear Charlotte, you're very quiet. Are you feeling ill?" asked Lady Sherborne in a low voice, under cover of the steady hum of conversation in the drawing room.

Charlotte shook her head. "I'm very well," she murmured. Which was true, as far as it went. There was nothing wrong with her physically, but she was feeling increasingly uncomfortable under the strain of being on display in front of Jeffrey's friends and acquaintances.

Today, as had happened every day since her arrival, the local gentry were calling at Cortona in droves. By now, Charlotte suspected, her coming betrothal was an open secret. Most of these callers were coming to have a closer look at the future Marchioness of Sherborne than they might be likely to obtain amid the large crowd of people at the Christmas Eve ball tomorrow night. Charlotte also suspected that every one of these people today, and every caller of the past few days, had compared her drably dressed self with the ethereal golden-haired beauty in the portrait over the mantelpiece.

She glanced up to see Jeffrey threading his way toward her with a newly arrived visitor in tow.

"Charlotte, I don't believe you've met my old friend, Sir Richard Bainbridge," Jeffrey said, introducing the stout, ruddy-faced gentleman. "Sir Richard is a pillar of the county, one of our justices of the peace."

Sir Richard bowed. "How d'you do, m'dear. From Lancashire, are you? A bit different from Oxfordshire, eh?" He was brisk but cordial, although, unlike the other callers today, he apparently had no interest in Charlotte as the next Lady Sherborne. After his brief greeting, he turned back to Jeffrey. "Been wanting to see you, Sherborne. Just got back from the quarter session. Thought I should tell you that we've had to raise the poor rate." He shook his head. "Hated to do it, I can tell you. It's all because of this increasing unemployment since the end of the war. Can't let these people starve, of course."

"I hope, now that the justices have decided to raise the rates, that they also plan to pay a family of four more than eight shillings a week," said Charlotte clearly.

Sir Richard stared down at her. "Pay them more money? Certainly not, my dear. We'd be forced to raise the rates for our landowners even higher."

Charlotte rose slowly to face the baronet. "Sir Richard, do you realize it costs a shilling to buy one loaf of bread?"

Sir Richard's expression grew chilly. "That I do, better than you, Miss Kinley, I'll warrant. Some years back, the Speenhamland magistrates proposed to assist the unemployed out of the rates at an agreed minimum amounting to the price of three gallon loaves a week for each man and one and one-half loaves for a wife and each child. The formula has now spread to every county except Northumberland and has been most successful."

Charlotte had a sudden memory of Jessie Reeves's thin little face, tattered clothing, and bleeding bare foot, and erupted. "Successful for whom? Not the poor, I assure you. A family of four can't keep body and soul together on eight shillings a week. You might as well condemn them to slow starvation. Is this the way a great country like England treats its unfortunates? We ought to be ashamed of ourselves! You justices ought to be more ashamed than the rest of us!"

Her voice had risen, and the other people in the room fell silent, staring at her and Sir Richard. The justice, his eyes bulging from his head, opened and shut his mouth several times, rather like a fish out of water, but no sound emerged.

"Charlotte!" gasped Lady Sherborne.

His face masklike, Jeffrey said in a low voice, "Charlotte, perhaps this isn't the time . . ."

Charlotte looked around her at Jeffrey's guests, seeing the shocked faces, the avidly curious eyes. She pushed past Jeffrey and Sir Richard, and walked swiftly out of the room. In the great marble atrium-hallway, she paused uncertainly, and then, almost without thinking, she headed down the long, glass-enclosed corridor toward the conservatory, where she sank down on a bench beneath some trellised vines. She leaned forward, elbows on her knees, and placed her hands over her hot face.

Why, why, hadn't she guarded her unruly tongue? Of course something should be done to assist the poor and the unemployed, but Lady Sherborne's drawing room wasn't the place to broach the subject. The dowager's guests would soon be spreading the word that her son's future wife was not only a female of inferior social position, but was also a wild-eyed troublemaker with no manners who had publicly embarrassed a respected magistrate. The dowager would doubtless find it difficult to forgive an affront to a guest. And what would Jeffrey say or do about her outburst?

Charlotte lingered in the conservatory, unwilling to see anyone until she felt calmer. After a quarter of an hour, she heard footsteps in the corridor and rose, anticipating the arrival of one or more of the gardeners. Instead, she caught the sound of a familiar voice and abruptly sat down again behind the concealing screen of vines.

"Jeffrey, you're being ridiculous, and yes, rude, practically running away from your own mother," protested Lady Sherborne as she hurried into the conservatory after her son.

"I don't walk to talk about Charlotte, Mama."

"But that's being even more ridiculous. We *must* talk. My dear boy, after what happened today, surely you don't intend to go on with this mockery of a marriage to Charlotte? I've tried to hold my tongue about this dreadful mésalliance, but now — ! Jeffrey, every feeling must be offended at the thought of that ill-mannered, forward young woman taking the place of our darling Cicely. It's bad enough that Charlotte's a nobody who doesn't know how to dress or act in polite society. Now she's insulted one of our oldest friends — in my own drawing room! Cicely, sweet, gentle, considerate Cicely, must be restless in her grave."

"Cicely is gone, Mama."

"But I know you've never stopped loving her, never stopped thinking about her." The dowager's voice softened. "Arabella is so much like her, it sometimes takes my breath away. Jeffrey, have you ever thought you might marry Bella? She'd be so perfect in every way. Oh, I know you're worried about money, but Bella will have a very respectable portion, you know. And it isn't as if you'd publicly announced your betrothal to Miss Kinley."

"That's enough, Mama." Jeffrey's tone was distant. "I've told you why I felt it necessary to marry Charlotte. The necessity still exists. Her manners, or lack of them, have nothing to do with the matter."

"But Jeffrey, how can I hold up my head — ?"

"Mama, I said that's enough."

"Oh, very well. If you insist on being so stubborn . . . I'll go, then. But please, my dear, think about what I've said."

Instead of leaving with his mother, Jeffrey began slowly sauntering through the greenhouse, his head bent as if in thought, his hands clasped behind his back. Charlotte could just glimpse him through the screen of vines. As he approached her hiding place, she shrank back in a reflex action against the iron bench, causing it to scrape slightly on the stone floor.

"Is someone there?" Jeffrey called.

Charlotte rose and walked out to him, feeling a little like a child who has been hiding under her bed to escape the wrath of her nanny.

Jeffrey wheeled on her, his expression torn between annoyance and dismay. "Charlotte! Did you — ?"

"Yes, I heard what Lady Sherborne said," she replied stonily. "I can't say your mother's opinion of me surprises me very much. I heard what you said, too. I apologize for my — how did you put it? — for my lack of manners."

Jeffrey looked harassed. "I didn't mean — Look, Mama was angry, embarrassed. Charlotte, what possessed you to bring up the subject of the Poor Laws with Sir Richard? I've never seen him so distressed. He felt you were personally attacking him."

Charlotte's blood began to boil again. "Distressed? I'm the one who's distressed!" She launched into a description of her encounter with Jessie Reeves, finishing angrily with, "And it makes no difference how little the county chooses to pay Jessie's father. *You* should have made some provision for the man when he lost a leg in your employ. But no, I'm forgetting. Your

343

bailiff manages your property, doesn't he? You're too busy to pay attention to details. You may spend some time at Cortona, Jeffrey, but you're no better than an absentee landlord!"

With a toss of her head, she stalked past him. He put out his hand to catch her arm as she went by. "Charlotte, is that what you really think of me?"

Panicking at the electric thrill that went through her at his touch, she tried to wrench her arm away. "Oh, God, more talk? Haven't we had enough talk today?"

His lips tightened. With a sudden swift movement, he pulled her against him, grinding his lips against hers in a savage kiss that went on and on until Charlotte felt as if she were sinking into a delirious abyss of delight from which she never wished to return. At last he released her. "Perhaps that's our problem. We talk too much," he said evenly and swung around on his heel to leave her.

As Sarah was leaving the bedchamber the next afternoon with a luncheon tray that her mistress had barely touched, Charlotte was tempted to call the abigail back to say to her, "Bring out the portmanteaux, Sarah, and pack my clothes. We're leaving." But she didn't say the words, and Sarah left the room.

Charlotte walked to the windows overlooking the park. Through the leafless trees she could glimpse the dome of the little classic folly. Her heart contracted as she remembered the handful of magic moments she'd spent there with Jeffrey, feeding the deer. Could it be a mere few days ago that she'd believed there was some small chance she and Jeffrey could become friends, if not lovers?

But that had always been an empty dream, she could see now. Yesterday in the conservatory, while Jeffrey had refused his mother's plea to cry off from his engagement, he hadn't denied his attachment to Cicely's memory, and he certainly hadn't defended Charlotte's conduct toward Sir Richard. No, Jeffrey was closing his eyes to Charlotte's flaws, social unsuitability, and lack of appeal to him. He was going through with

344

his marriage because he was determined to save Cortona from financial ruin. And it was no use thinking about that kiss. It hadn't meant anything, except that Jeffrey had taken out his anger and frustration in a physical way.

Sighing, Charlotte turned away from the window. Her eye fell on the dress hanging from the door of the wardrobe. The gown, which had belonged to Lady Sherborne and had been altered by a seamstress in Banbury, had arrived yesterday. It was made of *crêpe lisse* in a delicate shade of pale violet, trimmed with flounces of lace and knots of satin ribbon in a slightly darker shade. What was more, it was immensely becoming. Charlotte would wear the gown tonight at the Christmas Eve ball, when her engagement was to be announced, unless . . . She clenched her hands tightly together, admitting to herself that she didn't have the courage to cut her losses, to tell Jeffrey flatly that they wouldn't suit, and leave Cortona before the ball. No matter what he felt, or didn't feel, for her, she still wanted him.

A knock sounded at the door. Charlotte hunched her shoulders impatiently. She hadn't gone down to dinner last night, pleading a headache, and she'd had breakfast and lunch in her bedchamber, because she hadn't wanted to see anyone after the embarrassing scene yesterday with Sir Richard in the drawing room. Which was ridiculous, of course. She couldn't remain in her bedchamber like a wounded lioness in her lair. She called, "Come in."

Jeffrey entered the room. "I was sorry to hear you had the headache. Are you feeling better?" His tone was polite and impersonal. He certainly showed no disposition to kiss her! But obviously he'd made up his mind to ignore their quarrel of last night.

"The headache's gone, thank you."

He handed her a worn velvet-covered box. "I thought you might like to wear these tonight. They belonged to my godmother."

Charlotte opened the box, which contained a necklace of amethysts and pearls.

"Mama told me you were going into colors tonight," Jeffrey

345

continued, glancing at the ball gown hanging on the wardrobe. "I think the amethysts will go well with your dress."

"The necklace complements the gown perfectly. I promise to take very good care of it."

"No, no, the necklace is a gift, not a loan," Jeffrey said quickly. "My godmother wanted my future wife to have it."

"Did you—" Charlotte choked back the words. She'd been about to ask, "Did you also give the necklace to Cicely?" That would not only have given away her feelings for him, it would have marked her as a jealous shrew. "Thank you," she said, ignoring his faintly puzzled expression.

The abigail, Sarah, rushed into the bedchamber. She paused, looking confused, when she saw Jeffrey. "Excuse me, my lord. I didn't know you was here."

"No need to apologize. I was just leaving." Jeffrey turned to Charlotte, bowing. "Until tonight, then."

When the door had closed behind him, Charlotte asked, "What is it, Sarah?"

"Well, ma'am, that little girl, Jessie Reeves, she's here. Says ye told her to ask for me if she wanted to send ye a message. She's in quite a state, she is. Looks worried to death. Will you see her?"

"Oh, dear, what—? Yes, of course. Where is she, in the kitchens?"

"No'm." Sarah coughed. "I thought as how ye mightn't like his lordship's servants to know about the child, so I whisked her out of the kitchens and brung her up here by the servants' staircase. I'll jist go fetch her."

Entering the bedchamber behind Sarah, Jessie Reeves seemed to forget her cares for a moment as she gazed in awe around the large, well-appointed room. The child wore the same thin dress and tattered shawl in which Charlotte had first seen her, but there was one change. Jessie was wearing a pair of shoes, purchased, most probably, with some of the coins Charlotte had given Mrs. Reeves. Jessie was also limping badly.

Charlotte exclaimed, "My dear, surely you didn't walk all the way from the village on that injured foot?"

"Not all the way. I sneaked over the estate wall and took a short cut across the park." An expression of desperation settled over the girl's face. "Sorry I am ter bother ye, Miss Kinley, but ye did say that ye'd help us."

"I certainly will if I can. What's the matter? Have the gamekeepers been threatening you?"

"No. No. It's me mum. The baby's coming. I mean, it's trying to come. Mrs. Bass—that's our neighbor in the village, she's helped with many a lying-in—Mrs. Bass says mum's babe is turned the wrong ways, like, and it can't get born by itself. Mrs. Bass says we needs a doctor real bad. And the nearest doctor's in Banbury."

Charlotte responded to the pleading in the child's eyes. "You want me to go to Banbury for the doctor. Of course I will, child. Sarah, order the carriage."

The abigail glanced at Jessie with misgiving. "Begging yer pardon, ma'am, it might be better if ye and Jessie was to go direct to the stables by way o' the servants' staircase."

"Heavens, yes, that would be better," Charlotte exclaimed as she hurriedly put on a pelisse and jammed a bonnet on her head. She had a mental image of Lady Sherborne's face if the dowager were to see her climbing into a carriage with a ragged village child in front of the magnificent entrance of Cortona.

A faint cry sounded from beyond the closed door of the bedchamber. Jessie scrambled to her feet from her huddled position on the floor next to Charlotte's chair and stood staring at the door. The child, unstrung with worry about her mother, had begged Charlotte to remain even after the doctor's arrival, and Charlotte had felt unable to refuse the request. Jessie's father straightened tensely in his chair, disturbing the toddler clinging to his remaining leg. The cry was repeated, stronger this time.

The slow moments ticked by. Finally the doctor appeared in the doorway of the bedchamber, smiling as he pulled down his shirtsleeves. "You have another son, Mr. Reeves. A Christmas baby, no less!"

"My wife?" said the crippled farm laborer.

"Very tired, but I've no doubt she'll be fine."

"Oh, Miss Kinley," Jessie breathed, "Mum's going ter be all right." Her face shining with joy, the child dashed into the bedchamber to be with her mother.

"Actually, ma'am, it's your doing, as much as my medical skill," said the doctor in confidential tones to Charlotte. "If you hadn't fetched me, I doubt very much that either Mrs. Reeves or the child would have survived. It was a very difficult birth. I'm only sorry you had such a long wait for me at my surgery. As I explained to you, I was at a farm some ten miles outside Banbury in attendance on another confinement. I'll confess to you, if I'd been delayed even slightly longer, I don't think I could have come in time to save either Mrs. Reeves or her baby."

Charlotte reached into her reticule. She pressed several bank notes into the doctor's hand. "Let's be thankful you were in time. Thank you for coming, Doctor."

The doctor glanced at the denominations of the notes and beamed. "A pleasure, ma'am."

Charlotte walked over to Jessie's father. "Congratulations, Mr. Reeves. If I can help in any way, please call on me."

"God bless you, ma'am. We'll never forget this."

"That's all right. Goodbye, Mr. Reeves. Say goodbye to Jessie."

Charlotte stepped out of the cottage and paused abruptly as she realized with sudden dismay that night had fallen. She'd lost all track of time since Jessie had come to Cortona to ask for help. It must be very late. It was full dark. Already the guests must be gathering at Cortona for the Christmas celebration that would culminate in the announcement of her betrothal. By the time she reached Cortona and dressed for the ball, it would be half over. The dowager would probably never forgive her. Jeffrey? Perhaps this latest example of Charlotte's social ineptitude would convince him, finally, that she'd never make him a proper wife. Well, she couldn't change anything that had happened, she reflected with a dragging sense of weariness and dejection. Nor would she have wanted to. She'd helped to save two lives.

She walked slowly out to her waiting carriage, where her coachman was pacing back and forth in the dim light of the side lamps. She noticed that the horses were draped in blankets and hoped that neither the driver nor the team had become too chilled during their long wait.

As she approached, the coachman hurried to open the door of the carriage and let down the steps. At the same time, a curricle and pair rounded a curve into the village street and was reined to an abrupt halt beside the carriage. The driver jumped down, tossing his reins to his diminutive tiger.

"My God, Charlotte, are you all right?"

"Jeffrey!" Charlotte gasped. As he came nearer, she could see he was wearing full evening dress beneath his caped driving coat. "What are you doing here?"

"Looking for you, naturally," he snapped. "When I finished dressing tonight, I came to your bedchamber to escort you downstairs. You weren't there, and your abigail—what's her name? Sarah?—clamped her mouth shut like a damned Sphinx and refused to tell me where you were."

Charlotte repressed a quick grin. Dear Sarah, with her sturdy Lancashire sense of loyalty.

"So then I went to the stables," Jeffrey continued, "where I learned you'd ordered your carriage in midafternoon and had gone off in the company of a tatterdemalion child. You'd been gone for so many hours, the grooms were worried that you'd had an accident. So I ordered my curricle and came out to look for you." He paused, glancing at the Reeves cottage. When he resumed speaking, the anxiety in his voice had changed to anger. "Have you forgotten our engagement ball? Or am I to understand that you prefer to spend your time visiting the villagers?"

Before Charlotte could reply, Jeffrey shot a look at the attentive coachman and another look at his equally attentive tiger, and said curtly, "We can't talk out here. I'll ride back to the house with you. My tiger can drive my curricle."

As the carriage rolled along toward Cortona, Charlotte told Jeffrey about Jessie's frantic request for help and described

349

the nerve-racking wait in Banbury for the doctor to return to his surgery and the long hours she'd spent at the cottage trying to comfort Jessie during Mrs. Reeves's difficult delivery.

She finished by saying, "I'm sorry if I've embarrassed you, Jeffrey. Truly, I didn't forget the Christmas Eve ball, or not exactly, anyway, but—"

"But you'd do the same thing all over again tomorrow, wouldn't you?"

In the gloom of the carriage, Charlotte stared at him in amazement. She couldn't see his face clearly, but she could hear the ripple of amusement in his voice.

"You're not angry with me?" she faltered.

"How can I be angry with the kindest, most loving woman I've ever met in my life?" Suddenly Jeffrey slipped his arm around her shoulders and kissed her. His lips fluttering against her mouth, he murmured, "I'm a little jealous, that's all. I want you to love me, too."

Charlotte gasped. Then she blurted, "Oh, Jeffrey, you idiot, I adore you." She locked her arms around his neck and returned his kiss with a passion that left them both breathless. Afterwards, she leaned back against his arm, looking up at him with dazed eyes. "You really mean it, you do love me?"

"From the first moment we met."

"But—why didn't you tell me?"

He bent his head, brushing her lips with his. "Because, my dear pea goose, you were so cold, so collected. You held me off every time I tried to get close to you."

"I didn't want to give myself away. I thought you were only marrying me for my money."

"I forgot all about your money five minutes after I met you." Charlotte turned her face away, and Jeffrey said anxiously, "My darling, what is it?"

"Oh, Jeffrey, you can't possibly love me the way you loved Cicely. She was so beautiful, so—so perfect in every way."

He was silent for a long moment. Then he said, "I've never told this to anyone. Cicely *was* beautiful and sweet and devoted. But after she died, I admitted to myself what I'd never allowed myself to think while she was alive, that she'd bored me to tears." Jeffrey's arms tightened around Charlotte. *"You'll* never bore me, my love. You'll go on, to the end of my life, irritating me and calling me to account and making me realize my responsibilities."

"And loving you."

"That, too. The most important thing of all."

ELEGANCE AND CHARM WITH ZEBRA'S REGENCY ROMANCES

A LOGICAL LADY　　　　　　　　　　　　　　(3277, $3.95)
by Janice Bennett

When Mr. Frederick Ashfield arrived at Halliford Castle after two years on the continent, Elizabeth could not keep her heart from fluttering uncontrollably. But things were in a dreadful state. Frederick had come straight from the Grange, his ancestral home, where he argued with his cousin, Viscount St. Vincent. After his sudden departure, the Viscount had been found murdered.

After an attempt on his life Frederick knew what must be done: he must risk his very life, and Lizzie's dearest hopes, to trap a deadly killer!

AN UNQUESTIONABLE LADY　　　　　　　　　(3151, $3.95)
by Rosina Pyatt

Too proud to apply for financial assistance, Miss Claudia Tallon was desperate enough to answer the advertisement. But why would any man of wealth and position need to advertise for a wife? Then she saw his name and understood why. *Giles Veryland*. No decent lady would dream of associating with such a rake.

This was to be a marriage of convenience—Giles convenience. Claudia was hardly in a position to expect a love match, and Giles could not be bothered. The two were thus eminently suited to one another, if only they could stop arguing long enough to find out!

FOREVER IN TIME　　　　　　　　　　　　　(3129, $3.95)
by Janice Bennett

Erika Von Hamel had been living on a tiny British island for two years when the stranger Gilbert Randall was up on her shore after a boating accident. Erika had little patience for his game of pretending that the year was 1812 and he was somehow lost in time. But she found him examining in detail her models of the Napoleonic battles, and she wanted to believe that he really was from Regency England—a romantic hero that she thought only existed in romance books . . .

Gilbert Randall was quite sure the outcome of the war depended on information he was carrying—but he was no longer there to deliver it. He must get back to his own time to insure that history would not be irrevocably altered. And that meant he must take Erika with him, although he shuddered to think of the havoc she would cause in Regency England—and in his own heart!

Available wherever paperbacks are sold, or order direct from the Publisher. Send cover price plus 50¢ per copy for mailing and handling to Zebra Books, Dept. 3583, 475 Park Avenue South, New York, N.Y. 10016. Residents of New York, New Jersey and Pennsylvania must include sales tax. DO NOT SEND CASH.